EYE CANDY INK: SECOND GENERATION

SHAW HART

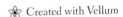

AMES

EYE CANDY INK: SECOND GENERATION

*

Ames Bronson must have a death wish.

In his defense, how was he to know that the girl he hooked up with one night when he first got to town would be his new boss's daughter? I mean, Zeke seems like a cool guy, but no one is that cool.

His only saving grace is that Zeke doesn't know about him and Maxine.

His brothers tell him he should be thankful for this small miracle and forget that he ever met her. That should be easy enough. They work at different Eye Candy Ink locations. He'll just do his best to avoid her and to push her out of his mind.

There's just one problem.

He's pretty sure that he's in love with her.

Will pursuing Maxine ruin everything? Or will he finally get the happily ever after that he's been dreaming about ever since he first laid eyes on her?

ONE

Ames

I FINISH WIPING down my room, tired but somehow full of energy after my first day working as a tattoo artist at Eye Candy Ink.

I moved to Pittsburgh for this job a few weeks ago and it's been a whirlwind of moving boxes, meeting new people, and trying to find my footing here in the shop.

Eye Candy Ink is a legendary tattoo shop and when I learned that they were opening a second location, I had jumped at the chance to apply. I'm a great tattoo artist but a bunch of great artists applied and I was a little surprised when I got the call from Zeke Miller, the owner of Eye Candy Ink, offering me the position.

That was two weeks ago and I had to pack and move up here in a hurry. Luckily, I was only coming from Philadelphia.

"Hey, are you headed home now?" Harvey asks as he shoves some papers into his backpack.

"Yeah, I'm almost done here," I tell him.

Harvey and Rooney had been nice enough to let me crash with them for a few days until I could move into my own place. They even helped me get settled in this last weekend. I have a feeling that was because I told them that I would buy them all of the pizza and beer that they could eat if they did, but it was still nice of them to give me a hand.

They're the co-owners' sons and their dads are legends in the tattoo world. I've been obsessed with Atlas Warner and Mischa Jennings work for as long as I can remember.

"Hey! Are we going out tonight?" Rooney asks as he skids to a stop, bumping into Harvey.

Harvey doesn't even react, and I'm sure that he's used to his best friend running into him. They did grow up together and I've heard from Banks that they've been thick as thieves literally from birth.

Rooney is like an overgrown puppy. He's hyper and energetic, a real handful. He's also absolutely hilarious.

Harvey is his counterpart. Where Rooney is wild, Harvey is calm and collected. He's a bit of a dreamer but both of them are good, solid, guys.

"Going out? Where are we going?" Banks asks, coming up behind the other two.

Banks is Nico Mitchell's son. His real name is Zeke but it got confusing with the other one and he's so secretive that everyone joked that he could actually be the street artist Banksy, so that's how he got the nickname.

"Let's go to Seven," Rooney says, and I search my brain to see if that place sounds familiar.

"I'm in," Banks and Harvey say at the same time and I smile.

"Me too."

I was looking forward to heading home and crashing but

I'm still trying to make friends here and I like hanging out with these guys.

"I'll drive!" Rooney says, heading for the front door and I laugh when Harvey and Banks both scream no.

"*I'll* drive," Harvey says and I follow after the guys, letting Banks lock up the front doors.

We head across the lot and I climb into my car. Banks heads to his and I watch Rooney and Harvey wrestle over the car keys for a minute before Harvey dives for the driver's side door and locks Rooney out. I laugh as I see them have some kind of argument and then Rooney slides across the hood of the car, only making it halfway. I can see Banks doubled over from here and Harvey just shakes his head, grinning at the maniac that he calls his best friend.

We finally pull out and I follow them a few blocks away to the club. Se7en is a nightclub not far from my apartment and I park near Banks and climb out.

"Are we going to be able to get into this place?" I ask, studying the upscale building before I look down at my casual attire.

Everyone is dressed in black jeans and t-shirts and I doubt that we will fit in with the other club goers.

"Yeah," Banks says with a laugh. "Our uncle Max owns it and his daughter Cat runs it."

We cross the street and I follow the other guys up to the front doors. Banks was telling the truth and we breeze in without incident.

The inside of the club is dark, the bass almost shaking the walls and I have to blink to get my eyes to adjust to the darkness. There's a bar running the length of one side and we head in that direction.

"What do you want, Ames? First round is on me," Harvey says, so I order a beer as I look around the place.

The place is packed and it's hard to make anyone out. There are some tables and booths on the opposite wall and then a stairway leads up to the second floor which I think is some kind of VIP area.

Rooney passes me a beer and then nudges me to get me to follow after them as we wind our way through the dancing crowd and over to one of the booths on the far wall.

"How are you liking Pittsburgh and Eye Candy Ink so far?" Banks asks me, and I take a sip of beer before I answer him.

"It's good. I like the city and my first day was good. Is the shop always this busy?"

"Oh yeah. We book months out, so expect to have back-to-back clients every day," Rooney says as he takes a long pull of his own beer.

"What about the other two artists? Gray and Ender?" I ask, wondering if those names are real.

"They're cool. Gray is wrapped up in his roommate. She's his best friend or something from his hometown and now they live together," Harvey says.

"Yeah, and he's totally in love with her but is pretending that he isn't," Rooney adds.

"What about Ender? Is that his real name?" I ask.

"He's cool. He's a few years older than us and tends to stick to himself, but he seems solid," Banks says.

"I think Ender is a nickname. The dude was in the Army or Navy or something. I think he was a real badass but then he got out and picked up tattooing."

I nod at Rooney as a waitress comes up to see if we want anything else. She's pretty in an overdone kind of way but she doesn't do anything for me. She still tries to flirt with all of us but we all brush her off and just order another round of beers.

"What about you?" Rooney asks as the waitress leaves.

"What about me?"

"Any special girl in your life?"

"Uh, no. I only moved here like two weeks ago. I don't move that fast," I joke.

We hang out for another hour but by then we're all exhausted. Banks is the first to leave and Harvey and Rooney follow soon after. I tell them that I'll see them tomorrow as I pay for the last round of beers, and they wave before they disappear into the crowd.

I'm turning to head toward the door myself when my eyes lock with an angel.

She's in the middle of the dance floor, her blue eyes sparking as the blue lights pass over her, and I'm frozen, entranced. Her blonde hair is slightly mussed around her flushed face as she dances to the music. Her body moves rhythmically. It's like she's a siren, drawing me to my ruin.

I'm moving toward her before I even realize that my brain told my feet to move and as I get closer, she gives me a slow grin and my heart thuds loudly in my ears, even over the music.

I stop in front of her, my heart racing as I search my brain for something to say.

TWO

Maxine

MAYBE IT'S the two margaritas that I downed when I first got to the club, but I'm pretty sure that this is the hottest guy that I've ever seen in my life.

Normally I'm not really the nightclub type, but when my best friend, Cat, invited me out to celebrate me graduating college and starting my new job managing Eye Candy Ink in a few days, I couldn't say no. I didn't *want* to say no.

I needed to blow off some steam after finals last week. I've been busting my butt for the last four years, making sure that I kept up my grades and graduated at the top of my class. I knew that I had a job lined up afterward at my parents' tattoo shop, but I still wanted to do well and make them proud.

My mom and dad have always told me that they wanted me and the other kids to eventually take over the Eye Candy Ink tattoo shops from them when they were ready to retire. My sister, Nichole, can draw but she was never interested in learning how to tattoo. She'd much rather study art and she's living in France now with her girlfriend, working at some small art gallery there.

Me, I can't draw a stick figure, so I knew that I was never going to be an artist. Numbers have always been my sweet spot, which is why I went to school to study business management. I knew that I would never be working at Eye Candy Ink as a tattoo artist or even a piercer, so my contribution is going to be running the place.

My eyes scan over the hot mystery stranger and my whole body starts to tingle. I've been focused on my studies for so long but now that I've graduated, maybe it's time that I start to think about dating or at least losing my virginity.

My mystery man sways closer to me, and I grin up at him. He's giving me space, letting me make the move and I like that. There's been a few other guys in this club who have hit on me but I turned them all away. None of them did it for me and I didn't like how they just pushed into my space, their sweat and beer scented breath in my face.

This guy isn't like that.

I step closer to him, my hands going around his neck as we start to move together to the beat of the music.

"I'm Ames. What's your name, angel?" he purrs in my ear and a shiver runs through me.

"Maxine," I whisper into his ear, letting my lips brush against the shell of his ear.

His whole body tenses and I look at his face, surprised at the lust that I can see in his eyes. Power surges through me and I grow bolder. My hands burrow into his hair and I step closer to him, our bodies rubbing together now.

We grind together, both of us getting lost in the music and each other. Sweat coats both of us as more people join the dance floor, but neither of us makes a move to leave.

I've never really done anything crazy in my life. My sister was the free spirit, the wilder one of the two of us. I was the one who stayed home on Friday nights to do extra credit. I volunteered at a soup kitchen and animal shelter all through high school and college. I even lived at home during college to save on costs and I only recently moved into my own place.

I always think things through, weighing the pros and cons of every decision. I never jump unless I know where I'll be landing.

So, why am I thinking about going home with Ames tonight?

Maybe it's because I've just graduated college and I'm about to start working and being a real adult. Maybe it's because Ames is the only guy that I've ever had this kind of reaction to.

Tingles start to spread throughout my body as I stare into Ames' eyes, our skin brushing against each other. The crowd and the rest of the club starts to disappear as I get lost in his dark blue eyes.

Before I know it, we're both leaning in and our lips meet in a soft caress. Our bodies are still moving together to the beat and the kiss deepens as the next song starts to play. My hands are buried in his hair and his are holding tight to my hips, pressing me closer against him.

We pull away to suck in a breath and I can't pull my gaze away from his.

One song bleeds into the next and it isn't until the club lights start to flicker on that I realize that it's almost two a.m. and Se7en is closing. Ames blinks, looking like he's coming out of a dream as more lights come on.

"What are you doing right now?" I ask, not wanting tonight to end.

"Whatever you want me to," Ames replies right away and I laugh.

"Come with me."

I take his hand and we head out with the rest of the clubgoers and down the sidewalk.

"Where's your car?"

He points across the street and I let him lead me over to it and I smile as he opens the door for me. As he heads around to the driver's side of the car, I pull out my phone and text Cat. She drove me tonight and I want to let her know that I'm headed home with some guy named Ames.

MAXINE: So, I met a guy.

Cat: OMG! It's finally happening!

Maxine: Shut up, you've never been on a date either.

Cat: Uh, yeah. Have you seen the fuck boys that come into this club? Where am I going to meet a nice boy?

Maxine: Maybe you should get out more.

SHE SENDS BACK the cat with its tongue out emoji as Ames slides behind the wheel and I laugh.

MAXINE: Anyway, I'm going home with him so I won't need a ride from you.

Cat: YASSSSS! Get it girl!

Maxine: OMG, you're so embarrassing.

Cat: You love me. Now go get some loving from this Ames guy. I want details tomorrow!!

· · ·

I ROLL my eyes as I tuck my phone away and turn to study Ames. He's handsome with chiseled features, dark brown hair tousled from my fingers and our dancing.

"Where to?" he asks and I bite my lip.

Do I really want to lose my virginity tonight? Yes, yes, I do. As long as it's with this guy. Maybe I can do something crazy tonight. Something to look back on after I start working and go back to having no life.

I can have a one-night stand. If things get weird or the sex is bad, then I'll just sneak out after and I'll never have to see him again.

My heart pangs as I think about not seeing Ames again and I try to push those feelings away. I just met this guy. I can't already be getting attached.

"How about your place?" I ask, trying to sound seductive.

Ames grins, leaning over the center console and surprising me by kissing me hard and fast.

"Anything for you, Maxine."

I smile, sitting back as he drives us down the mostly deserted streets. He doesn't live far from me and I'm happy to find that if I have to make a run for it, I can just walk home from here.

He takes my hand as he leads me up three flights of stairs and down a short hallway to the last door on the left. I wait while he unlocks it and then steps inside.

His apartment overlooks Main Street and downtown, the faint glow from the streetlights and shop signs casting colorful shadows on the walls.

"It's a little..."

"Bare?" Ames supplies and I nod.

"Yeah."

"I just moved in a few days ago," Ames explains and I

turn to spot the pile of boxes still lined up against the hallway wall.

"Well, it's still a nice place," I say as he heads into the kitchen.

"Thanks. Did you want something to drink?"

"No, I'm alright."

My earlier bravery seems to have dimmed slightly in the brighter lights of his apartment.

"Do you want me to take you home?" Ames asks and I swallow hard, shaking my head no.

"Can I see your bedroom?" I whisper, licking my lips as he studies my face.

"We don't have to do anything, Maxine. We can just talk."

I think I fall a little in love with him right then.

"I want to, do stuff," I say, starting to unzip the back of my mini dress.

Ames licks his lips, his blue eyes darkening as he watches my every movement. He takes a step toward me and I back up, giving him a sly smile. I love the way he looks at me, like I'm the best thing that he's ever seen in his life. That look is what has me so emboldened and acting so brave.

I take another step back and he follows. One more step and I'm against the wall. Ames takes one last step and just before he can cage me in with his body, I let the dress drop. It slithers down, getting snagged on my wide hips and I shimmy a little to get it to fall.

"Fucking hell, Maxine," Ames breathes in awe and I forget all about how this is the first time that a man has seen me half naked.

I know that I don't have a model-perfect body. I'm never going to be a size zero, I'll always hover around a size twelve, but I've always been okay with my looks. It's obvious that Ames likes what he sees too if the stiff ridge in his pants is any indication.

"Your turn," I tell him, my voice coming out husky.

Ames reaches behind his neck and tugs his shirt off in that sexy way that guys do. I never really got the appeal but watching Ames do it has my mouth watering and my whole body heating.

Tattoos snake up his right arm and I want to trace each one with my tongue. All of his are tastefully done and that tattoo artist daughter in me loves them. It looks like he has a few more on his back and I want to see them, but not as much as I want to watch him take his jeans off.

He unbuttons them and tugs down the zipper before he pushes them down his thighs and kicks them off. His black boxer briefs are clinging to his thighs, the front tented with his impressive erection.

"Come here," he says, and the next thing I know, I'm in his arms, my legs wrapped around his waist, his cock rubbing against me in the most mind-blowing way as he carries me down the hallway and into his bedroom.

His lips find my neck and I close my eyes, my head tilting to the side to give him more room. I can feel his fingers on my back but I'm too wrapped up in his kisses to realize what he's doing.

He lays me down on the bed, dragging my bra down my arms and tossing it aside. His lips move down my neck, over my clavicle until he captures one of my nipples in his mouth. His mouth is so warm, his tongue teasing as he flicks it back and forth over the stiff peak. Soon my hips are rising off the bed, trying to rub against him as he continues to play with my breasts.

He switches to the other one as he reaches down and

frees his cock from his underwear. I don't know what I expected a dick to feel like, but it's better. It's like velvet steel brushing up against me, and it doesn't take long before he's covered in my juices.

"I need you," Ames murmurs against my skin, and I spread my legs in invitation.

"I need you too," I moan as his cock slides against my clit, driving me wild.

"I want a taste first."

I groan in frustration, wanting to feel him filling me, but then his mouth is on me and my groans turn to moans in an instant as my mind blanks.

His tongue is even better between my legs and it isn't long before I can feel a strange pressure filling me.

"I... I'm—"

I don't get the words out before I'm coming on his lips, my legs wrapped around his head like a vise as I ride out my pleasure.

"You taste like heaven," Ames says as he kisses his way back up my body.

I'm not sure when he ditched his underwear but my eyes widen as I get a glimpse of his cock.

"You're pierced," I breathe as I see the barbell running just under the head of his cock.

"Yeah, is that a problem?" he asks hesitantly as he grabs a condom out of his bedside table.

"No, just a surprise."

He grins at that and rolls the condom down his length. Then he's back between my legs and I dig my nails into his biceps as he starts to sink inside of me.

I suck in a breath and he freezes.

"Are you a virgin?" he asks, sounding surprised, and I nod.

"Yeah, is that a problem?" I ask, trying to break any tension.

"No, just a surprise," he repeats my words with a smile.

He leans down, kissing me, and I focus on that instead of the slight sting of pain as he sinks inside of me completely.

Ames pulls away, hissing in a breath like he's in pain, and I freeze.

"Am I hurting you?" I ask, alarmed.

"I've just never felt anything so fucking good before. Jesus, Maxine. You're heaven, my fucking heaven."

My face flushes as his words hit me, and I clench around him involuntarily. I can feel that piercing of his rubbing against my wall and I moan, trying to move my hips so that I can feel it rub more.

Ames takes my hint, his hips sliding back before he thrusts into me once more. My nails dig into his shoulders as he starts to move and soon my legs are wrapped around his hips as we move together.

Ames kneels between my legs, changing the angle slightly and I scream in ecstasy as he hits some secret spot deep within me. His piercing rubs against the spot and I burst apart, coming all over his cock as he pounds into me.

"Fuck, fuck, fuck," Ames chants, his eyes squeezed shut tight as he finds his own release and I moan as he slowly rocks into me.

I can't stop smiling as he gently pulls out of me and rolls onto his side. He leans over the edge of the bed, taking care of the condom and then he's back beside me, pulling me into his arms so my back is to his front and presses kisses against my shoulder.

"Do you need anything?" he asks and I can hear the sleepy tone of his voice.

"No," I say, faking a yawn.

He kisses my shoulder one last time and I wait until his breaths even out before I slip out from under his arm and gather up my clothes. I take one last look at Ames in his bed before I pad to the front door and head downstairs.

It's almost four a.m. as I make my walk home and collapse into my own bed. I can't help but wonder if I'm making a mistake with every step I take away from Ames' apartment, but that doesn't stop me or make me turn back.

I unlock my apartment and head straight for my bed. My eyes are heavy and I close them. I know that I should probably get up and take a shower but I don't want to wash Ames and our one night together off. Not just yet.

I want to remember tonight forever. I want to remember the man who took my virginity and a small piece of my heart.

THREE

Ames

I'M DISTRACTED the next morning, my mind still occupied with thoughts of my dream girl, Maxine, from last night. I can't believe that I fell asleep like an idiot and let her get away. I don't even have a last name or anything to go by and if she's on social media, it must be private because I can't find her.

"Hey, whoa, dude. You look like shit. Are you sure that you're ready for us to open in a few minutes?" Harvey asks as he wanders past my room and stops in the doorway.

"Yeah, I'm fine. Just didn't get a lot of sleep."

Yeah, because you woke up and found Maxine missing, so you've spent the last three hours scouring social media for her.

"Luckily, I've got my designs done for the next few days."

"I heard that!" Rooney yells from down the hall and I

laugh, picturing him bent over his desk, hurrying to finish up his designs for his clients today.

Harvey laughs and heads back to his own room as the front door opens. A second later, Banks hurries past my door, looking like he slept in. Rooney calls to him a minute later, probably giving him shit for almost being late, but I tune their bickering out, my mind already going back to last night with Maxine.

It had been perfect.

Until I woke up alone this morning. I wonder why she slipped out without saying goodbye. Did she not feel this connection between us like I did? Did I hurt her last night?

The questions are killing me and I pick up my phone once again, pulling up my social media sites again and typing in Maxine. I scroll through the hundreds of results, growing frustrated when I don't recognize her in any of the profile pictures.

We open a few minutes later and I put my phone aside and try to get lost in my work so that I can forget about my dream girl. It doesn't quite work but it keeps me from stewing about not being able to get in touch with her again.

I go out to grab lunch for everyone and I find myself searching the street, hoping to spot Maxine in the crowd. No such luck though and I head back to the shop with my appetite gone.

I'm trying to keep my eyes open as I pack up for the day when Zeke, my boss and the owner of Eye Candy Ink, comes into the shop.

"Hey, Ames. How's it going?" he asks me as I stop in my doorway for him to pass.

"Pretty good."

"Are you headed home for the night?"

"Yeah, I just finished up with my last client."

"Well, before you go, I wanted to introduce you to my daughter. She's going to be taking over as manager of this Eye Candy Ink location," he says with a proud smile.

I paste on a smile as I turn and my heart drops as my eyes lock on my dream girl from last night. She's walking toward me down the hallway, laughing at something that Rooney is saying to her. She hasn't seen me yet and I wonder if she'll be happy to see me and to find out that I work here too.

I get my answer a minute later when her head turns and our eyes lock. Her smile falters, her eyes widening in surprise as she freezes.

I'm not sure how to react. Do I pretend like I don't know her? That seems like the best option since trying to explain to my boss how I know his daughter seems like a bad idea.

"Nice to meet you," she says, seeming a little nervous and off-kilter.

"You too," I tell her, shaking her slim hand.

"She'll be running this place for me. She just graduated from college last week," Zeke says, smiling down at his daughter.

It's obvious that he loves his daughter and is happy to be including her in the business.

"Congratulations," I tell Maxine and she nods, giving me a strained smile.

"Thanks."

"Well, you two can get to know each other better later. I still wanted to show you around the office."

"Yeah, it was nice to meet you," she says, looking relieved that this conversation is over.

"You too," I tell her, watching her turn and head down the hallway.

She disappears into the back office a minute later, but not before she turns and looks back at me one last time.

I head outside and across the street to my car, pulling out my phone as I go. I don't really have anyone else to talk to about Maxine since Harvey, Rooney, and Banks are practically her brothers. Ender is the quietest guy in the shop and I still don't know him very well, so I don't really feel comfortable going to him.

I open up my text messages and bring up the group chat with my two brothers, Alexander and Anthony. They're both older than me, but we've always been close. Alexander is married now to his assistant and living in New York City. He's a real estate developer and the only one in our family who didn't do something artistic for his career.

My other brother, Anthony, is a comedian living out in Los Angeles. Although I heard that he's headed to New York soon to audition for some comedy club.

They're good guys, but they're also my brothers and I know that while they'll try to help me, they're still going to give me shit about this too. That's why even as I type out my message, I know that I'm going to regret this.

AMES: I need some advice.

Anthony: Who is this?

Alexander: I don't have time for this.

Ames: You guys are the worst.

Anthony: I'm going to tell mom that you said that.

Alexander: What do you need?

Ames: I met someone.

Anthony: Okay, I'm going to tell mom THAT. She'll

be calling you in five minutes wanting to know every detail about her.

Alexander: Do it. Then he can stop bothering us.

Ames: There's a problem.

Alexander: Let me guess, she doesn't feel the same way.

Anthony: Bummer, man.

Ames: She's my boss's daughter.

Anthony: Oh shit.

Alexander: Fuck, man. You sure know how to pick them.

Ames: Fuck you, Alex. You got drunk and married your assistant in Vegas.

Anthony: Yeah, but he was in love with her for like years first. Does your boss know?

Ames: No.

Alexander: Then what's the problem?

Ames: I like her.

Alexander: Well stop liking her. Just forget about her. It's for the best. Unless you want to find a new job.

Anthony: Yeah, I'm with Alex. Count your blessings that no one else knows and pretend like it didn't happen.

I SIGH, tossing my phone to the side. I know that they're probably right. Nothing good can come from me pursuing any kind of relationship with Maxine, no matter how much I like her or how amazing last night was.

There's just one problem.

I'm not sure that I can.

FOUR

Maxine

MY DAD finally leaves the shop and I settle back into my new office chair. I'm supposed to be getting settled in here and organizing the office so that it's all set for me to get to work tomorrow but I can't stop my racing thoughts.

What are the chances of my one-night stand being the new tattoo artist at Eye Candy Ink?

It had been quite the shock when I looked up and saw Ames standing there in the hallway. He looked like he didn't know how to react either and I'm glad that he went with it when I pretended not to know him. That would have been awkward to explain to my dad how I knew him.

That leads to a new problem though.

Can I really work here with him every day and not have it be weird? It was difficult enough just passing him in the hall and not letting on that I knew him and had just had him between my legs a few hours earlier.

Maybe it wouldn't be so strange for most people but I

work with people who are like my brothers. My aunts and uncles will be stopping by, plus my dad, and I don't really want them to know that the guy that I lost my virginity to is working right down the hallway.

I sigh, picking up my phone and trying to figure out the time difference in my head as I bring up my sister, Nichole's, phone number. She's living with her girlfriend in France and working at a small art gallery there. I'm happy for her but it's hard not being able to see her that often and it's always tough to find time to talk to her.

She answers on the third ring, sounding like she was sleeping, and I wince.

"Hey, sis," I say, trying to inject some enthusiasm into my voice.

"What's wrong?" she mumbles right away and I sigh.

"I slept with this guy named Ames and then found out today that he works at Eye Candy Ink and I'm supposed to be managing him and it's a whole mess."

I blurt everything out and she's silent, listening, or maybe she fell asleep again. I tell her about meeting him at Se7en and going home with him. I leave out most of the explicit details from our night together and get to me sneaking out while he was asleep and then pretending to meet him in front of our dad earlier tonight at the shop.

After I finish telling her everything, there's a beat and the Nichole lets out a big breath of air.

"Jeez, Maxine. That was a lot."

"I know," I groan pitifully, resting my head on the desk. "What am I supposed to do now?"

"Well, I think you need to figure out how you feel about this guy first. I know you, and you wouldn't just go off and spend the night with someone if you didn't have some sort of feelings for him. Do you like him? Do you want a relationship with him?"

I think about it and I know the answer. Yes, I would like to go out with him again, but dating him just seems like too much right now. I'm just getting my feet under me. I'm just getting set up here at work. Plus, it would be my first relationship and when it inevitably went sour, wouldn't that just make it more tense and uncomfortable around here than it already is?

"Yes, but I'm not sure that it's worth the risk."

"You and your risk analysis," Nichole says and I can picture her rolling her eyes at me in her head.

"I know, I know, but if I see him and we break up, it's just going to be miserable around here."

She thinks that over and I can hear Michelle, Nichole's girlfriend, getting up. It must be about time for them to get ready for work and I check the clock, seeing that it's close to eleven p.m. here. I must have been so lost in my thoughts that I lost track of time.

"If that's how you feel, then I know that you can do it. You can do anything. You're so strong, Maxine, and I know that you're going to rock being the manager there. You could handle a little awkwardness if things go bad, but who is to say that they'll go bad? Maybe you'll both fall in love and grow old together."

"You and your romantic fantasies," I tease her. "I guess you're right though about me being able to handle it," I say, starting to grow more confident that Ames and I can move past this.

"Besides, if it does get to be too much, you can just fire him," she jokes and I laugh.

"I don't think I'm quite ready to fire anyone yet."

"You should try it on Rooney tomorrow," she says with a laugh and I join her.

I talk to her for a few more minutes, listening as she tells me about her and Michelle's plans for this coming weekend. I miss seeing both of them and I mention that it would be great to see her in person. I'm hoping that she comes home for a visit soon.

"I'll talk to you later. Good luck!" she says.

"Thanks, I'll text you later!"

We hang up and I lean back in my chair.

"You can do this. It will be fine. Just talk to Ames tomorrow and let him know that you want to keep it professional. No big deal."

I finish up my pep talk and begin to gather up my belongings and head for the door, smiling when I see Rooney, Harvey, and Banks all hanging around outside the shop's front door.

"Were you guys waiting for me?" I ask as I lock the front door behind me.

"Nah, we were just grabbing something to eat and saw your car. We thought we'd stop and see if you were okay," Rooney says as Banks passes me a takeout box.

"Thanks," I say as we head across the street to where my car is parked next to theirs in the lot.

They wait until I'm inside and buckled up before they wave and climb into their own cars and I know that I'm lucky to have them for my makeshift brothers.

FIVE

Ames

I COULD BARELY SLEEP last night and I'm not sure if it's because I couldn't stop thinking about Maxine, or if it was because her scent was still clinging to my sheets. Either way, I figured the only way to stop all of this craziness was to just come in early to talk to her.

That plan may have worked, except Maxine didn't come in until we were opened and by then I was busy with a client. It was like that all day and I would have thought that she was avoiding me, except we both seemed to be slammed with work.

It isn't until closing time when I have a chance to head back to her office. Banks, Maxine, and I are the last ones in the shop now since Harvey had today off and Rooney and Ender finished their last client over an hour ago.

I've been thinking about how to approach her all day. What do I say? I'm glad now that it's just us in the back because I don't really want to have this conversation in front of people that she considers her brothers.

"Hey, got a minute?" I ask, rapping on her open office door.

She looks up, her blue eyes unfocused for a minute. She looks at me, and then past me and when she sees that there's no one else nearby, she nods.

"Sure."

I step inside her office and close the door, taking a seat in the chair across the desk from her.

"I thought maybe we should talk about the other night."

"Yeah, me too," she says, pushing the papers that she was going over to the side as she gives me her undivided attention.

"I didn't know who you were that night," I blurt out and she nods.

"Me either. If I had..." She trails off and I know that neither one of us wants to say that we wouldn't have gone home together.

"That night was great but I really love working here and I don't want that to change."

"Me either."

"So, we're just going to keep things professional?" I ask, motioning between the two of us, and she nods, looking relieved.

"Yes, I just started working here and I wanted to get settled before I start dating or all of that. And I definitely don't want to see someone who I work with. That would just be too messy."

"Right," I say but her words don't sit right.

I especially don't like the idea of her with someone else. She's too good for anyone. Doesn't she realize that?

"Good, then we'll keep it professional."

"Good."

"Good," I repeat, feeling way out of my depth. "Are you done for the day?"

"Yeah, I was just getting ready to head home."

"Can I walk you to your car?"

"Sure, that would be nice," she says, her voice nothing but polite indifference and I hate it.

I want to hear her scream my name while I'm buried deep inside of her. I want to hear her moan and pant in my ear, and I kiss my way down her neck. She should only ever sound like that around me. Not like she's talking to some stranger.

She gathers her purse and stands from the desk and I follow suit, pushing my chair forward so that we can both get to the door. She smiles up at me and it looks a little forced. I do my best to return it as she steps into my space.

I reach past her and I swear it was just to open the door for her, but the next thing I know, our lips are molded together, her tongue is in my mouth and I've got her backed up against the office door.

I know that I should pull back, that we just agreed to *not* do this, but I can't stop. Not when she's making those breathy sounds that I love or when she digs her hands into my hair and tugs on the ends the way that drives me wild and leaves me panting and aching for more.

My hands tangle in her hair and I tug on the ends, tilting her head back so that I have more access to her mouth. Her lips part beneath mine and we waste no time in tangling our tongues together and deepening the kiss.

She tastes like chocolate and honey and I can't get enough. I've got her pinned to the door and she's wrapped around me tight. I'm about two seconds away from wrapping her legs around my waist and dry humping her against the door.

Before I can though, a knocking sound interrupts us and we both pull away to stare at each other in wide-eyed horror.

"Maxine? Are you still in there? I'm done for the night and was going to walk you to your car," Banks calls, and I back away from her as Maxine tries to straighten her mussed hair.

Her lips are still red and puffy from my own, and I'm sure that we're both flushed. It's going to be obvious to Banks what we were doing in here.

I'm so screwed.

"Maxine?" Banks calls again and she looks at me in panic.

I shrug, not knowing what to do either.

"Yeah, be right out!" she calls and I look at her like she's nuts.

She glares at me, and I reach down and grab her purse for her. She opens the door and Banks steps back. He's so engrossed in his phone and whatever message he has there that he doesn't even look up until we're all headed down the hallway.

"Oh, I didn't know that you were still here, Ames."

"Yeah, I just finished up a client and came to see if I could walk Maxine to her car too," I lie, looking at him over my shoulder as we head out the front door.

"Oh, well if you're walking her, then I'm going to take off. I parked over there," he says, pointing in the opposite direction.

"Sounds good, man. See you tomorrow," I tell him, thankful that he didn't seem to suspect anything between Maxine and me.

"Bye, Banks," Maxine calls but he's back to looking at his phone and frowning.

"Think he's going to go spray paint some building?" I joke and she laughs.

"Who knows with him."

I walk her over to her car, waiting for her to unlock the door and climb in.

"I'll see you tomorrow," she says and I nod, not trusting myself to speak.

My fingers itch to hold her again but I force myself to close the door as she starts the car and I step back. She waves as she drives off and I head over to where my own car is parked, climbing behind the wheel and trying to ignore my still tingling lips.

I have no idea what is going on between Maxine and me. Can we really keep things professional between us if we can barely keep our hands off of each other? Do either of us really want to?

One thing is sure though.

I'm so screwed.

SIX

Maxine

SO, I'm not going to be able to keep things professional between Ames and me.

I think that much is obvious after the way that we made out in my office last night. I forget about my reaction to him. I'm so used to not feeling anything around guys that I thought being around Ames and keeping it strictly professional would be a piece of cake. But then I stare into those blue eyes of his and my whole body just comes alive.

Being near him is like standing in the middle of a field during a bad storm. I know that I should probably run for cover but there's something so beautiful and magnetic about it that I can't move.

I've never done anything crazy before in my life. I don't take risks, I plan everything out, and I've had my future mapped out for years. My sister Nichole is the wild one. The one who bucked tradition and ran off with her girl-friend. Who moved across the ocean to a country that she barely spoke the language of. My parents are happy that she followed her dreams, but I'm jealous.

I could never do that. I would have to take language classes, get a job over there, an apartment, everything would have to be lined up and thought through.

I hate being the boring sister. That was part of the reason why I went home with Ames. I wanted to have a one-night stand. I wanted to do something wild before I got back to my five-year plan.

I liked being crazy with Ames. Maybe that's why I don't want to keep things professional between us. I don't want to give up the way he makes me feel. Besides that, the allure of sneaking around and doing something forbidden is intoxicating.

I head into work early the next day. I hadn't been able to sleep much last night, my body too worked up from Ames and his kisses and my mind racing with thoughts about the two of us.

I'm surprised when I walk in and see Banks sitting in his room. He's busy working on some tattoo design and I leave him alone, heading back to my office. My phone rings as I hang up my purse and I dig it out, smiling when I see Nichole's name on the screen.

"Hey, are you calling to tell me that you're coming home soon?"

"Not yet," she says and I can hear the smile in her voice. "I was calling to see if you had figured out your thing with that Ames guy."

"I did, but then..." I trail off, trying to think of how to word it.

I already know what Nichole will say. She's always trying to get me out of my shell and part of me knows that she's right. I should try to live a little more.

"What happened?"

"He came to talk to me and we agreed that we should just keep things professional between us. Then he went to get the door for me to walk me to my car and we ended up making out. Banks knocked and interrupted us and then we both just went home."

"What did you want to happen?" she asks and I bite my bottom lip, thinking about how worked up I was last night.

"I wanted to go home with him again."

Nichole gives an excited little scream and I giggle. I can feel the blush staining my cheeks.

"So, you're into him then?"

"Yeah, he's hot for sure, but he's also just a cool guy. He makes me laugh and feel a little bit crazy, but also safe."

"Then why don't you ask him out? There's no rule that you can't date someone in the shop."

"Because Dad will freak out!"

Nichole sighs and I know that she knows that I'm right.

"You're an adult, Maxine. If you want to date him, then there's nothing that Dad can do about it. If you want to be with him, then be with him."

I hear Rooney and Harvey laughing as they burst through the front doors of the tattoo shop and I know that it's time for me to get to work.

"We're opening now. I should go but I'll call you soon."

"Okay, I love you. Text me if you need anything!"

"I will. Love you too."

I hang up and toss my phone aside, leaning back in my chair and stretching. Banks shows up in the doorway a minute later and I smile at him. Banks has always been close to Nichole and me. He even pretended to date Nichole until her and Michelle were comfortable with coming out to everyone.

"Hey, Banks. Got all of your designs done?"

"Yeah," he says, coming into the office and closing the door behind him. "I wanted to see if you wanted to talk about Ames."

That's the good thing about Banks. He's straightforward.

"There's not much to say. We, uh, we hooked up one night and then I found out that he worked here. We tried to keep it professional and I just..." I trail off, not knowing what to say.

"But you don't want to."

"Yeah."

"Then don't. Ames seems like a good guy. Besides, he'd be an idiot to hurt you when he knows that we all love you and would pick your side."

"That's what Nichole said too. She thinks I should ask him out."

He nods, looking thoughtful and I wait for him to work things out in his head.

"Then ask him out. I won't tell anyone and you'll be able to see if there's anything between you two before Rooney or your dad gets wind of it."

I smile gratefully at him and nod. A second later, Rooney bursts through the office door and I can't help but laugh as he almost tackles Banks in the process.

"Hey, Maxine. I just wanted to see if you needed anything."

"Thanks, Rooney, but I'm good."

"Are we having a meeting?" Harvey asks, appearing in the doorway behind Banks.

"No," I say as Rooney tells him yes and takes a seat in the chair across from my desk.

"Did I miss something?" Ames asks as he comes up behind Harvey.

"No," we all say at once and Ames looks suspicious for a minute before his eyes meet mine.

He gives me a smile and I can tell that he doesn't know how to act around me now.

"Alright, everyone. Get out. Get to work," I order and Rooney makes a whip-cracking noise as he leaves.

Ames is the last one to go and I clear my throat, motioning for him to come into my office.

"Hey," he says quietly with an almost shy smile.

"Hey. I know that we said that we would keep things between us professional but after last night, it doesn't seem like I can do that. So, I was wondering..."

"Yes."

"If you would go out with me sometime."

"Yes," he says again, smiling wide now.

"Cool. Then you can pick me up tomorrow night."

He grins, leaning over the desk and kissing me quickly before he stands up and heads back to his own room to get to work.

My heart races and I smile all day.

SEVEN

Ames

"BE HONEST. You picked this for our date so that you could show off for me," Maxine says with a laugh as I lead her into the paint and pour class.

"Maybe," I say, shifting the wine bottles and glasses to my other hand so I can sign us in at the front counter. "It also sounded fun and not like the standard old dinner and a movie date."

"I've never been on one of those. Is it boring?" she asks shyly and I look at her in surprise.

I knew that she was inexperienced with sex but I thought that she had at least been to a movie with a guy.

"Well, I'll take you out on that date next time," I promise her.

She gives me a shy smile, the kind that I love. Maxine is such a wonderful mix of sweet, timid, and sultry vixen. She's more reserved around everyone else, but with me, especially when I've got my hands or mouth on her, she's a wildcat. A temptress. My dream girl.

We head into the big craft room at the back of the art store and I take a seat on the side of the large table set up, pulling out the chair next to it for Maxine. There's a another table up front with supplies laid out and Maxine heads over to grab us a canvas and some brushes.

There are a few other people here for the class, one other couple up front and then a few groups of women who all already seem like they're a little buzzed. They laugh loudly as they take their seats at the table next to ours, and I smile. I can already tell that they're going to be a lot of fun.

"What kind of wine did you want? I brought a pinot grigio, a rosé, and a cabernet sauvignon."

"I'll take some of the rosé, please," Maxine says as she looks around the room. "The picture looks really advanced," Maxine whispers, sounding nervous and I pour her a little more wine, hoping that it helps her relax.

"You'll do great. This is just supposed to be for fun. No one is grading it."

She takes a deep breath, nodding as she grabs her glass of wine and takes a big gulp.

"What kind of wine is that?" one of the older ladies sitting next to us asks and I have to check the label.

"It's called Summer Water Societé," I tell her and she oh's.

"I love the pink wines," she says with a wink, and Maxine and I laugh.

"Want to try some?" I ask and the next thing I know, she and her friends are all crowded around us, talking wine.

I hear one of them ask Maxine if we're together and when she says yes, I can't hold back the grin that threatens to split my face.

"Lucky you. He sure is fine. Do you kids still say that?" Louise asks.

"No, they say thick now," her friend Thelma says, eyeing my butt.

And no, I'm not making those names up.

I step a little closer to Maxine and she laughs. I'm just happy that she seems to be having a good time and finally stopped worrying about doing well on the painting.

Maxine has seemed stressed for the last few days with work and I wanted to do something fun and silly with her to help her relax.

The class starts soon after and I take my seat next to Maxine, smiling encouragingly as they start to walk us through how to make our trees. We spend the next few hours drinking wine, trying our best to follow the instructor's directions, and laughing with Thelma and Louise.

By the time that we're ready to leave, we're both a little buzzed and we have plans to meet our new friends at the next paint and pour night. I promised them that I'd bring more of the wine that they liked.

Our paintings are still a little wet so I lay them in the trunk and then hurry to get Maxine's door.

"Should we walk for a little bit?" she asks and I close the door, taking her hand as we start to stroll down the sidewalk.

The cool night air helps to clear my head and we pass a cart selling pizza slices.

"I'm starving," Maxine says.

"Me too," I say as I buy us each a slice before we start walking once again.

"That was a lot of fun," Maxine says when we eventually make it back to my car and start to head back home.

She doesn't live that far from me and I love that she's

close by. I wish that the night didn't have to end but it's already close to midnight and I know that we both have to work tomorrow.

"I'll walk you up."

She smiles as I help her out of the car and up to the third floor. She has a small apartment. I saw a bit of it when I picked her up and I wonder if she'll invite me in now. Things went well tonight but I'm not sure how fast Maxine wants to take things. I know that we didn't exactly start in the most conventional of ways.

"I had a lot of fun tonight."

"Me too," I tell her as she hesitates outside of her door. "Can I take you out again? We could go see a movie and grab dinner."

"I'd really like that. It's just, I'd like to keep things quiet about us for now. If Rooney finds out, well…" She trails off but she doesn't need to finish that sentence.

If Rooney finds out, then everyone will know. That guy can't keep a secret to save his life.

"I understand and I get it."

She nods, looking relieved and I smile, leaning down and brushing my lips against hers. She seems to want to take things slow between us and I'm alright with that. I just want to spend time with her.

Her hands wrap around my neck and she pulls me back toward her until our lips meet again.

This kiss is different from the one in her office the other night. The passion is still there, but the urgency is gone. Our lips move together leisurely, like they were made to. My hands wrap around her waist, pulling her closer to me as her fingers burrow into my hair.

Our tongues move against each other lazily as we rest

against the doorframe and it isn't long until we're consumed by the other, wrapped up in our embrace.

An apartment door slamming on the floor below has us slowly pulling apart and I smile when I see her love drunk eyes and puffy lips. I'm sure that mine look similar.

"Good night, Maxine. I'll see you tomorrow," I promise her as I lean in and brush my lips against hers one last time.

"'Night, Ames."

I stand and wait until she's locked the apartment door behind her before I make my way slowly back down the stairs and out to my car. I make the short drive back to my place and head up to my apartment.

Tonight, I smile as I bury my face in the pillow and breathe in Maxine's sweet scent. I dream about her in my sleep and wake excited to head to work to see my girl.

EIGHT

Maxine

AMES and I were supposed to go out on our dinner and a movie date tonight but then we heard Rooney and Harvey talking about going to see the newest superhero movie so we had to change plans.

We still went out to dinner. He took me to eat at this cute little Italian place. It was out of the way and I know that he chose it because we were unlikely to run into anyone that we knew there.

We had gotten to know each other more over dinner. He told me about his family and I told him about mine. I met one of his brothers briefly when he stopped by the shop last night right before close. Ames told me that Anthony was headed to New York to try out for some special comedian venue there. His other brother, Alexander, already lives out there. He's some big real estate developer and seems to be doing well for himself. I laughed as he told me about some of the funnier stories from growing up with them. His parents live down in Philadelphia and Ames said that he tries to see them at least once a month.

I love that he's so close with his family since I'm so close with mine. I talk to my mom two to three times a week and my dad even more, although some of that is just about the business. We have weekly Sunday dinners with everyone over and spend holidays together every year.

When we left the restaurant and Ames asked me if I got seasick. I had laughed thinking that he was joking. He wasn't. I didn't even know about the tiki boat rides offered at Allegheny Park. It's late and besides the bartender, we have the boat to ourselves.

The little tiki bar is in the center of the boat. Well really, it's more like a floating platform, and I grip the bar top hard as we take off out onto the water.

"What can I get you two?" the bartender asks with a practiced smile and I look over the menu.

"I'll take a beer," Ames says.

"I'll have a blue Hawaiian cocktail," I tell him.

The bartender gets to work on our drinks and Ames and I take in the views as we float over the calm water.

"You know, I've lived in Pittsburgh all of my life and I've never been out here. It's cool to see the city like this," I tell Ames and he grins at me.

"Glad I could be here when you experienced something new."

I let Ames take my hand and we ride in silence for a few minutes. Soft Hawaiian music plays over the gentle lapping of the water on the side of the boat and I've never felt more relaxed in my life.

"So, you just graduated college then?" Ames asks and I nod, taking a sip of my drink.

"Yeah, I went for business management here in Pittsburgh."

"You wanted to stay close to home?"

"Yeah, I love it here. Plus, I didn't want to leave my family and friends. I always knew that I would be managing Eye Candy Ink, so why not just set up my life here. What about you? Do you miss Philadelphia?"

"Not really. We lived in New York for a bit and I like the bigger cities but I've wanted to work at Eye Candy Ink for as long as I can remember. Zeke, Atlas, Mischa, Nico, Sam, Trixie, those guys are all legends. I wanted to work with them, or at the very least, for them."

I smile, proud of my parents and how talented they are and what they've built. I grew up knowing that my parents were different. For starters, there was about a sixteen-year age gap between them. My dad is covered in tattoos and he's always worn his hair long. My mom loves to dye hers, especially pink, and she has her own collection of tattoos. They were unlike any parents at my school or that my friends had and I had always liked that. They were cooler, and that made me cooler by extension.

"What do your parents do? Were they upset when you wanted to become a tattoo artist?"

"Nah, my mom is an artist and my dad is an art history professor. They were both thrilled that I loved to draw and paint and they've always been really supportive."

"That's good. It seems rare in this career field."

Ames nods as the bartender starts to steer us back toward the dock. I didn't even realize how much time had passed and the sun is just starting to set now. I'm glad that we both worked the earlier shift today because I don't want tonight to end just yet.

I finish off my third blue Hawaiian and thank the bartender as we dock and Ames helps me onto the dock.

"Thanks," I murmur as he keeps my hand held in his.

He's been letting me set the pace and part of me wanted to take things slow, to really see if this thing between us was real or just a physical attraction but I like Ames. He's sweet and thoughtful. He's talented and gets along with everyone. Rooney, Harvey, Banks, even Ender, they all seem to like him. He values family, just like me, he makes me laugh and feel cherished. Most importantly, he's the only man that I've ever met that has made me feel this way. He's the only guy that I haven't been able to forget.

"I was going to take us to the Carnegie Science Center, but I think it's closed now," Ames says as he checks the time on his phone.

"That's alright. We can go some other time."

He leads me over to his car and instead of getting the door for me like I expect, he backs me up and cages me in with his body.

"I don't want tonight to end yet," he murmurs as he stares down into my eyes and I feel myself growing bold.

"Who said it has to end?"

"I don't want to rush you—" he starts and I interrupt him, placing my lips against his.

"You're not. I want you, Ames. What do you say? Take me home?"

He doesn't answer me, just pulls me away from the car so he can open the door and help me inside. He leans down once I'm buckled in, his lips brushing over mine in the hint of a kiss before his lips find the shell of my ear.

"I'll do whatever you want, Maxine. Anything and everything for you."

A shiver runs down my spine and I turn to see the

promise in his eyes before he stands, shuts the door, and rounds the hood. I barely have time to get myself under control before he's climbing behind the wheel and steering us out of the parking lot.

I know that as soon as we're at his place, I'm not going to be able to hold back.

And what's more, I don't want to. I'm all in with this man. I just hope that he feels the same way about me.

NINE

Ames

MAXINE and I crash into my apartment together, both of us too wrapped up in each other to care about waking the neighbors. She's already tugging at my clothes and I hurry to slam the door closed before I help her.

"I love your body," she moans, her lips like a brand as they trail over my skin.

"Fuck," I grit out through clenched teeth as my cock presses painfully against the zipper of my jeans. "Need you."

She hums and my dick pulses at the sound. I grab at her clothes, desperate to feel her skin on mine and she wiggles her way out of them, giving me what I want, giving us what we both want.

"I've been dreaming about you, about this," she whispers in that breathy voice of hers, and I swear that I almost come right then and there.

"Yeah? What did you dream about, Maxine? All of the ways I'm going to make you come?"

She nods frantically, unhooking her bra and reaching for my boxer briefs as we stumble our way down the hallway and into my bedroom.

"Were they dirty dreams? Any fantasies that I need to fulfill?" I whisper into her ear before I nibble along the shell.

"I just need you to fuck me," she half cries as I wrap my arm around her hip, my fingers dipping into her panties to cup her slick pussy.

I slide a finger inside of her wet heat, fucking her with it slowly and she wiggles against me, only growing more frustrated when her ass grinds against my thick erection. My aching cock wants between those sweet globes but I hold back. I want to drive her crazy for me before I sink deep inside of her.

"Like this?" I purr against her shoulder and she shakes her head.

"More."

I add a second finger, pumping slowly and her head falls back against my shoulder. I kiss her shoulder, up her neck, stopping to suck on her pulse point. I moan as I feel it fluttering against my lips.

She's riding my hand now, her juices coating my palm and I need a taste. I pull my fingers out, pushing her soaked panties down her legs and turning her around. I lick my fingers clean, intending to drop to my knees to get a taste between her legs but she beats me to it.

"Maxine," I start but she's already opening wide around my length and I can only groan as her tongue flicks against my piercing. She doesn't tease me long, opening her mouth wider as she takes as much of me into her mouth as she can.

Her hands move over the last few inches and I groan, my fingers twisting and tangling as I fist her hair. She moans, the sound vibrating through me, and I have to look up at the ceiling. The sight of her naked, on her knees before me, my cock stuffed in her mouth is the hottest thing that I've ever seen in my life.

"I need you. I need to fuck you," I grit out as she sucks me harder and she shakes her head but I can't wait another second.

"I promise that I will let you suck my cock literally any other time that you want to, but right now, I just really need to be inside that tight fucking pussy."

She nods, sliding onto the bed and spreading her legs wide for me.

"Fucking hell. How did I get so damn lucky?"

She smiles as I join her, slipping between her thighs and sliding my cock up and down her slit.

"I want you bare," I say against her lips and she nods.

Her hips buck at my words as a moan slips out of her sweet lips. I claim her mouth, thrusting my tongue inside at the same time my cock enters her. We both groan into the kiss, our bodies falling into sync as we move together.

Maxine rolls her hips, grinding down on my cock and I have to think about my grandma to keep from spilling right then and there.

"Fuck, you feel so good," she moans as I start to rut inside of her.

"Jesus," I grunt, pounding into her, drilling her body into the fucking mattress.

Maxine screams, her nails digging into my shoulders as she holds onto me and I pound into her. I can tell that she's close to the edge already and I grit my teeth. I want her to come on my dick at least twice tonight, and I bury my face in her neck as I feel her come.

Her muscles tense and her pussy clamps down tight around my dick, her little walls fluttering around me, trying to milk my cum from me.

"Fuck, that's it. Come all over my cock, Maxine."

Her climax seems to go on for minutes and I smile as she starts to come down only for me to lean up more on my knees and start to fuck her roughly again.

"Oh god!" she cries and I grit my teeth, trying to hold back my own release until she's come again.

"That's it, angel. You feel me owning this pussy?"

"Uh huh," she says, her blue eyes glazed over with lust as I rock into her.

Her pussy starts to clench around me once again and I can feel the familiar tingle at the base of my spine and I know that it won't be long.

"Ames!" she shouts a second later as she finds her release once more and I can't hold back any longer.

"Fuck, yes, that's it. Milk me dry."

She cries out, her orgasm intensifying as I come with her. When we're both down from our peaks, I pull out of her, collapsing on my side and pulling her into my arms.

"No sneaking out this time," I murmur against her damp skin and she nods.

"I don't think I can move even if I want to," she says with a happy giggle and I smile.

"Good, then my plan worked."

She laughs, her head resting on my chest and I smile. We're both still trying to get our breath back and I close my eyes, letting sleep claim me as my angel curls up against my side.

TEN

Maxine

AMES and I have settled into a new routine over the last month. We spend most nights together, usually splitting which apartment we stay at. Then we split and head home to get ready for work and both show up at Eye Candy Ink and act friendly but professional.

It's been heaven.

It's also been getting harder and harder to not be obvious that we're together. I can't tell you how many times I've reached out to hold his hand only to catch myself at the last minute or how many times I've almost leaned in to kiss him, only to remember that we couldn't do that.

I know that keeping our relationship a secret was my idea, but I'm really starting to regret it now.

I love Ames. I think maybe I've been in love with him since the first night that we met. I don't care who knows it, but maybe I should work up the courage to tell him first.

It's Sunday so I'm at my parents' place for our weekly

family dinner. Banks, Harvey, Rooney, and Cat are all hanging out on the back patio and I kiss my mom and dad hello, waving at my uncle Mischa and Atlas, and Aunt Indie and Darcy before I join them. My uncle Nico and aunt Edie must be running late.

"Hey," I greet everyone, taking the mimosa that Cat holds out to me.

"Long week?" I ask her as she downs her own glass.

"Yeah, we had two of the new hires quit after three days, so I've been trying to manage the club and work the floor to help out."

"You should have come to work at Eye Candy Ink, Cat. We're easy to manage. Tell her, Maxine!"

"It's like herding cats."

Cat laughs at that and I see Rooney grinning like the loon that he is out of the corner of my eye.

I stretch out my legs, content to get some sun and catch up with everyone. My dad is making lasagna, some new recipe that he's really excited about, and Uncle Nico and Aunt Edie show up a little bit later, two things of garlic bread in hand.

"Hey, kid. How's it going?" Uncle Nico asks me when I head inside for another drink.

"Pretty good. I've got the office set up the way I like it now and things are running smoothly."

He nods, always a man of few words and soon after Mischa talks him into coming outside for a game of croquet. My mom has been obsessed with playing for the last few weeks and I see that the course is still set up. Seeing Nico, who is almost six and a half feet tall, with one of those little mallets is pretty funny.

"Hey," Banks says as he comes up behind me and I smile. He is so like his dad.

"Hey, how's it going?" I ask, offering him the bottle of champagne but he shakes his head no.

"Pretty good. I was about to ask you the same thing. Are you and Ames doing okay?" he whispers, looking around to make sure that we're alone.

"Yeah, we're great," I tell him and I wonder if that sounded as love-struck to his ears as it did to my own.

"Are you going to tell everyone about you two yet?" he asks, nodding to the back door where everyone is now gathered around to watch Mischa beat Nico at the last hole of croquet.

I can hear the cheers from here and I know that we'll be listening to Uncle Mischa joke about the game for the rest of the night.

"Not yet. I need to talk to him first before we go public. I'm, uh, I'm not sure how my parents are going to take it," I admit.

"You mean your dad?" Banks clarifies with a smile and I laugh.

"Yeah, I mean my dad."

"You might want to do it soon. I think Rooney and Harvey might be on to you two."

I nod. I had a feeling that they were too and I want to be the one to tell my dad. Hopefully he takes it better that way. I just need to work up the courage to actually do it.

"I'll talk to Ames soon. Then this will all be out in the open."

"Do you think he's your one?" Banks asks after a minute and I nod.

There's a legend in my family that everyone takes one look at their person and they just know that they're meant to be. I had never bought into it, but now that I have Ames, I wonder if it's true.

"You think the legend is true?" Banks asks thoughtfully and it's like he can read my mind.

"Maybe. Why? Did you meet someone special?"

"Maybe," he says and when he doesn't elaborate, I know that it's best to let the subject go.

Banks is the type to talk about things on his terms and if you try to push him, he'll just shut down. He has to get it straight in his head before he says it out loud.

"I'll see you out there," he says as another cheer goes up and I wonder who won the game.

"Yeah, I'll be right behind you."

He nods and takes a beer before he heads back outside to join the others. I pull my phone out of my pocket and smile when I see that I have a new message from Ames.

AMES: My mom is dying to meet you.

Maxine: You told her about us?

Ames: Of course. She wanted to know why I couldn't stop smiling.

Ames: Besides, Anthony was dying to tell her about me and my girlfriend.

Maxine: LOL!

I START to type out a response, to ask him if maybe it's time that we tell my parents and family too, but before I can, my name is called from outside. I smile, tucking my phone back in my pocket as I head outside to join the others.

My uncle Mischa wraps his arm around my shoulders

as soon as I step outside and I laugh as he starts to tell me all about how he trounced my uncle Nico at croquet.

"When are you going to bring someone home?" Uncle Mischa asks and I know that he's just trying to get a rise out of my dad but I still tense under his arm.

"Never," my dad says, glaring at him.

"I'm focused on work right now, Uncle Mischa. Where would I find the time to meet someone?" I try to joke.

"Maybe someone at the shop," he suggests with a wiggle of his eyebrows and I wonder for a second if he knows.

"Ha! You know the rule. No fraternization at the shop or you're fired," my dad says, authority ringing in my ears.

My stomach drops at his words. I had never heard of that rule but dating was never really a concern of mine.

What am I going to do now?

I fake a smile and slip out from under Mischa's arm as I cross the porch and take a seat next to Cat on one of the recliners. She and Banks both give me sympathetic looks and I smile back at them, though I know that it's forced.

Looks like I'll have to have a talk with Ames. It's just going to be a different one than I thought.

ELEVEN

Ames

I'M HEADED into work the next day when my brother, Alexander, calls.

"Hey," I answer the phone. "What's up?"

I can hear other phones ringing and people talking in the background and I know that he's at work. He and his wife are both workaholics, although they've both slowed down since they got married in Vegas a few months ago.

"Hey, are you at work?" he asks and he must have closed his office door because the background noise is gone now.

"No, I'm headed there now. What's up?"

"Just hadn't talked to you in a bit. Wanted to see how things were going."

I pull into the parking lot across from Eye Candy Ink and put the car in park when my phone beeps in my ear.

"Anthony wants to FaceTime," I tell Alexander and he hangs up on me.

I roll my eyes as a second later, I answer Anthony's FaceTime call and see that Alexander is already there.

"Hey, what's up?" I ask, looking up to see if I can spot Maxine's car in the lot.

Maybe I can sneak inside and we can have a few minutes alone before everyone else gets here. I could have her pressed against the door, my cock buried deep inside of her in two minutes and she'll be coming right after that. I don't see her car yet though and I frown, turning back to my brothers.

"Did you get your lady problems figured out?" Alexander asks Anthony and my eyebrows rise.

"Anthony has lady problems? I must really be out of the loop."

"Yeah, he showed up at my place with her a few weeks ago. Uninvited," Alexander stresses and Anthony grins at him.

"Emerson?" I ask him, remembering how he had stopped by the shop with her when he was driving through town a few weeks ago.

"Yeah, and yes, we're fine now," Anthony says, rolling his eyes.

"You're a 'we' now?" I ask, surprised.

"Yes, but that's not why I called."

"Why did you call?"

"I wanted to talk to you about *your* lady problems."

"We're fine," I promise him.

"Mom and Dad said you couldn't stop talking about her," Alexander says and I smile.

"Yeah, things are really good between us. I'm in love with her," I tell them and I can see them both just staring at me on the screen.

"Well," Alexander says, breaking the silence. "I'm going

to be in town for a few days at the end of the week. Why don't we meet up? I can take you out to dinner. Check this girl out."

"Are you trying to get me to invite you to stay at my place?" I ask him.

"God no, I'll be staying at the nearest five-star hotel."

Anthony cracks up and I roll my eyes.

I see Harvey and Rooney pull into the lot. Rooney is air drumming in the passenger seat and Harvey is cracking up. I can't help but smile as they drive and park next to me.

"I've got to get to work but I'll talk to you guys later. I'll see you in a few days, Alexander."

"Bye," they both say and I disconnect.

I bet that they're both still on the call, probably talking about me, but I don't care. Ender looks like he's already inside the shop and Banks is off today. I'm climbing out of my car when some nice Audi pulls up next to me and Gray climbs out.

"Thanks for the ride, Nora," he says and I crane my neck, trying to get a better look at his friend.

Everyone at the shop can see that he's in love with her. He's always talking about her but when you try to ask him about why he doesn't just ask her out, he clams up. There's some kind of history there but Gray is hard to get to open up about things.

"Nora?" Rooney asks, almost tripping over himself to get out of Harvey's car. "It's so nice to finally meet you! This one never shuts up about you," Rooney says as he tries to elbow his way past Gray to the passenger window.

"See you later, Nora," Gray says, trying to hold Rooney back and I join Harvey at the trunk of his car to watch the show.

"How was your weekend?" Harvey asks as Rooney

shouts questions to Nora who is laughing inside her car. Gray is doing his best to shut him up but he can't seem to get a good hold on Rooney.

"Pretty good. I went down to Philly to see my parents. What about you?" I ask him.

"I had to work on Saturday and we had family brunch on Sunday. You should come next weekend. You can meet the rest of the family and we can talk tattoos."

I'm afraid to look at him, too busy wondering if he suspects that Maxine and I are dating. I don't mind if people find out about us, in fact, I'd love to scream it from the rooftops that this girl is mine, but I haven't heard Maxine say anything more about us going public.

"Sounds good," I tell him as Nora waves and drives off.

Gray is glaring at Rooney who is backing away with his hands held up. I start to go over to help Harvey break them up when Maxine pulls into the lot and I freeze.

Her eyes lock with mine and we both grin at each other before she spots the guys and quickly looks away. I'd be lying if I said that seeing her look away from me like that didn't hurt. It also means that I have my answer about us going public.

I turn away from her, trying to smile as I joke around with the guys and head toward the front doors of Eye Candy Ink.

TWELVE

Maxine

IT'S BEEN a busy few days and it's Wednesday before I have a minute alone with Ames. He sneaks into my office just before closing and I smile tiredly as I stand up and move to give him a kiss.

"Are you done for the day?" he asks me, and I shake my head.

"My dad found some new software so that we can book things easier and it's been a nightmare to set up. I should have taken my aunt Indie up on her offer to get it running."

"Want me to see if I can help?" he offers and I shake my head.

"I have it up and running now. I just need to test it a bit more."

"Are you coming over tonight?" he asks and I shush him, eyeing the open door.

It's only opened a crack but I don't know who else is still

around. My dad has already been acting suspicious the last two days and I wonder if someone told him. I know that I should break up with Ames before he does find out and one of us gets fired, but I can't seem to bring myself to do it. I don't want to lose Ames.

"We're the only ones here. Ender just left and I told him that I was going to walk you to your car."

He looks a little hurt by my reaction and I feel like crap.

"Sorry, I just..."

I don't know what to do here. Do I break up with him and save his job? Or do we just try to keep this to ourselves? At least for a little bit longer.

Either way, I know that this is going to hurt.

"You just what, Maxine?" he asks after a minute, sounding a little annoyed and a little hurt.

I still don't know how to answer him and I stare at him, my heart starting to race.

"I'm not ashamed or afraid for people to find out about us. I know how I feel about you and that's not going to change because Rooney knows and teases us a bit."

"I know—" I start but he cuts me off.

"I want to take you out and not have to worry about ducking into an alleyway or something. I want to go to dinner and not have to pick someplace out of the way so that we don't run into anyone. I want to be with you. What I can't figure out is why you don't seem to want that too. Are you embarrassed of me? Are you ashamed to be dating me?"

"No!" I tell him right away and I hate that I ever made him think that. "It's just complicated."

I don't know what my dad will do if he finds out that I'm seeing Ames. *Will my dad really fire him because we were dating? What if he knows that I'm in love with Ames?*

I know that it was Ames' dream to work at Eye Candy Ink and I don't want to be the reason that he lost his dream.

"No, it's not. It's not complicated at all. Do you want to be with me, Maxine?"

"Yes, but... I don't want you to get fired. I know that my parents, my dad especially, will get all protective of me."

"I can handle your dad," he says confidently but I shake my head.

"You don't know my family. I'm the youngest and they still treat me like a baby."

"Maybe this will help them see you in a different light."

"There's also kind of a rule that you can't work at Eye Candy Ink and date each other. I just found out about it this weekend at brunch. If we told them, one of us would get fired and I don't think that it will be me."

"Shouldn't that be my decision?" Ames asks and I don't know what to say.

"I don't want that for you. I don't want you to have to choose between me and your dream job."

"You're worth it, Maxine," he says, taking both of my hands in his. "I'm all in with you. I have been since the first night. You have to know that. It's just you that needs to make a decision."

"Please, can we just keep it between us for a little bit longer?"

"For how much longer, Maxine?"

"I... I don't know."

He stares down at me, and I can see the hurt and disappointment in his eyes. It breaks my heart and I want to take the words back but before I can, he drops a kiss on my lips before he heads for the door, leaving me debating what I should do.

What's the right answer here?

I'm not sure that there is one. All I know is that I don't want to lose Ames. I'm in love with him. I just need to work up the courage to tell my family now.

THIRTEEN

Ames

I HAVEN'T SEEN Maxine outside of work for the past few days. She said that she was busy and I was trying to give her space to make her decision. I wanted to walk back into her office right after I left and tell her that I would stay a secret for as long as she wanted to. I didn't want to lose her but I also know that I can't keep hiding with her.

Sometimes I think that maybe she's right and we should keep our relationship a secret. I don't want to lose my job here or the friends that I've made, but I know that she's worth it. Being with her is worth it. I can find a different job in the city if it came to that.

I've been keeping busy, trying to distract myself. Getting ready for Alexander's visit and staying up on all of my upcoming client's designs have helped but it's still not enough to distract me from how much I miss Maxine.

At home, I can smell her on my sheets. Her toothbrush is still in my bathroom, some of her clothes still folded on top of my dresser. Everywhere I look, I can still see her. The only time that I'm at peace is when I'm at Eye Candy Ink working.

I can get lost in tattooing but I think a big part of it is knowing that she's right down the hall. I'm starting to live for those brief glimpses of her, even if things are a little strained between us.

I can hear her shoes squeak out in the hallway and I crane my neck, hoping to catch sight of her as she passes. Rooney pops up in my doorway just as she's walking by though and I sigh, trying not to show how frustrated I am as I look over to Rooney.

"Hey, what's up?" I ask him as he bounces into my room and up onto my tattoo table.

"You have a guest. Some suit. Want me to tell him to get lost?"

I can't help grinning at that. I wonder what Alexander would say if Rooney told him to leave. Unfortunately, I'll never know because Alexander appears in my doorway a second later.

"Hey," I greet him, standing up and making a show of wiping off my hands before I go in to hug him.

He still glances down at his suit after I've stepped back and I roll my eyes. He must be going to another meeting after this if he's still dressed up and worried about his appearance.

"Rooney, this is my older brother, Alexander. Alexander, this is Rooney. He works here too."

"Looking to get a tattoo?" Rooney asks with a grin and a wiggle of his eyebrows and I see Alexander frown at him.

"No thanks."

"I've been offering him one for years and he always turns me down too," I tell Rooney.

"Maybe he just wants one from the best," Rooney suggests and I roll my eyes.

"You're not the best. Maybe your dad..." I say, trailing off. I know that this will get a rise out of him.

"Psh," Rooney starts but before he can continue, the front door of the shop slams open and I hear someone scream my name.

Rooney slides off of the table, his eyes wide as he stares out into the hallway.

"What the fuck did you do?" Rooney and Alexander ask at the exact same time and I shot both of them a glare before I look back toward the doorway.

"Uh, I'm guessing that Zeke found out that I've been dating Maxine," I say slowly.

Rooney laughs, looking at me like I must be joking but when he sees my face, his laughter cuts off.

"Oh, dude. You're so fucking screwed."

My brother is leaning against my desk, smiling and I glare at him. Looks like I won't be able to count on him helping me out.

"Thanks, I can see that you're going to be a lot of help here. So much for family loyalty."

"Eden is pregnant, and if it's a girl, then I can kind of see where this Zeke guy is coming from," Alexander says calmly and I gape at him.

"Congratulations, Alex," I say sincerely, stepping forward to hug him and he claps me on the back.

"Thanks."

And that's when Zeke bursts into my room.

Harvey and Banks are both lurking in the hallway, their eyes wide as they peek around the corner at a raging Zeke.

Alexander steps back, leaning against the desk once

more and crossing his arms over his chest as he gets ready to watch the show.

Rooney, for his part, tries to leave but Zeke is standing in the doorway, blocking his exit so he inches along the wall behind me. That turns out to be a bad move because when Zeke takes a step toward me, I step back, and now both Rooney and I are trapped in the back corner.

"How do I keep ending up in these situations?" Rooney mumbles and I try not to laugh at how upset and confused he sounds.

That only seems to make Zeke angrier and I hurry to school my features.

"Hey, Uncle Zeke!" Rooney says, trying to break the tension and Zeke just points a finger at him.

"Did you know?" he asks with a glare.

"Only for like the last twenty seconds, I swear," Rooney says, holding his hands up in a don't shoot gesture.

Zeke turns his attention on me and I hold my hands up too, my heartbeat pounding in my ears. He takes another step toward me and I gulp, but I'm saved by an angel.

My angel.

Maxine comes sliding around the corner and hurries into the office. Her wide eyes meet mine and I give her a strained smile.

"Yeah, so, your dad knows about us now."

FOURTEEN

Maxine

"YEAH, I CAN SEE THAT," I say, only slightly panicked as I try to pull my dad away from Ames and Rooney.

"That's right!" My dad says, glaring at Ames.

"How did you find out?"

"Uncle Max saw you two out one night. He just told me. He thought that I already knew."

"That explains the text I got from him a few minutes ago," I mumble, remembering the text that just said I'm sorry in all caps.

"So, it's true then? You've been seeing him?" my dad asks, looking at me like I'm crazy and I roll my eyes.

"Yes, and before you ask me why I didn't tell you, well..." I trail off, waving my hands at him. "I didn't want to have to deal with this!"

"I have every right to be upset. You kept this from me. You know the rules around here."

"So, you're going to fire me?" I ask, crossing my arms over my chest and glaring back at him.

"Am I interrupting something?" comes a soft voice from behind me and it takes me a second to place it.

I gasp and whirl around to spot Nichole and Michelle standing in the hallway, suitcases in hand.

"Oh my gosh!" I yell, forgetting about my dad and Ames momentarily as I run over to throw my arms around her neck. "What are you two doing here?"

"We wanted to surprise you."

"Mission accomplished," I say as I hug Michelle.

She laughs and I look over to see my dad hugging Nichole and glaring at Ames over her head.

"So, you finally found out about these two, huh?" Nichole asks and I glare at her.

"*Finally*?" my dad yells and I see Rooney hide behind Ames.

"Yeah, they've been dating for ages now," Nichole says helpfully and I want to strangle her.

"Ages?" my dad asks, growing more agitated.

"Dad! Stop. I'm allowed to have a life and Ames is a good guy and I'm in love with him. You don't get to come in here and scare him away. I want to be with him."

The whole room is silent, everyone staring at me wide-eyed.

"I love you too," Ames says, his eyes locked on me and I realize that I just blurted that out for the first time in front of everyone.

"You do?" I ask quietly, turning to face him and he grins at me.

"Yeah, of course I do. How could anyone not?"

Ames steps toward me and cradles the back of my head

in his hand. His lips are lowering toward mine when a throat clears behind me, and I realize that I still have to deal with my dad.

"Ames and I are together and we're in love. I know that it's against your shop rules and that you might not be happy about this, but I am. Oh, and if you try to fire him, then I'll quit too."

I raise my chin, gripping Ames' hand tight in mine as I stare down my dad. He studies my face and I swear it's like everyone in the shop is holding their breath, waiting to see what will happen.

"You really love him? *Him?*" my dad asks quietly and I smile, shaking my head.

"Yeah, him. I really love him."

"Alright, but you and I need to get some things straight," he says, pointing at Ames and motioning for him to follow him back toward my office.

I want to object, but before I can, Ames squeezes my hand and kisses me quickly. He follows after him, and I watch him go, wondering what my dad could possibly have to say to him and why can't he say it in front of me?

"So that was Ames, huh?" Nichole asks after a beat and I can't help but laugh out loud.

Leave it to Nichole to break the tension.

"Yeah, aren't you glad that you came home now?"

"So glad," she says, wrapping her arm around my shoulders and tugging me into her side.

"It's good to have you here," I whisper as we all stare down the hallway at the closed office door.

"Missed you, Maxine."

"Missed you more, Nichole," I say as everyone pretends to work while keeping an eye on the back office door.

I'm about two seconds from storming back there when the door opens and I hold my breath, waiting to see Ames' face.

FIFTEEN

Ames

I FOLLOW Zeke into the back office and close the door behind me. He seems to have calmed down since he first came into the shop but I still stay close to the door, just in case.

"Maxine is my baby girl, and she's never been interested in boys. I guess, as her father, I was hoping that maybe she never would, but that's not fair. She has been happier these last few weeks and I suppose that has to do with you."

He pauses and I don't know what to say, so I just nod.

"As long as you continue to make her happy, then we don't have a problem. You seem like a nice guy, everyone at the shop likes you, and I guess that's good enough for me. But I will be watching you."

"I understand, sir. I love your daughter. I would never do anything to hurt her."

He studies my face for a moment and I hope that he can

see how sincere I am. I would never do anything to hurt her or jeopardize my relationship with her.

He nods once more and stretches out a hand toward me. I eye it for a second before I place mine in his and we shake.

"Now get back to work," he orders and I nod, hurrying back to my room and my girl.

"All good?" she asks when I reach her side and I smile.

"Yeah, we're all good."

Rooney has left and so have Banks and Harvey.

"Ames, this is my sister, Nichole, and her girlfriend, Michelle. Guys, this is Ames."

I smile, taking the hand of the girl who looks like a slightly older version of Maxine. She grins at me, and I like her instantly. Her girlfriend is the opposite of the Miller girls, her hair midnight black and with big brown eyes. She shakes my hand with a smile and turns to look at Nichole.

"Should we go get settled in at the house?" Michelle asks and Nichole nods, taking her hand.

It's obvious that they love each other and I look over to Maxine to see her smiling up at me.

"Oh, yeah, and this is my brother, Alexander," I say when I spot him still in his spot by my desk.

He rolls his eyes at me, and I grin.

"Alexander, this is Maxine."

"It's nice to meet you," Alexander says, sounding formal and I roll my eyes at him.

"Nice to meet you too," Maxine says with a smile.

"I'll catch up with you two later," Alexander says as he checks his watch and I wonder what meeting he's going to now since it's almost seven p.m.

"See ya, and congratulations again!" I call after him and he smiles once more before he heads for the door.

I'll have to remember to text Eden later on and tell her congratulations and see how she's feeling.

"So, now that we're official, what should we do first?" Maxine asks, and I grin down at her.

"Well, I can finally take you out on the dinner and a movie date."

"Oh, sounds exotic," she jokes and I laugh.

"And you could also move in with me."

She stares wide-eyed up at me, and I lean down and kiss her lips.

"I love you, Maxine. I want to spend all of my free time with you. What do you say? Will you move in with me?"

"Yeah," she says, almost shyly and I grin.

"I love you."

"I love you too," she whispers against my lips and I can't wait any longer to seal my mouth against hers.

SIXTEEN

Maxine

ONE YEAR LATER...

I SMILE as I look outside to see my dad and fiancé standing side by side at the grill. It's Sunday and we're all at my parents' house for weekly family brunch.

It's taken my dad a while to come around to the idea of Ames and me. We used to try to avoid touching or kissing in front of him but I think seeing us together has actually helped. He knows that we're committed to each other and that we really do love each other. Ames even asked my dad for his approval before he proposed to me a few months ago. I knew then that he was finally okay with us being together.

My mom has been supportive from the start but I was never really worried about her reaction. She's just happy to see me so happy and Ames definitely makes me happy.

The wedding is set for this fall and I'm so excited to

have Nichole and Michelle back for the wedding. There's even talk of the two of them getting married when they're back home and I'm fully on board with having a double wedding weekend.

Nichole and Michelle have both agreed to be my brides-maids and Ames has asked his brothers, Anthony and Alexander, to be his. Rooney had been outraged at that but Ames promised him that he could plan the bachelor party and he got over it.

"Need anything?" Ames asks as he passes by me to head into the kitchen and I shake my head.

I see his eyes dip to my half empty glass of lemonade though and I know that he'll be bringing me some more. He's so attentive and sweet to me.

I moved in with him a month after he asked me to. I had to wait until my lease was up on my place but by then, I was basically already moved in with him since I slept there every night. I'm pretty sure Ames was moving stuff while I was at work some days too and I love that he was so excited for us to be living together.

"Hey," Cat says as she joins me on the deck.

She takes the Adirondack chair next to mine and I look over to see her fiancé, Ender, standing behind her. It's always like that with them. Wherever Cat is, Ender is never far behind.

"Sorry we're late," Sayler says as she rushes in with Rooney hot on her heels.

Harvey and Coraline are right behind them and my stomach starts to growl as I smell the appetizers that Cora-line made for today. She'll probably have to leave soon to get back to her restaurant, Wild Thyme, but it's always nice to see her, even for just a little bit.

Banks and Palmer should be here in a little bit. It takes longer now that their baby boy is finally here.

"Banks just texted and said that Palmer just got done feeding Kya, so they're on their way now," Ames says as he walks out with a bottle of barbeque sauce and a new lemonade for me.

I smile as he passes me the lemonade and kisses the top of my head. We've been talking about having kids of our own. Banks and Palmer's little girl is so adorable and seeing her has given me the itch.

I know that Ames would be an amazing dad, and I want to start a family with him. I want everything with him.

Ames heads back over to the grill and I smile as I look around at my family all gathered together. My mom is talking with Aunt Indie and Aunt Darcy. Uncle Nico is cuddling Aunt Edie over by the garden and she giggles, elbowing him as she pulls away. Aunt Cat and Uncle Max are both talking to Harvey and Coraline by the kitchen door and Rooney is chasing Sayler around the backyard, trying to tickle her.

I turn my face up to the sun, enjoying the cool breeze until I feel his eyes on me. Even now, feeling him watching me still causes me to shiver. I smile, peeking one eye open to see him grinning at me. When he nods to the house, I grin, knowing exactly what he means.

I stretch, making sure that my shirt roams up before I stand and casually walk toward the kitchen door. I can hear his footsteps behind me and I grin as I pick up my pace and head inside and up to my own room.

We pass by Banks and Palmer in the kitchen so I know that everyone will be distracted and no one will notice that we're gone.

Ames grabs my hand and takes the stairs two at a time

up to my old room. I laugh as he closes the door and pushes me up against it, his lips claiming mine right away.

I get lost in his touch, his embrace, and I'm about to reach for his pants when I hear my dad call my name.

Ames groans and I laugh.

"Later. I'll make it worth the wait," I promise him, and he gives me another quick kiss.

"It's always worth it with you, Maxine."

"I love you," I say, my insides melting and he smiles down at me softly, love shining in his eyes.

"I love you too."

SEVENTEEN

Ames

FIVE YEARS LATER...

"BE GOOD FOR GRANDPA ZEKE," I tell my son, Ansel, as I give him a hug goodbye.

He's about to start preschool but Zeke and Edie have been watching him for the last few years while Maxine and I were at work. They loved spending time with their grandson and they were cheaper than any daycare around town.

My parents come up at least once a month to see us now too. Even Anthony and Alexander have been making a point to see the family more. We're headed up to a cabin with them after work this weekend. It will be nice to get the kids together and to see everyone for a few days.

We still have the weekly Sunday brunches at Zeke's house. Most of the original Eye Candy Ink tattoo artists are either retired or thinking about retiring, so I spend my time between the two shops. Maxine is working hard to find new tattoo artists to fill their places but it's taking longer than she thought it would.

"I'll see you guys tonight. Want me to pick up dinner?" I ask Zeke as he helps Ansel take off his shoes and line them up by the door.

"Pizza!" Ansel screams and I grin.

"You got it, buddy. Grandpa Zeke was just telling me that he was hungry for it."

Zeke gives me a glare and I grin. I know that he eats pizza at least once a week because it's Ansel's favorite food right now. Before that, we practically lived off of peanut butter sandwiches and macaroni and cheese.

"I'll see you later," I say, waving as I jog down the front porch steps and head back to my car.

Maxine calls me as I'm parking at Eye Candy Ink and sounds terrible.

"Are you alright?" I ask, hurrying out of my car and up to the shop. "I'm just walking in now."

"Ugh, I can't stop throwing up," she says, sounding miserable and I backtrack to my office, grabbing the Sprite that I have in my little office refrigerator.

"Was it something that you ate?" I ask her as I open up the bathroom door and see her sitting next to the toilet, her back against the wall.

"No," she says with a grateful sigh as I pass her the bottle of pop.

"Want me to take you to the doctor?"

"Not yet."

"You're kind of scaring me, Maxine," I say, crouching down next to her and brushing some of her hair away from her face.

"I'm throwing up because I'm pregnant."

"Really?" I ask, a smile threatening to split my face.

"Yeah, I found out last night but you had just fallen asleep."

"You should have woken me! We could have celebrated."

"How?" she asks with a laugh and I join her.

"I don't know, birthday cake and pickles?"

She laughs and then groans and I hold her hair back just in time.

"I'm sorry, I'll never mention food again," I promise her as she throws up again.

When she's done, I pass her some wet paper towels and join her on the bathroom floor.

"I'm so happy," I say as I pull her against my side and wrap my arm around her shoulders. "Should I cancel the trip this weekend? Everyone will understand if you're not feeling up to it."

"No, the morning sickness should pass soon. I'll be alright."

"We're going to have to get a bigger place," I say as I think about our already cramped apartment.

"I know. I want a house. Something cute with a big backyard so we can get a dog or two."

Maxine starts to list off everything that she wants with the new house and I just smile. I know that half of the things are probably just the hormones talking but I still make a list to circle back to in a few weeks.

"Love you, Maxine. And I love you too," I say, leaning over and talking to her belly.

"We love you too," she says and I see her eyes starting to drift shut.

"Why don't I drive you home? You can take a nap and then do some work once you have some more energy."

She gives a sleepy nod and I stand, helping her to her feet.

"Let's get you home," I say as I help her outside to her car and buckle her up.

She's asleep before I've even pulled out of the lot and I smile as we head home. Our families are going to be over the moon excited for us and I can't wait to tell Ansel that he's going to be a big brother.

I park and carry my sleeping wife upstairs to our place, smiling as she mumbles my name as I tuck her in.

Who would have thought that all of this would come from a one-night stand? That one night and I got the love of my life, the best family, and the happily ever after that I didn't even know that I wanted.

All thanks to Eye Candy Ink.

DID YOU LOVE AMES? **Please consider leaving a review! You can do so on Amazon** here or on Goodreads.

ARE **you curious about the Bronson Brothers? Read Alexander's book, For Better or Worse. Anthony's book, Cocky Comedian, is part of the Cocky Hero Club and will be releasing June 27th!**

. . .

DID you miss the original Eye Candy Ink series? You can read the boxset here.

GRAB the next book in the series, Harvey, here!

ALSO BY SHAW HART

STILL IN THE **mood for Christmas books?**
Stuffing Her Stocking, Mistletoe Kisses, Snowed in For Christmas

LOVE HOLIDAY BOOKS? **Check out these!**
For Better or Worse, Riding His Broomstick, Thankful for His FAKE Girlfriend, His New Year Resolution, Hop Stuff, Taming Her Beast, Hungry For Dash, His Firework

LOOKING **for some OTT love stories?**
Fighting for His Princess, Her Scottish Savior, Not So Accidental Baby Daddy, Baby Mama

LOOKING FOR A CELEBRITY LOVE STORY?
Bedroom Eyes, Seducing Archer, Finding Their Rhythm

IN THE MOOD **for some young love books?**

Study Dates, His Forever, My Girl

SOME OTHER BOOKS BY SHAW:

The Billionaire's Bet, Her Guardian Angel, Every Tuesday Night, Falling Again, Stealing Her, Dreamboat, Locked Down, Making Her His, Trouble

HARVEY

EYE CANDY INK: SECOND GENERATION

Harvey Warner might have lost it.

His mind, that is.

His heart he just willingly gave away as soon as his eyes landed on the curvy chef working in her food truck outside of Eye Candy Ink one night.

In his defense, he's never been great at talking to women, but now that he's met the girl of his dreams, the stakes are higher than ever, so blurting out his name and the cheesiest pick-up line ever isn't a great start to their relationship.

The only saving grace is that the voluptuous chef seems to find his clumsy attempt at flirting endearing.

The pick-up lines shouldn't work on anyone, but somehow Coraline seems to kind of dig it.

Will pursuing Coraline ruin everything? Or will he finally get the happily ever after that he's been dreaming about ever since he first laid eyes on her?

ONE

Harvey

"DO you want us to wait and walk you out? Banks is still here but he's got another hour or so with his client," I tell Maxine as Rooney and I lean against her office doorframe.

"No, that's okay. Ames drove me to work this morning and he just texted to say that he was almost done grabbing groceries and he's going to swing by and pick me up."

"Alright, I'll see you tomorrow," I say before we both wave and head toward the front door.

We pass Ames as we head out and he nods, giving both of us a light punch on the shoulder.

"Hey, guys, how's it going?" he asks.

"Pretty good," I say, shifting the backpack in my hands to my shoulder.

"Is Maxine almost finished up in there?" he asks and I shake my head with a grin.

"I doubt it. The computer went down around lunch, so

she's working on getting caught up with that," Rooney tells him.

"Great," he groans and I laugh as I head out the door.

"I'll see you tomorrow," I call as Rooney and I head down the sidewalk toward my parked car in the lot across from Eye Candy Ink.

Rooney has been my best friend since birth. Literally. Our parents are best friends and we were raised together. We're also roommates and so I drive us to work most days. Rooney has gotten more than his share of tickets and he's also terrifying to ride around with, so it works out for both of us.

The two of us could probably pass as twins with our lanky frames, messy dark brown hair, blue eyes, and dark tattoos. That's where the similarities end though.

I'm the dreamer of the two of us and Rooney is the prankster. We balance each other out since I tend to take things too seriously sometimes and Rooney hardly ever does.

We're almost to my car when the wind shifts and the scent of fried meat and spices hits my nose. My stomach growls, and I look over to Rooney. Without saying anything to each other, we both change directions and head over to the far side of the parking lot.

There's a food truck parked there that I've never seen before but if the smells coming from it and the line of people waiting to order are any indication, I'll be stopping here every night after work.

We stop at the back of the line and scan the menu on the side of the truck. It looks like this place serves fancy comfort food and while I don't know half of the ingredients listed on the board, it all sounds good. Tonight's special is chicken and waffles, and my stomach growls again as a customer walks by with a takeout box.

The food truck is called The Culinerdy Cruiser and the name is stretched across the side of the pale blue truck, done to make it look like it was graffitied in bright bold colors. The artist in me likes it and I laugh at the name, looking up right as the girl working inside of the truck turns around.

My heart stops for one brief second and then takes off like a shot. She's passing the customer a takeout box and she gives him a smile. She looks up, her eyes locking on mine for just a minute and I almost lose my balance.

Oh shit. Is this it?

I grew up listening to my dad tell me that he took one look at my mom, Darcy, and just knew that she was it for him. My Uncle Mischa used to tell us that falling for his wife, Indie, just snuck up on him. I always used to wonder how I would fall. Would it be like my dad or like Uncle Mischa?

Looks like it's going to be like my dad.

My food truck girl, she's gorgeous. Even flushed from the heat, she's perfect with her platinum blonde hair twisted up into a messy bun and sticking out of the back of her baseball hat. It's hard to tell how tall she is with the truck window only showing her from mid-torso and up, but she seems petite.

Her eyes are the clearest blue and they twinkle in the lights from the nearby streetlights. She gives me a little nod, a shy smile on her lips before she turns back to the grill and I think if I hadn't fallen in love with her at the first look, I definitely would have after that.

"Rooney. She's mine," I whisper and he straightens next

to me, looking over at the girl who has captured my attention.

He knows without me elaborating what I'm talking about. I guess growing up together and being best friends will do that. We're like an old married couple who don't need words to communicate.

"Are you sure?" he asks, studying my girl, and I nod.

"Positive."

I spend the rest of my time waiting in line, studying her. She's efficient, taking orders and making food like she was born to do it. By the time it's my turn, I've already run through a million different opening lines.

Maybe that's why it's so disappointing when I get to the front of the line and open my mouth only for "Hi, I'm Harvey. What's your name? And are you a fan of shotgun weddings?" to come out.

"Oh my god," Rooney groans, taking a step away from me like he's afraid that he might get second-hand embarrassment.

The girl blinks at me and then to my, and I'm sure Rooney's, complete surprise, throws her head back and laughs. The sound is rich and wraps around me like a blanket leaving me feeling warm and at ease.

"That was a good one, Harvey. It's definitely the most creative pick-up line I've ever heard before."

"Oh my god. She's just as crazy as you," Rooney mumbles to himself and I want to glare at him but I refuse to take my eyes off my girl.

"I'm Coraline and this is my truck. What can I get for you two?"

Rooney hurries to order tonight's special and I ask for the same thing then step to the side and watch her as she works.

"Did you just open this truck? I haven't seen you around here before," I ask, trying to strike up a conversation. I want to learn everything about her.

"Yeah, I used to be over in New York but my best friend just moved here and she convinced me to come up here too. This is my first night that I'm opened over here. I used to park over by Phipps Conservatory but there wasn't that much foot traffic there late at night. This seems to be a better spot."

She passes Rooney and I our takeout boxes and Rooney thanks her and then steps over to grab some napkins from the little condiment section on the side of the truck. I hesitate, not wanting to leave her just yet.

"I'll see you around, Harvey. I hope that you stop by again soon."

"We work over there at Eye Candy Ink so I definitely will, Coraline," I promise.

She moves to take the next customer's order and I head over to join Rooney.

"It's really good," he says around his bite of food and I open my own box, taking a bite of the waffle and nodding.

"We'll have to come back again," he says and I nod.

I know that I'll be back again. Probably every night.

We finish our food and I reluctantly follow after Rooney as we head back to my car. I can't help but take one last look over my shoulder as I climb behind the wheel. Coraline's eyes meet mine and I smile as I head out of the lot and toward my apartment.

Maybe I'm not the only one who caught feelings tonight.

TWO

Coraline

I'M a sweaty mess the next morning, bent over the grill and scrubbing everything until it sparkles and looks brand new. It's only ten in the morning but I've already been up for a few hours. I hit up the farmer's market first thing and grabbed some more produce for the rest of the week.

I had grown used to ordering supplies for when I was on the other side of town and I almost ran out of ingredients last night. The traffic is a lot higher over here next to the clubs and I'll need to prepare for it from now on.

"Hey, boo!" my best friend Sayler says as she climbs into the truck, scaring the crap out of me in the process.

"Hey, Say. What are you doing here?" I ask her.

Sayler has been my best friend since grade school. When she moved up to Pittsburgh a few weeks ago, I had come with her, wanting to stay close to the last bit of family that I had left.

Sayler works as a freelance graphic designer and

website developer. She's always been good with computers and is a phenomenal artist. I had asked her to draw a design for The Culinerdy Cruiser and she knocked it out of the park. I'm pretty sure it's the reason why I get half of my business.

She also designed a website for me and helps with my social media and in exchange, I cook for her. She gets free food from the truck whenever she wants it. Which just so happens to be most nights.

"Just thought I'd see if you needed any help. You left this morning before I could ask how last night went," she says as she grabs an extra sponge and starts to wipe down the front counter.

"Thanks. Last night was busy. I got like triple the customers over here, so I had to run to the farmer's market right when it opened. I was so tired that I didn't clean as well as I should have last night."

She hums, scrubbing at a particular spot by the front window.

"Are you going to hire some help soon?" she asks as I move from the grill to the prep counter.

"I wish. Right now, I'm still barely making enough to cover all of my expenses and share of the rent. Maybe after a few more weeks over here on this side of town, I'll be able to swing it."

"I can cover your share of the rent for a bit," she offers but I'm already shaking my head no.

I know that Sayler would do anything to help me out, but I don't want to take advantage of her. Her parents are loaded, both lawyers, but they tend to try to buy her love and she's sick of it. That was part of the reason why she moved to Pittsburgh. She wanted to get away from them and stand on her own two feet and while I know that she's doing better than me, she's still growing her business too.

"I'll be fine," I promise her and she just sighs, shaking her head in exasperation.

She's used to me refusing help. I've always been independent. That probably stems from a lifetime of having to do everything myself. My mom and dad were always too wrapped up in their drama or latest argument to remember that they had a daughter most of the time.

They were like that for as long as I can remember. Miserable, tearing each other down instead of working together. They should have gotten divorced, hell, they never should have been together in the first place. They were way too toxic and growing up in that environment certainly left me with more than one hang-up about relationships. That's probably why I've never tried to date anyone before.

"Have any interesting customers last night?" Sayler asks and my mind flashes back to the hot tattooed guy.

"Yeah, this one guy who works at that tattoo shop over there. Said his name was Harvey. He was pretty entertaining."

"Yeah? Does he have tattoos?" Sayler asks curiously.

"Yeah. He asked me what my name was and if I'm a fan of shotgun weddings," I say with a laugh and Sayler cracks up.

"Marry him."

I laugh at her and she grins at me.

"I'm being serious!"

"Yeah, yeah," I say as I move onto the last stretch of counter.

"I can't wait to meet him. Was he hot?"

I don't answer her right away but I think my blush answers that question for me.

"So, you've met the tattooed love of your life then? You lucky duck."

I roll my eyes, cleaning up the last of the cleaning supplies and storing them in the back of the truck. Sayler is the romantic of the two of us. She also knows that I'm not interested in guys or settling down right now. I just got out of culinary school a year ago and I need to make my little food truck a success and hone my craft. Or better yet, get a job working in a restaurant so that I don't have so much on my plate.

That's always been my dream but I couldn't find any restaurants hiring a chef, or even a sous chef, back in New York. I've applied to a few places here in Pittsburgh but haven't heard anything back yet. That's why I'm still working at The Culinerdy Cruiser.

Sayler meanwhile has been dreaming about her happily ever after since we were kids. Too bad she'll never get it since her parents have been planning her wedding to their rich friends' son, Trevor, since before she was born.

I pull some of the vegetables from the fridge and get to work prepping some of the food for tonight.

"What's tonight's special? I'll put it up on the website and your social stuff while you cook."

"Since it's Tuesday, I'm going to make crispy pork belly tacos with my chili lime sauce. I'll also have regular tacos and burritos with my homemade guacamole and queso sauce."

"Ugh that sounds so freaking good," Sayler says, pretending to wipe drool off of her chin.

"I'll make some for you right now," I tell her, firing up the grill.

I make the pico de gallo and set that back in the fridge before I move onto the chili lime sauce. Sayler hums some pop song to herself as she updates all of my accounts and I reach over her, turning on the little fan I have clipped to the top of the food truck window so that we both don't die from heatstroke.

We work for the rest of the afternoon. Her on some new client work that she has due soon and me on prepping everything for tonight. I make my own guacamole and queso, then move on to making taco shells.

It's starting to get late and Sayler puts her laptop away and pulls over the iPad and little card reader that we use to collect payments.

"Are you staying to help?" I ask her and she nods.

"Yeah, I have a feeling that you'll be busy. Besides, maybe your tattooed hottie will come by and I can see if he has any friends."

She gives me a wink and I laugh, passing her another taco as our first customer of the night comes up to the counter.

THREE

Harvey

"IT LOOKS SO HOT, RIGHT?" Sally, or Susan, asks as I finish up with her lower back tattoo.

"Totally," I say unenthusiastically.

Sharon, or whatever her name is, giggles, wiggling slightly and I try to hold in my sigh as I stop tattooing her yet again. This girl, whose name I could swear starts with an S, can't stop moving. She whined and shifted for this whole freaking session and when she wasn't whining, she was trying to flirt with me.

I'm used to this.

I've never been that interested in dating. Being a tattoo artist always attracts the girls looking for a fling with a "bad boy" and working at a tattoo shop called Eye Candy Ink might actually encourage it more. I know that most of the women that walk through the door are only interested in a fling and I didn't want that. I want the real thing. I want love.

I finish the last of the shading and turn off my tattoo machine, grabbing the ointment and bandages so that I can get what's-her-name out of here.

This is my last client and I can hear the other tattoo artists getting ready to close up and head home too. I drove Rooney and I to work again today so I know that he'll be hanging around until I'm done. I wonder if I can convince him to grab some dinner from The Culinerdy Cruiser.

I haven't been able to get Coraline out of my mind. Her food had been delicious but it had been my reaction to her that had stuck with me for the last twenty-four hours. I even dreamed of her last night.

"You're all set," I tell my client as I snap off my gloves and stand from my chair.

She takes her sweet time standing up from the table and gathering her purse from the chair in the corner. She bends over, giving me a good look at the bandage above her ass and I roll my eyes, turning away from her and stepping out into the hallway.

Rooney, Gray, and Banks are all cleaning up the front waiting area and I lead my client up there, hurrying through the payment process. Gray offers to walk her to her car for me and I give him a grateful smile as he leads her out.

Rooney and Banks follow me down the hall to my room and lean in the doorway as I clean up the mess from my last tattoo.

"Did she ask for your number?" Rooney asks as I wipe down the table and I roll my eyes.

"No."

"Did she offer you hers?" Banks asks and I flip him off as he laughs.

Banks, Rooney, and I have been friends since birth. Our parents are all super close and they all worked at the original Eye Candy Ink tattoo shop. Uncle Mischa, Rooney's dad, and Uncle Nico, Banks' dad, still work over at the other location.

Banks' real name is actually Zeke but with our uncle Zeke, it got too confusing. We used to tease him, asking him if he was the street artist Banksy. We could never prove it either way and since we needed a nickname, Banksy was shortened to Banks.

I finish cleaning my room and grab my backpack, trailing after Rooney and Banks as we head up front. Gray is back, typing away on his phone. He's probably texting Nora, his roommate and best friend. Those two are insepa-rable... and perfect for each other, although neither of them seems able to see that.

"You guys want to grab a late bite to eat?" Banks asks as he digs his keys out of his pocket.

"Yeah, I'm headed over there," I say, pointing across the street to the food truck.

"To see your girl or to grab something to eat?" Rooney asks and I grin at him.

"Can't it be both? You know how I love to multi-task."

Everyone laughs at that. I'm a notoriously horrible multitasker. I just like to concentrate on one thing at a time so I can make sure that I've done it perfectly. It does make things hard though. I mean, I can barely walk and talk sometimes.

"I'm in. I'm starving," Gray says as he continues to text on his phone.

"Me too," Banks says and we all take off across the street.

There's another line and I see that the special has changed to tacos. My stomach growls as the scent of spicy meat and zesty lime hits me. Coraline is working the grill and there's a new girl taking orders. She's pretty with pitch-black hair and big green eyes but she does nothing to me.

Only my Coraline can do that.

"What are you guys going to get?" Gray asks and I pull my eyes away from Coraline to answer him.

"I'm going to try one of those pork belly tacos and then get two of the regular."

We both look over to Rooney and I'm surprised to see him staring at the food truck with a dumbstruck look on his face.

I look over and see that he's staring at the girl taking orders and I start to grin. Then a thought hits me. *Did I look that lovestruck when I saw Coraline last night?*

"Nora says to grab her some tacos. She must be working late."

I roll my eyes at Gray, biting my tongue before I can point out that he should just take her out on a real date instead. I know that it wouldn't do any good.

Rooney is silent, in a daze, until it's our turn to order and then he steps in front of Gray and me and gives the girl he's been staring at a wide smile. Gray looks surprised and I realize that he must have missed the looks Rooney has been giving this girl.

"Hi," Rooney says and the girl leans on the counter, giving him a grin.

"Well, hey there," she says with a grin.

Coraline must hear her because she looks over her shoulder and our eyes lock.

"Hey! Shotgun wedding!"

"What?" Gray and Banks ask at the same time, both sounding confused and maybe a little alarmed.

"I'll explain later," I mumble as I step up to the window, trying to elbow Rooney out of the way.

"Back for more?" Coraline asks as she passes a takeout box to the last customer.

"Yeah."

"Well, what can I get you all?" Coraline's friend asks.

"How about your number?" Rooney says smoothly and I want to kick myself for not saying something like that last night to Coraline.

"How about we start with your order, boo?" she asks with a laugh.

"If you want to take this slow, then I can do that. I'll take two of the pork belly tacos and two of the beef ones," Rooney says before he steps aside and Gray steps past him to place his order.

"I'll take six of the beef tacos and four pork belly ones please."

Banks goes next and then it's my turn.

"Two beef and a pork belly, please," I say last, elbowing Rooney to pay.

He rolls his eyes at me but passes over his debit card.

"Rooney Jennings, huh?" the counter girl asks as she reads his card.

"Yeah, what's your name?"

"If I tell you, are you going to say something cheesy like it would sound better with Jennings at the end?"

"Maybe..."

She laughs and then relents.

"I'm Sayler."

Gray starts humming the theme song to Sailor Moon almost instantly and I want to ask him how he knows that but my eyes stray to Coraline, and I get distracted.

Rooney is busy doing his best to flirt with Sayler and I tune them out as I watch Coraline cook. She has a soft smile on her face and I wonder if it's because she loves to cook so much or if Sayler and Rooney's conversation is really that amusing.

When she starts to box up all of our tacos, I know that my window to talk to her is rapidly closing and I straighten, determined to make this time count.

"Here you go," Coraline says, sliding our boxes over to us.

Gray and Banks take theirs and step over to the side. Gray is busy texting Nora on his phone and Banks has already started to eat his. Rooney thanks Coraline and then goes back to flirting with Sayler.

There's no one in line behind us so I lean against the food truck window and try to give Coraline my most charming smile.

"No pick-up line tonight?" she asks with a laugh as she leans on the counter and I search my brain for a good one.

"I wish I were cross-eyed so I could see you twice."

"Jesus, you're bad at this," Gray says, giving me a horri-fied look.

Banks and Rooney snort out a laugh, used to how bad I am at talking to women. Coraline laughs too and I try to think of another one.

"Do you like raisins?" I ask her and she gives me a wide grin.

"Sure."

"How about a date?"

She laughs hard at that one and I grin, feeling more at ease.

"That was a good one," she says as she giggles and I vow to hear that sound every day for the rest of my life.

Sayler is looking between the two of us like she's never seen what's happening before and I wonder if that's a good sign.

"Oh! I've got one," Coraline says excitedly and I lean closer. "If you were a chicken, you'd be impeccable!"

I laugh at how bad it is and Coraline almost doubles over.

Fuck, she's adorable.

I look over to see Gray, Banks, and Rooney staring at the two of us like we're insane but I don't care.

Some more customers come up to the window and I'm forced to step to the side.

"See you around, Harvey," Coraline says with a wave as she goes back to her grill and I wave, wishing that I had gotten her number or something.

"Bye, Rooney," Sayler says, sliding him a piece of paper before she turns to help the next customers.

The three of us turn and head across the parking lot and Rooney flicks the paper at me. I flip him off and he laughs.

"You guys are the worst," Gray grumbles as we head toward our cars, and Rooney and I crack up.

Banks laughs and Gray flips us off as he climbs into his car and takes off out of the lot.

FOUR

Coraline

THE RUSH HAS FINALLY SLOWED and I take a break, leaning against the counter with the fan blasting at my face. It's got to be close to ninety degrees out and it's even hotter in the food truck with the grill and fryer going.

Tonight's special is an aioli burger with aged sharp cheddar cheese, applewood smoked bacon, caramelized onions, tomato, lettuce, and a roasted garlic aioli. I was surprised when almost every customer so far has ordered it. It comes with a serving of fries and I'm glad that I portioned those out earlier today so that I just have to dump them in the fryer and then I can work on the burgers.

My eyes stray across the parking lot toward the neon pink glow of the Eye Candy Ink tattoo shop and I wonder if Harvey will be stopping by again tonight.

As if my thoughts have conjured him, he steps out of the shop and our eyes lock from across the street. I raise my hand and wave and he grins, jogging across the street.

"Hey, Coraline. Did you just come out of the oven? Because you're hot," he says with a mischievous smirk.

"Hey, Harvey. What can I get you?" I ask with a laugh.

"I'll take the special. I've been smelling it for the last hour and it smells delicious."

My face flushes from the compliment and I give him a smile before I turn and get started on his order. I dump an extra serving of fries into the fryer and get started making the best burger of my life. I want him to think that I'm the best chef that he's ever had cook for him. I want to give him a reason to keep showing up every night, although I suspect that he would do that even if my food was shit.

"How has tonight been?" he asks after a beat.

"Good. Pretty steady crowd over here. If it wasn't so hot, it would be perfect," I joke, fanning my face.

"Want me to grab you a cold bottle of water or something?" he offers and my heart melts at how sweet he is.

"No, I've been sticking my head in the cooler every few minutes, so I'm alright," I joke and he laughs.

I finish his order and pass the box over to him. He looks inside and smiles.

"Extra fries, Coraline? You better be careful or people are going to think that you've got a crush on me."

"It's not that. I'm just trying to fatten you up. You're so skinny and it looks like the last time you ate was sometime in the nineties."

"I've got to give the ladies what they want."

"What ladies? I don't know anyone who is searching for this look," I say with a grin, eyeing him from his shoes up to his messy hair.

"I took a poll. Tall and lanky is hot right now."

"I think maybe you should retake that poll," I tease.

"Haha. You know, if you really wanted to fatten me up,

you could give me a slice of that cheesecake," he says, pointing to the dessert menu for tonight.

I take a step closer and lean over the food truck window.

"I can't do that, Harvey. People might get the wrong opinion and think I have a crush on you or something."

He throws his head back, laughing up at the dark sky and I join him. I've never had this kind of easy relationship with a guy before. I'm used to sexist pricks or fuck boys. No one like Harvey.

Culinary school was filled with a bunch of cocky guys and even if I had been interested in one of them, it was too competitive to really nurture any kind of relationship. Before that, I was busy trying to keep a roof over my head and save up for school. I didn't have time for boys or dating.

I technically still don't.

I need to get this food truck off the ground or find a chef position at a restaurant around here. I need to hone my craft and become the best chef that I can possibly be. The best chef in Pittsburgh.

A few more customers head my way and my mood sours. I don't want to help them right now. I just want a few more minutes with Harvey.

That's how I know that he's dangerous.

Sayler couldn't stop talking about Harvey and Rooney last night and she kept up that conversation long after we had shut down the truck and gone home. I know that she's already started planning double dates out in her head and I hate having to tell her that I don't have time for dating right now. I know that she'll try to get me to change my mind.

"Hey, um, I was wonder if maybe you'd—" He's cut off by the arrival of the next round of customers and he gives me a sad smile, shifting out of the way slightly.

"I'll see you tomorrow night?" he asks as he steps out of the way more and I nod, giving him one last smile.

I try not to watch as he crosses back to the shop and heads inside. He stops when he reaches the door and looks over his shoulder.

For one brief moment, our eyes meet and cling. Even in the dim light and with the distance, I can see the fire burning in his eyes and it calls to me. I want to go to him. I want him to wrap those lanky arms around me. I want to feel his lips on mine, his body on mine.

I force myself to look away and paste on a smile as I take the next round of orders and get back to work.

Sayler shows up a few minutes later and I give her a grateful smile as she takes over the counter. We work for half an hour before we get another break and I know what she's going to ask before she opens her mouth.

"Has Harvey been by yet?" she asks and I nod.

"You just missed him. He came by right before you got here."

She frowns and I pass her a water, aiming the fan at her for a few minutes.

"Did he ask you out yet?" she asks and I shake my head.

"I think he was going to tonight but we got interrupted."

"Maybe next time. It's obvious he's into you. We just need to get the timing right."

She scrunches her nose and I swear I can almost see her doing the math in her head of when would be the ideal time to run into Harvey.

"It's not like it matters. I can't go out with him."

"What? Why not?" Sayler demands, frowning at me.

"I've got this truck and I need to get my business off of the ground. I don't have time to worry about guys right now."

Sayler sighs and takes a drink of her water.

"You can't always predict everything, Cora. Especially not when you'll meet 'the one.'"

"I know. It's just like you said. I just need our timing to be right."

Sayler frowns, not liking me using her words against her but we get another few customers then and I'm saved from her arguments.

Still, as I turn back to the grill to get cooking, I can't help but steal one last look at the front doors of the Eye Candy Ink shop, hoping to get one last look at Harvey before I push him from my head once again.

FIVE

Harvey

TODAY IS my last night of work for the week and I'm exhausted. I've been looking forward to stopping by Coraline's food truck before I head home and pass out. It's been a long week, filled with back-to-back clients and I'm desperate to catch up on some sleep.

I step out of Eye Candy Ink, locking the door behind me before I look across the street to The Culinerdy Cruiser. There's a long line tonight and I smile, happy that people seem to be recognizing how talented my girl is. As I get closer though, I realize that something is wrong.

Everyone in the line seems a little annoyed and when I glance up to the truck window, it looks like the guy ordering is yelling at my sweet girl. He's leaning over the ledge, gesturing to the takeout box and I can see that Coraline is trying to calm him down. I can also see that she is trying to hold back her tears and I react without thinking.

I head up to the food truck door and knock. The guy

who was yelling at Coraline has stormed off and I don't have to wait long for Coraline to open the door for me.

Her cheeks are flushed, her eyes shiny with a sheen of unshed tears, but her face seems to relax a bit at the sight of me.

"Thank god. I thought you were another customer coming to yell at me."

"Has that been happening a lot tonight?" I ask carefully and she nods, her eyes still a little glassy.

"Apparently the Cajun Chicken Gnocchi isn't a big hit," she says, trying to make a joke but I can hear the pain in her voice and I can't stand it.

"Well, it smells really good."

"It's too spicy. That's been the complaint all night but I marinated the chicken last night and I can't really change that now. I'd have to make more of the cream sauce to go with it to tone it down a bit but I can't leave to go get more ingredients."

"Let me help. I'll text Rooney to run to the store. You cook and use more of the cream sauce for now and I'll help you make more once Rooney gets here."

"You don't have to do that, Harvey. I know that you've been working all day."

"I want to help you, Coraline."

"Why?" she asks as the crowd starts to grow more annoyed.

"Because I like you and I can't stand to see you upset. Now, what does Rooney need to get?"

She eyes me for long seconds and then she rattles off a few ingredients and I text Rooney. He tells me he'll be there in twenty minutes and I climb into the truck and head to the window. The checkout system is pretty easy and I pick it up quick.

We were together in unison, making a good team as we clear the line. We're just finishing with the last customer when Rooney pulls up and heads over with a few grocery bags. I let him in and hurry to show him how to work the credit card machine before I move to help Coraline at the back counter.

I wash my hands, sliding on a pair of gloves and a baseball hat before I take my spot next to her at the counter.

"Can you keep stirring the sauce? I don't want it to burn. I'll cut up the onions and green peppers."

I take the spoon from her and start stirring, watching as Coraline quickly slices and dices the onions and green peppers. She's a master with that knife, the blade moving so fast that it starts to blur. She adds the vegetables and some herbs to the pan that I'm stirring and then has to get back to work when a few more customers walk up.

We finish the sauce and I start helping Coraline box up the food. The three of us work together in tandem for the next two hours. I didn't realize that her busiest hours seemed to be right as Eye Candy Ink was closing. There's more people out, club hopping or heading to bars and so there's a lot of hungry, slightly drunk club goers out and they all seem to gravitate to The Culinerdy Cruiser, probably drawn by the delicious smells.

We don't close down until one a.m. and by then I'm beat. I don't know how she does this every day. And by herself most of the time.

"Thank you so much for helping me out tonight," she tells Rooney and me, and we both nod.

"Anytime," I tell her, leaning over and giving her a side hug.

"Do we need to clean anything up? I was trying to wipe

down the counter when I could," he says, looking around the truck.

"Oh, you don't have to do that. I can take care of it later."

"Let us help you," I tell her. "Then we'll walk you to your car."

She nods, giving us a grateful smile before she asks us to take care of the condiments outside of the truck and to wipe down the counters. She cleans the grill and Rooney heads outside, so I grab a towel and start to wipe down everything in sight.

By two a.m., we're finally done and I follow Coraline outside and wait while she closes the truck door and locks up.

"You know, if you want to work later hours, for less pay, I can totally hire you two."

Rooney and I laugh and then Rooney yawns, I can tell that he's exhausted too and I definitely owe him one for spending his night inside the food truck with us.

"See you later, Coraline. See you at home, Harvey," Rooney says before he waves and heads toward his car.

I turn with Coraline and head in the other direction toward an older model Ford Edge.

"Thanks again for helping me out tonight," she says sweetly and I nod.

"Anytime, Coraline."

We reach her car and she digs her keys out of her pocket. We both shift and I like to think that it's because we both don't want to say goodbye to each other.

"Do you ever take a night off?" I ask.

I'm sick of dancing around how I feel for this girl. I need to ask her out. I need to make her mine.

"Yeah, I take Monday and Tuesday nights off."

"Maybe I can take you out for dinner then? You can let someone else cook for you for a change," I ask and she gives me a smile that looks slightly brittle around the edges.

"I'd love to Harvey, but I can't. I'm just too busy here and I need to make the food truck a success before I worry about anything else."

I try not to let my disappointment show as I nod and shuffle my feet.

"No worries."

"I really am sorry," she says and I nod again. "I'll, uh, I'll see you later," she says, unlocking her car and I nod again, feeling lame and more awkward than I ever have before.

"See you later," I echo as I hold her car door open for her.

She slides inside and I close the door, waving one last time before I head across the parking lot and climb into my own car. I wait until after Coraline has driven out of the lot and turned onto Main Street before I rest my head on the steering wheel and let out the groan that I was holding in.

SIX

Coraline

HARVEY HASN'T BEEN by for the last two nights and I wonder if I scared him off or upset him when I turned down his date. I know it has only been a few days since I met him, but he's already become a part of my daily routine.

Most of my days are just filled with work, but seeing Harvey was a bright spot in them. He could always make me laugh, make me feel better. Now that I haven't seen him for a few days, I can see just how boring my days are.

I miss him.

I can't help but glance over to the Eye Candy Ink tattoo shop. I've been stealing looks in that direction all night, hoping to catch a glimpse of Harvey's lanky frame.

Sayler clears her throat and I jerk my eyes away from the tattoo shop to meet her laughing eyes.

"Looking for something? Or should I say someone?" she asks with a sly smile and I can tell that she's onto me.

"Nope," I say, turning my back on the shop and wiping down the counter for the tenth time in the last half hour.

The weather is a little overcast tonight so foot traffic and customers have been slow. Normally I would be grateful for the break in the hot weather but the downtime has only given me more time to think and wonder if I made a mistake the other night in turning Harvey down.

"Do you want to talk about that person that you're not looking for?" Sayler asks and I snort out a laugh at the way she worded that question.

"There's not much to talk about. He asked me out. I don't have time to date right now, so I turned him down," I say but the words sound sour to my ears and I have to swallow hard around the lie.

"Maybe you'll get one of those chef positions that you applied for."

"Then I'll have even more to do to get an entire kitchen used to me and the way I run things."

"So, basically you're just never going to date anyone," Sayler says dryly and I sigh.

"Guess so."

She gives me a hard look and I turn away. I know that it won't stop her from saying whatever is on her mind.

"What are you so afraid of? That you'll get hurt? Or that you will find out that you were wrong this whole time. I know that you like to think that everyone is just better off alone because of your parents. But you're alone right now and are you really happy. The only time that I've seen you smile lately is when Harvey is around. I think that means something."

I know that she's right, that I'm making excuses, but I can't help it. I don't have the best example of a healthy relationship. My parents fought constantly. They made each other miserable and I never understood why they stayed together just to be angry all of the time.

Sayler's parents are still together and they argue nonstop. They say that it's just because they're both lawyers but Sayler and I stopped buying that excuse years ago.

Her parents just aren't great people and part of me wonders if they corrupted each other, or if they only wound up together because they both were corrupt. Either way though, isn't that proof that you'll just end up being happier alone?

"Not every relationship ends in disaster, Coraline. You're not your mom and I highly doubt that Harvey is like your dad."

Her words hit home and I know that I shouldn't be surprised. Sayler knows me better than anyone and she's well versed in all of my hang-ups and issues.

"I know. In my head, I know that, but I still just can't seem to find it in me to pull the trigger and take that leap."

"That's what you have me for! You just have to say yes and then we double date. I'll be there to help you in case he turns out to be a jerk and vice versa. It's the Meyers and Jones girls against the world!" she says excitedly, holding her closed fist out to me.

I laugh, fist bumping her and then go back to cleaning the counters as I mull over her words.

Maybe it's time that I started dating. I never had much interest in dating or men before, but there's something about Harvey that draws me in. It feels like he's already under my skin and I'm not sure that I want to get him out.

By ten p.m., the truck is spotless and it's starting to rain so we close up the truck and get ready to head home. Sayler has work to do still, so I offer to make us something to eat and stay up with her.

She loves my truffle macaroni and cheese and I'm planning on making it for the truck sometime this week so I figure that I'll practice now.

I start the water to boil and then move over to my own laptop. I need to update my expenses and check my email. I've been applying to a few chef positions over the last few weeks. Owning a food truck was never really my plan. I liked the freedom of it originally but it's a lot of work. Besides, I want the notoriety of running my own brick-and-mortar place. I want people to line up for a chance to dine at one of my tables. Not to stand in line at my tiny truck window.

I open my email first and my heart drops when I see the name on the first message.

Maxwell Schultz.

Maxwell is a huge name in the restaurateur business. He's even bigger here in Pittsburgh. Working for him would be a dream come true and while I had applied, I never thought that I would get even an interview.

I hurry to open the email and my breath stalls in my lungs.

"Oh my god," I whisper and Sayler looks up at me.

"You alright?" she calls from the couch and I turn wide-eyed to stare at her.

"I got an interview for the new restaurant that Maxwell Schultz is opening."

"Woohoo!" Sayler screams, vaulting over the back of the couch to almost tackle me in a hug. "That's my best friend! Kicking ass!"

I laugh with her, jumping up and down in the center of our tiny kitchen. I only stop when the water for the macaroni and cheese starts to boil over.

"That's awesome, Coraline! Maxwell is going to hire

you as soon as he takes a bite of your food. You're going to kill it and be rich and famous and everyone will be dying to eat your food."

Sayler has always been my biggest supporter and I grin at her now, adding the macaroni to the pot and stirring it.

We stay up for hours talking about the interview and what I'll be making. Sayler is already making plans for how to sell the food truck and how she's going to have to insist that she has a standing reservation every day.

It's after three in the morning when I head to bed with a smile on my face but the last thought that I have before I fall asleep is that I wonder if Harvey would come and see me at the restaurant.

SEVEN

Harvey

"HEY," Ames says as he drops down onto the spare chair in my tattoo room.

"Hey, what's up?" I ask him as I go back to finishing up the sketch that I'm working on.

"I have a question for you," he says with a grin and I groan, already knowing what's coming.

The whole shop has been asking me if I'm a fan of shotgun weddings ever since Rooney spilled the beans about my first conversation with Coraline. They also keep trying to give me pick-up lines to use on her.

News also spread to my entire extended family and my uncle Mischa keeps trying to send me dating articles. My mom and dad keep asking when they can meet her.

Meanwhile, I can't even get my girl to let me take her out to dinner.

"Is Mischa still sending you those dating articles?" Ames asks and I nod, ignoring him when he starts to laugh.

Gray wanders into my room, hopping up on top of my table and I nod at him.

"I have a question for you, Harvey," Gray starts and Ames cracks up.

The sound draws Rooney, and I groan as he comes into my room too with his usual maniacal grin stretching his lips.

"I thought of another one," Rooney says and I toss down my pencil. It looks like I won't be finishing this sketch right now.

"What?" I ask.

"Did you just come out of the oven? 'Cause you're hot," he says, grinning wider.

"Good one," I say dryly.

He just laughs and Ames rolls his eyes. Gray is busy texting on his phone and if I had to bet money, I would say that he was talking to Nora.

Ender wanders by my door and when he sees everyone hanging out, he stops and leans against the doorframe.

"Hey, man," I say.

Ender has been here for close to a year now and I still feel like I know nothing about him. He's super quiet and he doesn't usually hang out with us. He does his work and then disappears.

"Hey," he says, his deep voice making mine sound like I haven't gone through puberty yet.

"Are you here to give me shit about my way with the ladies too?" I joke and he shakes his head, crossing his big arms over his chest.

"Are you here for some tips yourself, Ender?" Rooney asks, wiggling his eyebrows at him.

I think Rooney might have a death wish. Ender is at least twice his size and looks like he could snap Rooney in two. Ender's lips twitch and I breathe a sigh of relief that thc guy has a sense of humor and isn't going to kill my best friend.

"Listen, as the only guy here with a girlfriend," Ames starts and Rooney rolls his eyes.

"How do you know you're the only one?" Gray asks and we all look at him with interest.

"Did you finally pull your head out of your ass and realize that you love Nora?" Ender asks and I'm shocked that he knows about Gray and his best friend and roommate.

"No," Gray says. "I meant that I saw the way Rooney was looking at Sayler the other night."

"I'm surprised that you caught that since your face was glued to your text messages with Nora," Rooney mumbles.

"Hey, are any of you working?" comes a voice from behind Ender and we all jump, turning to see Zeke standing there.

"I was trying to, Uncle Zeke," I say, sucking up to our boss and the other guys boo me.

"We were trying to work but Harvey's lack of a love life distracted us," Rooney says.

Uncle Zeke tries to cover his smile but I still see it and roll my eyes.

"Is that why you're here too?" I ask Zeke and he shakes his head no.

"I came to grab the bank deposit from the office so Maxine doesn't have to do it later. They're talking about your love life over at the other Eye Candy Ink location too and I thought that I would give you a heads up. It seems Mischa has found some new tips, so you have those to look forward to later," he says with a laugh and my phone buzzes on my desk.

"Great."

"You're just in time, Uncle Zeke! Ames here was just about to tell us all how he was able to win your daughter Maxine over," he says with a shit-eating grin and I see Ames wince and Gray grin. Ender looks like he's trying not to laugh as Zeke levels a death glare at Ames.

Ames had a one-night stand with Maxine a few months ago and then found out that she was the daughter of his new boss, Zeke, right after. To say that it was a terrifying mess would be an understatement but everyone seems to be getting along well now. Well, until Rooney starts to push people's buttons again.

"Get back to work," Zeke says, turning to head back to the office. "Good luck with your girl, Harvey!" he calls over his shoulder and I sigh, turning back to the guys.

They wait until Zeke has left before they turn their attention back to me.

"In all seriousness, what are you going to do?" Gray asks me curiously.

"Yeah, do we need to take you out to a club or something? You can get drunk and forget all about Coraline," Ames suggests.

"Max's club?" Ender asks, sounding interested and I wonder why he cares if we go to my uncle Max's club.

"Sure," Rooney says with a shrug, looking at Ender curiously and I can see the wheels turning in his head.

"I'm in," Ender says and even though I don't really want to go to a club, get drunk, or forget about Coraline, as if I ever could, I still feel like I have to say yes.

"I don't want to forget about Coraline but I'm up for a guy's night," I tell them and they nod and start to make plans for tonight.

We still have a few hours until the shop closes and they all have at least one client left to do today so they head back to their rooms soon after. Ames stays back a beat and closes my door slightly.

"If you really like her, then you should wait for her. Ask her out again and if she still tells you that she's too busy right now, then tell her that you're willing to wait for her. She'll either say okay and then maybe you really do have a chance with her, or she'll let you down easy again and you'll know that it's not meant to be."

His advice is surprisingly romantic but it makes sense. I nod, giving him a grateful smile.

"Thanks, Ames," I tell him honestly.

He just smiles and nods before he heads back to his own room.

I turn back to my desk, picking up my pencil and getting back to work on my design. I already know that I'll be stopping by The Culinerdy Cruiser tonight to see Coraline and I'll ask her out again, just like Ames suggested.

And if she says no again, then maybe I really will be getting drunk tonight.

EIGHT

Coraline

I'VE BEEN BUZZING all day thinking about my upcoming interview. I swear that I haven't stopped smiling since I read the email. Sayler is here tonight at the food truck running the counter for me.

We've been trying to brainstorm ideas for me to cook for my interview but I think that she's really here tonight because she knew that I was making my truffle mac and cheese. She's already had two bowls and I know that she'll be grabbing a slice of the cinnamon cheesecake that I made for dessert soon.

I'd never admit it, but I've been looking out for Harvey all night. For some reason, I can't wait to tell him my news about the interview. I'm not used to wanting to share things with other people, besides Sayler of course. I know that if I told Sayler about wanting to see Harvey, that she would only push me to go out with him.

I've been mulling over her words for a while and I know

in my heart that I want to go out with him. It's my head that I'm having a problem with.

"Hi, what can I get you?" Sayler asks and I look up to see two older couples standing outside the window.

"We'll all take the special," one of the women says, her eyes locked on me and I give a small smile.

I get to work on their order, trying not to be obvious as I sneak glances across the street to Eye Candy Ink to see if I can spot Harvey.

As if my thoughts have conjured him, I look up and see him headed across the street. A few of the other guys who work at the shop are locking up the front door and I wonder if they'll be stopping by to grab something to eat too.

"Mom? Dad?!?" Harvey asks, sounding shocked and a little embarrassed to see his parents crowded around the food truck.

"Dude, this must be so embarrassing for you," Rooney says with an evil chuckle as he rounds the side of the food truck and I see Harvey nudge him, nodding over to where Sayler is standing inside the truck taking orders.

"That's your parents right there," Harvey points out and he flushes beet red.

"Mom and dad! What are you doing here?" He asks, hurrying over to their side.

"We were just in the neighborhood and we're hungry," the woman who ordered says innocently but no one seems to be buying that.

"It's nine pm! You guys should be in bed," Rooney argues, trying to herd his parents to their car.

"We can still party," one of the guys protests with a frown.

"Yeah! We're hype, we boogie."

"Oh my god," the guy and Rooney say at the same time

only the guy is grinning at his wife and Rooney looks like he wants the earth to open up and swallow him whole.

"We just wanted to meet your lovely lady," Harvey's mom says, giving me a warm smile and I look past his parents to see that Harvey seems to have relaxed now that he sees that I'm okay with them being here.

"Well, we better go," Harvey's mom says and I give them a little wave as they take their food to go.

They stop and say something to Harvey and Rooney before they wave and head towards their car.

"Sorry about that," Harvey says with a wince and I laugh.

"They were sweet."

We're silent for a minute until Harvey breaks the tension.

"Do you have a Band Aid? I just scraped my knee falling for you."

"Good one, Harvey," I say with a laugh as he gives me a wide smile and leans over the window.

"Hey, Sayler," he says, waving at my friend as she steps aside to chat with Rooney. "It smells awesome."

"Truffle mac and cheese," I tell him and he reaches for his wallet, placing an order.

"Where are you guys headed tonight?" Sayler asks him as I get started boxing up his food.

"To Seven," he says, naming a popular nightclub down the road.

Max Schultz owns that place too and it's the perfect opening for me to tell him about my interview.

"Are you sure that you can get into that place?" I tease him and he chuckles.

"My uncle Max owns the place so fingers crossed."

My stomach drops when he says that Max is his uncle.

"Did you tell him to give me an interview?" I blurt, my voice coming out accusatory.

Harvey's brow scrunches and he looks confused.

"What? What interview?"

"I got an interview for the new restaurant that Max is opening. Did you ask him to give me one?" I ask.

"No, I haven't talked to Max for a few weeks. And I don't really keep up with his business ventures. That's awesome about the interview though! You're going to kill it!"

He seems so sincere that I know that he's telling the truth. My shoulders relax and I can see Sayler grinning between the two of us.

His friends are approaching now and he swallows hard before he blurts out, "Maybe I could take you out to dinner to celebrate."

"I wish I could, but I need to keep this place running and prepare for my interview."

Even as the words leave my mouth, I know that I'm making a mistake.

"It's okay. I can wait, because I know in my heart that you're it for me. You're worth waiting for, Coraline."

He says it so quietly that I want to pretend like I didn't hear him but I can see the honesty in his eyes and I don't want to hurt him.

"Okay," I whisper and his eyes widen.

"Okay?" he asks and Sayler leans forward, her whole body hanging on our every word.

"Okay, I'll go to dinner with you."

"Really?" he asks, sounding surprised but happy.

"Yeah, does Monday night work for you?" I ask with a laugh.

"Yeah, yes," he says right away, pulling out his phone.

"What's your number?"

I rattle it off as his friends join us and Harvey gives me a smile.

"You said yes?" Rooney asks as he stops beside Rooney and I nod. "Are we still going to Seven?"

"Yes." A tall man standing slightly apart from the group says and Rooney eyes him for a minute.

"Alright then," Rooney says slowly.

Sayler only has eyes for Rooney as he orders his food and I try to give them some privacy as I box up the food and hand it off to her.

I want to say more to Harvey and as if he heard my thoughts, my phone buzzes in my pocket and I pull it out to see a message from an unknown number.

UNKNOWN: **You look beautiful.**

I LOOK OVER MY SHOULDER, biting back a grin when I meet Harvey's eyes.

CORALINE: **Thanks**

I ADD the kiss face emoji and hit send before I slide my phone back in my pocket, wash my hands, and get back to work.

A few more customers walk up and so we say goodbye to the guys and get back to work. As I work, I wonder if I'm more excited and nervous for the interview with Max or for my date with Harvey.

NINE

Harvey

I'VE NEVER BEEN this nervous in my entire life. I know that it's just a date, and while I've never actually been on a date before, they never seemed this freaking scary. I guess maybe I should have paid more attention to the tips that Rooney, Ames, and Gray were trying to give me last night.

We went to Se7en after we left The Culinerdy Cruiser and even Banks came out to hang out with us. I have a feeling that Rooney called him and told him where to meet us because he showed up at our table with a grin on his face right as the other guys started to tease me about Coraline.

Cat, Max's daughter and the manager of Se7en, even joined us for a round and as soon as I saw the way that Ender was looking at her, I figured out why he wanted to go to the club so bad.

I'm supposed to be picking up Coraline in like fifteen minutes and she lives a few blocks away, so I take one last look at myself in the mirror before I head for the door.

Luckily for me, Rooney is at work so he's not here to give me shit before my big date. I mean, he's still been texting me, but those I can ignore.

I try to give myself a pep talk the whole way over to Coraline's apartment. She lives a few blocks away from me, close to Eye Candy Ink. I manage to nab a parking spot right out front and I jog up the stairs to the fourth floor and knock on Coraline and Sayler's door.

I dry my palms off on my dark jeans as I wait for someone to answer the door. I don't have to wait long and I swear I almost swallow my tongue when I get a look at Coraline.

She's dressed in a pair of black leggings that mold to her legs and lush hips. She's got a lacy tunic with a pale pink tank top underneath and it gives me just a hint at the curves hiding beneath. Her pale blonde hair is pulled up into a high ponytail and she's got something dark and smoky on her eyelids that only make her blue eyes seem bigger and bluer.

"Whoa," I whisper and Coraline laughs.

"Thanks, you don't look so bad yourself," she says as she steps out into the hallway and pulls the door closed behind her.

"Ready to go?" I ask her, reaching over and grabbing Coraline's hand in mine.

She nods, ducking her head to hide her blush and seeing the pink stain on her cheeks puts me at ease. It means that I'm not the only one who's feeling nervous about tonight. *That has to mean that she has feelings about me too, right?*

I open the car door for her and Coraline smiles at me as she slips inside. I planned for us to go to an escape room before we head to Il Tettoo, a rooftop restaurant in down-town Pittsburgh. It was the most romantic place that I could think of with its tiny twinkling string lights and the view of Penn Avenue. The food is supposed to be great too which is a major plus. Coraline cooks for people all of the time, so I want to take her out someplace good.

"Where are we headed?"

"Have you ever been to an escape room?" I ask her.

"Uh, no... but quick question."

"Sure," I say with a smile.

"Um, should I be worried that for our first date you're taking me someplace where I'll literally be trapped with you?" she asks with a laugh and I join her.

"I hadn't thought of that," I admit. "It just sounded like something fun and I've never been before, so maybe it would be a new experience for both of us."

"It sounds cool. Are we grabbing food too?"

"Yeah, I made reservations at Il Tettoo at seven-thirty so hopefully we're out of the escape room by then."

Coraline laughs as I pull into the parking lot of Dido's Escape Rooms and hurry out of the car and around the hood to open Coraline's door for her.

"You look gorgeous, Coraline," I whisper in her ear as I lean past her to close the car door.

I could swear that she shivers at my words and my confidence grows. These feelings can't be one-sided.

I take her hand again as we head inside and get checked in. Our escape room is designed like a prison and we listen to the instructions before the energetic employee locks us inside and starts the timer.

"Where do you want to get started?" Coraline asks me, and I look around the small room.

"Those shelves over there?" I suggest and we start to search the room for the first clue.

We only have forty-five minutes to find all of the clues

and the key and get out. It's fun to watch Coraline get competitive. She's so cute and smart. She finds most of the clues and we make it out of the room with five minutes to spare.

Coraline high fives me as we head up to the front counter and I grin. I've never seen her so happy and carefree and I love that I was able to put that look on her face. I want to do it again and again every day of my life.

Things are easy between us as we drive the few blocks to Il Tettoo and ride up to the rooftop in the elevator. Coraline's eyes widen in wonder as she looks around the cozy restaurant.

Twinkling lights are strung criss-cross around the space and small tables are set up all over the rooftop. There's some low music playing and the soft murmur of other couples talking adds an intimate feeling to the space.

"The view is incredible," Coraline murmurs as we take our seats near the edge of the roof.

You can see most of the Pittsburgh skyline from here and the traffic from down below is just a distant hum.

"I've never been here before but it is pretty. I'm glad that you like it."

"I do. I'd love to be the chef at a place like this," she says, looking around the space once more.

"You don't like running The Culinerdy Cruiser?" I ask her.

I thought that the food truck was her dream, but I should have realized when she mentioned she had an interview with Max.

"Not exactly. I love being a chef but I want my own brick-and-mortar place. I couldn't find that in New York and, so far, I haven't found it here in Pittsburgh either. The food truck was the next best thing."

I mull this over as we both look over the menu. I love learning new things about her and I want to help her achieve all of her dreams.

The waitress comes by to get our orders and as soon as she's gone, I start asking Coraline more about herself.

"Do you have any brothers or sisters?"

"No, I was an only child, although Sayler feels a bit like a sister at this point. What about you?"

"I'm an only child too, but it's the same way with me and Rooney. Actually, all of the kids are like that. I grew up with my uncle Zeke, Nico, Mischa, and Aunt Sam. They own the Eye Candy Ink shop and all work together over at the other location. All of us kids basically lived at each other's houses and we took family vacations and all that together."

"Sounds like a tight-knit family," Coraline says with a smile but I can see something in her eyes. Some kind of pain or longing.

"What about you? Did you have a big family?"

"No, just me and my parents."

"Are they back in New York?"

"No, they're dead," she says flatly and I can tell that she doesn't want to talk about them anymore.

"I'm sorry for your loss," I murmur.

The waitress comes over and drops off our drinks and we move on to lighter topics.

"What kind of restaurant would you like to run? Would you still make your fancy comfort food?" I ask her and her smile brightens.

Her whole face lights up as she talks about menu and different food and drink combinations. I listen to her chatter about food for most of the meal and I love it. She glows when she talks about her passion, her whole body growing more animated and she somehow looks lighter.

"Sorry, I just blabbered on like that," she says as I pay the bill and we stand from the table.

"I loved it. I'll have to let you order for us on our next date."

"You think there's going to be a next date?" she asks as we step into the elevator and I crowd her against the back wall as we start to descend.

"I hope so."

Coraline smiles, tilting her face up to me and I take her invitation, our lips meeting in a soft caress that's over far too soon.

The elevator doors open and I step back, taking Coraline's hand and leading her outside to my car.

"Are you nervous for your interview?" I ask her as I merge with the late-night traffic and head back toward her apartment building.

"A little. I really want it, so I feel like there's more pressure on it. I'm interested to hear what Mr. Schultz's vision is for the new place."

"I wish I could tell you more, but I haven't seen him in a few weeks. He's been busy getting the new place set up."

"It's okay, I want to do this on my own," she says, giving me a warning look and I hold up my hands.

"I told you before. I stay out of his business. When you get the job, it will be because he realizes that you're the best chef ever."

Coraline smiles, ducking her head but I can see her reflection in the passenger side window and I smile.

We pull up to her place a few minutes later and I open her door, helping her out of my car and up the stairs to her place.

"I had a lot of fun tonight," she says shyly and I grin.

"Me too. Does that mean that you'll let me take you out again?"

"Yeah, I'd like that."

"Good," I say, closing the space between us and sealing our lips together.

She sighs, leaning into me more and I wrap my arms around her, molding her to me. I lick along her lips and she opens for me. She moans as our tongues tangle together and I press her harder against her front door.

Coraline runs her hands up my arms and I shiver as her short nails scrape along my skin.

"Coraline," I whisper against her skin as I kiss a path down her neck.

She arches, giving me more access to her neck and that's when the door opens behind her and we both stumble into her apartment.

"I'm so sorry! I thought I heard something and I didn't even think that it would be you," Sayler says, looking apologetic.

"It's okay," Coraline says and I give Sayler a nod, making sure that Coraline is steady on her feet before I step away from her a bit.

"Well, good night," Coraline says, obviously ready for me to leave and I give her a smile.

"See you later," I say, leaning in and brushing my lips against hers once more.

I pull back to see a red blush staining her cheeks and I grin.

"Have a good night, ladies."

My lips tingle the whole way home.

TEN

Coraline

I TAKE a deep breath before I open the front door of the address that Max emailed me. He's waiting for me in the empty dining area and my heart starts to race. I've always dreamed of working in a restaurant like this but as I walk through the front doors and get my first look at the still-unnamed restaurant, it feels more real.

I need this job. I want to run this place.

"Hey, you must be Coraline," Max says, holding a hand out to me.

I shake it, taking in his button-down shirt and jeans. He's dressed more casually than I had expected but it puts me at ease. He's got dark salt and pepper hair and warm blue eyes and the friendly look in them also help me relax.

"It's so nice to meet you," I tell him with a smile and he nods.

"Kitchen is this way."

He points out the bar area and the hallway that leads to

the back office. The kitchen door is right next to the hallway and I follow him inside, almost weeping when I get a look at the pristine kitchen.

It's a chef's dream and only strengthens my resolve to nail this job interview and become the chef of this place.

"My daughter, Cat, loves your food truck. I think she eats there at least four times a week," he says with a grin and I try to remember any regulars that I have/

"Does she have purple hair?" I ask him and he grins.

"I think it's teal now, but yeah, it was purple for a while."

I smile as I head around to the other side of the counter and look at some of the ingredients that are laid out.

"So, I haven't thought of a name yet, but we're narrowing it down and I'm hoping to be open for business in a month. I did interviews all week and you're actually the last one. I'm hoping to make a decision in the next few days."

"Do you have the rest of the kitchen staff hired yet?" I ask, wondering about the process.

"No, I want to leave that up to the chef since they're the ones who will be in charge of this domain."

I nod, running my fingers over the stainless steel countertop.

"My vision for this place is to be different from my other restaurants. I have Abernathy Brewery, which is more of a pub or bar, Salitos, which is tapas, Risel, which is more upscale, and then this place. I want it to be more of a comfort food menu and more laid back than Risel."

I nod. That's my sweet spot and what I want to cook too, so it's a perfect fit. Now I just need to make the best meal of my life to show Max that.

"That's what I make at The Culinerdy Cruiser. Americana comfort," I tell him with a smile and he nods.

"Love the name. If you become the chef here, maybe I should let you name this place too," he says as he leans back against the opposite counter.

"I've got a few ideas," I say with a grin as I get my chef knives out and a few of the other supplies that I brought with me.

"What will you be cooking today?"

"I thought I would make my truffle mac and cheese, my Americana burger, and my bacon-wrapped meatloaf."

"Sounds delicious."

I get to work laying out my ingredients and it's easy to get into the zone then and do what I love to do. I talk with Max as I cook and he tells me more about some of his restaurants and how he found his way in the business. I tell him more about my food truck and moving up here.

"Ready for the first course?" I ask him and he nods, pulling up a barstool and taking a seat.

"It smells delicious," he compliments me and I beam.

"Thanks," I say, sliding the plated truffle mac and cheese over to him.

I watch him take a bite before I tell him more about what's in it.

"So, this is my truffle mac and cheese with my special goat cheese cream sauce, truffle oil, some fresh herbs, and finished off with toasted bread crumbs on top. I would have this be an entrée on the menu since it's so heavy that it would be hard to pair with something else. Another option is that we could offer to add chicken or shrimp or some other protein to it."

He nods, taking another bite and I take that as a good sign.

I finish up the burger while Max makes a few notes on the first dish. I made my Americana burger with garlic parmesan fries to go with it.

"This is one example of a burger that we could make. It has white cheddar, crispy fried onions, Dijon aioli, tomato jam, and hickory smoked bacon on one of my homemade buns. For the side, I made garlic parmesan fries."

I watch as Max takes the first bite and he nods before he takes another bite. I smile, turning around to plate the final dish.

Things seem to be going well as I finish plating the mini bacon-wrapped meatloaf.

"Here's the mini bacon-wrapped meatloaves with mashed potatoes and crispy sauteed green beans and scallions."

I set the final plate in front of him and wipe my hands off, watching as he takes a bite of each item on the plate.

"I added my own zesty BBQ glaze to the meatloaf but I thought we could add it to the menu with different options. Maybe a honey BBQ glaze and a spicy one."

Max nods, finishing off the meatloaf.

"The mashed potatoes have cheddar and chives added and then the garlic sauteed green beans with crispy fried scallion on the side."

"It's delicious, Coraline," Max compliments and I grin.

"Thank you."

I clean up while Max finishes eating and making notes. I'm just packing up my dishes, leftover ingredients, and knives as he sets the barstool back by the kitchen door and comes back over to me.

"Thank you so much for coming in, Coraline. I'm going to go over my notes and then I'll let you know my decision in the next few days."

"Thank you. It was an honor to even be considered for this position," I tell him as I shake his hand and follow him back to the front door.

"Thanks again," I tell him as I nod and head outside to my car.

I set my bag into the back seat and then climb behind the wheel, pulling out my phone to text Sayler and Harvey about how it went.

It isn't until after I hit send that I realize that I never even hesitated to tell Harvey my good news. I've only known him a few weeks and already he's become so important to me that he's one of the first people that I want to talk to.

That thought should make me nervous. I should be worried that I'll become like my parents and we'll get so miserable that we'll destroy each other, but somehow, the panic never comes.

Harvey is the sweetest man that I've ever met and I know that he would rather die than hurt me. He's funny and goofy, and so supportive.

He's not my father. He's not going to make me miserable.

I think he might just be the man of my dreams.

ELEVEN

Harvey

IT'S a week after our first date and while I've been going to The Culinerdy Cruiser almost every night to grab dinner and see her, it's not the same as getting to be with her one on one.

I worked an earlier shift today, so I'm leaving Eye Candy Ink to head to her place. I park outside of Coraline's apartment and head up to her floor. She must be waiting for me because she opens the door a few seconds after I knock.

"Hey, you look beautiful," I tell her and she grins up at me.

"Thanks," she says, rising up on her tiptoes and brushing a kiss across my lips.

It's over far too quick for my liking and I promise myself that I'll rectify that later in the night.

We're both dressed casually which fits perfectly for what I planned for our date tonight. I take Coraline's hand and lead her down the stairs and out to my car.

As soon as we're both buckled up and I'm headed across the river to Allegheny Commons Park, I ask her more about how her interview with Max went.

"I think it went well. He seemed to like what I cooked," she says and she seems excited about it.

I ask her more about what she cooked and what her plans would be for the menu if she got the position. She's so happy, so animated, as she describes everything that she wants to do. I love seeing her so excited and I relax and let me tell her all about her big plans as we drive.

I park close to the entrance of Allegheny Commons Park and hurry to get Coraline's door. We're going to get dinner later, but for right now, since the weather is so nice, I thought that we would grab some shaved ice from the cart by the entrance and take a stroll through the park.

We both choose cherry and I take her hand once more as we start to walk.

"I've never been here before. This place is beautiful," Coraline says and I'm glad that I could experience another first with her.

We walk over a little pedestrian bridge and take in the view of the Pittsburgh skyline as we finish off our shaved ice.

"How was work today?" she asks after we toss out our trash.

"Good. Busy, but we're always busy."

"Yeah, I heard that you guys book like a few months out," she says, letting me intertwine my fingers with hers.

"I don't keep up with the schedule. Maxine handles all of that and just hands us a list each week with our clients on it and what they want done."

"Good system, I guess," Coraline says with a smile and I grin.

"Yeah, I don't really want to be in charge of the admin stuff but Maxine excels at it. Plus, she's Zeke's daughter and he owns the shop, so it's nice that it's all been kind of kept in the family."

I tell her more about my family and extended family. She asks how I got into tattooing and I tell her that it's kind of a family thing. She asks more about tattooing and the process and I love that she's taking an interest in what I do and what I love.

"Ready for some dinner?" I ask as we make it back to the entrance to the park and she nods.

"What would you like to eat?"

"Pizza," Coraline says right away and I'm surprised that she didn't say something more upscale or fancier.

"From Basic Kneads?" I ask, naming a local favorite pizzeria.

"Duh," she says with a laugh as I open her car door and I laugh too, falling a little more in love with her.

Basic Kneads is only a few blocks over from my place and when I see that it's packed inside, we decide to get the pizza to go and head back to my apartment.

Rooney is still at work, thank god, so we sit on the couch and eat. It's only six p.m. and when Coraline's phone buzzes as we're cleaning up, I tell her to take it. I'm loading the dishwasher when I notice how still she is.

The first thing I think is that something is wrong. I'm on my way to her, to console her or help in any way when she says thank you and spins around to face me with a huge smile on her face.

"I got the chef position!" she screams, launching herself at me.

I catch her, letting out a whoop as I spin her around.

"I'm so happy for you. You deserve this," I tell her, dropping a kiss on her lips before I hug her tight to me.

"Thank you," she murmurs, wrapping her arms around my waist.

"Are you going to get rid of The Culinerdy Cruiser then?" I ask and she nods against me.

"No sense in keeping it."

"It's going to be weird to not be able to walk across the street every night to see you."

"The restaurant that I'm working at is a block away from Eye Candy Ink," she says and I laugh.

"Alright, I can make it a block."

She laughs, pulling back to smile up at me.

"Are you sad to get rid of the truck?" I ask, brushing some loose hair away from her face.

"A little, but I'm not going to miss the heat or having to do everything by myself," she says with a small chuckle.

"It was super hot in there," I admit, remembering the night that I helped her out. "Still, it was your first successful business venture."

"That's true. Maybe I'll get a tattoo to remember my time with the Cruiser."

"I'll do it for you," I offer right away.

"Alright I'll call tomorrow to make my reservation," she says with a laugh.

"I'll fit you in before or after we open so you don't have to wait that long. Just let me know when you want to get it done."

She smiles up at me and I can feel the attraction between us grow. I'm not sure who moves first but one minute we're grinning at each other and the next our mouths are locked together and we're making out hot and heavy.

Coraline presses closer to me, her lush curves molding to me and I moan, loving how soft she is everywhere. My hands slip under her t-shirt and my fingers graze over her smooth skin, leaving goose bumps in their wake.

Coraline squirms against me, her fingers diving into my hair and holding me close to her. I'm surprised since normally this is the part where we get interrupted or she pulls away.

I've been letting her set the pace between us because I know that she's it for me and I don't want to do anything to mess this up with her. I smooth my hands up and down her spine as our lips continue to move together, waiting to see what she'll do next.

Her hands slip down my front and my cock rises, dying to feel her hands on every inch of me.

"Should we, um, go to the bedroom?" Coraline whispers against my lips and I pick her up and almost run to the bedroom.

Coraline giggles as I kick the door closed behind us and set her on her feet next to the bed.

"Are you sure about this?" I ask her, wanting to make sure that she's comfortable before we go any further. "We don't have to do anything toni—"

Coraline's lips land on mine, cutting me off and I pull her closer to me, letting her grind against the stiff ridge in my jeans. Her fingers dip under my shirt and I step back, helping her pull it over my head before I reach for the hem of her shirt.

She seems to grow a little uncertain, a little self-conscious, as soon as the shirt is off, and I frown.

"You're perfect, Coraline. Every inch of you is a fucking dream come true. You're my dream come true."

She relaxes at my words, giving me a small smile as she

slowly lets her hands drop to her sides so that I can look my fill. She reaches behind her and unhooks her bra and my dick hardens even more as her ripe breasts are revealed to me.

The round globes are topped with cherry red nipples that have my mouth watering.

"Fuck, Coraline."

She's emboldened by my words and lustful gaze and I watch, mesmerized as she tugs down her black leggings, taking the lacy black panties with her.

Then she's naked in front of me and I've never seen anything prettier in my entire life.

"You're a work of art, Coraline. So fucking pretty."

"Your turn," she says with a sexy little grin as she runs her fingertips down my naked chest.

I hurry to tug my jeans and boxers down and then we're wrapped around each other once again. It's even better feeling her full curves against me, skin to skin.

I take a step back, not realizing how close we are to the bed and we both go tumbling down onto the mattress. Coraline giggles against my mouth and I grin.

"I'm so smooth," I joke.

Coraline laughs before she kisses her way down my neck. My hand finds her breast and I roll my thumb over her stiff nipple. She moans as it hardens against my fingers and I can't hold back any longer.

I move between her legs, my mouth finding her stiff peak and I suck her nipple into my mouth, loving it with my tongue and teeth.

"Harvey," Coraline sighs and my cock pulses at the sound.

Her hips are lifting off the mattress, desperate for something, some friction, and I'm eager to give it to her.

I move between her legs, gritting my teeth when the soft slick flesh brushes against the tip of my cock, leaving me panting. My balls are drawn up tight against my body, my teeth clenched, and I have to think about baseball to keep from coming right then and there.

"You drive me so crazy," I murmur against her skin as I kiss my way down her round stomach and settle between her thick thighs.

Her honeysuckle scent hits me as I lean in, taking one long slow lick up her dripping center. She's so small, so tight, and I know that she must be a virgin. I'm going to have to loosen her up before I try to fit my dick inside of her.

I take another lick, rolling my tongue over her clit until her back arched off of the bed and she lets out a needy moan. That sound does something to me and I moan too, suddenly ravenous, and bury my face in her slick folds.

"Harvey!" Coraline calls, her fingers tangling in my hair as her legs clamp down around my head.

She holds me to her but she doesn't need to. I'm not going anywhere until she comes all over my face. Until she's screamed my name so many times that she's hoarse.

It doesn't take long.

Coraline has a hair-trigger and I lick her to two orgasms before she's tugging on my hair, urging me up her body.

"I want you," she says, her voice low and sultry and I'm powerless to deny her.

I line my cock up with her snug opening and kiss her as I start to sink in slowly. I can feel her stretch around my length as I push inch after inch inside of her. I reach her cherry and push my tongue inside her mouth as I pop it and bury the last few inches inside of her.

I have to close my eyes and bury my face in her neck to keep from coming right then and there. Coraline mewls, her fingernails scratching my back as she wiggles under me, trying to get me to move.

"Fuck," I moan, giving her what she wants.

I pull out slowly, my face still buried in her neck, her honeysuckle scent filling my nose as I start to make love to her.

"Oh my god," Coraline moans, starting to move with me and soon we're settled into a rhythm.

"You feel incredible," I tell her, my lips moving against hers as we rock together.

"I'm-I'm coming!" she screams and her pussy clamps down around my length, triggering my own orgasm.

"Fuck!" I shout, coming with her.

Her fingers dig into my back and I love it, pounding into her harder until both of our peaks have passed.

"Whoa," Coraline says as I slowly ease out of her.

"I know. It was even better than I imagined."

"You imagined having sex with me?" she asks, sounding surprised.

"Only every day since I met you. I told you before, Coraline. You're the girl for me. You and I are forever."

She smiles up at me, giving me a soft kiss and I roll onto my side, gathering her up in my arms and wrapping around her.

Her breathing evens out a minute later and I say the words that have been on my tongue for weeks.

"I love you, Coraline."

TWELVE

Coraline

I DON'T SEE Harvey again for another week. I cleaned out the food truck and sold it this morning to someone who's going to change it into a BBQ place. I'm glad that I was able to sell it so fast, but seeing it go hit me harder than I thought it would.

Sayler took me out to a late dinner to celebrate me starting my next chapter in life and then dropped me off at Eye Candy Ink so that I could meet Harvey. He's supposed to be giving me my tattoo today since I'll be crazy busy for the next few weeks getting the restaurant and staff ready.

I've been talking to Max almost every day and I love that he's letting me give so much input into this place. He even let me name it and the sign and logo for Wild Thyme should be ready next week. We're working on finalizing the menu and arranging for interviews for staff next week too and then it will be time to order supplies and everything else that we need. It sounds overwhelming but I'm still so excited for this opportunity.

Rooney is just walking out when Sayler pulls up outside the front door and we both wave at him as I climb out of the car.

"Hey, Coraline! Congrats on the new restaurant," Rooney says, sounding happy for me and I smile.

"Thanks, I'm excited."

"Hey, Sayler," Rooney says and Sayler grins and waves at him.

"Hey, Rooney. How's it going?"

"Good," he says and things seem a little awkward between them.

I'll have to ask her what's going on between them later.

"I'll see you later," I tell them both as I head inside, and Sayler waves at both of us before she merges back with traffic and heads back to our apartment.

I open the tattoo shop door, turning to see if Rooney is following me in, but he's staring after Sayler's car, a look full of longing on his face. I don't want to interrupt him, so I just head inside the shop.

There's a front waiting area and then a hallway leading to the back of the building and so I head down the hallway, peeking into a few of the rooms until I find Harvey in one of the last ones.

"Hey," I say, stepping inside his room.

He's sitting at a crowded desk next to the door and he spins around in his chair at my voice and gives me the biggest smile. I love seeing him smile like that.

He stands up and pulls me into his arms, dropping a sweet kiss on my lips before he smiles down sweetly at me.

"How was your day?" he asks and I sigh.

"Good. Harder than I thought that it was going to be."

Harvey nods, looking concerned and I want to put him at ease.

"You'll just have to make sure that my tattoo is perfect so that I can always remember my little food truck era," I joke, trying to lighten the mood.

"I will. It's going to be perfect," he says, kissing my forehead before he steps back over to his desk and grabs some papers.

He passes them over to me and my breath catches as I study the design that Harvey has drawn for me.

It's perfect.

I knew that Harvey had to be talented if he worked at Eye Candy Ink. I mean, the place is a legend and they have that insane waiting list. I heard that they even tattoo celebrities sometimes, so they have to be incredible artists.

"I love it," I tell him, taking one last look at the miniature version of my food truck.

"Good. Where did you want it?" he asks and I mull it over.

I don't want it to be visible, so it has to be somewhere under my clothes or something that I can hide easily.

"How about right here?" I ask, rubbing the spot on my side over my ribs, where my bra lies.

"I can do wherever you want it. It might hurt a little bit going over your ribs," he warns me and I nod.

"I want it there."

Harvey gets to work then, asking me to take off my shirt and bra and lie on the tattoo table. He does something with the tattoo, transferring it onto a different kind of paper and lining up a few cups of ink, gloves, ointments, and paper towels.

I climb up onto the table and wrap one hand around my

breasts, covering them and moving my arm out of the way so that he has room to work.

"Alright, I'm going to get it in place and then you can take a look at the stencil on you before we get to work. Sound good?"

"Yeah."

He takes his time lining it up on my side and I love how focused and patient he is. He hands me a mirror and I check it out, nodding when I see that it's exactly where I wanted it.

He pulls on a pair of black latex gloves and fits a needle into his tattoo machine before spinning around to me.

"Here we go," he says, giving me a reassuring smile and I try not to tense as he starts to outline the tattoo.

We're silent for the first part of the tattoo, Harvey because he's concentrating on getting the lines perfect, and me because I'm trying to get used to the sting of the needle.

"Are you getting everything set for the restaurant?" he asks me after a few minutes.

"Yeah, we finalized the menu, and the sign and logo for the menus and social media stuff should be here soon. We just have to hire staff, order supplies, and then train everyone."

"Oh, is that all?" he jokes and I laugh.

"I know, but I love it and it doesn't seem like work. You know?"

"Yeah," he says, finishing up the outline.

The tattoo is small and won't take him long to finish up. The Culinerdy Cruiser is written in a circle around the pale blue food truck. He added some stars along the circle and then a fork and spoon above the truck so that it looks more like a logo.

He stops the machine and trades out colors, dipping his needle into the light blue color.

"Are you doing alright?" he asks as the needle moves along my skin.

"Yeah, I think I'm starting to get used to it."

"Is it making you want to get more?"

"Maybe," I say, looking at him with a grin.

"I'll tattoo you any time that you want."

We talk more about the new menu as he works and soon, he's all done. He grabs the ointment and wraps up the tattoo.

"You're all set," he tells me as he helps me sit up on the table.

We're eye to eye and he leans in, dropping a kiss on my lips.

"You did great."

"Thanks. It wasn't as bad as I thought it was going to be."

I wrap my arms around his waist and my core starts to tingle in my leggings. We haven't had any alone time since last week. Living with roommates makes it hard to find time where we're the only ones there. Plus, our work schedules can be rough to navigate. Sure, we text and talk on the phone every day, but it's not the same as seeing him face to face.

"I missed you," he tells me, our lips getting closer and closer together.

"I missed you too," I say and then our lips meet and I get lost in my man.

I'm already half undressed and I need to feel his skin on mine, so I tug at his shirt. He picks up on what I want and pulls his shirt off over his head. His lips land back on mine but I want more. I'm dying to feel him moving inside of me again.

"Can we... do it here?" I ask, my fingers trailing down to the button of his jeans.

"God yes."

I laugh as Harvey scrambles to undo his jeans and strip. I slip off the table to pull my leggings and panties down and then I'm dropping to my knees in front of him and taking his thick cock in my hand.

I look up at him, feeling like a queen as he stares down at me with such reverence.

"You don't have to," Harvey says as I lean forward and take a small lick up the underside of his dick.

Harvey groans and I grow more confident, licking another path, my tongue tracing the vein there.

"Fuck," Harvey grits out, his finger tangling in my hair as I open my mouth wide and take as much of him as I can.

I moan, my head bobbing as I lick and slurp along his length. Harvey moans, his fingers tightening in my hair with each pass I make along him.

"I need you," Harvey says and then he's reaching down and picking me. I gasp as he lays me down on the tattoo table and then Harvey comes down over me and I spread my legs, desperate for what he does to me.

He's about to drop to his knees but I stop him.

"Trust me. I'm wet enough. I need you inside of me."

"One lick. I need one taste."

He's between my legs a second later and I moan, squirming on the table as he eats me out.

"Harvey!" I scream as an orgasm crashes down on me.

He's standing a second later and pushing into me. We both moan long and low as he seats himself fully inside of me. Then we just act on instinct, moving and grinding together as we both chase our release.

"Jesus, Coraline. You're my everything."

I can only moan, the wave of pleasure rising up inside of me.

"More, more," I chant as my nails dig into his arms.

Harvey's pace picks up and he pounds into me as the wave finally breaks, spreading through my body. I come and then come again as Harvey continues to rut into me.

"Fuck, Coraline. Fuck. Jesus, I love you," he says as he finds his own release.

Hearing him say those three words sends a shockwave through my system. I should probably be freaked out that it happened so soon, but all I feel is excitement. I want to say it back but then the doubts hit me.

Did he just say that in the heat of the moment? Did he really mean it?

I open my mouth to say something, but the words won't come and I hurry off the table, grabbing my clothes as my phone rings.

"I should get this," I tell him, tugging my clothes on. "Thanks for the tattoo."

I turn and jog toward the door then, ignoring Harvey when he calls after me. It isn't until I'm outside in my car that I start to panic.

What the heck do I do now?

THIRTEEN

Harvey

"I TOLD Coraline that I loved her," I blurt out as soon as I walk into Eye Candy Ink the next day.

Rooney drops the case of Clorox wipes that he's carrying to the back office. Gray and Ender both just stare at me blankly, while Banks looks confused and I realize that I haven't seen him in a few days so he's probably behind in gossip. Ames doesn't even look up, he's too busy nuzzling his fiancée, Maxine's, neck.

"Congratulations, Harvey. Does Aunt Darcy and Uncle Atlas know yet? I know they were telling my dad that they still haven't really met her. They're super upset that Uncle Max and Aunt Cat have already talked to her a bunch and they haven't."

I groan, knowing that I'm going to be hearing more about that from my mom and dad, probably tonight.

"She didn't say it back," I tell the room before this conversation can get too far off the rails.

"Oh," Gray says with a wince.

"Bummer," Banks says and I think he's still trying to keep up with the conversation.

"Maybe she didn't hear you?" Maxine suggests and I shake my head.

"She definitely did. She ran out of here afterward like the place was on fire."

"Maybe she just needs more time," Ames says, wrapping his arms around Maxine's waist.

"Yeah, you did just meet her like three weeks ago. You probably freaked her out," Rooney chimes in and I glare at him.

"So, I shouldn't have told her how I felt?" I ask the group and everyone looks around.

"I think that you should have," Ender finally says and I'm surprised that he was the one to answer.

"Yeah, maybe she just needs time to process it," Maxine suggests, shuffling the papers in her hands.

"Maybe you scared her off," Rooney says and I see Banks shoot him a glare.

"I don't think you should take any of Rooney's advice. It's not like he has a girlfriend," Banks says and Rooney eyes him.

"And you do?" Rooney asks and we all turn to look curiously at Banks.

He squirms in his chair and looks away and I know that Rooney is never going to let this go now.

"What's her name?" Gray asks.

"And when do we get to meet her?" Rooney asks with a wicked grin.

"You? Never."

"So, you do have a girlfriend?" Maxine asks as she heads behind the front counter to boot up the computer there.

"Not yet," Banks mumbles and I take mercy on him.

"So back to me and my problems."

"Just go talk to her. Tell her that you love her again but that you recognize that it might be too soon for her," Ames says and I nod.

"That could work."

I wonder when I'll have time to see her. She's been super busy with opening the new restaurant and I have a feeling that she might be avoiding me now after last night.

I couldn't sleep last night. I just kept going over and over what happened in the shop. Maybe I should have just kept my mouth shut but I couldn't hold the words back any longer.

But now I rushed things and could have pushed her away. I don't know what I'll do if she breaks things off with me over this.

"Thanks, Ames," I say, getting ready to head back to my room.

"What about me? I offered you advice too!" Rooney calls after me.

"Your advice sucks!"

He laughs and I hear him follow after me and head into his room. A second later, he comes into my room and tosses me a bottle of Clorox wipes.

"Thanks."

"No problem."

He hops up on my table and I eye him for a second but when he doesn't say anything, I go back to working on my tattoos for today.

"Are you going to talk to Coraline?" he asks a few minutes later and I nod.

"Yeah, I can't lose her."

"I know," he whispers and I stop drawing to turn and look at him.

"You do?" I ask him and my mind flashes back to the way that he was looking at Sayler. "Did you ask Sayler out?"

"Yeah," he admits after a minute.

"Cool, man. When are you going out?"

"We aren't."

"What? Why not?"

"She turned me down. It's just... I could swear that she wanted to say yes."

"Do you want me to ask Coraline about it?" I ask him and he nods, not looking at me.

"Yeah, if you don't mind. I just, I can't stop thinking about her and if it's something that I can fix, then I'd do it for a chance with her."

I nod, knowing the feeling well.

"I'll talk to Coraline," I promise him and he gives me a grateful smile before he hops off the table and heads back across the hall to his room.

My first client is supposed to be here soon, so I push thoughts of Sayler and Rooney and Coraline from my mind the best I can and get to work.

A knock at my door has me looking up and I smile when I see my mom and dad standing there.

"Hey! What are you guys doing here?" I ask them as I get up to hug them.

"We haven't seen you in a few days and we were in the neighborhood."

"Yeah, I've been busy."

"We heard," my dad says and I know that he's talking about Coraline.

"When do we get to meet her?" my mom asks and I know that that's why they were really here.

"I don't know. I'll have to ask her and we can grab dinner sometime soon."

My mom nods and I start to relax, glad that they aren't going to push the issue. My parents have the perfect marriage, the perfect relationship. My dad worships the ground that my mom walks on and they have always been close.

Maybe that's why I don't share my girl trouble with them.

I catch up with my parents for a bit but then Eye Candy Ink opens a few minutes later and my parents say they'll call me soon as they leave and I turn to get back to work. My first client arrives a few minutes after that and I get to work, eager to get lost in tattooing.

It doesn't quite work. I'm distracted all day, planning out what I'll say to Coraline when I go to see her tonight. By the time Eye Candy Ink closes, I've got everything set in my head.

Now I just need to go find my girl and make things right with her.

FOURTEEN

Coraline

I'M CHECKING things off on my clipboard when the kitchen door opens and Harvey pokes his head in.

"Hey," I greet him with a nervous smile.

I've been thinking about how I freaked out and ran away from him all day and I was just about to stop for the night so that I could go talk to him. I need to tell him how I feel and apologize for running away from him. I just hope that he doesn't think I'm too much of a weirdo for freaking out like that last night.

"Hey, you got a second? Am I interrupting anything?" he asks, looking around the dark, empty kitchen.

"No, the staff just left for the night and I was just finishing my nightly checklist."

"Cool. It looks really good in here," he says.

"Thanks."

I shift anxiously on my feet, wanting to bring up last night but not knowing how.

"How's the tattoo?" he asks, giving me the perfect opening.

"Good, I love it."

I could swear that he winces at those words and I want to smack myself.

"I'm glad that you stopped by. I was about to come find you when I was done."

"You were?" he asks, sounding surprised and I nod.

"I'm sorry about last night—"

"I shouldn't have rushed you," he cuts in and I shake my head.

"No, you should never have to apologize for how you're feeling. I just, well I haven't heard those words a lot in my life and I thought that maybe you just said them in the heat of the moment. I didn't want things to be weird if you didn't mean them, but then I ran away and made it weird anyway."

"I didn't just say it in the heat of the moment. I meant it, Coraline. I love you."

His words warm me like a good cup of coffee or a shot of tequila and I smile shyly at first but soon I can't stop my lips from stretching wide.

"Say it again," I ask him and he swallows and takes a step toward me.

"I love you, Coraline. I love you more than anything."

"I love you too, Harvey. So much," I tell him as he wraps his arms around me and our lips crash down on each other.

His tongue pushes into my mouth and I open for him greedily. He tastes like mint and something that is all Harvey. His lips mold to mine and he backs me up until I hit the counter. I know that we would be breaking about a million health code violations if we did it in here but I still find myself reaching for the hem of his shirt.

And that's when Max, my boss and Harvey's uncle, walks into the kitchen.

Harvey and I jump apart and I can feel the blush heating my face.

"Hey, Uncle Max. Looks good in here," Harvey says and I can see Max trying to hold back his smile.

"Thanks, Harvey. I just came to see if I could walk Coraline to her car before I left for the night but I see that you've got that covered. I'll see you two crazy kids later," he says with a smile as he waves and heads back out the kitchen door.

"Oh my god," I groan and Harvey laughs.

"Why don't you let me take you out to dinner and then we can head back to my place and I can check on your tattoo."

"Right," I say with a grin and he laughs.

"Alright, take me home, shotgun wedding."

Harvey wraps his arm around me, laughing as he leads me out of the restaurant and over to his car and I sink into him. Into the man that I love.

FIFTEEN

Harvey

ONE YEAR LATER...

I GRAB the last few bags of groceries before my fiancée can. She glares at me slightly and I just lean over and kiss her quickly before I head up the stairs to our apartment. Coraline is still the most independent woman that I've ever met but she's starting to learn that she can lean on me and other people more.

"Can you grab the door?" I ask her and she steps around me, pulling open the apartment building's door.

I follow her up the stairs to the apartment that we just moved into. My lease was up with Rooney and now that he's living with Sayler, Coraline and I decided to move in together. Sayler and Rooney live next door and as I head toward our front door, I see Sayler pop her head out and grin when she sees us.

"Did you get it?" she asks Coraline and my fiancée nods, scurrying into the apartment with Sayler hot on her heels.

"Get what?" I ask her but she just gives me a sly smile and grabs one of the bags for me.

It just had some cosmetics and shampoo in it and I frown after her confused as she and Sayler giggle and head into the bathroom. I let them go and head into the kitchen to put the groceries away when there's a knock on our door.

"Hey!" I say when I answer and see my mom, dad, Aunt Indie, and Uncle Mischa standing there. "What's going on?"

Uncle Mischa and Aunt Indie squeeze their way inside and I laugh, hugging my mom and dad.

"We were in the neighborhood and wanted to see if you and Coraline wanted to go out to dinner with us?"

"Rooney is supposed to be home soon too, right? We were going to ask him and Sayler too," Aunt Indie says as I start to close the apartment door.

"Hey!" Rooney says, sounding outraged as I close the door in his face.

"Sorry, didn't see you there."

He glares at me but I was being sincere.

"Is Sayler here?" he asks and I huff out a laugh.

"Coraline is home. Where else would she be?" I joke.

Coraline works crazy hours as a chef which means that when she's home or has a day off, the girls are usually together.

"Hey guys," Rooney says as he greets our parents and heads over to open the fridge.

He pulls out the potato salad that I just put away and grabs a spoon from the drawer and I roll my eyes.

"We wanted to take you and the girls out to dinner," my

mom tells him and he shoves the spoonful of potato salad into his mouth before he puts it back.

"Where are we going? And where's my girl?" he asks.

"Bedroom with Coraline," I tell him as the girls come out of the bathroom.

They're both smiling from ear to ear and they smile wider when they see our parents standing there.

"Hey," Coraline says, hugging my mom and dad before she switches with Sayler and hugs my aunt Indie and uncle Mischa.

I smile. My parents, my whole family, loves Coraline and Sayler and I'm glad that the girls have the family that they deserve now. A family who loves them and just wants them to be happy.

"What are you two so happy about?" Rooney asks as he hugs Sayler to him.

"We have some exciting news," Sayler says, sharing a look with Coraline.

"What's going on?" I ask, pulling Coraline into my side.

She smiles up at me and I get lost in her eyes for a minute.

"We're pregnant!" Sayler screams and I gape at Coraline.

"We are?" I whisper and she nods, tears in her eyes.

"Yeah, we are," she whispers back and I wrap my arms around her, crushing her to me before I panic and loosen my grip.

"Congratulations!" my mom and Aunt Indie cry, swarming us and wrapping the girls up in a hug.

Our dads are next and then I'm pulling Coraline back into my arms.

"How are you feeling?" my mom asks and I hold my girl close as my mom and aunt bombard the girls with questions.

I smile through it all.

This is everything that I wanted in life. My family, the love of my life, and now we're going to have kids of our own.

"Let's go eat and celebrate," Uncle Mischa says and I take Coraline's hand as we head down the stairs.

"Are you happy?" she asks me as we follow everyone outside and I squeeze her hand.

"I couldn't be any happier. I love you, Coraline."

"I love you too," she says, leaning up on her tiptoes and brushing a kiss across my lips.

SIXTEEN

Coraline

FIVE YEARS LATER...

"YOU NEED to behave for Grandma and Grandpa," I tell my kids as I help them with their overnight bags.

Our son, Graham, and our daughter, Lila, both nod at me as they skip after each other and I sigh, knowing that they're going to be hyper most of the night. They've been excited about having a sleepover at their grandparents' house all week and I know that Atlas and Darcy are just as excited to spend time with their grandkids.

Harvey and I are headed out for dinner and a night alone for our anniversary. We've been married for four years and since we had our kids, we don't get as much alone time as we'd like.

Both of our hours are crazy and we're usually rushing in the morning to get the kids ready for preschool.

We still live next door to Rooney and Sayler, although both of us had to move to a new apartment building with bigger apartments. They had two kids too, both boys and they're best friends with our kids.

It's Sayler and Rooney's anniversary today too. Sayler and I actually shared a wedding. It was Sayler's big dream and since I never pictured my wedding, I was more than happy to let her plan it for the both of us. My only contribution was the food and liquor.

"Hey!" I greet Darcy as she opens the door for us and she grins at me.

"Hey guys! Go ahead and go in. Grandpa is setting up the living room so we can have a movie night tonight," she informs the kids and they take off.

"Bye guys! I'll see you tomorrow!"

They yell bye back and laugh.

"They're very excited about tonight."

"Oh, we are too," Darcy promises and I smile.

Darcy and Atlas are the parents that I wish I had growing up. They are so supportive and loving and I swear I've never seen them argue.

"Thanks again for watching them. We'll be back tomorrow morning with breakfast."

"Sounds good! Have a good night, honey," she says as I wave and head back to my car.

I still work for Max Schultz at Wild Thyme and over the last five years, I've turned it into one of the hottest spots to eat in all of Pittsburgh. I have a great sous chef who covers for me twice a week so that I can be home with my family. Harvey always takes the same two days off at Eye Candy Ink so that he can be home with us too and I love how into family he is.

He's a great husband and an even better dad. He's the

one who helps them get dressed and ready for bed. He reads to them every night before bed and takes them to the park most mornings. Him and Rooney even have play dates most weekend mornings before Sayler watches them for the rest of the day.

I hurry back to the apartment and pull up just as Harvey does. He had to work today but he must have finished with his client early if he's home already.

"You ruined my surprise!" I tell him as he comes over to open my door.

"Want me to wait in my car for a little bit?" he asks, passing me a bouquet of flowers and a box from my favorite bakery.

"Cinnamon roll cookies?" I ask him and he nods.

"And those macarons that you love."

"You're the perfect man," I say with a sigh and he grins.

"I try."

He takes my hand and I let him lead me inside and up to our apartment. I had planned on being home before him. He'd come inside and I'd be wearing that lingerie that I picked out last week. We'd end up ordering dinner later. Hopefully much later.

"Where did you want to go to dinner?" he asks as I set the flowers down on the kitchen counter.

"I'd like you to give me five minutes and then I'll tell you."

"Alright," Harvey says with a confused smile on his face.

He takes the flowers from me and grabs a vase and I kiss his cheek.

"Be right back," I promise him.

I hurry into the bedroom and then grab the lingerie and

hurry to get dressed. I fluff my hair and apply another layer of mascara before I take one last look at myself in the mirror.

I look hot. The purple lace and silk hugs my curves and I know that Harvey is going to go crazy when he sees me in it.

I head out into the kitchen, my high heels clicking on the hardwood floor but Harvey doesn't look up from the flowers.

"Know what you're hungry for yet, babe?" he asks me and I lean against the kitchen doorway.

"I'll let you decide. What are you hungry for?" I ask and Harvey finally looks up at me.

His mouth drops open and I can see his eyes heat from across the room.

"You," he murmurs. "I'm hungry for you."

I giggle, letting him pick me up and carry me to our bedroom where he lays me out on the bed and devours me.

DID YOU LOVE HARVEY? **Please consider leaving a review! You can do so on Amazon or on Goodreads.**

DID **you miss the original Eye Candy Ink series? You can read the boxset here.**

GRAB **the next book in the series, Rooney, here!**

ALSO BY SHAW HART

STILL IN THE **mood for Christmas books?**
Stuffing Her Stocking, Mistletoe Kisses, Snowed in For Christmas

LOVE HOLIDAY BOOKS? **Check out these!**
For Better or Worse, Riding His Broomstick, Thankful for His FAKE Girlfriend, His New Year Resolution, Hop Stuff, Taming Her Beast, Hungry For Dash, His Firework

LOOKING **for some OTT love stories?**
Fighting for His Princess, Her Scottish Savior, Not So Accidental Baby Daddy, Baby Mama

LOOKING FOR A CELEBRITY LOVE STORY?
Bedroom Eyes, Seducing Archer, Finding Their Rhythm

IN THE MOOD **for some young love books?**
Study Dates, His Forever, My Girl

SOME OTHER BOOKS BY SHAW:
The Billionaire's Bet, Her Guardian Angel, Every Tuesday Night, Falling Again, Stealing Her, Dreamboat, Locked Down, Making Her His, Trouble

ROONEY

EYE CANDY INK: SECOND GENERATION

Rooney Jennings is out of his mind.

To be fair, a lot of his friends would claim that he was never in his right mind.

He was raised by two carefree pranksters who fell head over heels in love and he grew up hearing about their love story and wondering if he would ever just see someone and instantly know that they were meant to be.

He had just about given up on that happening when he spots Sayler Jones, the spunky graphic designer who can make him laugh like no one else.

They should be happy together, they're both interested in one another and they just click.

There's just one problem.

Sayler has been promised to another.

Will pursuing Sayler ruin everything? Or will he finally get the happily ever after that he's been dreaming about ever since he first laid eyes on her?

ONE

Rooney

MY PHONE BUZZES as I'm finishing cleaning up from my last client and I tense. I already know who is texting me and what they want and I really don't want to get into this right now.

I also know that if I ignore her, then my mom will just keep texting, or worse, she'll just show up here.

MOM: **So, when are you going to meet your girlfriend??**

Rooney: She's not my girlfriend.

Mom: You could bring her by on Sunday.

Rooney: She's not my girlfriend.

Mom: Still.

Rooney: I love you. Got another client, so talk to you later.

Mom: Love you too, boo bear!

I TOSS my phone back onto my desk, sighing as I run a hand through my messy black hair. My mom has been dying for me to get a girlfriend since I turned twenty. I think she always thought that it was weird that I never dated in high school, but the truth was that I didn't want to.

I wanted a love like theirs. I wanted to see someone and just know in my bones that we were meant to be together, and I never felt that way about any of the girls in my high school.

My best friend and roommate walks by my room, smiling down at his phone and I turn away before the now-familiar surge of jealousy can hit me.

I love Harvey. We might not actually be related, but he's my brother in every way that counts. We've been best friends since birth and I want him to be happy.

It just sucks that the woman that he fell in love with is also my dream girl's best friend. Now he's on cloud nine and I'm busy panting after the girl who stole my heart with just one smile.

Coraline and Harvey are perfect together though and he deserves to get everything that he wants in life, so I suck it up, forcing the jealousy down and just being happy for him.

My next client is going to be here soon and so I force my mind off of Harvey, Coraline, and my girl Sayler and get back to work.

It doesn't last long.

I've already got the tattoo designed and on the tracing paper. I just need to pour the colors that the client wants and I'll be good to go.

I've wanted to ask Sayler out since the night that we met. I had been grabbing a bite to eat with Harvey at The Culinerdy Cruiser, the food truck that Coraline used to run that was parked across the street from Eye Candy Ink most nights.

Harvey was going there to eat because he was already head over heels in love with Coraline. I was going because I was hungry and also to make sure that Harvey didn't crash and burn with his girl too much. The guy has no game.

Then I had looked up and spotted Sayler through the food truck window and that had been it. One look was all it took for me to know that she was it for me. I could feel it in every fiber of my body. I could feel it in my soul.

She was my one.

I left that night with her phone number but she had seemed a little hesitant to start anything so I've been taking it slow instead. I've been trying to take my cues from her, but that's getting harder now.

I used to see Sayler almost every night at The Culinerdy Cruiser food truck, but ever since Coraline started working as the head chef at Uncle Max's new restaurant, Wild Thyme, and closed down the food truck, I've had to resort to texting instead.

I pull up our messages, scrolling through the ones from the last few days. There are some GIFs, a few pictures of my latest tattoos, some funny ones of her pretending to cry over her computer, and then a bunch of texts in between.

We talk about our days, what we need to get done and when I'm getting off of work. She works from home, designing book covers, graphics, and websites. Sometimes she asks my opinions on some of her work and I'm always blown away at how talented she is.

Mixed in with those messages are a few of me inviting her out to eat.

She always turns me down gently.

Harvey walks back past my room, whistling, and I look over to see him shooting me a grin. I roll my eyes, glaring at him and he laughs, heading up front to grab his next client.

It's late and this is my last client of the night. I yawn, stretching my arms over my head to work out any kinks and tight muscles before I stand and head up front to grab my client.

When I see that it's two girls, both a few years younger than me and probably still in college, I groan. They're already eyeing me like I'm a piece of meat and I paste on a smile. Looks like I'm in for another few hours of dodging flirty banter and listening to giggles.

"Ready?" I ask them with a smile and they both giggle as they stand and head my way.

I barely manage to hold back a grimace as I turn and lead them down the hallway toward my room.

My eyes stray to my phone as I walk in and I wish that I was texting with Sayler instead of tattooing this rose onto this girl.

Luckily, the tattoo doesn't take long and I'm packing up all of my stuff and heading for the door a little over an hour and a half later. I pass by Harvey's room and see that he's just wrapping up his client too.

"I'll meet you at the car," I tell him and he nods, wrapping up his client's arm with plastic wrap.

I push outside, waving at Gray as he checks out his last client at the front counter. I head across the road, leaning against Harvey's car. He drives us pretty much every day since I'm not the best driver. I tend to have a bit of a short attention span and I talk with my hands a lot, neither of which are great for driving.

I pull out my phone as I wait for Harvey to finish up and open up my messages with Sayler. The last one was from this morning but she was busy with work so we didn't talk for long.

I debate for a second, but I'm weak, especially when it comes to her, so I give in and send her another text.

ROONEY: **Get everything that you wanted to get done today?**

I wait, wondering if she's busy but she replies right away.

SAYLER: **Almost! The rest I'll be able to get done tomorrow for sure though. How was your day?**

Rooney: Good. Busy. I miss seeing you every day.

Sayler: Me too. Plus, now I have to go to Wild Thyme if I want to eat some of Coraline's food!

Rooney: She doesn't cook for you at home?

Sayler: Sure, when she's here but she's always at the restaurant or with Harvey now.

Rooney: Ugh, true love is the worst.

Sayler: LOL! Right?

Sayler: I wish I had what they do *insert dreamy sigh*

.   .   .

I WANT to text back and tell her that I'll give her anything that she wants but I bite my tongue.

ROONEY: **Me too.**

I TUCK my phone back into my pocket when I see Harvey headed my way. He and Gray finish locking up Eye Candy Ink and as Harvey gets closer, I head around to the passenger side.

"Pizza?" Harvey asks as he unlocks the car and I nod.

"With extra cheese."

"Duh," he says as he starts the car and pulls out of the lot.

I smile as he drives us down the mostly deserted streets.

TWO

Sayler

I SCROLL THROUGH NETFLIX, bored out of my mind. Ever since Coraline took the head chef position at Wild Thyme, my nights have been long and monotonous. Don't get me wrong, I'm so happy for her, and I know that she deserves it, but I miss hanging out with her every night.

I don't have any other friends in this city since we just moved here a few months ago and I work from home. I've been trying to keep myself busy, but I'm not doing a great job of it.

I tried watching a few different television series, but nothing was able to hold my interest. I even tried working and now I'm two weeks ahead and still bored.

The only time that I'm not tired of being alone is when I'm texting Rooney. He always knows what to say to make me laugh and I love the way his mind works.

My phone rings and for a second, I wonder if my thoughts conjured up Rooney. My stomach flips and I hurry to grab my phone. Then I look at the screen and see my mom's name on the screen and my stomach drops.

I really don't want to answer it. It's late and I know that she must just be getting out of some fancy event. It also means that she's probably at least a little drunk. My mom isn't the nicest, but when you put a few vodka martinis into her, she turns downright nasty.

I don't want to answer it, but if I don't, then she'll just keep calling until I do. She would never even consider that I could be busy or that I don't have time to drop everything and answer her calls. It's always been like this. What my mom wants, she gets.

"Hey, Mom."

"Sayler, what took you so long to answer?" she snaps and I bite back my sigh.

Because I didn't want to talk to you.

"Sorry, I was sleeping," I say instead.

My mom is big on beauty sleep so I know that she won't have anything bad to say about that excuse.

"Hmm, you don't sound like you were asleep."

"Well, I was. Did you need something?" I ask, hoping to wrap this conversation up fast.

"Yes, your father and I wanted to know when you would be coming back to New York. The Radcliff's son has finally graduated from medical school and it's time to start planning your wedding."

My stomach cramps, turning into knots at her words.

My parents had a deal that I would marry the Radcliff's son, Dalton, pretty much since the day that I was born.

The Radcliffs are a big deal in New York society and it was an even bigger deal that they agreed to this union. My parents are both lawyers and while they're extremely wealthy, it's nothing compared to the Radcliff's oil fortune.

"I don't know, Mom. I just moved to Pittsburgh and I really love it here."

"In Pittsburgh?" she says, derision dripping from each word.

"Yeah, it's a cool city. You should come visit and check it out."

She laughs outright at that and the sound grates on my nerves. It's cruel sounding, filled with malice and absolutely no real humor. I should be used to the sound. She's always either putting on a fake laugh, one that's high pitched and phony sounding, or laughing like she just did.

I'm not sure which one I hate more.

"We expect you to come home soon. This silly fantasy of yours is a waste of time. Dalton is waiting on you and it's time for you to fulfill your commitments."

I want to scream that it's not my commitment and that I don't want to be married to Dalton Radcliff. The guy is a sexist asshole with a god complex and a circle of friends who are just as uptight and materialistic as he is. If I were to marry him, my life would be hell and I would be miserable.

"Is that understood, Sayler?" my mom asks, her voice hard and filled with a warning.

It's not really a question.

It's a warning to behave, to toe the line or face the consequences.

"I understand," I say, my heart sinking as tears sting the back of my eyes.

"Good," she says, hanging up on me without saying goodbye or that she loves me.

She didn't even bother asking me how I was doing. I can't remember the last time that she asked me how I was or what I was working on.

I hang up, turning off the TV and resting my head

against the back of the couch. I don't even want to think about my parents or the life waiting for me back in New York. Luckily, my phone dings and this time it is a message from Rooney.

ROONEY: **So, I was thinking. How would you like to join me for dinner at Wild Thyme sometime? I know that we're both missing Coraline's cooking and I miss seeing your face.**

I BITE MY LIP, rereading his words. I know that Rooney is interested in me. That he's been interested in me since we first met, but I didn't want to get tangled up in him only to be summoned back home to fulfill "my duty."

Maybe I should though. Maybe this is my one chance to date someone that I choose. Someone that I actually like.

"Whew!" Coraline says, dumping her purse and a few takeout containers down on the kitchen counter as she breezes into the apartment.

"Hey!" I say, abandoning my phone and jumping up to see what goodies she brought home. "How was work?"

"Awesome," Coraline gushes, a big grin on her face and I smile.

I love how happy she is. She deserves to be the head chef, to reach all of her dreams and I'm so happy that she's getting it here in Pittsburgh.

Can I really leave Coraline behind and go back to New York? She'd have to choose between me and Harvey then and I never want to ask her to do that. Or maybe Harvey would move too, although then he'd be leaving Rooney and his own family behind.

Does any of this matter? Can I actually marry Dalton? I'd be in hell for the rest of my life if I did. Plus, do I really want to give up my new life in Pittsburgh to go back to New York. The whole reason why Coraline and I moved was to get away from my parents and their stifling wishes.

"What did you bring me?"

"I made this new meatball recipe! I was thinking about adding a gyro to the menu since they seem to be so hot right now. I can make my own mint tzatziki sauce to go with it and maybe make my own pita bread."

Coraline talks excitedly about different ingredients or variations she can make and my mouth starts to water as I listen to her. She hands me a takeout box and I spear one of the meatballs and take a big bite.

"Oh man, it's so good," I say, moaning around the bite in my mouth.

"Thanks," Coraline says, beaming at me as I finish off the meatball.

"I talked to Caroline today," she says and my mood picks up at the mention of our friend.

"How is she doing?" I ask.

"Better. Or at least as good as can be expected. She said that she found a diner for sale in some small town called Cherry Falls. She's moving there with Charlotte in a few weeks."

"We should go help her move."

Coraline nods and I make a mental note to call Caroline soon. The three of us had been close all through high school. She was always close with her brother so while Coraline and I left New York as soon as we could, she stayed behind to be close to him and his daughter.

Her brother just passed away along with his wife about a year ago, leaving her the guardian of their daughter, Charlotte. I know that it's been an adjustment for her and we've been trying to help as much as we could while not being in the same state.

Coraline passes me another container and I open it to see the truffle macaroni and cheese that she makes. It's my favorite and I give her a quick hug before I dig in.

She smiles, her grin widening when her phone dings and I know that it must be her boyfriend, Harvey.

My stomach starts to sink as I watch her text him back. Things are changing here. She's going to be moving in with him soon and then I'll be alone here.

I want what she and Harvey have. I want to be part of a couple. I want to be in love.

And I know that I'll never have it with Dalton Radcliff or anyone else that my parents pick for me.

But maybe I could with Rooney.

I finish off the macaroni and cheese and say goodnight to Coraline before I head to bed. His texts are still fresh in my mind and I realize that I never responded. I'm torn though. Do I give in to this attraction between us and see where it leads? Or do I protect him and tell him that I'm promised to another?

I'm still undecided by the time that my eyes drift closed and sleep finally takes me.

THREE

Rooney

"DO YOU WANT A MIMOSA?" my uncle Nico asks and I can't tell if he's messing with me or not.

"Nah, I'm good," I say, holding up my beer bottle, the label half hanging on from where I was picking at it.

He grunts as he sinks into the deck chair next to me, stretching out his long legs.

"Where's Banks?" I ask, referencing his son and Nico shrugs.

"He said that he was on his way a bit ago. He should be here soon."

I nod, moving my legs as my uncle Atlas and Zeke both come over and take the other two deck chairs. When I see my dad and Harvey both dragging over chairs, I know that something is up.

"What's going on?" I ask the guys and they all shoot me varying amused looks.

"Your mom wants grandkids," my dad says seriously and I almost choke on my beer.

"Oh my god," I grumble and I start looking for an escape route.

"Not so fast," my dad says, blocking my exit with his chair.

"I was just going to get another beer," I lie and Nico looks down pointedly to my half-full beer bottle.

I quickly down the last of the beer.

"Mom wants to know when we're all going to get to meet Sayler," my dad says and I try not to groan.

"You already met her," I point out, referring to the night that they came to The Culinerdy Cruiser a few weeks ago.

They were really there to meet Coraline but since Sayler was there, they technically already met her too.

"We want to meet her again. Plus, Zeke, Nico, Trixie, and Edie haven't met her yet," my dad says and I slouch farther in my chair.

"We're not dating, so it would be weird to bring her over here."

"Ask her out then," Uncle Nico adds helpfully and I glare at him.

"I did. She hasn't replied yet."

"She left you on read?" Banks asks as he joins our group and I roll my eyes.

Great. *Now* he shows up.

"Yeah," I grumble, my leg starting to bounce as I grow more agitated.

"Maybe you should move on then?" Uncle Max says and I sigh.

"I can't. She's stuck in my head like a bad idea," I say, more to myself than to anyone else.

"How did you ask her out?" Harvey asks and I want to ask him whose side he's on.

"We were texting and she said that she missed Coraline's food now that she's working at Wild Thyme, so—"

"What about my restaurant?" my uncle Max asks as he joins our group and I sink another inch down in my chair.

"Rooney asked Sayler out for a date there. She didn't respond," Uncle Atlas summarizes.

"Oh, ouch," Uncle Max says with a grimace and I sink even lower in my chair if possible. At this rate, I'm dangerously close to just sitting on the ground.

"That's rough," Uncle Nico says, clapping me on the shoulder.

"Thanks," I say dryly.

"Want me to try to set you up with someone else?" Uncle Max offers and I shake my head right away.

I want Sayler or no one at all.

"No, I just need to figure out a different way in with her. She's hiding something, I just don't know what it is."

"Want me to ask Coraline?" Harvey offers and I shake my head again.

I want Sayler to trust me enough to open up to me.

"Just give her time. Being friends first is always a good thing. You're building a strong foundation," Uncle Atlas says and I perk up a bit.

Going any slower might kill me, but if it gets me Sayler in the end, then it will be worth it.

"Why don't you ask her out in person? You kids nowadays with your texting and—" Uncle Zeke starts.

"And your Razr scooters," my dad finishes, trying to sound like a crotchety old man.

I laugh at that, laughing even harder when Uncle Zeke flips my dad off.

"I'm not that old," Uncle Zeke grumbles and I grin.

"Maybe you should ask her out in person," Uncle Nico says.

"Yeah, if nothing else, you might be able to get a better read on her," Banks offers and I nod.

Maybe they're right. Maybe she thinks that I'm not that interested or serious about her because I'm just texting her. I can step it up. Do it right.

I'll bring her flowers and ask her if she wants to go to dinner with me. It doesn't even have to be at her best friend's restaurant.

"Time to eat!" my aunt Darcy calls and we all stand and start to make our way over to the kitchen.

"Thanks, guys," I murmur to the guys and they each pat me on the back or fist bump me as we head inside.

I pause before I step through the doorway, pulling out my phone one more time to see if she's responded yet.

My mood plummets when I see that there are still no new messages. I shove my phone back into my pocket, determined to come up with a game plan before I contact her again.

"Come on, boo bear!" my mom calls and I force a smile as I step inside and take the plate from her.

"Thanks, Mom," I say, giving her a side hug and a kiss on the top of her head before I start to load up my plate.

Now I just need to figure out how to win over my girl.

FOUR

Sayler

WHEN MY PHONE rings the next day and I see that it's my mom calling again, my whole body tenses. Two calls in two days? This can't be a good sign.

"Hey, Mom!" I say, trying to infuse as much cheer into my voice as I can.

"Sayler, I'm calling to see if you've thought any more about our conversation last night."

"Um, what about it, Mom?" I ask.

She sighs like I'm really putting her out and I can feel my heart starting to beat faster. *Why does she always do this? Make me feel like a nuisance and a burden instead of like her daughter?*

"When are you coming back to New York? It's where you belong and you have responsibilities here. Do you have any idea how embarrassing it is to explain to all of our friends that our daughter is off in *Pittsburgh* working on some computer programming? I mean, my god, Sayler." She whispers the last part like she's embarrassed or worried that someone can hear her and I grip the phone tighter in my hand.

"I'm not working on a computer program, Mom," I say through gritted teeth. "I'm a graphic designer. A damn good one."

"Language, young lady," she warns and it's her tone of voice that has me snapping.

It's like she's talking to a wayward puppy and she's trying to bring me to heel. There's no love here. The only reason that I tolerate them or still talk to them is because I don't want to lose my family. We might not have anything in common, but they are my parents. Shouldn't that mean something?

I always thought that it did, but lately... well, I'm not so sure anymore.

Plus, they'll cut me off if I don't do as they order. My business is doing alright right now, but I don't have that much in savings and a few bad months and I could be out on my butt.

"I don't want to marry Dalton Radcliff," I tell my mom, schooling my voice until it's nothing but pleasant, no hint of the anger simmering inside of me.

"It's already been decided, Sayler Ann."

Oh, the middle name. She's serious about this.

"But I don't love him," I try, one last time.

She scoffs at that.

"Love, Sayler? He is wealthy and from a good, prominent, family. He will be able to provide you with a good life. A *comfortable* life. He'll support you, give you everything that you need. He is the right choice. The decision has already been made."

I don't have anything to say to that, or at least nothing

that will change her mind, so I remain silent, my throat on fire from the words lodged there.

I want to scream at her, to tell her that I'm her daughter and she should care about what I want but I know that it won't be any use.

"Your father and I expect a date when you will be moving back to New York soon. Very soon," she warns before she hangs up on me.

"Ugh!" I growl, standing up off of the couch and starting to pace.

My phone is gripped tight in my hand, digging into my palm and I want to scream.

Before I can stop myself, I pull up my text messages, find Rooney's name, and text him back.

SAYLER: **I'd love to have dinner, but it might be a while before we can get into Wild Thyme. Their head chef is kind of a big deal and I heard that the waitlist is insane.**

Rooney: I could pull a few strings. I'm kind of a big deal too. I've got connections all over this town.

Sayler: Do you mean just your Uncle Max?

Rooney: Maybe….

Rooney: Okay, yeah. It's just him and maybe Harvey.

Sayler: LOL!

Rooney: Don't worry, if we can't get into Wild Thyme, then I have a few other ideas. What day works for you?

Sayler: Let me look at my schedule and I'll text you tomorrow?

Rooney: Sounds good. Talk soon

I TUCK my phone back into my pocket, some of the angry energy leaving my body after talking to Rooney. He can always brighten my day.

Coraline comes in a few minutes later, her chef clothes stained with something red and I join her as she comes over and sinks down onto the couch.

"How was work?" I ask and she yawns.

"Busy. My sous chef had to leave early for a family emergency so I had to pick up the slack."

"You should have called me!" I joke and Coraline laughs.

I can't even boil water and we both know that I wouldn't have been any help.

"What have you been up to?" she asks.

"My mom called. Again."

"Again?"

"She called me last night too."

"Ugh, I'm sorry. She's the worst," Coraline grumbles, toeing off her shoes.

I nod. She really is.

"What did she want?"

"The usual. When am I moving back to New York? I have responsibilities and Dalton Radcliff is finally ready to settle down, so I need to be done with my silly fantasies and come home to marry him."

"Dalton Radcliff," Coraline half snarls, and I lean my head on her shoulder.

"I know. He's so... slimy."

"And he's a sexist pig who thinks that he's God's gift to women. Plus he's a serial womanizer. I mean honestly, how can your parents think that he's a good choice?"

I raise my hand, rubbing my fingers together to show money and she scoffs. I'm not looking at her but I know that she just rolled her eyes.

"I know. And my mom is trying to convince me that I'm the lucky one for getting to be Mrs. Dalton Radcliff."

"Please promise me that you won't marry him. He'll be cheating on you before you even finish your wedding vows."

"I could never marry him. He's disgusting."

"Good," Coraline says, leaning her head against mine.

"Rooney asked me out," I say after a minute.

"Yay!" she says, her whole energy changing as we get back to a more pleasant topic. "Did you say yes? Where is he taking you?"

"I said yes, but I don't know when or where we're going. I need to look at my schedule."

"I'm so excited for you! We can even go on double dates now!"

She hugs me and I laugh, hugging her back. We sit like that for a while and it's exactly what I needed. Everything is changing around here and my future seems so uncertain but it's nice to just sit on the couch with my best friend and ponder all of the possibilities.

FIVE

Rooney

I HAVE a hard time sitting still most days but waiting until six pm to go pick up Sayler for our first date is harder than usual. I've been dancing around Harvey and my apartment all afternoon. I had today off so I've already run all of my errands and had plenty of time to plan out our date.

"Dude, you need to calm down," Harvey says as he comes into the apartment and sees me bouncing up and down.

"I can't," I say, vaulting over the back of our couch.

"You're going to scare her away," he warns and I scoff.

"Who could turn this down?" I joke, motioning down my lanky frame.

"Probably most women?"

I snort at that and he grins.

"Are you all set for tonight?" he asks me, setting his backpack down on the kitchen counter.

"Yeah, I've got it all planned. It's going to be great. The start to an epic romance."

"Do you want to maybe run a few laps or something? Burn off some of this energy?"

"Nah," I say, my foot tapping away on the floor as I lean against the back of the couch.

"Alright, well have fun! I'm sure that it's going to be great," he says, fist bumping me and then heading down the hallway to his bedroom.

"Thanks," I call and I smile when I see that it's time for me to leave to go pick her up. "I'm taking your car!"

"No!" Harvey yells back and I grin as I swipe his keys and head out the door.

Sayler only lives a few blocks away from me and the traffic is light so I make it there right at six p.m. I take the stairs two at a time and knock on their door.

Waiting for Sayler to answer feels like it takes years but when she does, my impatience melts away and my mouth drying as I take in my girl.

Her pitch-black hair is pulled back into a messy pony-tail and she's wearing an old t-shirt and a pair of leggings that mold to her legs and have my cock hardening in my pants.

"Hey, sorry, I wasn't sure what to wear. I can be ready in five minutes though!"

She darts back into the apartment and I follow after her, taking in her and Coraline's tidy place. Their apartment is a lot like Harvey's and mine. A small, two-bedroom, one-bath-room place with old hardwood floors, dark wood cabinets in the kitchen, and a modest size living room.

I wander over to a group of pictures hanging on the wall and I smile when I see the ones of a young Coraline and Sayler, both grinning with their arms around each other. It's obvious how much they love and care about each other and I love seeing her so happy.

There are a few more pictures, mostly of the two of them but there's one of Sayler with an older couple who must be her parents. They look just like her, but while Sayler seems to radiate light, they both look stern, their faces in a permanent frown, their posture stiff as they stand next to their daughter.

"Is this alright?" Sayler asks and I spin around to face her.

"Whoa," I murmur, my eyes widening as I take in the fucking goddess before me.

Her hair is down and hanging in gentle waves past her shoulders. She must have put something on her eyes because they look fucking huge and so much greener than before. Her lips are a vivid red and my eyes snag there, wanting to taste them. I want to see that lipstick smeared all over my body.

She's wearing some silky-looking tank top that dips low in the front, giving me a glimpse of her perfect tits. Her dark jeans hug her hips, accentuating her curvy hourglass figure and it has my mouth watering for a taste.

"You look fucking perfect," I tell her honestly. "Most beautiful thing that I've ever seen."

She blushes prettily at my words and it has my cock stirring in my jeans.

"Ready to go?" she asks, grabbing her purse from off of the kitchen counter and I nod, trying to break free from the lustful stupor that I'm in.

I lead her down the stairs, helping her into the passenger seat of the car before I slip behind the wheel.

"I thought that we could grab drinks before dinner?"

"Sounds good."

I drive us over to Letmein, a Prohibition-era-like bar that serves old-fashioned cocktails. It's a rundown-looking building that honestly looks boarded up from the outside. Harvey and I stumbled upon this place with Gray one night and thought it was cool. We come back every now and then for a cocktail and to go to a bar that isn't too packed.

"Are you going to kill me?" Sayler jokes as I park and I laugh.

"It's actually a really cool bar," I promise her as I take her hand and lead her across the street to the front door.

We head inside and I turn to see Sayler's delighted expression. My pride swells and I'm glad that I was able to put that look on her face.

"This way," I tell her, tugging her over to the bar.

We find seats on the end of the bar and look over the menu.

"It all looks so good," Sayler says, grinning as her eyes scan over the list of drinks.

The bartender comes over a few minutes later and I order one of the local brewery's beers. Sayler orders some fancy cocktail that has blueberries in it.

"What time is the reservation at Wild Thyme?" she asks as we each take a sip of our drinks.

"Max said to show up anytime between seven-thirty and eight."

"So, we don't have to chug these then?" she asks with a laugh and I join her.

"Nah, we've got time."

She grins at me and if I wasn't in love with her before, I would have been right then and there. The way her eyes sparkle with mischief and joy, the way her red lips spread, every little thing about her just does it for me.

"How's work going?" I ask, trying to change the subject

before I embarrass myself and blurt out how obsessed with her I am. How I love her already and would do anything to make her smile like that at me every day for the rest of our lives.

We sit and talk for the next hour, ordering another round of drinks. She tells me about some of the cool work projects that she has coming up and I tell her about some of the designs that I've done lately for clients.

"Did you always want to be a tattoo artist?" she asks and I nod.

"Yeah, it's kind of a family thing, but I've always been drawn to it."

"So, your parents didn't push you into it then?"

I swear that I can hear a strange tension in her voice but I don't question it.

"No, they've always been super supportive. I always loved to draw and I used to go watch my dad, uncles, and aunt tattoo and loved it. They were my heroes."

She smiles but there's a strange forcedness to it. I'm about to ask if she's alright when the bartender interrupts and asks if we want another round.

"No, we need to get going," I say and he slides the bill across to me.

I pay quickly, taking Sayler's hand as we head outside to the car.

"What about your parents? Are they excited that you're a kickass graphic designer?" I ask, trying to pull us out of this weird funk that we've found ourselves in.

"No, not at all."

She sounds so sad and defeated so I immediately change the subject. I ask how she and Coraline met, figuring that that's a safe subject.

Sayler beams, her whole energy changing and I drive us to Wild Thyme as she launches into the story.

"Best friends since kindergarten then. Well, Harvey and I have you beat."

"Oh yeah? When did you two meet?" she asks, relaxing into the booth at Wild Thyme.

"Since birth."

"Really? Like literally since birth?" she asks with a laugh and I nod.

"Yeah, he was born a few days before me, so literally since my birth."

"That's so cool!"

We chat more about our childhoods and share funny stories with each other about our friends. I love that she's just as adventurous as I am, that she can see the humor in things, and doesn't seem to take herself too seriously.

Our food comes and Coraline joins us for a minute. Harvey appears out of nowhere, smooshing me farther into the booth and I laugh.

"Were you following me, you stalker?"

"You wish. Coraline can usually take a break about now. I came to see her."

Sayler is whispering to Coraline, both of them smiling and I take that as a good sign, leaning back in the booth as I watch my girl and hang out with my best friend.

Best. Date. Ever.

SIX

Sayler

I'VE BEEN DODGING phone calls from both my mom and my dad for the past few days. I called them back when I knew that they would be sleeping and said that I had lost my phone and would talk to them later so hopefully that buys me a few days before they try to contact me again.

Rooney and I have been texting even more than before and we've been planning our second date since the night of our first one. He had dropped me off after dinner and kissed me goodnight. When we came up for air, he had asked me out on another date and I had eagerly agreed in between him sneaking in some more kisses. I went to bed that night with a smile on my face and my lips still tingling.

Drinks and dinner with him had been a blast. He's so funny, so interesting, and I love learning more about him. A lot of people think that I'm strange. I have a lot of energy and a weird sense of humor that can throw people off. None of that throws Rooney off though. If anything, he seems to click with me better than anyone else.

I think maybe it's only hurt more because when I'm in New York, I'm forced to dress like some uptight socialite and that's just not me. I like wearing casual clothes. I like my curves and I'm never going to be a size two which in New York is like committing a crime.

All just more reasons to prove that I don't belong in New York or with my parents.

We had to wait another week until Rooney's next day off to get back together. We ate breakfast together a few times before he had to run to work but that's not the same as a real date where we both aren't rushing off afterward.

There's a knock on the door and I grin, skipping over to answer it. Rooney is standing there, a crazy smile curving his lips and I immediately know that I'm in for a good time tonight.

"Are you ready?" he asks, taking my hand and tugging me out into the hallway.

I giggle, locking the door and running with him down the hall. We laugh, jumping steps as we head downstairs and out onto the street.

"Where are we going?" I ask him and he grins wildly at me as he opens the car door for me.

"It's a surprise."

I smile, settling into the car seat as he starts the car and takes off. We wind through the city and get on the highway, heading toward Acme, Pennsylvania. He turns off the highway and we wind our way through a forest until I spot a sign for some restaurant.

"Tops Restaurant," I read out loud and Rooney nods.

He's practically vibrating with energy and I love it. I

love that he's so excited to show me something or take me somewhere.

"It's a treehouse! We're going to eat in a treehouse!"

"Oh my god!" I scream back, so excited that now I can't sit still in my own seat.

We must look insane as Rooney parks, drags me out of the car, and takes off skipping toward the entrance.

We have to walk up a few flights of stairs and then we come out onto a wooden deck. There are wooden walkways connecting the hostess stand to the different private tree-houses and I squeeze Rooney's hand, excited to see which one we get to sit in.

It's beautiful up here. You can see all of the Laurel Highlands and I take a moment to study the scenery.

I had never even heard of this place and I wonder how long it took Rooney to find. I love how much effort he puts into our dates to not just take me to some fancy restaurant or to a movie or something.

For a second, I think about where Dalton would take me, if I were to marry him. A five-star restaurant, I'm sure. He would never be caught dead in a place like this. He probably wouldn't even step foot in Wild Thyme, even though my best friend runs it.

I don't really need to think much about it to see the differences between Rooney and Dalton. I also don't need to think at all to pick which one I would rather marry.

"Right this way," the server says, leading us down a wooden walkway, past a few treehouses, until we finally turn into one.

It's only two walls, with two exits, and a roof. That way, servers can come in and out and we still get the amazing views.

Rooney passes me a menu and I look it over. It's fancier

than I had anticipated and I scan over the menu to see what looks good.

"What are you getting?" I ask him.

"The steak and a whiskey," he says, setting his menu aside.

"That sounds good, but I don't want the whiskey. I'll get an old-fashioned instead."

The server appears before we can start a conversation and we place our orders.

"This place is so cool. How did you find it?" I ask him once the server is gone.

"I was doing some research, trying to find different places that we could go to. This one popped up and I knew that we had to go."

"Well, I'm glad that you found it and that you brought me here."

He grins at me, leaning over the table to brush a gentle kiss on my lips. I chase after his lips when he starts to pull away and Rooney laughs, leaning back in and pressing his smiling mouth against mine.

The waiter comes back with our drinks and we pull away. I pick up my drink, taking a big gulp as I stare at Rooney over the rim. He's still smiling at me. He always seems to be smiling and I love it.

His hand reaches across the table as he tells me about how he thought Ender was going to strangle Ames earlier this week because he kept blasting his music and their rooms are right next to each other. I laugh, letting him play with my fingers as he asks me about my day and the newest website that I'm designing.

The sun is starting to set as the waiter sets our food down and I smile, loving the view. Little twinkle lights start to come on as the sun sinks lower and I don't think that there could be any more romantic place on Earth.

We finish off our food as Rooney tells me about some vacation that the whole family took when he was a kid. I laugh as he tells me how everyone ended up sunburned, covered in aloe vera and cat scratches because Harvey and him had found a few stray cats outside their rental house who hadn't been a fan when they tried to give them a bath.

"Was that the last family vacation?" I ask him after the waiter has cleared away our empty plates.

"Oh no, we try to go on one every year together. Harvey and I just aren't allowed anywhere near animals now and we always pack like ten things of sunscreen."

I laugh at that and Rooney smiles at me.

I don't have any experience with men but suddenly, as I watch Rooney give me a teasing grin, I realize that I want him. Rooney is so unlike any other man that I've ever met. He makes me laugh, makes sure that I'm happy and have everything that I need, and he already seems to know me better than anyone, besides maybe Coraline.

I really like Rooney. Hell, I know that I could fall in love with him if I just let myself. In fact, I may have already fallen for him.

Rooney takes my hand in his, his fingers playing with mine and I smile, relaxing even more as the sun completely sets behind the trees and we're left sitting in a tree, surrounded by tiny Christmas lights.

SEVEN

Rooney

WHEN SAYLER INVITED ME UP, I had said sure, thinking that we were just going to watch TV and talk some more. That's why I'm so caught off guard when she closes the apartment door behind us and then backs me up against it, her lips crashing down on mine.

I should probably tell her that we can take this as slow as she wants, but then my mind blanks and I can only focus on her mouth on mine.

Her hands are in my hair, then my shoulders, then fiddling with the button on my jeans and for a second I think that maybe I died and went to heaven. My cock is so stiff that I swear I could cut diamonds with it and it gets impossibly harder when she shoves her hands into my boxer briefs, her smooth little hand wrapping around my length.

"Are you pierced?" she asks, breaking the kiss and I can only nod dumbly at her, all of my attention still focused on her lips.

"That's so hot," she moans, her lips moving to my neck as I wonder what else I can get pierced for her.

She sucks a path down my neck and I groan as her hand tightens around my dick.

"Fuck," I hiss as her fingers tease the piercings along the underside of my cock.

"I want to feel it in me," Sayler moans and Jesus fucking Christ, I want that too.

This girl is a genius.

"Naked," I grit out and I wonder where all of my brain cells went. I swear I used to be able to form coherent sentences.

Sayler steps back, her hands pulling at her clothes as she hurries to get naked and I rush to do the same. I'm sure it won't always be this way between us. I'll be able to slow down, to savor every minute of making love to her, but not tonight. Probably not for the next hundred times that we have sex.

She's naked first and I hurry to kick off my shoes and socks, working on my boxers when she drops to her knees before me.

"Say," I start but the words escape me when she wraps those fucking cherry red lips around the tip of my cock and sucks.

I let out a string of expletives, my eyes closed tight as she takes more of me into that perfect mouth of hers.

I look down, and wow. She's looking up at me, her big green eyes locked on my face in wonder.

"I've never done this before," she says, her hand gliding up and down my length, her fingers playing with the piercings of my Jacob's ladder.

"You're fucking perfect at it."

She grins, liking my praise and I want to flip her onto

her back and spread her legs. I want to worship every inch of her body but before I can do any of that, she's taking me back into her mouth.

She sucks hard this time, her cheeks hollowing and I almost fall to my knees at the pleasure. Her head bobs, her clever hands stroking the rest of my cock that she can't get into her mouth and I groan.

I can feel my balls starting to tighten, that familiar tingle in the base of my spine and I reach down, grabbing her and pulling her up.

"My turn," I say, staring into her wide eyes. "I've never done this either, but fuck, I promise to practice until I'm the best fucking pussy licker in the world."

Sayler's pupils dilate at my words and we stumble back over to the couch. She falls over the armrest, her ass still on it and I hurry to throw her legs over my shoulders and bury my face between her legs.

We both moan as I get my first taste of her. She's like honey and something that is all Sayler and I want to taste it every day for the rest of my life.

"Rooney," Sayler cries, her hands tangling in my hair and I moan against her wet folds.

My tongue wiggles inside her opening and Sayler's back arches, her hips growing restless on the edge of the couch.

I lick up, finding her clit and rolling it under my tongue until I see her eyes roll back in her head. She's so tiny, so tight and I know that I need to stretch her so that she can take me.

I slide one finger into her cunt, pausing as she tenses around the digit. My mouth goes back to work, licking and sucking her clit until she's relaxed and I can fit another digit into her.

"Oh, Rooney," she cries, a blush covering her body. "Don't stop."

Never.

I double my efforts, hooking my fingers inside of her until I find that sensitive patch of skin and rub her there. Her legs tense up around my ears and she sucks in a breath as her body tenses.

Then it's like everything speeds back up. She squirms against my face, her head thrashing against the couch cushions as she comes.

She's fucking beautiful.

I lick up her release, not wanting to miss a drop and when I stand, she's staring up at me with lust-filled eyes.

"Bedroom," we both say at the same time and I grab her hand, pulling her up and laying a kiss on her before we take off for her room.

We crash down onto the bed together and she looks up at me as I roll her under me.

"I'm on the pill," she murmurs and my cock weeps at the thought of taking her bare.

"Are you sure?" I ask and she nods.

"I want to feel you."

"Fuck."

She grins at me, spreading her legs wide in invitation and I move closer, my cock rubbing through her slick folds. My tip bumps at her entrance and I lean down and kiss her as I start to sink inside of her snug channel.

"Fuck," I grit out as her pussy grips me like a vise.

Sayler moans, her eyes falling closed as I reach her virginity. I don't want to hurt her, so I kiss her, my thumb moving between us to find her clit as I thrust once, popping her cherry and making her mine.

Sayler cries out but she only tenses for a moment and then her hips are moving against mine, searching for relief.

I start to move, tentative at first and then with reckless abandon. She feels so good, so hot, so tight, so wet. It's better than I ever could have imagined.

"Fuck, Say. I'm going to—"

"Come!" she shouts as she finds her release.

Her pussy grips my cock even tighter, so tight that I have no choice but to follow her over the edge. I come deep inside of her and it seems to last for minutes, hours.

When the black dots have finally faded from my vision, I look down to see Sayler smiling shyly up at me.

"That was—"

"I love you," I blurt out and she seems surprised but not for long.

"Yeah?" she asks and I nod, my heart feeling like it's going to burst.

"Yeah."

"Good, because I love you too."

My whole body sags with relief and Sayler giggles under me, the movement causing the bed to move and we both groan.

"Once more?" she asks and I growl, burying my face in her neck as I start to move.

As I start to make love to the girl of my dreams. The girl that I love.

EIGHT

Sayler

"I KNOW that you already met my parents and Harvey's parents that night at the food truck, but I just want to be sure that you know what you're getting yourself into. It's going to be *everyone*. And they're going to be a real handful."

"I'll be fine, Roon," I say with a laugh as I let him lead me up the front walkway to his uncle Zeke's house. "They can't be that bad and besides, Coraline is supposed to be here for a little bit."

Rooney nods, his black hair flopping into his eyes like a puppy and I smile softly as I push it out of the way.

"They're going to love you."

"Just like you love me?" I ask, dying to hear him say it again.

He's been saying it almost nonstop for the last few weeks and you'd think that I would be used to it by now, but hearing those words from him still gives me such a rush of emotion.

"God, no! That would be weird. I *love* you, love you. They're just going to love you."

"Ha ha, get the door, funny man."

He laughs, opening the front door and ushering me inside.

"Are we early?" I whisper when I don't see anyone in the front room.

"No," Rooney says slowly, his brow furrowed as he frowns and looks around, confused. "This may be a trap..."

"What?" I ask, not sure that I heard him correctly.

He doesn't get the chance to answer me.

"She's here!" Rooney's mom, Indie, yells as she pops around the corner.

"Jesus!" Rooney says, startled and I barely have time to laugh at him before several other women join us in the front room.

"She's so much prettier than you let on, Rooney," a girl about our age with bright blue hair says and Rooney rolls his eyes.

"I literally said she looks like a goddess from heaven, so that's not possible."

I can feel myself blush at his words and I give him a nudge with my knee. He looks down to me, smiling happily as he wraps his arm around my waist.

"Okay, Sayler, this is my family. This is my mom, who you've already met, my aunt Darcy, Aunt Edie, Aunt Trixie, Aunt Sam, and then that's Maxine and Cat. Guys, this is my brilliant, definitely too good for me, girlfriend, Sayler."

The other girls all aww at that and I blush again. Harvey, Coraline, and a guy that I've seen with the other guys at The Culinerdy Cruiser before come inside and I'm saved from having to answer any questions by their arrival.

"Hey," the guy that I don't know says as he nods at me and I give him a small wave back.

"Hey, Banks. This is Sayler. Sayler, this is Banks. He's Nico and Edie's son and works at Eye Candy Ink with me."

"Nice to meet you," I say and he gives me a small smile back.

"Are the guys outside?" he asks and Rooney shrugs.

"We haven't made it that far yet," he says dryly and his mom swats his arm.

"Right, let's let them get settled. Then we can have girl talk."

I like Rooney's mom. She's just as hyper as her son is and her sense of humor is delightful.

My parents would hate her on sight.

They would hate all of these people on sight and look down their noses at them because their bank accounts aren't big enough to rival theirs.

I guess it's a good thing that they'll never be meeting.

Rooney leads me farther into the house. We pass through a kitchen and head out onto the back porch where a group of guys are all gathered around the grill.

"Hey, guys," Rooney greets them and they all wave, turning our way with big smiles.

"Uh oh," Rooney whispers under his breath and I look to him to see what's wrong.

"What?" I whisper to him.

"They might give us shit."

"Why?" I whisper back, starting to get a little nervous.

"Because I give them shit."

That startles a laugh out of me and I turn to face the guys.

"So, this is her," one of the guys says and Rooney squeezes my hand.

"Yep, this is Sayler. Sayler, this is my uncle Zeke, Uncle Nico, Uncle Max, my dad, and my uncle Atlas."

"Nice to meet you," I tell them, relaxing into Rooney's side.

"You too. Did you grab something to drink?" Zeke asks and Rooney tugs me over to a table of refreshments.

He pours each of us a lemonade, passing me a glass with a smile.

"Doing alright?" he asks and I love that he's checking on me and making sure that I'm comfortable.

He has no idea that I was born and bred to be able to make meaningless small talk with strangers at charity events or other social parties.

"I'm great," I tell him honestly, leaning in to kiss him.

"Love you, Say."

"Love you too, Roon."

He takes my hand again and we head over to some deck chairs. He takes the one next to mine and soon, we're surrounded by the rest of his family.

"Are we out of orange juice?" Harvey asks, looking over the table.

"Yeah, why don't you and Rooney go grab some from the store," Mischa, Rooney's dad says and Rooney stands, kissing the top of my head before he whispers that he'll be right back.

Coraline plops down in Rooney's abandoned chair and I smile at her.

"Long time no see," I tease her and she grins.

"I've been busy. My boss is a real perfectionist."

I laugh as Cat, Maxine, and all of the other women pull chairs up next to ours.

"So, why don't you tell us about yourself, Sayler?" Rooney's aunt Sam asks and I take a sip of my lemonade before I answer her.

"What would you like to know?"

"Where are you from? What do you do?" Indie, Rooney's mom, starts to list off questions and I see Darcy shoot her a look, trying to rein her in.

"Well, I'm originally from New York but I moved to Pittsburgh a few months ago with Coraline and love it here. I'm a graphic designer by trade, mostly freelance right now."

"How did you and Rooney meet?" Trixie asks and I tell her the story of us meeting at The Culinerdy Cruiser.

"What do your parents do?" Darcy asks.

"They're both lawyers. They have their own firm in New York."

"Do you go back home often?" Indie asks and my stomach cramps at the thought.

"No, not really."

"That's too bad. Your parents must really miss you," Darcy says sympathetically and I have to bite back a laugh.

My parents don't miss me. They only want me back to do their bidding and secure their spot in New York's elite.

I take another sip of lemonade instead of answering.

They must realize that they hit a nerve because the conversation turns to Coraline and then funny stories about Harvey and Rooney when they were younger.

The day passes by quickly and is filled with laughter, conversations, and sunshine. By the time we leave, I'm slightly buzzed and my stomach hurts from laughing all day.

I'm also surer than ever that what I have with my own parents is a joke compared to what Rooney has with his entire extended family.

I also know that I don't want to give up Rooney or the family that I could have if I was with him.

NINE

Rooney

"HEY, Rooney? You have some, uh, visitors."

That strange sentence from Gray is my only warning that my life is about to go terribly wrong.

I'm at Eye Candy Ink and in between clients, so I finish cleaning up my room and disinfecting from my last client before I head up front to see who could be here to see me.

Standing in the lobby of the shop is an older couple who stands out like a sore thumb. They're way overdressed, for one. The man is wearing a suit and tie and the woman has some expensive looking dress and high heels on.

They're both also glaring around the shop, looking disgusted, and if their noses got any higher in the air, I don't think that they'd be able to see where they were going.

I can't figure out why they would be here to see me. Not until the woman turns, her blue eyes glaring with hate and disgust. I've never seen that look on my Sayler's face, but the blue of her eyes is exactly the same.

"Hi," I greet them.

I didn't even know that they were going to be in town or that Sayler had told them about me. She never really talks about them and as I meet their icy stares, I start to realize why.

Sayler's mom looks me up and down, her lip curled in disgust and I cross my arms over my chest, already knowing that there's no way in hell this is going to go well.

"What can I do for you?" I ask after a minute of them just glaring at me.

"We're Mr. and Mrs. Jones. Sayler's parents, and we wanted to talk to you. In private," Sayler's dad stresses and I nod, leading them back to my room.

I close the door behind us and turn to face them. It feels like I'm headed for my doom but I don't know how to stop it.

"What can I do for you?" I ask as they look around my tattoo room.

"It's recently come to our attention that you've been seeing our daughter," Mrs. Jones starts.

"Yeah, I am," I say, frowning at the way they said that.

They don't sound impressed by me and they're making it sound like Sayler wasn't the one to tell them about us.

"Well, that's a problem."

"Why?" I snap, starting to lose the patience that I never really had.

"Because she's engaged to someone else," Mrs. Jones replies back tartly and my whole world seems to drop out from beneath me.

My heart stops and my brain seems to short circuit as I try to make sense of their words. They grin at me and I can tell that they know they hit a nerve.

"She's been engaged to Dalton Radcliff for years now.

She wanted to see the world a bit first but now it's time for her to come back and plan her wedding."

"She's never mentioned him," I half whisper to myself, my brain still trying to make sense of all of this.

"Why would she tell her sidepiece about her fiancé?" Mr. Jones asks, a cruel smile on his face.

"Sayler isn't a cheater. She wouldn't do that."

"She's just sowing her oats before she gets married. She's engaged to Dr. Dalton Radcliff, of the New York Radcliffs," Mrs. Jones explains like that should mean something to me.

"I don't know who that is and Sayler has never mentioned him," I repeat.

"He comes from a prominent family in New York. They're one of the wealthiest families in the state and have been family friends for years. Dalton and Sayler were high school sweethearts and are meant to be. He will be able to provide her with the best life, with the life that she deserves. She has a bright future with him," Mrs. Jones says and I can get her point with her spelling it out for me.

She doesn't have one with me.

"With Dalton, she'll be comfortable and taken care of. He can offer her a beautiful penthouse, her choice of seat on any board in the city, and she'll be close to her family and friends. What can *you* offer her?"

My mind races. I don't have any of those things. I'm never going to be rich. All that I can offer her is me.

"Love," I say and they actually laugh at that.

I can feel my face heating as my hands tighten into fists.

"You're a phase. It's time that Sayler grew up and came back home. If you care about our daughter at all, you'll let her go."

With that, they push past me and out the door. I watch them leave, feeling numb.

"Hey, you alright?" Harvey asks as he walks by my room and sees me standing there.

"Yeah, I'm fine," I lie.

"Who was that?"

"That was Sayler's parents."

"Yikes," Ender says, coming up behind the others and I'm so shocked that he said anything, that I laugh.

Ender is the strong silent type and he tends to stick to himself most of the time. No one in the shop really knows him that well, though I do see him and Gray talk every now and then since their rooms are right across from each other.

"Yeah, they were a real nightmare," I tell my friends, leaning back against my desk as I think about everything that they said.

"What did they want?" Harvey asks and I can see him starting to get angry on my behalf.

"They told me that Sayler is engaged to some other guy and that he's rich and can give her everything that she wants."

"They have to be lying," Harvey says and Ender nods.

"Yeah," I say, but part of me can't stop thinking about what they said.

"Hey, Rooney, your next client is here," Ames says as he walks by with his client.

"Thanks," I say and we all turn to get back to work.

Harvey is the last to leave and he grabs my shoulder.

"Are you alright?" he asks and I can see the concern in his eyes.

"Yeah, I'll be fine."

He doesn't look like he believes me but he lets me go and I head up front to grab my next client.

I can barely concentrate for the rest of the night and I know that I need to talk to Sayler about all of this, but I find myself hesitating. If it's all true, do I really want to know? Or would it be better to live like nothing changed for a little longer?

I know I'm only thinking that because I want to protect my heart but it can't last long. Not knowing is bound to drive me crazy.

I push every thought except for tattooing out of my head as I get back to work.

TEN

Sayler

ROONEY HAS BEEN ACTING SO strange the last few days and I can't tell if something is wrong or if he's picking up on my attitude.

I've been stressed the last few days too, trying to get everything sorted. My mom called me again Sunday night after Rooney had dropped me off at home and informed me that she and my dad would be coming to Pittsburgh to see me.

I know that this can't lead to anything good.

I've been bracing for a fight for the last few days. I know that I can't marry who they want me to. I'm in love with Rooney and the life that I have here and I don't want to force myself to live the life that they want for me when I know that I'll be miserable.

It's time for me to stand up for myself but that's easier said than done with my parents. They're both lawyers, so they're master debaters and they also know all of my weak spots. The only thing that they don't know is that I've met someone else and that I'm not going to give him up.

I've been getting ahead on my work and busy with deadlines, so Rooney and I haven't seen each other all day today. In fact, we've barely texted the last few days and I know that I need to talk to him soon and find out what's going on with him.

My parents' flight should be landing any minute now and I hurry around Coraline's and my apartment one last time, picking up any messes that I missed. I'm shoving the last of the dirty clothes in the washer when there's a knock on the door.

I take a deep breath, trying to calm my racing heart as I answer the door, pasting a smile on my face when I see my mom and dad standing there. They don't look impressed with my place and they haven't even stepped foot inside of my apartment yet. I'm really glad that I spent all afternoon cleaning the place. I should have known that that wouldn't really make a difference.

"Hey, Mom, Dad," I greet them, leaning in to air kiss my mom on her cheek.

My dad pats me on the shoulder and I can't help but compare it to how Rooney's whole family greeted me.

"We should get to dinner. Your father made reservations at the best restaurant in town. Although, I'm not sure how good it could possibly be," my mother says, and I know that even if it was the best meal in the world, she would never admit it.

"Did you want to come in and see my place?" I ask them and they both just stare at me like I'm crazy. "Right. Let me just grab my phone."

I hurry inside, grabbing my phone and purse before I head back out to meet them. They're already headed back toward the stairs and I hurry to lock the door and catch up with them.

I send a text to Coraline, knowing that she's at work and won't be able to check her phone for a few hours at least. Still, she's the only one to know my parents and what kind of a night I'm in for.

I had debated inviting Rooney over to meet them but I knew that it was going to be a fight when they tried to get me to come back to New York and since I haven't told Rooney about my parents, New York, or the man that they've been trying to set me up with for years, I decided not to.

My parents hired a town car and I squeeze into the back, sitting between them. They're both busy on their phones for the whole ride and I stare out the window at the dark Pittsburgh streets. We drive past Eye Candy Ink and I look for Rooney, knowing that he's at work right now.

I'm starting to wish that I had invited him. He would have made tonight a lot more fun. When my parents got to be too snooty, he would have stuck his nose in the air and tried to mimic them. He would have made a fool of himself if it got me to laugh and I smile at the thought.

"Dalton sends his love," my mom says with a smile and I try not to grimace.

"That's nice," I say, thinking about the fact that he hasn't tried to get in contact with me for years.

I'm sure that he didn't send anything. He doesn't care about me, just like I don't care about him. My mom just wants to remind me about why she's really here and I know that tonight will be filled with more comments just like that.

We pull up outside of some fancy glass and marble building and I slide out after my parents. My high heels are already starting to pinch my toes and I keep pulling on my dress. I feel like an imposter in these clothes after not having to wear anything this dressed up in close to a year.

Inside, the place is hushed, done up in dark colors with tuxedoed waiters carrying shiny trays past us.

I hate it instantly.

Rooney would never take me to a place like this. It's the epitome of everything that I am not. If I marry Dalton, I would be stuck going to a place like this at least once a week.

A shudder runs through me at the thought.

We're led to our table and I smile at the hostess as she seats us. My mom purses her lips as she studies the menu and I turn to see my dad still busy on his phone. I try not to sigh as I pick up my own menu and try to decide on what to get.

"The strawberry salad looks good. Don't you think, Sayler?" my mom asks and I know what she's trying to say.

My mom has always hated that I wasn't a size zero. When I was a teenager, she made me diet and even set me up with personal trainers. I think that fact that Coraline cooks for me is another reason why they don't really like her. Her lack of pedigree from an influential family would be the other reason why.

"Sure, Mom," I say.

My stomach is in knots so I'm not that hungry anyway. Besides, maybe if I let them win that battle, I'll be able to win the war.

"You should start dieting now before we go wedding dress shopping in a few weeks. Try to lose some of those pesky pounds."

"I'm not marrying Dalton, Mom. I don't love him."

My dad looks up from his phone at that statement and both of my parents frown at me.

"You have responsibilities, Sayler Ann," my dad reminds me, his voice like a knife as it cuts through the silence at our table.

"I know, but none of my responsibilities are to marry a man that I don't love or to move back to New York. I'm happy here. I have my best friend, a job that I love, and a great boyfriend."

There's another beat of silence and then the waiter interrupts us to take our order. My father orders for my mom and me and I grit my teeth when my mom pulls the rolls away from my side of the table.

The rest of dinner passes in an icy silence and I know that they still haven't given up on bullying me into doing as they want.

They drop me off outside of my apartment building, claiming to be too tired from their travels, and that's fine with me. I can't wait to get away from them either.

I force a smile and wave as their town car drives away before I head inside to crash on my couch.

ELEVEN

Rooney

IT'S BEEN three days since my run-in with Sayler's parents and I know that she had dinner with them last night. Part of me expected to get a call or text from her telling me that it was over and that she was going back to New York, but that never came.

I'm not sure if I should be relieved by that or if she's waiting to break up with me in person.

"Alright, man. What the hell is going on with you?" Harvey asks as he drives us to work and I jerk out of my thoughts about Sayler to turn to him.

"What are you talking about?" I ask even though we both know what he's talking about.

"You've been all mopey for the last few days. What's going on?"

"I'm fine," I grumble, turning back to the window as he pulls into the lot across from Eye Candy Ink.

"No, you're not. You've been boring the last couple of days and that's definitely not like you."

He parks and I hurry to climb out before he can question me anymore.

It doesn't work since he just climbs out after me.

Banks parks next to us and I can already see Gray, Ames, and Ender by the front door, headed inside. I practically sprint away from Harvey to the door. Not that it helps. He just follows after me, trailing me down the hall and jamming his foot in the doorway before I can slam the door in his face.

"Lover's quarrel?" Gray jokes as he passes and I hear Banks and Ames laugh. I bet Ender didn't even crack a smile.

That guy needs to get laid.

"No, Rooney is just being a dickhead," Harvey growls, trying to push the door open.

"Real mature, asshole," I yell back and he huffs out a laugh.

"Just tell us what's going on. Why are you being so difficult about this?" he yells back, managing to push the door open half an inch.

I brace my foot against my desk, trying to close it when all of a sudden, it pushes open and I'm plastered against the wall behind the door.

Ender peeks around the corner, sighing and I wave at him. That earns me an eye roll but at least he lets the door go and I can breathe again. Ames, Harvey, Gray, Banks, and Ender are all in my room now, their arms crossed over their chests and I know that I won't be able to get out without explaining what's been going on.

"So Sayler might be engaged to someone else," I blurt out and I watch as the news hits my friends.

Banks and Ames look confused, while Gray just looks pissed. Harvey and Ender are both just staring at me. They already knew that.

"You didn't ask her about that yet?" Harvey asks, frowning at me as I shake my head no.

"What do you mean she *might be* engaged to someone else?" Banks asks and I rest against the edge of my desk as I explain.

"Her parents came in to see me a couple of nights ago. They told me that she's been engaged to some hotshot super rich doctor back in New York."

"But you don't know if it's true?" Ames asks and I shake my head.

"I've, uh, I've been too nervous to ask Sayler about it."

"It can't be. You two are disgusting together," Ender says, his voice low and scratchy.

"Thanks?" I say, not sure if that's a compliment or not and he just shrugs in return.

"Just ask her. Then you can stop moping around," Gray says, seeming to grow impatient with me, and I glare at him.

"It's not that easy. You should know."

"What's that supposed to mean?" he asks, his voice hard.

"You've been in love with Nora for-fucking-ever! Why don't you just tell her so that you can stop chasing around after her."

"You don't know what you're talking about."

"Sure, I do. *Everyone* knows how you feel about her but instead of doing something about it, you just settle for being friends. What's going to happen when she starts to date someone else? When she kisses someone else. *Sleeps* with someone—"

Ender cuts me off then.

"Dude, you're about to get your ass beat," he warns and I can see Gray glaring at me.

"You know I'm right," I say, quieter and the fight seems to leave him.

"Yeah, I know," he says, running a hand through his hair as he looks away.

We're all silent then and I know that it's almost time for us to open. I know that I need to get ready for the day and push thoughts of Sayler and what her parents said aside.

"I'm alright, guys. I promise. I'm going to go see Sayler tonight. We'll get it all sorted out."

They all study me for a moment before they nod and head back out into the hallway to get ready for the day.

I don't tell them about what else Sayler's parents said about me not being good enough for her. I know that they're right, but I highly doubt that this guy in New York is good enough for her either.

Still, Sayler deserves the very best... and I don't think that that's me.

I have back to back clients all day and for once, I'm grateful to be so busy. It keeps my mind occupied and it isn't until the shop is closing that I remember the mess that I'm in.

"Want me to drop you off at Sayler's?" Harvey offers and I nod.

We ride the few blocks to her apartment building in silence and I know that he can feel the nervous energy coming off of me.

"It's going to be okay, Rooney."

I nod, not wanting to argue with him.

"Do you want me to wait for you here? You can text me if you're going to stay."

"Sure. Thanks, Harvey."

He nods and I ignore the worried look that he gives me as I climb out of the car and trudge up to the front door.

It feels like it takes me no time at all to reach her door and I still don't know what I'm going to say to her as I lift my hand and knock.

She answers a few minutes later, smiling wide when she sees me standing there.

"Hey!"

"Your parents came to see me a couple of nights ago," I blurt out and her smile drops.

"What? Why?"

"They told me that you were engaged to someone else."

"Oh my god. No, I'm not. They keep trying to push one of their friend's son on me, but I'm never going to marry him."

Part of me relaxes at her words, but I know that it still doesn't change what has to happen.

I have to clear my throat before I say the next words.

"They also said that I'm not good enough for you, that I can't give you the life that you deserve, and that we needed to break up."

She huffs out a laugh that's filled with absolutely no humor, her eyes hard.

"Of course, they did. I'm not even surprised. Just pissed. I'm so sorry, Rooney. I know that they can be assholes. I should have warned you."

"No, they're right," I say, the words like shards of glass as they come up my throat. "I'm never going to be able to afford a penthouse apartment or whatever in New York. I can't even afford one in Pittsburgh. I don't want to leave this city and it sounds like you have a life that you are supposed to get back to in New York, so maybe it's best if we just end things now."

The words taste like dirt on my tongue but I force myself to say them anyway. All I want is for her to be happy, and if that means being with someone else, then I'll have to be okay with that.

I expect her to say something else, maybe to even fight me on it.

Instead, she glares at me before she slams the door in my face.

I stare at her door for a long minute, wondering if I made the right choice. In my head, it feels right, but my heart breaks with each step I take away from her.

Harvey must be able to read what happened on my face because he starts the car and heads to our favorite pizza place without me having to say a word.

TWELVE

Sayler

I SLAM the cupboard door closed, grabbing the ice cream out of the freezer before I slam that door closed too.

I can't believe this.

Normally I'm a pretty upbeat person but after the last few days. I'm done.

I'm annoyed with everyone. With my parents for going to Rooney and saying all of that shit to him, and for being such crappy parents. With Rooney for thinking that I care about money and being "comfortable", as my parents would call it, instead of love and happiness. Even with Coraline because she's happy and with her dream guy when she was never even interested in love or dating.

I know that the last one isn't really fair and truthfully, I am happy for her. I just wish that I had my dream guy too.

"Give me five minutes and I swear that I'll be ready to go!" Coraline shouts as she runs into the apartment and heads for her bedroom.

"Ready for what?" I yell around my bite of ice cream.

"Girl's night!" she calls back and I groan.

I completely forgot that Cat had texted Maxine, Coraline, Nora, and me about getting together for a girl's night last week. At the time, I had been thrilled. I was making new friends and growing my roots here. Now I'm just reminded of Rooney and I get mad all over again.

I think of a way out of going. I can't say I'm sick. I don't look it and I'm currently stuffing my face with ice cream. Maybe I could say that I have a lot of work to do?

"Why aren't you dressed?" Coraline asks as she hops back into the living room, tugging her shoes on as she goes.

"I'm not going."

"Why not?"

It's on the tip of my tongue to lie and say something about work, but instead, I blurt out the truth.

"Rooney and I broke up," I tell her, bursting into tears and she is instantly at my side.

"What? What happened?"

I tell her about my parents' visit and how they had apparently gone to see him before they came to see me. I tell her about dinner and them talking nonstop about Dalton. How Rooney had been acting weird for a few days and now I knew why. Then I tell her about him showing up here last night and us breaking up.

"That idiot," she huffs out and I nod.

"I can't believe that he thinks that I would choose money over the way that I feel about him."

She hugs me, letting me sniffle on her shoulder as she pulls her phone out with her other hand.

"What are you doing?" I ask.

"Texting the girls."

I thought that she meant to cancel for us, so I'm

surprised when everyone shows up at our place half an hour later, armed with junk food and enough alcohol that I'm legitimately nervous about the hangover that I'm going to have tomorrow.

Maybe it will help distract from the pain in my chest.

"What did Rooney do?" Cat asks, annoyed as she plops the boxes of pizza down on the counter.

Her hands land on her hips and she frowns. I'm surprised that she's on my side since Rooney is like a brother to her.

"He dumped me so that I could go back to New York and marry a sexist pig that my parents are trying to get me to settle down with because he's rich and has the right pedigree."

"What year is it again?" Nora asks and I laugh.

"I know. They're mad that I haven't come home yet to be Mrs. Dalton Radcliff."

I can't help the shudder that comes with those words and Maxine grabs a bottle of vodka, opening it and asking where our glasses are.

I get up and redo my messy bun as I join everyone in the kitchen. We crowd around the island there, reaching over each other for pizza or cookies. Someone hands me a glass of something pink and I take a drink, coughing as the alcohol hits my throat.

"Too strong?" Maxine asks. "I've never mixed drinks before."

"A little," I tell her and I see Cat grinning at me from behind her own cup.

"So, what are you going to do about Rooney?" she asks.

"What can I do? He broke up with me so that I could find someone with more money."

"Is that really what he said?" Nora asks, sounding outraged.

"Well, no," I admit.

"What did he actually say?" Maxine asks and I shove another bite of pizza in my mouth to stall for time.

"He said that my parents told him that I was engaged to someone else, which in their heads, is true, but I was never going to marry the guy they had lined up for me."

Everyone nods and I take another sip of my cocktail.

"Then he said that he would never be good enough for me, that he was never going to be able to afford a penthouse or New York, and that he thought that we should break up."

"Oh my god. He's such an idiot," Cat groans and I nod my agreement, finishing off my drink.

It doesn't taste so strong now and I pass my cup back over to Maxine, watching as she tries to mix me another one.

"He's an idiot, and he for sure should have just talked to you, but I don't know. I think that it's kind of sweet," Nora says.

"Yeah, I guess he was trying to do something nice for you. Just in a really roundabout way," Cat says, finishing the last of her drink too.

Maybe they have a point. I may, it's not like he cheated or lied to me. He just dumped me because he thought that I could do better.

Still, that should be my choice. I don't need Rooney to protect me from myself. I know who I am and I know who I love.

I can't beg him to take me back though. I have more self respect than that, so it looks like I'm stuck. At least until he pulls his head out of his ass and realizes that he made a huge mistake.

Man, I hope that he realizes that soon.

The conversation turns to the other girls and I try to pay attention but my brain is a little foggy from the drinks and I keep getting distracted with thoughts of Rooney.

When there's a knock on the door, my heart leaps into my throat.

Maybe it's Rooney.

Coraline looks over to me before she moves to open the door and I smooth my shirt, making sure that I don't have pizza sauce or chocolate smeared on my face as she opens it.

It's not Rooney though.

Instead, there stands Ender.

"He looks pissed," I mumble and I see Nora and Maxine both nod.

Cat looks cool as a cucumber though, smiling slyly as she downs the last of her drink.

"You like driving me crazy, don't you, kitten," Ender growls, stalking into our apartment, his eyes locked on Cat.

In the blink of an eye, he's got her over his shoulder, his hand wrapped around her upper thigh as he storms back out, the door slamming shut behind them.

"Uh, should we be concerned?" I ask after a moment of no one saying anything.

"Nah, I'm sure that she'll be fine," Maxine says, grabbing another slice of pizza.

Her phone rings and I see that it's after two in the morning. We're all going to be tired and hungover tomorrow, but I think it will be worth it.

I smile as Maxine hands me another cocktail, raising the glass to my lips as I look over my new friends.

THIRTEEN

Rooney

IT'S ONLY BEEN a few days since Sayler and I broke up but I'm dying. It feels like I'm in hell. I had heard that breakups were rough, but this is my first time experiencing it and I'm here to say that people have definitely been underselling how much it sucks.

I can't eat.

I can't sleep.

Nothing holds my interest or attention.

I keep thinking that I see Sayler everywhere that I look and my heart leaps up into my throat, only to fall again when it inevitably turns out to not be her.

I've thought about calling or texting her and even started to at least a dozen times, only to delete it before I could hit send.

"Why so glum, Rooney?" Uncle Max says as he sits down in the deck chair next to me.

It's Sunday and I'm at family brunch. Normally, I love

being around my family but right now, I'm afraid that I'm pretty terrible company. I've been sitting out on the deck by myself since I got here an hour ago.

"You feeling alright?" Uncle Nico asks as he joins us, taking the other deck chair.

"Yeah," I mumble but I can tell that they're not buying it.

"What's going on?" my dad asks as he leans against the deck railing.

"Rooney is grumpy."

"I'm not grumpy," I argue with my uncle Zeke.

"Right," he says back, taking a drink of his lemonade.

"Girl troubles?" Uncle Nico guesses and I hate how observant he is.

"Maybe," I hedge.

"What's going on?" Uncle Atlas asks as he joins us and I groan, slouching down in my chair.

"Sayler and I broke up," I admit.

Maybe it will help me to talk about it. Maybe they'll have some kind of advice that can fix the ache in my heart.

"What happened?" Uncle Max asks at the same time my dad asks what I did.

"I broke up with her."

"Why?" Uncle Atlas asks.

"I can't give her what she deserves."

"What the hell does that mean?" Uncle Zeke asks.

"Her parents came to see me at the shop. They have some other guy lined up for her. Some rich doctor that she's known all of her life. He can provide for her way better than I can."

There's a beat of silence as everyone takes in my news.

"You're an idiot," Uncle Nico says, breaking the silence.

"What?" I ask.

I hadn't been expecting that response.

"You're an idiot," he repeats.

"Yeah, I mean, if she's known him all of her life, then she's had her chance with him and she didn't choose him. She chose you," Uncle Atlas adds.

"But shouldn't I be doing what's right for her?" I ask.

"Oh, man," Uncle Max says, sinking down in his chair.

"You should never decide something for a woman," Uncle Atlas tells me.

"I just wanted to do what's right for her. She deserves the best of everything. I'm never going to be able to give her a penthouse in New York or anything like that."

Everyone groans and I drop my head back against the back of my chair, dreading whatever they're going to say next.

"Kid, you really are your father's son," Uncle Zeke says with a laugh.

"What's that supposed to mean?" my dad snaps, annoyed.

"Oh, come on, Mischa," Uncle Atlas says with a laugh.

"Yeah, you know that you and Indie broke up like ten times before you even got together," Uncle Nico adds.

"How is that even possible?" Uncle Max asks with a laugh as he leans back in his chair.

"I'm a ladies' man. You have to keep them guessing to land them. Look at me and Indie now!" my dad says and I roll my eyes as everyone laughs.

"Yeah, if we could get back to me and my problems for a minute?" I ask and they all turn back to me.

"You love her, right?" Uncle Nico asks, direct as always.

"Yes," I answer him right away.

"Then go get her. It's okay to be a little selfish in love," Uncle Zeke says and Uncle Max and Atlas both nod.

"They're right. If you want her, if you love her, then you need to fight for her."

Harvey, Ames, Banks, Maxine, and Cat all join us out on the porch and I let them take over the conversation as I mull over the advice that I just got.

Did I fuck up? Or do I just want to take their advice because it means that I can try to win Sayler back?

I spend the day with my family, still not much company, but it's nice to be around people who love me as I nurse my broken heart and think about my next move.

By the time I leave, I know that I can't go on like this. I messed up and I need to go see Sayler and beg her to forgive me and take me back.

It starts to pour as I drive down the traffic-filled streets toward Sayler's place. I have to circle her building three times before I find a parking spot and by then my nerves are frayed.

I park and get out, instantly soaked as I wait to cross the road. I'm headed for the front door when I spot Sayler parking her car in the lot and I change directions and head her way.

"Sayler," I say as I reach her in the parking lot but apparently, she doesn't hear me because she runs right into me.

"Whoa!" she says and I reach out, grabbing hold of her rain-drenched arms.

"Hey," I say as we stand and stare at each other.

"Hey," she says back warily, her voice getting swept away with the rain.

"I'm an idiot," I blurt out when it looks like she's going to walk around me and leave me standing here.

"Yep."

"A complete idiot."

"No argument here," she says.

"A complete idiot who is head over heels, hopelessly in love with you."

That stops her and she stares at me, her blue eyes wide, raindrops dripping from her eyelashes and running down her face. Her hair is plastered to her head, her clothes soaked and I'm sure that we both look like a mess, but I've never seen anything more beautiful in my entire life.

"I love you, Sayler. I'm so sorry that I let your parents get into my head. I'm never going to be a millionaire. I'm never going to be able to give you a penthouse in New York or a cushy life, but you will never find anyone who loves you more than I do. You will never find anyone who will try harder to make you happy every single day for the rest of your life."

I hold my breath, staring into her eyes as I wait to see how she responds.

"You shouldn't have chosen for me. I can make my own decisions and I never wanted to marry Dalton. He's a sexist prick who would cheat on me before the ink was even dry on our marriage certificate."

"I know. I'm so sorry, Sayler."

"I never wanted him. I only want you."

"I only want you too."

"But only if you can stop making decisions without me. We're supposed to be together and that means talking about things."

I nod, knowing that she's right. I would do anything that she asked if she would take me back.

"You're right. I'm so sorry. It will never happen again. I swear," I promise her.

She studies me for a moment before she gives me a smile.

"I love you," she says as she raises up on her tiptoes, her lips landing on mine.

The rain thunders down around us, soaking us to the bone, but neither one of us cares. Not with her lips on mine, her hands in my hair, and her curvy body pressed up tight against mine.

Her lips part and I don't waste a second in slipping my tongue into her mouth. She tastes like cinnamon and hot chocolate and I moan, cradling the back of her head as I pull her closer to me.

A car horn honks and we both startle, forgetting that we're still standing outside of her apartment building.

"Maybe we should go inside," Sayler says with a smirk and I nod my head.

"Yes, please."

She laughs, taking my hand and dragging me after her. We run through the rain to her front door and then I race her up the stairs to her apartment. She messes with her keys and I kiss my way up her neck, doing my best to distract her.

"Fuck, Rooney. I'm about two seconds away from saying screw it and letting you fuck me against this door."

Her elderly neighbor, Mrs. Griggs, gives us the stink eye as she passes and I laugh into the curve of Sayler's shoulder.

"Oh my god," she groans and I grab her keys from her, unlocking the door and dragging her over the threshold.

I slam the door closed and back her up against it.

"What are you doing?" she asks breathlessly as I nibble at her neck and undo her wet jeans at the same time.

"Fucking you against this door," I growl against her skin and I feel her heartbeat flutter under my lips.

"Okay," she breathes out and I grin.

"Always so agreeable."

She laughs at that, lifting her hands when I try to peel

off her wet shirt. She undoes her bra for me and then she's standing before me in just her panties.

"God, I'm one lucky bastard."

"Uh huh," she agrees, tugging her panties down and then reaching for my clothes.

I help her strip me and soon we're both standing naked in record time. I'm about to kneel before her, spread those curvy thighs and feast but before I can, Sayler jumps.

I catch her, pinning her between me and the door.

"I was going to lick that sweet pussy," I growl against her mouth and she grins at me.

"You can do that later. I need to feel you inside of me. Now."

I groan, angling my hips and pushing in until I'm buried balls deep in her sweet snug hole. My cock and piercings drag along her walls slowly and I grin, loving the way she moans when they slide over that particular spot inside of her.

"Did you miss me?" I ask as I start to thrust and she moans, nodding her head as my fingers dig into her thighs.

She'll have fingerprint-shaped bruises tomorrow and I find that I love that idea. I angle my hips letting her grind her clit against the root of my cock until she's gushing all over me.

"That's it. Coat me in your juices," I order and she moans.

"Oh god," she breathes, her eyes squeezed up tight and I know that she's going to come soon. "Right there!"

I fuck her harder, rifling her up and down my cock while I keep her pinned to the door. I'm sure that her neighbors from two doors down can hear us going at it and I smile.

"Rooney!" Sayler screams as her pussy clamps down

tight on my cock and I grit my teeth, as I battle with myself not to come.

I keep pumping inside of her, trying to prolong her orgasm. When she finally opens her eyes, giving me a lazy smile, I grin back.

"Hold on," I order and she squeaks as I grip her ass, turning and heading over to her bedroom.

I lay her down on the bed, giving her a quick kiss before I pull out and kiss my way down her lush body. She moans as I suckle at her tits, leaving each of them wet and red from my mouth.

I kiss over her stomach, making a beeline to that sweet slice of heaven between her thighs.

"Rooney," Sayler moans, her fingers tugging on my hair.

"You said later. It's later," I remind her as I use my fingers to spread her puffy folds and dive in.

We both moan as I take my first lick of her, trying to swipe up as much of her juices as I can. I don't want a single drop to go to waste.

I fit my tongue up against her little pearl, wiggling my tongue against that sweet button until Sayler is tensed on the bed, her back bowed, her whole body flushed.

"Give it to me, Say," I whisper and I slip two fingers inside of her, pumping them as I suck her clit into my mouth.

She cries out, sailing over the edge and coming against my mouth. I lick her through most of it but before she can come back to earth, I flip her over onto her stomach, drag her up onto her knees and plow into her from behind.

"Fuck!" we both shout and I know that I won't be able to last long.

I pound into her, rutting like an animal, and she cries out, her fingers tangling and twisting in the sheets.

"Oh god, fuck, Rooney!" she shouts as she comes and this time when her pussy cinches up around my cock, I don't hold back.

I come with her, moaning long and loud as I empty myself inside of her. She collapses on the bed on her stomach, her arm and one leg dangling off the side and I smile as I gather her in my arms, dragging her farther up the bed to cuddle with me.

"Love you, Roon," she whispers sleepily against my chest and I smile.

"Love you, Say."

FOURTEEN

Sayler

ROONEY and I have been back together for two weeks and everything has been perfect. We spend the night with each other every night and try to grab lunch or dinner together every day. We text nonstop and we've taken to exploring the city together, trying to one-up each other with a new restaurant or attraction each night.

We've hit up dive bars, seedy diners, and Rooney even took me to a playground that he claimed was haunted one night. We spent an hour trying to see who could swing higher on the swing set and I had laughed so much that my stomach ached the next day.

I think that we've been over every square inch of the city so far but I'm sure that Rooney has something else up his sleeve.

Tonight though, we're staying in.

Rooney and Harvey invited Coraline, Gray, Nora, Banks, Sam, and Ender over for a movie night. He's out picking up pizza for everyone and should be back any minute now.

My phone rings on the counter and I grin when I see Caroline's name on the screen.

"Hey, boo! How have you been?" I ask as soon as the call connects.

"Good," she says and she sounds more relaxed and at peace than I've heard her in over a year.

"Yeah, you sound good."

"Yeah, I uh... I met someone."

"What?" I yell, a grin stretching my face. "Tell me everything!"

She laughs and I listen to her tell me all about some guy named Heath that she met in Cherry Falls.

"He's so good with Charlotte. He's really outdoorsy, owns the Cherry Falls Trading Post and loves to camp."

"So you two are perfect for each other," I joke. I know that Caroline hasn't camped a day in her life.

She laughs and I can hear someone say something in the background.

"I don't mind camping so much now."

"Yeah, I bet. Not when you have some big, strong, man to take care of you."

"He really is," she says with a dreamy sigh and my heart melts.

"I'm so happy for you, Caro."

"Thanks. How are things with you and Rooney?" She asks and I spend a few minutes catching her up with everything that has happened here.

We've been texting so she knows all about what happened with my parents. She practically growls when I tell her that they still think that I'm going to be marrying Dalton.

I hear Charlotte call for her a few minutes later so I let her go, smiling as I hang up. It looks like all of us are getting our happily ever afters. I can't wait to meet Heath now.

I pour the bag of popcorn that I just popped into a bowl and carry it over to the coffee table just as the door opens and Rooney comes in, ten pizza boxes in his hands.

He sets it down on the counter, turning to smile at me and I grin back, rushing over to him. I jump, wrapping my arms and legs around him and he laughs as my lips crash down onto his.

"Missed you," I say and he grins at me.

"We should never be apart again then. Move in with me."

I freeze at his words. I did not see that coming.

"Are you serious?" I ask and he nods.

"Of course. We spend all of our time together anyway. You can move in here, save on rent, and we can see each other all of the time. Or at least every night."

"I'll have to talk to Coraline. I don't want to leave her with all of our rent."

"I'm pretty sure Harvey asked her to move in with him too," he says as he starts to kiss his way up my neck.

"So, I get to be with you *and* still live with my best friend?"

"Hmm," Rooney murmurs against my skin, right over my pulse point and I shiver.

"Then sign me up," I say, my voice coming out breathy and filled with heat.

Rooney backs me up against the wall and our lips meet. I open for him right away, letting his tongue into my mouth to tangle with mine.

My phone rings and we both groan, pulling apart.

"It's my parents," I say, my stomach dropping and my good mood souring instantly.

I've been putting off talking to them for a few weeks now. They still keep texting me, sending me updates on Dalton and demanding to know when I'll be back.

It's been driving me crazy.

"I should get this," I tell him and I look up into Rooney's worried eyes.

He comes over to my side, wrapping his arm around my shoulders as I hit accept and hold the phone to my ear. His grip on me tightens and I lean into him, letting him support me.

"Hello?" I answer and my mom lets out an impatient sigh.

"There you are. I'm getting sick of having to track you down, Sayler."

I tense, knowing that I need to stand up to them. I can't keep fighting with them over this. I'm never going to want to marry Dalton. I'm never going to want to move back to New York and I don't want the life that they want to force onto me.

"What did you need, Mom?"

"When are you moving back to New York? Dalton is getting impatient," she snaps and I snap too.

"Never. I'm never going to marry Dalton and I'm never coming back to New York unless Rooney is going there too."

"Rooney?" she shouts, and I straighten my spine.

"Yes, Rooney. I'm in love with him, Mom. He makes me happier than anyone else. I'm with Rooney and if you're not okay with that, then I understand. I thought that you would be happy for me for finding someone who makes me happy and who loves me just as much as I love him, but if you can't be okay with that, then we can't talk anymore."

I hold my breath, but deep down I already know what will happen next.

She hangs up on me, and I sag against Rooney.

"I'm so sorry, Sayler. They're idiots for not wanting you to be happy."

I nod against him, not trusting my voice right then.

"We can share my parents. My mom already loves you more than she loves me," he tries, doing his best to cheer me up and I laugh at that.

I turn in Rooney's arms, leaning my chin against his chest and smiling up at him.

"Okay."

"Okay?" he asks, looking doubtful and I nod.

"I'm going to buy her a world's best mom cup and start signing cards to her as from your favorite child."

Rooney laughs, his arms tightening around me.

"Love you, Say."

"I know, I love you too, boo."

The door opens and Harvey, Coraline, and Banks walk inside, pausing when they see Rooney and I hugging each other in the center of the room.

"Hey," I say, pulling away from Rooney to greet everyone.

I hug Coraline as Ender, Sam, Gray, and Nora come inside.

"Help yourself to pizza!" I call as I drag Coraline over to the bedroom.

"Are you moving in here?" I ask her and she bites her lip.

"I meant to talk to you about that," she starts and I grin.

"Rooney asked me to move in with him too," I tell her with a smile and she relaxes.

"So, we're still going to be roommates then?"

"Yep," I say with a big smile and she returns it, pulling me into a hug.

"Look at us. All happy and in love and shit."

She laughs, grabbing my hand as we head out to join the others. Everyone is already grabbing a paper plate and filling it with pizza as Rooney fiddles with the remote, turning the TV on and getting the movie pulled up.

I grab two plates, putting pizza on the plates for Rooney and I. He grabs us drinks and we sit down on the couch next to each other. The guys talk about work and I listen in as Cat says something about Se7en, the nightclub that she manages.

"Let's start the movie already," Rooney says, wrapping his arm around my shoulders as he hits play.

I lean against him, cuddling into his side as the opening credits play on the screen. I look around at our friends, happy even though I probably just lost all contact with my parents tonight.

I feel lighter now. I don't have to dodge their calls anymore or deal with their disappointed sighs when I inevitably don't live up to their standards or fall in line with their plans for me.

I have the family that I really want right here with me.

I look around at them, noticing for the first time that way the Nora and Gray and Ender and Cat trade sly glances with each other when they think that no one is watching.

I grin, wiggling against Rooney when he tickles me as I watch them.

I wonder which couple will be the next to fall.

FIFTEEN

Sayler

ONE YEAR LATER...

"ARE you sure that you're okay with this?" Rooney asks me as we move the last of our boxes out of the apartment that we used to share with Harvey and Coraline.

"It's going to be hard, but I think we'll get settled in soon," I say, pretending to wipe a tear away from my eyes.

"You two are ridiculous," Gray says, rolling his eyes as he pushes past us and heads next door to our old apartment.

"You know that you're just moving next door, right?" Harvey asks, carrying another box.

"We're dealing with a lot," Rooney cries, heading after him and I see Harvey grin and shake his head.

"It's going to be weird not living with you anymore," Coraline says, wrapping her arm around my shoulders.

"I know. It's the end of an era," I say with a sigh, leaning my head on her shoulder.

We head into Rooney's and my new apartment and look around. It's an exact replica of the one we shared with Harvey and Coraline, except everything is flipped.

When we found out that the old renter was moving out, we had jumped at the chance to rent it. Don't get me wrong, it's been awesome living with our best friends, but it was getting a little cramped.

"Is that the last of it?" Cat asks as we walk into the apartment and I nod.

"That's it. Now we just need to get everything unpacked."

Rooney groans and I grin at him. I have a feeling that he won't be letting me help with the unpacking.

We found out that I was pregnant a few weeks ago and ever since, he's been acting like I'm made of glass. I am more tired lately and my bladder feels like it's the size of a thimble, but I can still lift stuff. I know that Rooney likes to pamper me though, so I've been letting him do most of the heavy lifting.

Indie and Darcy, Rooney's and Harvey's moms are both over the moon about being grandparents. Even Atlas and Mischa were excited. They've already started looking at cribs and strollers. I get texts from Indie every day with some new cool baby gear and I wonder how we're going to fit everything that they've already bought us into our new place.

I love that I get to go through this with my best friend. We've already talked about our kids growing up together and started looking at daycares and good school districts.

I haven't told my parents but then, I haven't talked to

them in a year. It's probably for the better. I don't need their negativity in my life or my baby's life.

"We brought food," Mischa says as he, Indie, Darcy, Atlas, Zeke, Trixie, Nico, Edie, Sam, and Max all come into the apartment. There's barely room for all of us but I just laugh as I bump into Rooney as I hug his mom.

This is everything that I wanted my life to be.

I'm surrounded by people who love me, who just want to see me happy, and who are my family and best friends. Rooney is the best boyfriend that anyone could ever have and I'm so glad that I found him.

He smiles at me, giving me a wink and I know that he's dying to tell everyone. I wink back, pulling the diamond engagement ring that I've been hiding out of my pocket and slipping it on.

Rooney proposed to me two weeks ago, right after we found out that I was pregnant. He said that he had been carrying the ring around for weeks, looking for the perfect time to pop the question and that he couldn't think of a better way.

He wanted us to be a family and now that I was carrying our child, he thought that we should make it official.

I had said yes of course. I wanted to be Mrs. Sayler Jennings more than anything. He had slid the ring onto my finger and that's when my morning sickness decided to kick in.

I had promptly run to the bathroom and he had followed, holding my hair back for me and telling me how pretty I am and how much he loves me as I threw up everything that we had had for dinner.

Since then, he's stocked up on those morning sickness suckers, ginger ale, and saltines and I swear he's been buying all of that stuff in bulk. Just another reason why I love him.

"Everyone, Sayler and I have an announcement," Rooney says and everyone turns to look at us expectantly.

"We're getting married!" I shout, holding up my hand to show off my ring.

"Oh my gosh!" Indie shouts, almost tackling me as she hugs me.

"Congratulations," Mischa says, giving me a less tight squeeze.

"Thanks," I say with a grin and my cheeks hurt from how much I've been smiling lately.

I go to give Darcy a hug when my stomach rolls and I make a beeline for the bathroom.

"Did I squeeze her too hard?" I hear Indie ask as Rooney follows me into the bathroom.

"No, she just does this now," Rooney says and I glare at him. "I mean, she is a beautiful incubator and—"

I swat at his legs as he laughs and holds my hair for me.

"I'm just teasing, Say. I love you and you really are the most beautiful woman that I've ever seen. Even with your head in a toilet."

"You're the worst," I say, resting my head against his legs as I wait to see if my stomach is settled. "But I love you too."

SIXTEEN

Sayler

FIVE YEARS LATER...

"WHERE ARE WE GOING?" I ask my husband as he drags me down the street, pushing our two kids in their stroller with his other hand.

"It's supposed to be a surprise! Kids, tell Mom what a surprise is," he says and Mia and Jasper both turn in their car seats and scream boo at me.

"Not quite, but I'll take it," Rooney says with a laugh as he turns the corner and we continue down another block.

We've been married for a little over four years and it's been the happiest years of my life. Sure, we're not filthy rich, and we're never going to live in a penthouse or a mansion, but I've got everything that I need with him here.

We had Jasper a few months after we got married. We had rushed the wedding, not wanting to have a long engagement and also because I didn't want to be showing in all of our pictures. We had Mia a year after that and two under two was more than enough for us.

We still live next door to Harvey and Coraline and their kids, but we've been talking about getting a bigger place. Maybe something with a yard for the kids to play in. I've also been trying to talk Caroline and her husband, Heath, into moving closer but they both love Cherry Falls so I'll have to settle for seeing them a few times a year for vacations or get togethers.

I still haven't talked to my parents and while there are days when I miss them or more the fact that they never will meet their grandkids, I know that it's probably for the best. We were only going to make each other miserable.

Indie and Mischa, and really Rooney's whole extended family, have all welcomed me into the fold with open arms. I have girl's night once or twice a month with Cat, Maxine, Nora, and Coraline, although Coraline can't make it sometimes because of work.

I've also grown my business in the last few years. Rooney has always been my biggest champion, buying me a new computer when my old one broke, even though we couldn't really afford it. He even sold his car when he found out that I was thinking about hiring on some employees because I couldn't keep up with the work. I had been worried that I wouldn't have enough to cover expenses and he had assured me that he always just got a ride with Harvey anyway.

That was two years ago and I've hired on two more employees since then, making it a grand total of four, but still. I've come a long way from just me and my computer five years ago.

Our kids are about to start school and I know that that

will help to lighten the financial load. Preschool can be expensive, but I'm hoping once they're both in kindergarten that we can sit down and look at houses. Somewhere still close to town, and hopefully close to Harvey and Coraline, since our kids are best friends.

"Hurry, Say!" Rooney calls, speed walking faster and I huff out a laugh as he tugs on my hand, urging me faster.

"I'm coming, I'm coming," I promise him and he gives me one of those wild smiles that I love so much.

Rooney is still very much the carefree, adventurous, goofball that I fell in love with. He makes a point to take me, or me and the kids out on an adventure at least once a month and I know that that's what we're doing today. I can tell by his excitement and the glint in his eye.

We cross the road and round one more corner and then Rooney grinds to a halt. I almost run into his back, so I sidestep him, looking to see what he's staring at.

"Is that—"

"Yep," he says, grinning wide.

"Hey, guys!" Indie says as she drags Mischa along behind her.

I wave and the kids go crazy, wanting to get to Grandma and Grandpa.

"Are you guys excited to go explore?" Mischa asks as he takes over pushing the stroller from his son.

"Yeah!" they shout, their eyes wide as they stare across the road at the huge playground before us.

There's a castle off to one side with slides coming down and a drawstring moat. Then there's a rocketship and I can see Jasper is already trying to make a beeline for that. Rooney takes my hand, kissing the top of my head as I lean against him.

"How did you find this?" I ask him.

"I drove by the other week. It must have just opened but not many people know about it yet. Come on, I want to show you the best part."

I let him lead me around the park, past the swing sets and another playground, this one with a bunch of ramps and bridges. We head over to a grouping of trees and as soon as I see the ladder leading up one, I start to laugh.

"A treehouse!"

Rooney grins at me, letting me climb up first and I smile as I take a seat. I have to wedge myself into the corner so that he can fit up here too and he laughs as his elbow dings off the wall.

"I remember this being easier," he says as he gets situated in the other corner.

It's comical watching him fold his long legs up so that he can sit and I laugh as he wiggles around, trying to find a more comfortable position.

"I love it. Thanks for bringing us here."

"Of course, Say. I'd do anything for you."

He shifts again, digging into his hoodie pocket and he grins as he pulls out a bag of half crushed Goldfish crackers.

"Hungry?" he asks, passing me the Ziplock bag and I laugh, leaning back against the wall as I pop a few into my mouth.

It may not be some fancy meal, cooked in a five-star restaurant on the Upper East Side, but I swear, it's the best thing that I've ever tasted.

DID YOU LOVE ROONEY? **Please consider leaving a review! You can do so on <u>Amazon</u> or on <u>Goodreads</u>.**

. . .

DID you miss the original Eye Candy Ink series? You can read the boxset here.

GRAB the next book in the series, Gray, here!

ALSO BY SHAW HART

STILL IN THE **mood for Christmas books?**
Stuffing Her Stocking, Mistletoe Kisses, Snowed in For Christmas

LOVE HOLIDAY BOOKS? **Check out these!**
For Better or Worse, Riding His Broomstick, Thankful for His FAKE Girlfriend, His New Year Resolution, Hop Stuff, Taming Her Beast, Hungry For Dash, His Firework

LOOKING **for some OTT love stories?**
Fighting for His Princess, Her Scottish Savior, Not So Accidental Baby Daddy, Baby Mama

LOOKING FOR A CELEBRITY LOVE STORY?
Bedroom Eyes, Seducing Archer, Finding Their Rhythm

. . .

IN THE MOOD **for some young love books?**
Study Dates, His Forever, My Girl

SOME OTHER BOOKS BY SHAW:
The Billionaire's Bet, Her Guardian Angel, Every
Tuesday Night, Falling Again, Stealing Her, Dreamboat,
Locked Down, Making Her His, Trouble

GRAY

EYE CANDY INK: SECOND GENERATION

*

Grayson Mackleroy is probably going to regret this.

He's regretted a lot of things in his life. Not standing up to his dad, not moving away from Rosewood when he had the chance, but none of them come close to his biggest regret.

Not making Nora Mason his the second that he laid eyes on her.

Now too much time has passed and while he's been in love with her since he first saw her in the third grade, she sees him as nothing but a best friend and roommate.

Or does she?

Will pursuing Nora ruin everything? Or will he finally get the happily ever after that he's been dreaming about ever since he first laid eyes on her?

ONE

Gray

"I THINK that we should get a dog," Nora says as soon as I walk into our apartment.

"Okay, and what brought this on?"

"You love dogs. Why wouldn't you want one?"

"I didn't say that I didn't want one. I just wanted to know why you did all of a sudden."

"'Cause I volunteered at the animal shelter this afternoon. I'm going to redo their website for them and they had the cutest little puppies there."

"And how many did you already adopt?" I ask her as I toss my keys down on the table by the front door.

"Six."

"Six?!?"

"Nah, I'm just kidding."

I roll my eyes, about to take a seat on the couch when two little balls of fur come skidding into the room, dragging one of my shoes with them.

"I thought that you said that you were kidding?"

"Yeah, I was. I only adopted two. I also signed us up to be a foster home," Nora says, scooping up one of the puppies and pushing his nose against mine. "Aren't they cute?"

"Adorable."

"I think so too," she says, snagging the other one before he can completely destroy my shoe.

"What are they?" I ask, staring at the black, brown, and white furball in my hands.

"They're just mutts. That's the boy and this is the girl. I haven't named them yet. I thought that we could do that together."

"How about Moose. I have a feeling that this guy is going to be huge," I mumble, staring at the size of his paws.

"Aww, that's cute. And you can be Marley."

Nora kisses the top of Marley's head and I've never been so jealous of a dog in my entire life. I wish that she looked at me like that.

"Are they house trained?" I ask her, trying to hold on to the squirming pup.

"Not yet," she says with a serene smile as her puppy curls up against her chest. Meanwhile, Moose looks like he's experiencing some kind of demonic exorcism.

"Don't worry though. We have puppy training classes starting on Saturday and Sunday mornings. They'll be trained in no time."

I make a mental note to clear my mornings at work for the next few weeks as I settle in next to my best friend and the love of my life.

The puppies jump down and I watch as they drag my shoe with them.

"Did you buy them toys?"

"Yes, they hate them."

I laugh at that, leaning back against the couch cushions.

"But they're really enjoying chewing on your shoes," she adds.

"How many did you let them chew on?"

"Just the one and before you can say anything, I already ordered you a new pair."

I relax back against the couch, too tired to go see what other things they may be chewing on. I'm about to work my fifth shift in a row at Eye Candy Ink, which means that I have one more day before my day off. I had thought that I would spend it sleeping in and then doing nothing all day with Nora. Guess that won't be happening.

Nora and I have been best friends since elementary school. We both grew up in the same small town of Rosewood, Colorado. It wasn't a happy place for either of us, which is why we moved away as soon as we both were eighteen. It's also why Nora is always trying to get us to do nice, normal things like adopt a pet or learn how to cook. She can't help but go a little overboard each time though, which is why we now have two puppies and each know how to make macaroons but have a hard time making spaghetti.

We tried living in New York for a minute because Nora had always wanted to visit and I would live anywhere as long as Nora was there. New York is expensive though and much too cutthroat. When a position opened up at the new Eye Candy Ink location, I applied and when I got hired, I told Nora. She had been so happy for me and so we both packed up and moved to Pittsburgh.

Nora is a web and software developer and can do anything with a computer. She can also pretty much work from anywhere as long as it has Wi-Fi.

"I saw my brother today."

"Yeah, before or after you adopted the pups?" I ask her.

"Before. Niall was the one to give me the idea actually."

I'm not at all surprised. Niall likes to stir up trouble, especially if it's for me. He knows that I've been in love with Nora for decades and he wants me to make a move so that he can stop worrying about her.

"How's he doing?" I ask.

"Good. He's busy training for some fight."

I nod, watching as she closes her laptop and heads over to her desk to plug it in. Niall is an MMA fighter and trains around the corner from Eye Candy Ink at Kings Gym. He's always training for some fight or recovering from another one.

"Are you hungry? I got you some takeout from lunch."

"What is it?"

"Jerk chicken."

My stomach growls at that and Nora laughs, heading into the kitchen to heat it up for me. The puppies come running into the kitchen and Nora bends down to pet them.

"Do you need to go outside?" she coos at them and I grab their leashes off of the counter.

"I'll take them," I say and she grins at me.

"Thanks."

It takes me a few minutes to catch them and get their leashes hooked on their collars. They keep chewing on the leashes as we try to make our way down the stairs, so I end up picking both of them up and jogging downstairs and outside.

We start to walk around the block but they don't know how to walk on a leash yet either, so it's more like a fight and me dragging them. They do go to the bathroom though, so I guess that's something.

I carry them back upstairs and unhook them, watching

as they run over to Nora where she's warming up the food in the kitchen.

She looks up, smiling at me, and my heart races in my chest. Even after all these years, she's still the most perfect thing that I've ever seen. She can still have me feeling like I'm riding a rollercoaster with just one look.

"Ready?" she asks as she plates the food and I nod.

Yeah, I think I might finally be ready to do something about how I feel about Nora. How I've always felt about her. I just hope that it doesn't ruin everything between us.

TWO

Nora

I'VE MADE A TERRIBLE MISTAKE.

I know that the next morning as I wrestle the puppies down the street. I don't know how Gray made it look so easy this morning. We walked all the way around the block with them before he had to leave for work. I had thought that I could do it by myself before I left to grab lunch with my brother but it's been twenty minutes and we've only gone half a block.

"Alright, come on guys," I sigh, starting the process of half chasing, half dragging them back to our apartment.

At this rate, I'm going to be late to meet Niall. He's probably still at Kings Gym anyway. He's an underground MMA fighter and he spends most of his days training.

Niall and I have always been close. We had to be, growing up with a dad like ours. He's always been one of my closest friends and fiercest protectors. Maybe that's why he became a fighter.

My phone rings and I see it's a text from Niall.

NIALL: **Training ran late today. I'm just now heading to the showers. Meet you in twenty?**

Nora: Perfect. I'm still trying to get the dogs back up to the apartment.

Niall: What dogs?

Nora: It's a long story.

Niall: I can guess.

Nora: No, you can't.

Niall: I know you better than anyone, little sis.

Nora: Nu uh.

Niall: You volunteered at the animal shelter to try to distract yourself from the way that you feel about Gray and ended up adopting a dog.

Nora: Nope.

Niall: What part is wrong?

Nora: I adopted two dogs.

Niall: See you in twenty, sis.

SOMETIMES I HATE how well Niall knows me.

Niall has known how I feel about Gray since before I even knew. Sure, Gray and I have been best friends since like kindergarten, but somewhere over the years, he became so much more than just my friend.

It's true that I only started volunteering at the animal shelter to get out of the house more. I was spending too much time with Gray and it was only a matter of time before I blurted out that I love him as so much more than a friend.

Adopting the puppies may have backfired though, because seeing them cuddled up against Gray's strong chest almost made my ovaries explode last night. Not to mention, we'll be spending even more time together when we start the puppy training classes.

I'm so screwed.

Gray is the only man that I've ever fantasized about, the only one besides my brother that I've ever loved.

He's everything to me.

Which is exactly why I can't risk it and tell him how I feel.

Niall has been encouraging me to tell him for years, but he's been more insistent about it since we moved to Pittsburgh. I know that he just wants me to be happy. He's always liked Gray. He knows that Gray would do anything for me, that he's been protecting and keeping me safe for years. I think it was why Niall felt comfortable enough to leave after he graduated from high school. He knew that Gray wouldn't let anything bad happen to me.

I hurry to herd the puppies upstairs and into the apartment, locking them in the bathroom with their new toys, food, and water bowl. I have ten minutes to make it across town to Kings Gym so I grab my purse, phone, and keys and hit the road.

I have a bit of work to do tonight but I know that Gray is going out with Ender, Banks, and Ames from work so I'll have the place to myself.

I work for a few companies downtown but since I just manage their websites, I work offsite so I do most of my work from home and can make my own hours for the most part. As long as I get all of my work turned in on time, they don't say anything to me and I keep getting paid very well.

By the time that I pull out front of Kings Gym, my brother is already waiting for me, his hair still damp from his shower. I pull up alongside the curb, waving at Beck, one of his workout buddies as he heads down the sidewalk toward his own car.

"Hey, sis," Niall says as he slides into the passenger seat.

"Hey, how was training?"

Niall tells me about sparring with Beck and about the next big match that he has coming up soon as we head down the street to our favorite diner.

"Have you told him yet?" Niall asks as soon as we take our seats in our usual booth along the back wall.

"Told who, what?" I ask, playing dumb.

Niall groans, picking up a menu even though we both know what he'll be ordering. These weekly lunches are his only cheat meals of the week, so he'll be getting two grilled cheeses, tomato soup, a Caesar salad, and a Coke. Then he'll sneak one of my mozzarella sticks and a bite of my pie for dessert. I move my purse out of the way, already knowing that his food will take up half of the table.

"What will it be?" our waitress, Everly, asks.

We always get her since we always sit in her section and it's one of the reasons why I love this place so much. Niall starts to blush slightly and I bite back a grin.

Yeah, he's got it bad for her.

"The usual please, Everly," I say, pretending to put my menu back between the napkin holder and the wall.

"Me too," my brother grunts out and I want to groan.

Niall has always been so focused on getting us through our childhood and then on being successful at boxing. He's never shown an interest in women. Not until Everly.

Unfortunately for him, his lack of experience with the opposite sex means that he has absolutely no game.

"You got it," Everly says with a tired smile as she turns and heads back toward the kitchen.

Niall frowns after her and I let him watch her go.

I wonder what's better. Only being able to see the person that you're interested in once a week, or seeing them all of the time and not being able to be with them the way that you really want to.

"So, tell me about the puppies," Niall says, finally turning his attention back to me and I smile, forcing my thoughts away from the person that they always seem to be on.

For one hour, I try to focus on Niall and our conversation but just like always, thoughts of Gray slip in. As Everly drops off our bill and I argue with Niall over whose turn it is to pay, I can't help but wonder what Gray is doing right now.

THREE

Gray

IT'S Tuesday night and that means tacos. I swing by Nora's favorite place on the way home and grab a dozen, plus chips, salsa, queso, and extra guacamole. Nora always asks for extra guacamole even though she will end up eating three tacos and then snacking on the chips and queso.

I can't stop thinking about what Rooney said today. He had asked me what I was going to do if someone ever made a move on Nora or if she ever found a boyfriend. I know that he was upset because things weren't going well with him and Sayler, that he was just lashing out at me, but that doesn't make his words any less true.

I wouldn't be able to handle seeing her with someone else. Even just thinking that has my fingers strangling the steering wheel so hard that it creaks.

I don't know what to do. Do I tell her how I feel and risk losing her? Or do I keep the status quo and at least get to keep her in my life as my best friend.

I still don't have an answer by the time that I pull up outside of our apartment building and by then, I'm out of time.

Nora is outside trying to wrangle the puppies up the steps when I park and I hurry over to help her.

"How about I trade you?" I offer as I pass her the bag of tacos.

Moose and Marley must smell the food because they practically pull me up the stairs after Nora.

"They already ate," she tells me as she starts to unpack the tacos and I unhook the puppies, watching as they scramble across the floor toward her.

"I'm not sure that the puppy training class worked," I joke and she smiles, passing me a plate.

"Yeah, it's weird how one class didn't teach them everything," she says sarcastically and I laugh, nudging Moose down when he tries to sniff my plate.

I decide to put the dogs in the crate while we eat as Nora makes us margaritas. They whine as I put them in their little pen so I bend down, petting each of them until they lay down.

Nora has poured the margaritas into two cups by the time that I return and I grab mine, following her into the living room.

"What are we watching tonight?" I ask her as we both carry our plates and glasses of margaritas over to the couch.

"Outlander?" Nora says hopefully and even though I don't really care for the show, I know that it's one of her favorites.

"Sure," I say, pulling it up and hitting play.

Nora grins as the opening credits start to play, sitting cross-legged on the couch and balancing her plate on her lap. I lean back against the couch, watching her more than the TV screen.

We just started this show, so we're still on the first few episodes. I knew that it was supposed to be a little racy but nothing so far had prepared me for episode seven.

Nora and I don't speak as we watch Claire and Jamie on their wedding night. I can see Nora's face is heated and she keeps stealing glances at me as the two actors go at it onscreen.

The room is filled with sexual tension and even though I'm still hungry, I don't dare pick up my last taco.

When Nora licks her lips, her breathing coming faster, her chest rising and falling rapidly, I can't help it. I let out a little groan, coughing right after to try to cover it up.

"Pretty steamy, huh?" Nora asks, trying to change the energy that's taken over the room.

I will myself to urge down my erection before Nora can see it. Luckily, my plate is covering most of it.

"Yeah, I think this show might be interesting after all," I joke and she laughs, but I can see that she's still a little awkward about watching this together.

I wonder if she can feel how much I want her. I wonder if she can tell how much I want to do everything that Jamie just did to Claire, and so much more.

The dogs whine and the spell is broken.

"I'll walk them," I say, jumping up from the couch and hurrying into the bedroom to get them.

"Want me to help you?" Nora offers but I wave her off.

"Nah, I got it."

She nods, setting her plate aside and grabbing her laptop, and I leave with Moose and Marley. We head downstairs and start to make our way around the block when my phone rings in my pocket. I pull it out, hesitating when I see my brother's name on the screen.

We're not the closest. Not after he left me to fend for myself with our dad. Part of me knows that he had to leave, that his paycheck from the Army was the only thing keeping the roof over my head and food on the table, but it's still hard not to be angry with him, no matter how unreasonable that is.

"Hey, what's up?" I ask as soon as I answer.

"Hey, Gray," he says and he sounds tired, like he's a hundred years old instead of just twenty-nine.

"Hey, are you back in the states?" I ask him.

He's an Army Ranger and has been deployed for the past few months. I like to think that that's why we've only talked a handful of times in the last six months.

"No, but I'm headed back now. I got some news today," he starts and the tone of his voice lets me know that I'm not going to like it.

"Yeah?" I ask nervously.

"It's Dad, Gray," Jasper sighs.

"What about him?" I ask, every muscle in my body tight.

I don't even realize that I've stopped on the sidewalk until someone runs into me and I move over, leaning against the building.

"He's dead," Jasper says flatly, and it feels like the world drops out beneath my feet.

"What?" I ask and I can hear my brother talking, but it's like he's in a tunnel all of a sudden.

"...so the funeral is going to be this weekend. I'm headed home to plan it now. I didn't think that you would want to be there for the planning," he says, trailing off.

He's right. I have no interest in going home, but I definitely don't want to plan that monster's funeral.

"I can if you need me to," I offer, praying that he won't take me up on it.

"No, Gray. It's okay, I can take care of it."

Suddenly, I realize that this grudge that I've been holding against Jasper for leaving truly isn't fair. He never could have supported us if he stayed and worked in Rosewood. We would have had to move somewhere else where we could all find jobs, and I never would have left Nora.

Maybe he knows that. Maybe he was trying to help keep Nora and I together and support us. Maybe it was the only option.

"Thanks, Jasp. Let me know if you need anything before this weekend."

"Will do. Do you want me to pay for your ticket home?"

"No, Nora might come with me, so I'll get my ticket. But thank you."

He clears his throat and we both stay on the phone.

"I'll see you and Nora this weekend," he says finally and I nod even though he can't see me.

"See you."

The dogs are tangled up in the leash and I bend down, freeing them and turning to head back toward our building.

"Perfect timing! I just finished up with work," Nora says as I walk back in, letting Moose and Marley off their leashes.

"Did you want to watch another episode or..." She trails off as she gets a look at my face and she's over the couch and in front of me in an instant. "What's wrong?"

"My brother just called."

"Oh, god. Is Jasper okay?" she asks, concern etched into her eyes.

"Yeah, he's headed back to the states. Back to Rosewood."

"Then what's wrong?"

"My dad died. The funeral is this weekend," I blurt out and she reacts to the news just like I did.

Her body tenses, her arms tightening around my waist as she hugs me.

"I have to go back to Rosewood for the funeral."

She snaps out of it then, nodding firmly.

"I'm coming too."

This, this is why I love her. She has always and will always be there for me. Nora is loyal, smart, funny, and protective. I'm not even surprised that she's going back to Rosewood with me. Even though we both hate it there.

Nora hugs me tighter and I wrap my arms around her, resting my head on top of hers. It's then, as we hold each other, that I realize that I can't put this relationship in jeopardy. I need Nora. I wouldn't make it a day without her in my life, so I'm just going to have to be okay with us being just friends.

I know that that's a lie though. The thought of us only ever being just friends makes it feel like another piece of my soul just died.

It's time for me to man up.

FOUR

Nora

"ARE you sure that you don't want me to come too?" my brother asks for the millionth time.

"I'm sure. I know that you have that match coming up soon and you need to train. We're only going to be there for two days anyway."

"If you're sure," Niall says but he doesn't sound happy about it.

I know that he's just being a protective big brother. He knows how I feel about Rosewood and he wants to be there in case anything goes wrong.

"I'm sure. Gray will be there and his brother, Jasper. We'll be fine."

Niall relaxes a bit at that and leans back in his side of the booth. We're on our weekly lunch now but I'll need to leave soon so that Gray and I can head to the airport.

"Are you sure you don't want me to watch Moose and

Marley?" Niall asks as Everly heads our way with the check.

"Yeah, Gray said that Rooney and Harvey from work are going to watch them. Thanks though."

"Need anything else?" Everly asks and I silently will my brother to say something charming.

"No, we're good."

I bite back my sigh, rolling my eyes as I turn to grab my purse. It's my week to pay and I hurry to drop some cash on the table before Niall can beat me to it.

"I better go. Gray will be waiting for me."

"Let me know when you land. And if you need anything while you're there," Niall says, giving me a hard look as he bends to give me a hug.

"I will."

We part in the parking lot and I head over to my car. Niall lives a few blocks away and I watch him walk until he turns the corner.

I try not to yawn as I start my car and head toward home. I've been busy all week, trying to get ahead on work since I won't be doing any this weekend. The stress of going back home has also taken its toll on me. The thought of running into my father while I'm back has given me nightmares all week and I know that's why Niall has been asking if I'm sure I don't want him to go home with me.

"Ready?" Gray asks, his voice and face grim as he wheels his suitcase out of his room.

"Yeah, I'm already packed. Just need to grab my bag."

Gray nods and I watch him head for the front door. I'm going back for the funeral to support him, but I'm not sure that I'm doing a very good job so far. He's been distant and withdrawn all week and I've tried to draw him out but it seems neither of us can shake the sense of doom that comes with thoughts of Rosewood.

The trip to the airport and most of the plane ride is spent in tense silence. I try to ask him about his brother and the funeral plans but he doesn't seem to know much. When we land, Gray grabs our bags and I follow after him to the car rental counter.

It's after midnight and I know that both of us just want to get to the hotel and pass out. Still, driving down the streets of Rosewood is almost surreal.

The last time we were in town, we were packing up Gray's old beat-up Honda and peeling out of town. My dad had been on another bender and we had used his unconscious state to our advantage. There's no way that we would have been able to get out without a confrontation if he had been sober.

Gray's dad had pulled another one of his disappearing acts. He liked to take the money that Jasper sent home and leave for a few days. He would spend it on booze, drugs, women, and God knows what else. He always came back after a few days and slept off whatever high he was on.

We pull into the hotel parking lot and I look over to see Jasper there. He's staring across the street at a dark-haired woman. I squint, trying to see if I remember her from growing up.

"Isn't that Evangeline?" I ask Gray and he turns to look.

"Yeah, Jasper always did have a thing for her."

"Think he'll make a move now that he's home?" I ask as Gray shuts off the car.

"Maybe."

We climb out, catching Jasper's attention, and when he turns, I can't hold in my gasp.

"What the fuck?" Gray growls, stalking the few feet over to his brother. "You're hurt?"

"Yeah," Jasper says, his hand rubbing at the back of his neck.

His other arm, from the shoulder down to his wrist, is wrapped in some kind of bandage. There are scars on his neck and a few on the side of his face, and I wonder what happened.

"My unit got hit on our last mission. I was going to tell you but then I got the call about Dad."

"And you just decided to show me when I saw you?" Gray asks and I can tell that he's annoyed.

"We're just glad that you're alright," I say, laying my hand on Gray's arm. "It's good to see you again, Jasper. I'm sorry for your loss."

Those last words don't ring true and I know that no one thinks Rod Mackelroy's death is any real loss.

"Thanks, Nora. It's good to see you too. Are you guys all checked in?"

"Not yet. We're headed in now."

Jasper nods, following after Gray and I as we head for the hotel lobby. I let Gray check us in as I catch up with Jasper.

"Do you need me to do anything for tomorrow?" I ask, careful not to let Gray hear.

"No, I already made all of the plans. I don't anticipate it being a big funeral. Rod wasn't exactly a pillar of the community."

"It starts at ten, right?"

"Yeah, then I thought we could grab lunch downtown somewhere. I need to go over to the house and clean it out."

"Are you sure that you should be doing that?" I ask, nodding toward his injured side.

"I'll be fine."

"When do you go back to the Army?" Gray asks as he joins us.

"I don't. I was medically discharged."

"So, what are you going to do?"

"I thought I'd stay in Rosewood for a little bit. I need to clean up the house and take care of a few more things."

"Then what?" Gray asks with a frown.

"Honestly, I don't know. I think I might like trying to figure that part out though."

My mind flashes back to the way that he was looking at Evangeline, and I wonder if he has other reasons for wanting to stay in Rosewood.

"We're on the fourth floor," Gray tells me and I nod.

"I'm the third," Jasper says as he hits the button for the elevator. "Room 314, if you need anything."

Gray just nods, and I lean against him, my eyes starting to droop.

"See you in the morning," Jasper says as he exits and we both nod sleepily.

"Ready for bed?" Jasper asks as he opens the hotel room door.

"Oh yeah," I say, heading over to the bed. "Just a king?"

"What?" Gray asks as he turns from setting our luggage over by the dresser.

"It's just one bed."

"It was supposed to be two," he sighs and I can tell that he's exhausted.

"It's alright. It's not like we haven't shared a bed before," I say with a smile.

Gray mumbles something but I don't catch it, I'm too tired. I head past him, grabbing my pajamas out of my suitcase and slipping into the bathroom. I wash my face, brush my teeth, and change before I trudge back out to the bedroom.

Gray passes me on my way and I lay down, listening to the water run in the bathroom. I'm asleep before he comes back into the room.

FIVE

Gray

NO FUNERAL IS a happy event but my father's is especially depressing.

It's just Nora, Jasper, and I in the pews as the preacher begins the sermon. We're all dressed in black, the stark white bandages on Jasper's left side standing out like a sore thumb.

It's awkward in the small church as the preacher goes on about my dad being in a better place and walking with Jesus now. I don't know how to tell him that there's no way in hell my dad made it to Heaven.

It's an open casket and I was shocked when I saw my dad for the first time in over five years. He had seemed smaller, thinner than I remember. The drugs and alcohol had really aged him in the last few years. I'll admit, it was strange seeing the monster from my childhood look so, well, human.

Nora holds my hand, her dainty fingers wrapped tight

around mine. We haven't spoken about the way that we spooned all last night. I hadn't been surprised when I woke up this morning wrapped around her. There was no way that I could resist her soft curves in the same bed as me all night long.

I know that Rosewood doesn't hold many fond memories for either of us and it means a lot to me that Nora was willing to come back to support me. Driving through town last night had been strange.

Nothing much had really changed. Main Street was still the same old shops, the diner down on Fourth Street is still the popular hangout with the high school kids, and I still wanted nothing to do with any of it.

Nora squeezes my hand and I jolt out of my thoughts. The funeral is over and it's time for us to head over to the burial. Jasper rode with us this morning so he slides into the back seat and we drive around the block, following the hearse.

We pass by some new nursery, the flowers blooming in so many different colors and I'm surprised to see Evangeline moving some of the flower pots around. When I look in the rearview mirror, I see that Jasper has also caught sight of her.

None of us thought to bring flowers and his headstone seems bare next to the big ones on either side of him. The preacher says a quick prayer and then we watch silently as he's lowered into the ground.

Nora leans against my side and I can see her watching me, worry clouding her eyes.

"I'm alright. I promise," I whisper to her and she nods, grabbing my hand in hers once more.

"Did you want a minute?" Jasper asks, nodding toward the casket in the ground and I shake my head.

"Do you?"

"No."

Just like that, the funeral is over.

My father is dead and I should feel something, but all that's left is relief. We've never had much of a relationship, haven't spoken in the last five years, and even before then, we rarely talked about anything besides if Jasper had sent the monthly money for rent and food.

"I need to go by the house. See how bad it is," Jasper says as he tugs at his tie.

"We'll go with you, but maybe we should change first," Nora suggests and Jasper nods, taking one last look at the headstone before he turns and walks away.

We follow after him and I tug Nora into my side.

"Thank you," I whisper and she nods, squeezing me back.

"Anytime."

We pile back into the rental car and drive back across town to the hotel. It's still just as dead as it was when we got here last night.

"Meet back down here in twenty?" Jasper asks as we ride up to his floor.

"Sounds good."

He steps off and we ride up to our floor in silence.

"Did you want to shower or anything?" I ask Nora and she shakes her head.

"No, I just need to get out of these clothes."

I try to keep my mind off of the image of me helping her do just that. I can't stop thinking about how soft she was last night, how she had moaned as I pulled her back against me. She had felt so right in my arms and now I don't know how I'll ever be able to sleep alone again.

"Me too," I say, shrugging out of my suit jacket and

hanging it back up on the hanger. "I'll let you use the bathroom first."

"Thanks."

Nora heads into the bathroom with some more casual clothes under her arm and I collapse back onto the bed. It still smells like Nora and I take a deep breath, letting my eyes fall shut.

My phone buzzes and I pull it out to see that Rooney has sent another picture of Moose and Marley. He's been doing this about every hour and calling them proof of life. I think he was nervous about watching them but I didn't know anyone who would be able to keep up with them as well as Rooney.

"Is this alright?" Nora asks, coming out in a pair of jeans and a plain pink T-shirt.

"Yeah, you look great," I say honestly, then because I can feel the sexual tension starting to grow in the room, I show her my phone. "Rooney says that the kids are great."

Nora laughs, smiling as she takes my phone from me. I leave it with her, heading into the bathroom to change out of my suit.

"Where did you want to go for lunch? Jasper just texted to ask," Nora says through the door and I try to think of restaurants in town.

"Let's just grab Wendy's or something," I suggest.

I have a feeling that neither Nora or I really want to run into anyone from town so fast food seems like the best choice.

"Sounds good," she says and I tug my shirt over my head.

I head back out to the room. We have one more night to sleep here since I wasn't sure what Jasper would need help with. I wonder if we can get everything done this afternoon and I can move our flights up.

I'm not sure that I can handle the temptation of sleeping next to Nora again.

"Ready to go?" Nora asks and I nod.

Her jeans are molded to her thighs and ass and I try to look anywhere but at it as we head back to the elevator.

We really need to go home tonight. I know that I won't be able to resist Nora again.

If I'm honest with myself, I don't think that I want to.

I've been holding myself back from Nora for decades and it's starting to break through. I'm not sure how much longer I can hide how much I love her.

SIX

Nora

PULLING up outside the Mackelroy home is daunting. No one moves when Gray puts the car into park and I can tell that neither of the brothers wants to venture inside.

Their house isn't too far from my old one and I can't help but turn and stare down the street. I can just make out the imposing two-story house on the corner. My eyes stay locked on the place, the perfectly cut grass, the neat flower beds. My father was all about appearances, but I know that if you went inside, you'd notice the worn carpet, the outdated wallpaper, the chipped dishes.

"Don't, Nora. Take a deep breath," Gray says, grabbing my hand and urging me to look away from my old house. "We're not going there. I'm not going to let him hurt you," he whispers and I take a deep breath, trying to calm my racing heart.

"Let's get this over with," Jasper says, climbing out of the car and I turn my attention back to where we are.

"Ready?" I ask Gray.

"Yeah," he says, studying my face.

I can tell that he's worried about me, so I force a smile. I'm supposed to be here to comfort him, not the other way around.

I climb out and follow Jasper up to the front door. The porch is sagging a little and Gray grabs my arm, steadying me as we hurry inside.

"We'll have to fix that if we want to sell this place," Jasper mumbles, glaring around the place.

There isn't much left. I'm sure that Rod has sold or pawned everything of value. Gray is rooted to the spot, his grip firm on my elbow and I want to tell him that I'm in no danger of falling through the floor anymore but it feels like I'm anchoring him so I remain silent.

"Where should we start?" Gray asks, looking to his brother.

"I'm not sure there's much to do. I was expecting way worse but there isn't much left. I'll have to hire a crew or something to make repairs and then we can list the place."

"Do you want to look around? See if there's anything that you want?" I ask and they both shake their heads no immediately.

"I haven't needed anything here for the last five years so I can live without it now. Let's just go," Gray says and I nod, letting him help me back down the front porch steps and over to the car.

We all pile back in and drive down the mostly empty streets. I can tell that the brothers are upset, that this whole ordeal has been harder on them than they would ever admit and as we drive past my old house, I get it.

This town doesn't hold good memories for any of us. It's

why we all were so desperate to escape it when we were younger.

"Can you pull over here?" Jasper asks from the back seat and Gray nods, turning into the nursery parking lot.

"Doing some gardening?" Gray asks dryly and Jasper just rolls his eyes.

"We're going to need to fix up the outside to sell the house. I just want to see if they do landscaping. I'll be right back."

"Think he's going to get her number?" I ask as we watch Jasper walk up to Evangeline where she's crouched next to some plants.

"Not a chance. He's got no game."

I smile, thinking back to my own brother and his lack of skills with Everly.

"Maybe it's hereditary," I mumble.

"What's that supposed to mean?" Gray asks and I wince.

"I meant for me. Niall is terrible with the ladies too."

"Are you trying to get with someone?" Gray asks and I can't help but wonder about the hard edge that I can hear to his words.

"Maybe."

"Who?" he demands, his brow furrowed as he glares at me.

I shrug, turning back to watch Jasper and Evangeline.

"You don't want to settle down with someone?" I ask.

I keep my head turned away from him. I'm not sure that I can handle his answer and I don't want him to see me upset if he says he's been interested in someone.

"Sure."

"Anyone in particular?" I press.

It feels like my heart is teetering on the edge and I bite my lip as I wait for his response.

"Maybe," he says and I know that he only said that because I did but it still stings.

"Anyone that I know?"

"Maybe."

My mind races with every eligible female that I know. *Could it be Cat? Or maybe someone from work?*

Jasper heads back toward the car and we drive the remaining blocks back to the hotel in silence.

"What time are you leaving in the morning?" Jasper asks.

"Eight," Gray says.

I can see him staring at me in the reflection on the elevator doors and I try not to shift. He's watching me like I'm a puzzle and he can't figure out how to solve me.

"Did you want to grab dinner tonight?" I ask Jasper as we stop on his floor.

"I need to make a few calls and then I have a doctor appointment in the next town over in two hours. It was good seeing you both though."

"You too," I say, hugging Jasper and stepping aside so the brothers can talk.

"I'll talk to you soon. Let me know if you need any more help with the house or if you need anything else. Let me know how the doctor appointment goes," Gray says, his voice thick with emotion.

I know that today has been hard for him. Being back here is hard for both of us, but I know that he's also wrestling with his feelings toward his brother too. They're going to need to have an honest conversation soon, but today doesn't seem like the day to do that.

"I will. See you guys."

With that, the elevator doors close and we ride up to our floor, stepping off and heading into our room in silence.

"I'm going to take a shower. Unless you wanted to first?" I ask, turning to see Gray standing right behind me.

"I..." He trails off, his eyes dipping to my lips and staying there.

I can't help it. I lick my suddenly dry lips, my eyes locked on him. Can he feel this thing between us? Can he tell how much I want him, how much I've always wanted him?

Our heads start to move closer together and my breathing grows more rapid. I can feel his warm breath blow across my face and my whole body feels on edge.

Finally. Fucking finally, he sees me. He wants me too.

My eyes start to drift shut when suddenly, he pulls back.

"I'll let you go first," he says, his voice hoarse.

I can feel my face flame and I grab the first thing my fingers touch before I turn and bolt for the bathroom.

I lock myself inside, embarrassment flooding me and I drop my head back against the door.

Fuck, I'm an idiot.

SEVEN

Gray

GOD, I'm an idiot.

I've been thinking that same thought over and over again ever since I almost kissed Nora in our hotel room.

Things had been a little awkward since that night and I know it's because I couldn't control myself. I almost ruined everything because I couldn't keep my hands to myself.

We're back in Pittsburgh now and things are a little strained but I'm hoping that we can both forget about this soon. We picked the dogs up from Rooney and Harvey's place yesterday afternoon. Rooney and Harvey had surprised us by going to the puppy training class in our place but I don't think that it really helped. They were still as crazy last night as ever. It ended up being a good distraction though, so for once, I didn't mind them trying to lick my face.

Jasper had texted me to say that his doctor appointment had gone well and that he forgot to tell me that there had been some flowers at the funeral from Ender, Banks, Ames, Maxine, Rooney, and Harvey. It was nice of them to send anything, so I don't bother telling them that the funeral had been a bit of a joke and definitely more of a duty.

"Hey," Ender grunts out as he comes into the shop the next morning.

Out of everyone at Eye Candy Ink, I'm probably closest to Ender. We started on the same day, our rooms are right next to each other, and he's always been a great sounding board. He's almost twenty years older than me and some days I wish that I had someone like him as my real dad.

"Hey, thanks for the flowers," I say as I finish up the last of the tattoos that I'll be doing today.

"Sure. It was Maxine's idea," he says and I smile.

That sounds about right.

"Still. Thanks."

He nods, leaning against my doorframe and I turn to look at him.

"Everything alright? Did I miss anything around here?"

"No, not really. Just wanted to make sure that you're alright. You seem a little off. I'm sorry for your loss. Were you and your dad close?" he asks and I can't hold in the laugh.

"No, not even close. He was an alcoholic asshole who liked to smack us around when he was drunk, which was pretty much every night."

My words come out bitter and I see Harvey and Rooney have stopped in the doorway and are staring at me wide-eyed.

Ender doesn't seem at all surprised by my words and I wonder if he suspected something.

Banks comes into the shop then, stopping outside of my door too.

"Hey, Gray. Welcome back," he says distractedly and I nod. "Sorry for your loss, man."

"Doesn't sound like it was much of a loss," Rooney says, anger clear in his voice and I see Harvey elbow him.

"It wasn't," I promise him.

"Was it nice to see your brother at least?" Harvey asks and I shrug.

"We have kind of a complicated relationship."

"Are any of you guys working?" Mischa asks as he comes up behind everyone else. "Gray, hey, heard about your dad. Sorry for your loss."

I know that he's just being nice but if I hear those four words one more time today, I'm going to scream.

"Wasn't a loss," Rooney and I say at the same time and Mischa frowns.

"I see. Well still, it's good to have you back here."

"What are you doing here, Dad?" Rooney asks and Mischa smiles at him.

"I'm here to invite everyone over for Sunday brunch. It just occurred to us that we've been neglecting half of you, so I expect to see all of you at Zeke's house this Sunday."

"Nora and I have puppy training classes in the morning."

"Come after! Bring the puppies and your girl."

"She's not his girl," Rooney says, a devilish twinkle in his eyes and I glare at him.

"We can help with that too," Mischa says and I know for sure that I can't be bringing Nora around any of these guys. Not if I want to keep our friendship intact anyway.

Mischa and Rooney head down the hall toward his room and I sigh.

"Drinks tonight?" Banks suggests. "We can hit up Seven."

"I'm in," Ender says right away and I know exactly why the war veteran who hates loud noises and crowds is so eager to go to the club.

Cat.

"Yeah, I'm in too," I say.

"Me too," Harvey says and Banks nods, heading back to his own room with Harvey on his heels.

"Did anything else happen on the trip?" Ender asks, curiosity in his dark green eyes.

"Like what?"

"Like maybe you confessed to Nora that you're in love with her and can't live without her?"

"Do you really want to do this? Should I tell everyone why you love Seven so much?"

He crosses his arms over his chest and I bite back a curse.

"No, okay. Nothing happened, but I did almost kiss her."

"You should have."

"It would have ruined everything."

"No. It really wouldn't have," he says before he turns and heads across the hall to his own room.

I mull over his words all day and by the time that we are locking up later that night, I still wonder if maybe he's right.

I'm at the end of my rope here and something has to give. Either I tell her how I feel or I have to pretend to be happy for her when she finally brings around whoever she's been crushing on.

My hands tighten into fists as I think about how we had talked about settling down and how she had said that she had someone in mind.

"Gray."

I look up as Niall heads my way down the dark street.

"What are you doing here, Niall? Looking to get some more ink?" I ask Nora's brother and he shakes his head.

"No, not today anyway."

I've done all of Niall's ink. He was actually one of the first people to let me work on him. He knew that I needed to practice and let me use him as a guinea pig.

"What can I do for you then?" I ask as Ender locks up the shop behind me.

Harvey and Rooney are already joking around over by their car and I wonder what Niall could need.

"When are you going to tell Nora how you feel about her? I thought something would happen when we were all back in Rosewood," he admits and my stomach cramps.

"Aren't brothers supposed to warn guys away from their sisters?" I try to joke and he sighs.

"Not with you."

"Why not?"

"Because... because you're the only other person on the planet who loves Nora as much as I do. I know that she'll be safe with you."

I don't have a response to that. He's right, I am the only person who loves her as much as him, although mine is in a different way.

"Stop wasting time. You're going to regret it one day."

With that, Niall heads down the dark street, disappearing around the corner.

"You alright?" Ender asks and I forgot that he was even there.

"Yeah, I'm fine. You riding with me?"

"Yeah."

We head across the street in silence. Harvey, Rooney, and Banks are all in their car already, so Ender and I hurry up and climb into mine.

"Are you going to finally tell her? Seems like a sign if even her brother wants you too," Ender points out as we drive the few blocks to Se7en.

"You going to get on my case too, man?" I complain and he shrugs.

"You going to ask Cat out tonight?" I ask him and he shrugs again.

I sigh as I pull into the parking lot and we head across the street to the club. We follow after Rooney and Harvey as they breeze inside and over to the bar. Ender passes me a beer and I grunt out a thanks that I'm sure he can't hear over the music.

"Come on," Banks says and I follow them as we head over to a booth on the far wall.

"Do you want to talk about anything?" Harvey asks me as we sit down and I shake my head.

"Alright, well we're here for you if you do."

I give him a grateful smile. I haven't had many close relationships in my life. Nora is the closest by far but it's nice to know that these guys will have my back.

"Did you and Nora share a hotel room?" Rooney asks, wiggling his dark eyebrows at me.

"Yep."

He almost chokes on his beer and I grin.

"We just slept."

"Dude, what is wrong with you?"

I laugh, taking another sip of my beer.

"He chickened out," Ender says and I elbow him. "It's true." He glares.

"Yeah, I know."

"Why don't you just tell her? She's into you too, man," Banks says.

My heart soars at that but what does Banks know about girls. He's the most single out of all of us.

"She's been my family since we were kids. I can't ruin that. I don't even want to jeopardize it."

"But if she feels that same way..." Harvey starts.

"If I were to go home and she gave me some sign, then I would go for it. But she hasn't, so I'm not going to risk it."

No one seems happy with that answer, not even me, but what choice do I have?

I spot Cat up on the second-floor landing and I nudge Ender but of course, he's already spotted her. She disappears back into her office and Ender turns to study me for a minute before he comes to a decision.

"I'll be back," he says and I watch in astonishment as he heads over to the stairs and glares at the bouncers who both immediately get out of his way. He climbs the stairs and I watch him head into Cat's office.

If he can go after who he wants, could I maybe do the same?

EIGHT

Nora

GRAY HAS BEEN ACTING weird all week. At first, I thought that it was just because he was still upset about his dad's funeral and going back home. As the week went on though, that stopped seeming likely.

I would catch him staring at me, or my lips more specifically, when he thought that I wasn't looking. When we went out for breakfast one day, he glared at any guy who came near me.

If I didn't know better, I would say that he's acting like a jealous lover.

I wish.

I haven't been able to stop thinking about that almost kiss since we got back from Rosewood. It feels like we should talk about it, but every time I start to try to bring it up, I chicken out.

We're at puppy training class, trying to corral Moose and Marley. They've both slowly been getting better. We can walk with them on a leash now without too much difficulty and they're almost completely potty trained. They still chew on everything, but we were assured that they would grow out of that by the time they were two. We've stocked up on toys so that they don't chew on any more of Gray's shoes.

"Alright, class. We're going to work on some commands now," our instructor says and Gray and I line up with everyone else.

Moose and Marley are busy sniffing the ground and trying to make friends with the german shepherd next to us.

"Cute dog," the guy holding the german shepherd's leash says and I smile at him.

"Thanks. Yours too. How old is he?"

"Four months. What about yours?"

"Three months."

"I'm Nate, by the way."

"Nora," I say, leaning over to shake his hand, only for Gray to growl behind me.

I turn to see him glaring at Nate and I give him a look, but he ignores me and continues to glare at me. Part of me loves that he's trying to scare other guys away. It has to mean that he likes me, right? Although he probably just doesn't think this Nate guy is good enough for me.

The instructor gets our attention again and I turn away from the two confusing guys on either side of me and focus on getting Marley to sit.

"Do we need to grab anything for brunch?" I ask as we head back out to the car at the end of class.

"Are you sure that you want to go to that?" Gray asks as he wrestles Moose into the back seat.

Moose instantly scrambles over the center console and

plops his butt down in the driver's seat. I laugh as Gray glares at him.

"Yeah, I'm sure. Maxine, Cat, Sayler, and Coraline are all going to be there and I missed girl's night last week. I want to see them."

"Alright, come on. Rooney just texted to say that we should bring the puppies. He said that he misses his niece and nephew."

I giggle at that, sliding into the passenger seat and laughing when Moose and Marley both jump onto my lap. Soon they'll be too big to do this but for now, I don't mind.

Zeke's house is only a few blocks off of Main Street and we pull up outside at the same time that Ender does. He's carrying a few bouquets of flowers and I frown at Gray as we climb out.

"I thought you said that we didn't need to bring anything?"

"We didn't. Ender is just sucking up 'cause he wants to marry into this family one day."

Ender flips Gray off, passing me one of the bouquets and I shove Marley's leash at Gray as I take them.

"For me?"

"Yeah."

"Thanks, Ender," I say, breathing in the sweet floral scent.

"Yeah," Gray drawls, looking suspiciously at his friend.

Ender just grins back at Gray and I think it might be the first time that I've seen the man smile. Gray mentioned that he had seen some shit overseas and was still trying to work past some things. Looks like working at Eye Candy Ink with the guys is helping.

"Come inside!" Rooney yells from the front porch and the dogs both go crazy trying to get to him.

Gray takes Marley's leash from me so that I don't have to try to hold on to her and the flowers. I follow him up the stairs and inside. Cat, Maxine, and Sayler are waiting for me just inside the door and Ender passes each of them a bouquet of flowers. I smile when I see that Cat has the biggest one.

"Welcome," Maxine says. "Let me introduce you to everyone."

Gray is busy talking with Rooney and Ender while he tries to wrestle the dogs to stay still. He looks over, making sure that I'm alright and I smile, nodding slightly as I follow after the girls out onto the back patio.

"This is my mom, Trixie, and my dad, Zeke," Maxine says, starting the introductions.

I do my best to keep the names straight as we move around the backyard, meeting all of her aunts and uncles. When I meet Indie and Mischa, I know right away that they're Rooney's parents and it's not because they look alike, though they do. They have the same chaotic energy about them as their son and I like them right away.

Atlas and Darcy are more relaxed and sensible, just like their son, Harvey, and Nico and Edie remind me of Banks with his easy-going energy.

"Is Coraline coming?" I ask as I take a seat with Cat and Sayler.

"She has to work. Her boss is a real workaholic," Cat says and I see her mom and dad both laugh.

"Max is her boss," Sayler tells me and I nod, finally getting the joke.

My eyes stray to Ender and I wonder if Max and Sam know how he feels about their daughter. Ender bought every woman flowers and I can tell that he's trying to make a good impression on Sam and the rest of the family. He must be serious about him and Cat.

"Here you go," Gray says as he passes me a mimosa.

"Thanks," I say as he nods and bends down to let the dogs off their leashes so that they can go explore the backyard.

Rooney takes off after them, two balls and some other dog toys in his hand, and Gray groans and goes to join him.

I smile, taking a sip of my drink. It's stronger than I thought it would be but the orange juice is refreshing so I take another sip.

"How are things going between you two?" Sayler asks and I take a bigger drink.

Maxine and Cat laugh at that.

"Oh, that good, huh?" Cat jokes and I laugh.

"Everything is still status quo."

"That sucks," Sayler groans and I giggle.

I think the alcohol is hitting me already and I look around for something to eat.

"Food will be ready soon!" Zeke calls and looks over to see Rooney, Harvey, Ender, Banks, and Gray standing over in the yard, drinking and playing with the puppies.

"How are things with you and Rooney?" I ask Sayler, trying to change the conversation.

"Good, really good actually."

"Where did he take you for your first date?" I ask and she launches into the story.

Rooney has been into Sayler since he met her at Coraline's food truck. She finally agreed to go out with him and they had their second date just a few nights before.

"It was this treehouse restaurant and it was so cool! The food was great too," Sayler says dreamily.

"I didn't know that there was anything like that around

here," Maxine says, taking a sip of her own mimosa.

"Me either. Rooney found it somehow."

Indie joins us, passing around another round of mimosas and I down the last of my first glass quickly before I take the second.

"What are you going to do about Gray?" Maxine asks as she looks over to the guys who are still playing in the yard.

"I have no idea," I admit with a sigh. "I don't want to risk our friendship."

"He wants you too. Everyone can see it," Cat says and I notice her own eyes dip over toward Ender.

"But if everyone can see how I feel for him, then he probably can too, and since he hasn't done anything about it, then I think I have my answer," I say, rambling on.

Cat, Sayler, and Maxine all stare blankly at me after that, so I down the rest of my second mimosa.

"Maybe he can't see it?" Maxine suggests. "He could be scared to lose you too."

"Yeah, you should do something to push him and make him admit his feelings," Sayler says, getting excited about the idea.

I think the alcohol must really be hitting me now because their idea doesn't sound so bad all of a sudden.

"So, I'm just supposed to seduce him?" I ask as someone passes me another mimosa.

"Yeah!" Cat and Sayler say and I can tell that they're pretty tipsy too.

"Food is done!" Zeke calls and I stand, wobbling slightly as I follow everyone over to grab a plate.

I mull over their words, laughing and downing a few more mimosas as I enjoy hanging out with my friends. Gray comes to see if I'm ready to leave around four p.m. and by then, I'm pretty drunk.

We say our goodbyes and I let Gray help me out to the car. Moose and Marley are already inside and I giggle as they jump on my lap.

"Let me help you buckle up," Gray says, laughing at my inebriated state.

The dogs lick his face and that looks like fun. Gray is gone before I can try it myself and he drives us back home.

"We should walk them again before we go back upstairs. Maybe get you some fresh air."

"Okay," I say as he helps pull me from the passenger seat.

I take Marley's leash and we start to head down the sidewalk. I stumble a few times as we round the block and Gray reaches out to steady me as we come to a stop in front of our building.

"Those mimosas were strong," I say with a giggle and Gray grins down at me.

"I can see that."

I stare up into his eyes and marvel at the way his gaze makes me burn brighter than any liquor ever made me feel.

"Careful," Gray says and I notice that Moose and Marley have managed to wrap their leashes around us like in *101 Dalmations*.

I find that hilarious and I can't seem to stop laughing.

"Let's get you upstairs," Gray says, trying to untangle us.

I brush my lips across his cheek as he bends down to unwrap the leashes from around our legs.

"I love you," I sigh into his ear and I notice Gray's whole body goes stock still but I'm too drunk to care right now.

Gray doesn't say anything as he untangles us and I sigh happily as he takes my hand and leads me up the stairs.

NINE

Gray

NORA GROANS as she stumbles into the kitchen the next morning. I grin, taking in her tousled hair and wrinkled pajamas.

"'Morning," I say sunnily and she groans at me as she takes a seat at the kitchen counter and rests her head on her arms.

"I made pancakes," I try again and she reaches a hand out.

I hand her one and watch as she slowly eats it.

"I'm never drinking again."

"Yeah, yeah. I've heard that before."

"I mean it this time."

"I'm sure that you do. Here," I say as I pass her another pancake.

Moose and Marley are sitting by my feet and I rip a pancake in half, tossing it to them.

"I've got to work tomorrow night so I'll have to miss taco

Tuesday, but I was thinking that maybe we could do it tonight instead."

"Sure," Nora says, swallowing her last bite of pancake.

"Or, I thought that we could go out somewhere nicer. Maybe more romantic."

Nora's head snaps up and she studies me.

"Uh, sure."

That's not exactly the reaction that I was hoping for but maybe she's still just hungover. I had come up with the genius idea to ask her out last night after she told me that she loved me. It wasn't exactly clear if she meant as more than a friend so I thought I should ask her out but be a little vague about it too. Kind of test the waters.

"I've got to get to work. Let me know if you need anything," I say, rounding the counter and brushing a kiss against the top of her head.

I've done it a hundred times over the past twenty years so it should feel natural but we both seem to tense at the contact.

I head to work but I can barely concentrate all day. It feels like my life is on a precipice. Either tonight goes well, and I get my happily ever after. Or it goes terribly wrong, and I lose everything that matters to me.

My shift comes to an end right at five. I usually have Mondays off unless one of my clients insists on it. I only had to come in to do a back piece today. It took most of the day but it came out badass.

Nora is at home working when I walk in the door and she seems surprised to see me. That means that she got lost in her work and lost track of time. My dream of a romantic date is seeming less likely by the second.

"Hey, are you hungry?" I ask her and she bites her lip.

"Yeah, but I have another half an hour left here. Can we

just walk the dogs and grab tacos at that place on the corner?"

"Sure," I tell her as I head back to my room to take a shower and get changed.

She's just finishing up with work when I come back out and I hook Moose and Marley up as Nora tugs her shoes on.

"How was your day?" she asks and I tell her about the back piece that I did today as we stroll with the puppies toward the taco place.

"What about you?" I ask as we stop to let them sniff something.

"I got caught up with a programming project for that micromanaging client."

"Are you done working for him then?"

"Yeah, I hope so anyway. He's been such a headache."

She fills me in on an exciting project that she has up next and even though I barely understand all of the technology lingo, it's still nice to sit and listen to her talk about something that she loves so much.

"Want me to hold the dogs or run in and grab the food?"

"Food," Nora says, grabbing Moose's leash.

I chuckle and head inside, grabbing our usual. The sun is just starting to set when we turn around and head back to our place. We take turns juggling leashes and tacos and I laugh as I watch Nora try to eat queso and walk Marley at the same time.

We take our time walking back home, both enjoying being with each other and the warm weather. The food is gone by the time we get home and I reach over, taking Nora's hand in mine.

"This was nice."

"Yeah, it was," Nora says with a smile.

She squeezes my hand and I grin. This right here. If I

could just have this every day for the rest of my life then I would die a happy man.

My heart is beating so fast that it feels like everyone we pass should be able to hear it. It's now or never. Either I make my move now or I have to let this crush, this obsession go, and be okay with us just being friends.

I slow to a stop, tugging on Nora's hand until she turns to face me. She looks up at me and her eyes sparkle in the fading sun. She's the most beautiful thing that I've ever seen in my life and I know that it's now or never.

"Nora," I whisper and I see her breath catch as I move closer to her.

She licks her lips, just like she did in the hotel room after the funeral the night that we almost kissed. My heart starts to race as every cell in my body urges me closer to her.

The puppies are busy sniffing a nearby tree and I move closer to her, bending down until our lips are a breath away. Nora's eyes flutter closed and I close the remaining distance, my lips touching hers for the first time.

They're so soft against my own and I moan, kissing her more firmly. Our lips lock together like they were made to and I wrap my free hand around her waist, pulling her flush against my body.

Nora's hand is tangled in my hair, holding me to her as if I would try to get away and I lick along the seam of her lips. She opens for me right away and I waste no time slipping my tongue inside and exploring every inch of her.

Her tongue tangles with mine in an erotic dance and we both move closer until we're plastered together. I wonder if she can feel how hard I am, my erection digging into her stomach. Or maybe she can feel the intensity coming off of me in waves.

The dogs start to bark but it barely filters into my

subconscious as I continue to make out with Nora. It isn't until they tug on the leash, chasing after some squirrel that the spell is broken.

We pull apart then, both of us wide-eyed and breathing hard as we try to get the puppies and our racing hearts under control.

"Fucking finally," Nora says and I can't help but laugh.

She laughs too as I drag her and the puppies up the stairs and into our place.

TEN

Nora

GRAY KICKS the door closed behind us, pinning me to the wood as he licks his lips, his blue eyes darkening as he watches my every movement. The puppies are happy to be back home and disappear into their crate where they start playing with their toys, the constant squeaking making me giggle.

He smiles down at me and I slide my hands up his chest. Soon, we've both forgotten all about the puppies and are lost in each other once more. I love the way that he looks at me, even after all of these years. Like I'm the most important thing in his world.

I lean up on my tiptoes, my lips a breath away from his and he gets the memo. His lips come crashing down on mine and we both moan. Gray takes a step closer to me, caging me against the door with his firm body and I moan, loving the feel of him pressed against me.

"Fuck, Nora," Gray breathes against my mouth and I moan.

Gray reaches behind his neck and tugs his shirt off in one smooth movement and my eyes hungrily eat up every inch of exposed skin. His tattoos are on display and I run my fingers over them. I rarely get to see the ones on his torso and I don't want to miss this opportunity.

Tattoos snake up his arms and across his chest. I know that he has a few on his back as well and some running down his ribs on his left side. I don't know where to look first but when his fingers fall to the button of his jeans, I forget all about his tattoos.

He unbuttons his pants and tugs down the zipper before he pushes them down his thighs and kicks them off. His black boxer briefs are clinging to his thighs, the front tented with his impressive erection.

My mouth waters at the sight and I look up into his eyes. It's like we're finally on the same page because we both reach for my clothes and it's like I can't get naked fast enough.

Gray's hands go to my hips and I jump, wrapping my legs around his waist. His thick cock rubs against my folds and I try to remember when he took his boxers off. When his dick rubs against my clit, all thoughts leave my mind.

"You're pierced," I breathe as I feel the metal barbell running just under the head of his cock rub against me.

"Yeah," Gray says, his cheeks stained a faint pink. "I heard... it's supposed to be pretty great for the woman."

"Oh," I half say, half moan as he continues to carry me.

His cock rubs against me in the most mind-blowing way as he carries me down the hallway but I know that I need to tell him something before all of the fun starts.

"I've never, um..." I start as he carries me into his bedroom.

"I know. Me either," he admits and I smile up at him as he lays me down on the bed.

I want to tell him that I waited for him, but then his mouth is on my neck, his fingers in my hair and I shut up, just wanting to experience it.

Having Gray's hands and mouth on me feels like a dream. I've wanted this for so long that part of me expects to wake up in bed alone.

My fingers tangle in his dark hair as he sucks and nips at my neck. His cock is still between my legs and we move together. He's not penetrating me, just sliding along my folds and driving me wild.

He moves lower, his lips caressing over the swell of my breast until his lips capture one of my nipples. He sucks the stiff peak into his mouth, his tongue rolling over the pebble until my back arches off of the bed.

His mouth is so warm, his tongue teasing as he flicks it back and forth over the stiff peak. Soon my hips are rising, trying to rub against him, to take him inside of me where I ache for him, as he continues to play with my breasts.

He switches to the other one as he reaches down and I can't take it any longer.

"I need more," I half sob and he takes pity on me, sliding lower down my body until his face is level with my dripping pussy.

His fingers spread me as his tongue licks a path to my core.

"Gray!" I scream as he sucks my clit into his mouth, rolling his tongue over it until I see stars.

He licks another path up my core, his tongue swirling

around my opening, dipping inside slightly, teasing me before he circles my clit, sucking it into his mouth again.

I didn't think it was possible, but having Gray between my legs is even better than all of the times that I had fantasized about him.

It isn't long before I can feel a strange pressure filling me, cresting like a wave and I go sailing along with the surf, crashing down with the waves.

"I... I'm—"

I don't get the words out before I'm coming on his lips, my legs wrapped around his head like a vise as I ride out my pleasure.

"You taste so fucking good," Gray says as he kisses his way back up my body.

He kisses me and I can taste myself on his lips. It's erotic and has me ready for another orgasm.

"Are you ready?" Gray asks and I nod, trying to calm the nerves as he lines his cock up at my opening and slowly starts to push inside of me.

He leans down, kissing me, and I focus on that instead of the slight sting of pain as he sinks inside of me completely.

Gray pulls away, his brow furrowed as he sucks in a quick breath like he's in pain, and I freeze.

"Are you alright?" I ask, concerned.

"I've just never felt anything so fucking good before. Fuck, Nora. You're the best thing that I've ever felt in my life."

He starts to move and we both groan. I can feel that piercing of his rubbing against my front wall and I moan, trying to move my hips so that I can feel it rub me more.

My legs wrap around his waist, wanting to take him deeper into me. When the base of his cock grinds down on my clit, I gasp, my nails digging into his shoulders. That seems to spur him on because he really starts to move then.

"It feels so good," I cry out, my back arching off the bed as he pounds into me.

Gray grunts, his fingers digging into my hips as he ruts into me, losing any finesse that he had.

He changes the angle and I scream in ecstasy as he hits some secret spot deep within me. His piercing rubs against the spot and I fall apart, coming all over his cock as he pounds into me.

"Fuck, Nora, fuck," Gray grits out, his eyes squeezed shut tight as he finds his own release and I moan as he keeps slowly rocking into me.

We're both smiling as he slowly pulls out and falls onto his side next to me. I breathe out a laugh, my eyes falling closed as he pulls me into his arms.

He kisses my shoulder, his face nuzzling my neck and I feel myself start to fall asleep. I dream about Gray and I in the future and when I wake, it's with a smile on my face.

ELEVEN

Gray

WHEN I WAKE up the next morning with Nora spread out on top of me, I think that maybe I've died and gone to heaven. Her hair is in my face and I gently brush it away. When I catch my scent on her skin, I can't hold back any longer.

I kiss her shoulder, her neck, her pulse point and Nora groans in her sleep, her hips starting to rock on top of me.

I can feel how wet she is as she grinds on me but I know that she must be sore after last night so I wedge my hand between us, my fingers finding her clit and applying pressure.

"Gray... yes, don't stop," she moans.

As if I could.

I growl, slipping two fingers into her and curling them to find that spot that drives her wild. She presses down, grinding on the heel of my palm as her breath starts to come in choppy pants.

My cock is aching and having her squirming on top of me doesn't help, so I gently roll her onto her side on the mattress, still moving my fingers inside of her as I bend down and kiss a path from her neck down to her perky tits.

Her head falls back, her mouth open in a silent cry and I bite down on her nipple as she goes over the edge. My thumb circles her clit, trying to prolong her pleasure for as long as I can.

I nuzzle my face into her neck as she starts to wake more fully and pull back to meet her eyes.

"Hey," she whispers and I smile down at her gently.

"Hey."

"Last night really happened?" Nora whispers and I tense, wondering if she regrets it.

"Yeah, it did," I whisper back.

"And this morning... that wasn't a dream?"

"Nope."

"Hmm," she hums as her fingers circle around my thick length and I groan, my eyes rolling back in my head.

Nora laughs, the sound like a siren's call as she rolls me onto my back and licks a path down my chest.

"Nora," I moan, her name the only word in my head as her lips wrap around my tip. "You don't have to do this."

She only takes me deeper into her mouth and I shut up, letting her do whatever the hell she wants to me.

I'm still on edge from her grinding on top of me and it doesn't take long for me to feel the familiar tingles at the base of my spine.

"Fuck... I'm going to come," I warn her and she takes one last suck of my cock before she slides up my body.

"I want to be on top," she says huskily as she rolls her hips and takes me into her body.

"Yes, fuck," I hiss as she sinks down, taking all of me.

She's so tight, so fucking wet, that I swear I see stars. I have to grit my teeth to keep from coming inside of her the second that she's fully seated.

"So big," she moans, circling her hips and I try to think of math or baseball stats. Anything but what she's doing to me.

Her nails dig into my chest as she starts to move and I can't stop myself from looking then.

She's gorgeous.

Her thick brown hair is mussed around her face and shoulders, her cheeks are flushed, her mouth slightly parted as she moves. Her eyes are glazed and filled with so much lust that it threatens to burn me up.

She bucks her hips, lifting and falling on my length in a steady rhythm but when I lean forward, taking one of her nipples into my mouth, she starts to grow unsteady. I can tell that she's close now and thank fuck because so am I.

Two more thrusts and she's falling over the edge, her pussy clamping down around me and taking me with her.

"Shit," she says against my shoulder and I nod, too out of breath to form words.

"Oh shit!" she says, louder this time and I frown as she jumps off of me and races into the bathroom.

"Uh, is everything okay?" I call, starting to follow her and she mumbles something that I don't catch.

"I forgot about my meeting! I'm going to be late!"

I turn and head for the kitchen then, thoughts of trying shower sex with her disappearing as I move to make her breakfast.

She comes into the kitchen a few minutes later, her hair only partially dried. She's got her black business skirt and blazer on, her shirt still untucked and I pass her the bagel that I made for her and the bag of nuts.

"Thank you," she says, kissing my cheek and bolting for the door.

"See you tonight!" I call and she waves as she rushes out.

I grin as I eat my own breakfast and get ready for the day.

I basically skip into work an hour later and that catches everyone's attention right away but I can't even be annoyed by Rooney's sly grin.

"So, you finally told Nora then," Ender says as soon as he catches sight of me.

"What gave it away?"

"The fact that your face looks like it's about to split in two from you smiling like that."

I laugh at that and Ender smiles.

"I'm happy for you. So, how did you finally ask her out then?" he asks.

"Looking for tips, Ender?" Rooney asks as he joins us.

"Not from you," Ender says as he crosses his arms and leans against the doorframe.

"Well, just so you know, no one asks people to go steady anymore."

Ender grins at that and I laugh but suddenly his words hit me and my stomach drops.

The truth is that I didn't really ask her out. I mean, I did, but does she know that? We didn't actually go to the romantic restaurant that I had booked for us. Grabbing tacos with the puppies was still fun, but was it obvious enough that it was a date?

We did have sex after but even that was casual, especially this morning. Does she know how much I want her, how much I've always wanted her? Does she think that this was just a friends with benefits thing? Or that I was blowing off steam?

My good mood has plummeted and I try not to panic.

This has to be an easy fix. I'll just go home tonight and lay my cards on the table. Then we can be sure that we're together.

"Here's the schedule!" Maxine calls as she and Ames hurry in the front door.

She giggles, swatting his hand away and I want that.

Harvey is off today so Rooney hangs out with us as Ames disappears into the back office with Maxine. I'm sure that he's just trying to stay away from the room and any sounds that he might hear since Maxine is practically a sister to him.

"I've got four clients today. A rib, two on the feet, and finishing up that sleeve," Rooney says as he passes the schedule to Ender.

"I've got a chest piece and..."

"Two tramp stamps," Rooney says, cackling evilly.

It's no secret that Ender hates doing tramp stamps. I wince at him as he sighs and passes me the sheet of paper.

"What do you have, Gray?" Ender asks and I smile.

"A half sleeve and a chest piece."

"Lucky bastard," Ender groans as he heads into his room.

I smile after him and head into my room to get ready for the day. All day I practice in my head what I'm going to say to Nora when I get home tonight.

Ender is in a terrible mood as the two giggling girls leave. It's just me and him left in the shop since everyone else finished and left already.

"That bad?" I ask and he grunts.

He checks his phone as we lock up and head across the

lot toward my car. Usually Ender walks to and from work since he lives so close but this time he stops next to my car.

He's glaring down at his phone and I watch him curiously.

"Everything alright?" I ask.

"Nope. I need a ride."

"Sure, to where?"

"Sayler's place."

He yanks the passenger side door open and I wonder what the hell is going on. The car ride to Sayler and Coraline's place is filled with tense silence.

I park and Ender is already out of the car and headed for the front door.

"Okay then," I mumble, wondering if I should wait here.

I debate for a minute before I start to follow after him.

I only make it a few steps before my phone rings and I pull it out to see my brother's name on the screen.

"Hey, everything alright?" I ask as soon as the call connects.

"Yeah, yeah. I'm fine. I was going through the house stuff and well, we should talk about some of it. Are you still at work?"

"No, I'm just headed home now."

"Well, I talked to the realtor and she thinks that we should spend the money to fix the place up before we sell it. Well, first she asked if I was sure that I didn't want to keep it since real estate is such a good investment and this part of Rosewood is really trending up. Do you want the house?"

"Fuck no," I hiss out and he kind of half laughs.

"Yeah, I figured."

"Do you?"

"No. I think we should tear the place down and rebuild

though. It might actually be cheaper since Dad didn't keep up on any of it and the roof needs to be replaced along with at least half of the pipes."

Jasper sounds exhausted and a pang of guilt hits me. I've just left my brother to clean up another one of our father's mess.

"I'm sorry, Jasper," I whisper and the line goes silent.

"For what?" he asks after a beat and I swallow.

"For hating you so much for the past seven years. I know that you were just doing what you thought was right, what you thought would be able to provide for us and I've been an asshole. I was so mad at you for leaving me with him."

"I didn't have a choice. Not if we wanted to eat."

"I know. I know that, but I still kind of blamed you."

We're silent as those words sink in and I take a deep breath.

"Did you even want to join the military?"

"It was a job," he says after a minute and I feel like an even bigger asshole.

I've been holding a grudge against my brother for years, blaming him for leaving me with our dad, and here he was working and fighting, doing a job that he didn't even want to do to provide for me.

"I'm sorry, Jasper."

"It's alright. It's not your fault. You were just a kid."

"So were you."

We are silent as I lean against the side of the building, staring blankly across the street.

"I can come home and help you with the house."

"You don't have to do that."

"Yeah, I do. It isn't all your problem, Jasper. I'll talk to my boss tomorrow and see when I can take time off."

"Thanks, Gray," Jasper says after a minute and I can hear the emotion in his voice.

I can only imagine everything that he's been through in the past few years. I don't know how he doesn't hate me for the way that I treated him. I was so mean to him and he was sacrificing everything to give me a better, more stable life.

"I'll talk to you soon."

"Yeah," he says and we hang up a minute later.

I lean against the building for another minute, staring up at the starry night sky. The apartment building door bangs open and I look up in time to see Ender carrying Cat over his shoulder. He heads past me, nodding in my direction as he grabs Cat's keys from her and I laugh as I watch them go.

I forgot that tonight was girl's night. That means that Nora is probably upstairs too. For a second, I think about going to grab her just like Ender did, but I don't want to interrupt her night. I know how much she looks forward to hanging out with her friends every week. Looks like I'll have to wait until tomorrow to have that talk with her.

It's probably for the best. I'm not in a great place mentally or emotionally right now.

I sigh as I head back over to my car and head home.

TWELVE

Nora

I HAD THOUGHT that things were finally happening between Gray and me but after last night, I'm not so sure. It had been girl's night and I had been over at Sayler and Coraline's place for most of the night.

I expected Gray to be up and waiting for me when I got home, but he was fast asleep in his own bed. I had debated waking him but I was pretty drunk and just wanted to get some sleep. I thought that we would have time together this morning but then I overslept and by the time I woke up, he was already at work.

It feels strange, like our bubble has already popped and now doubts are starting to sink in.

What's going to happen now? Are we officially together? Why hasn't Gray brought it up? Was it just a friends with benefits moment? Does he regret it?

I know that Gray isn't like that. He would die before he hurt me, so he wouldn't be taking any of this lightly and he wouldn't risk our decades-old friendship for one night together.

Still, I need to talk to him soon before even more doubts start to hit me.

Moose and Marley both start barking and dancing around by the front door and I know that Gray must be home so I set my laptop aside and stand.

"Hey," I say as he comes through the door.

"Hey," he says and he looks and sounds exhausted.

"What's wrong?" I ask him, wrapping my arms around his waist.

"It's just been a really long day and I have the worst headache. I'm going to take some Tylenol and take a shower."

"Okay, want me to grab soup or something for you?"

"Sure, thanks," he says with a tired smile.

I watch him head back to his room with a frown and turn to grab my phone to order some food. It's then I see that I have a text from Cat. I had messaged her to see how last night went after Ender had stormed into Sayler and Coraline's apartment, growled at Cat, thrown her over his shoulder and left.

CAT: **Yeah, that was pretty wild, but I promise you that I'm more than fine.**

Nora: I'll bet

Cat: How are you and your beau doing?

Nora: I'm not sure.

Cat: Just tell him that you're in love with him already!

Nora: We kind of hooked up the other night.

Cat: What!?? And you're just telling me this now?

Nora: Sorry, I wanted to talk to Gray before I told other people but now things are weird between us.

Cat: How so?

Nora: We just haven't really talked or hung out since. He just got home and said he has a headache so he's in the shower.

Cat: Go nurse him back to health!

Nora: What if he regrets it?

Cat: He is literally head over heels in love with you so that's not an option.

Nora: But you don't know that for sure.

Cat: Anyone with eyes knows that. Trust me.

I BITE MY BOTTOM LIP. Could she be right?

NORA: **I've got to go. He's about to come out.**

Cat: Good luck! Let me know if you need anything!

Nora: Will do!

GRAY COMES out of his bedroom and I tuck my phone into my pocket before I remember that I never ordered the food.

"Chicken noodle soup? Or do you want broccoli cheddar soup?"

"Either works," he says and I pull up the bistro on the corner and order some soup and sandwiches.

"Are you feeling better?" I ask as he takes a seat on the couch.

"Yeah. I, uh, I got a call from Jasper."

"Is he alright?" I ask, alarmed.

"Yeah, but I need to go back to Rosewood and help him with the house for a week or two."

"Is that why you have a headache?"

"Yeah. It was hard working my schedule around so that I had enough time off. I'm going to owe everyone at the shop a huge thank you for taking on a few of my clients."

I let out a big sigh and Gray looks at me curiously.

"Everything alright with you?"

"Yeah, I just thought that maybe you had regrets or something about..." I trail off and Gray looks at me like I'm insane.

"Nora, I don't want there to be any confusion. This is something that I should have done a long time ago."

"Okay," I say, my palms sweating as I turn to face him on the couch.

"I love you, Nora. Of course, I don't regret it. I've wanted you my whole fucking life. I thought that maybe you didn't want me."

"I've always wanted you," I say with a laugh, relief flooding through me. "I've been in love with you since we were kids but—"

"But you were afraid to tell me because if I didn't feel the same, it would have ruined everything," he finishes and I nod.

"Yeah."

"Yeah," he says, his fingers tangling with mine.

"Say it again," I tell him as he pulls me closer to him on the couch.

"I love you, Nora."

"I love you too, Gray."

"Fucking finally," he says with a smile a second before his lips meet mine.

THIRTEEN

Gray

ONE YEAR LATER...

"READY?" I ask Nora as she finishes typing something on her computer.

"Yeah."

She leans over to kiss my cheek and I smile, taking her hand and admiring the diamond ring that I put on her hand ten months ago.

We've been saving up for the past few months for our wedding we're going to have next month and I can't wait. It feels like I've waited my whole life to make Nora mine and it's about damn time that it became a reality.

"Sit," Nora says and Moose and Marley both plop down, tails wagging against the ground as we hook their leashes to their collar.

"Want to go to the dog park?" Nora asks and I nod, taking her hand in mine as we head down the stairs.

Both puppies are grown and to be honest, they're a lot bigger than I thought that they would get. Luckily for us, they're trained now and pretty well behaved.

We turn left once we get outside and start to head the few blocks over to where the dog park is. We stumbled upon it a few weeks ago when we were out walking and the dogs love it. It's pretty close to where Rooney, Harvey, Sayler, and Coraline live and since they now have dogs, we like to meet them there and let them play.

"Jasper called today. He said that him and Evangeline are planning on coming up two Wednesdays before. She wanted to help you with any of the wedding plans that she could."

"That's so sweet of her," Nora says, swinging our hands slightly and I smile.

Jasper hadn't been surprised at all when I told him that Nora and I were together. I had gone back home for two weeks and the two of us bonded and tore down our child-hood home. Jasper had already hired a contractor to rebuild there and we sold the house for a profit last month.

I wasn't surprised when Jasper said that he would be staying in Rosewood. He was always obsessed with Evangeline when we were kids and it seemed his injury and being home for our father's funeral was the second chance that they needed to finally get together.

The two of them bought a house not far from her nursery and he's been helping her take care of her sick mother for the past six months.

Jasper and I got over the awkwardness of the past few years and have actually grown pretty close. We talk almost every week, catching up and learning about each other and we try to see each other every few months. He even let me tattoo him the last time that he was in town.

Business at Eye Candy Ink has been better than ever and now that everyone is settled with their fiancées and girl-friends, things seem better than ever. We still go to Sunday brunch at Zeke's house every week and now that Moose and Marley are trained, they're more welcome.

"Looks like Rooney and Sayler are here," Nora says and I look over to see Rooney wrestling with his Irish wolfhound puppy, Baxter.

"Harvey and Coraline too," I say, nudging Nora until she spots Harvey trying to get his sheepadoodle puppy, Theo, to sit.

It's not going well.

"Want to go show them how it's done?" I ask Moose and he wags his tail excitedly.

"Have fun!" Nora calls as she heads over to talk with Coraline and Sayler.

I give her a kiss before she can get too far and she laughs against my lips. I take Marley from her and head over to join my friends.

If you had told me five years ago that I wouldn't make Nora mine until I was twenty-six, I would have asked you what the hell took me so long, but the truth is that she was always mine. It was finally just the right time for us then. We were both mature, doing well in our careers, and stable financially.

I let Moose and Marley off their leashes and laugh as they head out to play with their friends. Harvey has given up on Theo's training for now and I smile as Rooney tosses a ball and all four dogs take off after it.

I never had much of a family. Nora was always enough for me, but it's even better now that I have my brother and his girl, Evangeline, and the family that I created at Eye Candy Ink.

This is the life that I always wanted but was too scared to even wish for.

Now that I've got it, I'm never letting it go.

FOURTEEN

Nora

FIVE YEARS LATER...

"THAT'S IT. ONE MORE PUSH," the doctor urges me and I glare at her.

She's said just one more push at least ten times now and I'm about to lose it. Gray squeezes my hand, helping me breathe and I try to focus on finally getting this baby out of me.

"Never again," I hiss at him and he nods solemnly. "I mean it. You're never getting that dick anywhere close to me again."

"Got it."

I take a deep breath and focus on the increasing need to push, bearing down as another contraction hits me.

"Fuck!" I scream, gripping Gray's hand so tight that I would be surprised if he doesn't have a few broken bones.

He doesn't complain though. He just keeps pushing my hair away from my face and telling me how incredible I am.

We've been married for four years now and are about to have our first child any minute now. I think both of us were a little apprehensive about becoming parents. We haven't exactly had the best role models but we've watched Rooney, Harvey, and Ames all start their own families and decided that it was time.

We've built a surrogate family here at the shop and with our friends, and I know that we have a pretty great support system. If we ever need anything, I know that we'll have people that we can call on.

Gray and Jasper have only grown closer over the years and I actually love hanging out with Evangeline on family trips too. They've been married for a few years now and are expecting their first child any day now too. I know that Gray is hoping that our baby and his cousin get along.

Jasper and Evangeline still live in Rosewood and while we've been back a few times over the years, we prefer to take trips with them to other places. The last time we were back in Rosewood, we ran into my dad and it was not a pleasant trip. Since then, we've had Christmas in Pittsburgh with everyone else. Evangeline and Jasper both get it and are happy to fly up here to see us or travel somewhere new with us each year.

"I can see the head. Just bear down and give me one big push, Nora!"

I snarl at the doctor, bending forward as I do what she says. I can feel a burning sensation and I swear it hurts like nothing I've ever felt before. Then the pressure is gone and I sag back against the hospital bed, breathing heavy.

Gray and I both hold our breath, our eyes locked on the

doctor and the tiny bundle in her arms until a piercing wail breaks the tense silence and I let out a relieved breath.

"Congratulations! You have a very healthy baby boy."

The doctor rests my baby on my chest and I can't help the tears that escape, rolling down my cheeks.

"You did so good, Nora," Gray whispers before he kisses my head. "I love you."

"I love you too."

We take a moment to admire our newborn baby boy before I hear raised voices outside the door.

"Want me to keep them out?" Gray asks and I laugh.

"I'm not sure that you could."

The door opens then and Rooney and Sayler come rushing in. Harvey, Coraline, Ames, Maxine, Cat, Ender, Banks, and Palmer all come filing in right after them and I smile. I'm not surprised when Mischa, Indie, Atlas, Darcy, Sam, Max, Zeke, Trixie, Nico, and Edie come in next, each carrying so many balloons and stuffed animals that I'd be surprised if the gift shop had any left.

"Have you called Jasper yet?" I ask Gray and he looks at me like I'm crazy.

"When would I have done that?" he asks with a laugh and I sigh.

"Hormones."

"I know," he says, kissing my cheek and then our baby's head.

He takes a step back as Coraline and Sayler come over. I see Gray move over to the corner of the room and make a call, presumably to Jasper and Evangeline. Rooney and Harvey are both trying to calm their own kids and I laugh out loud at the chaos that seems to follow our family.

They're loud and noisy, but I love them all and I know that they love us and would be there for us no matter what.

"So... what's his name?" Sayler asks and I grin, looking over to Gray as he joins me at the side of the bed again.

"Sawyer. Sawyer Weston Mackelroy."

The girls coo over him and I let them take a turn holding them. Gray must see me getting tired because he shoos everyone out after about an hour and places Sawyer back on my chest.

"You're a rock star," he says and I can hear the awe in his voice.

"Thanks. We should get you fed, huh boo?" I ask Sawyer and he buries his face against my breast.

As Gray helps me get settled with our baby, I smile. I don't know why we were worried about being good parents. With a dad like Gray, our kid is going to be just fine.

I can't wait until he's older and asks us how we met. I'm going to tell him that we fell in love when we were kids and that there was only each other for us.

He's going to know that his parents were meant to be.

DID YOU LOVE GRAY? **Please consider leaving a review! You can do so on Amazon, Goodreads, and Bookbub.**

DID **you miss the original Eye Candy Ink series? You can read the boxset here.**

GRAB **the next book in the series, Ender, here!**

. . .

ARE **you curious about Gray's brother, Jasper? Then check out his book, Always, <u>here</u>.**

ARE **you curious about Nora's brother, Niall and Everly? Then check out his book, Fighting Fire With Fire, here.**

ENDER

EYE CANDY INK: SECOND GENERATION

*

Ender Montrose definitely doesn't belong here.

In this club filled with college students and business people who are all half his age.

But he's still here.

Because of her.

Cat Schultz.

The bombshell vixen who stole his breath and his heart the first time that he looked at her.

He's old enough to be her father, but she calms those tortured thoughts in his head and he seems to calm the storm inside of her, too.

Will that be enough to convince her that he's the man for her, though?

Will pursuing Cat ruin everything? Or will he finally get the happily ever after that he's been dreaming about ever since he first laid eyes on her?

ONE

Ender

I TRY to school my features as I elbow my way through the crowd and back over to my friends. Rooney and Gray turn to look at me as I approach our booth with the next round of drinks and when they both look concerned, I know that I'm not succeeding.

I'm pretty sure that everyone that I work with at Eye Candy Ink sees me as the dad. At thirty-nine, I'm older than all of them by at least a decade. They've all been nice though, inviting me out for dinners or to the bar after work. Harvey, Rooney, and Banks are all from Pittsburgh too, so they helped me find an apartment close by and showed me around when I first moved here.

The slow song that was playing turns back to some loud techno beat and I wince, my shoulders tensing as the first note blares over the speakers. Gray nudges me discreetly and I nod at him, letting him know that I'm alright.

I hate clubs and most loud noises. Fireworks are a

freaking nightmare for me. All of that is a leftover scar from my time in the Marines, I'm sure. Every popping sound or loud blast and I'm right back there in the desert, sand and sweat in my eyes as I watch one of my friends get shot.

I blink away the memory and take a long pull of my beer, reminding myself why I'm here.

It's to hang out with my friends, but I also have an ulterior motive.

Her.

Cat Schultz.

My eyes drift up to the second floor and I stare at her office door, willing it to open so I can get a glimpse of my girl.

I wonder if her hair is still dyed that pale pastel orange or if she's switched it up. She probably has. It's been close to three and a half weeks since I saw her last and I know that she usually changes it after three weeks or re-dyes it to freshen up the color.

A cheer goes up over by the bar and I frown as I see a bunch of college kids getting rowdy. They only remind me that I'm the oldest person in this place by quite a few years. Even when I was their age, I never went to places like this.

Growing up, it was just my mom and me. I'm not sure that my mom even knew who my dad was. She wasn't exactly known for being safe with men, and she was terrible at picking them. There weren't many choices in our small town, but she always seemed to have some man around.

It was my mom who signed the forms for me to join the Marines when I was seventeen. I think that she was happy to get rid of me. She used to love to tell me that I was an accident, one that she regretted and between that and her shitty boyfriends that used to steal from us every time they broke up with her, I was itching to get out.

I think it was that life that caused me to crave order and structure so much. I like being in control and I don't need a therapist to tell me that it's because I had none growing up. Maybe that's also why when I think about being with Cat, it's in a different role than just her boyfriend or husband.

I knew that I was never going to have much of a life if I stayed. I'd probably wind up in the trailer down from them since the only jobs in town were at the plastic plant a few miles away.

So, I joined the military. I went through basic training and then was deployed. I moved around a lot, getting orders to different bases and then deploying another handful of times. I was used to that. We didn't always have money for rent, so I tended to keep my possessions to the bare minimum. It made packing up and leaving a lot easier.

I did my twenty and then retired. I knew that I would get money every month, but I wanted something else to fill my time. I had always liked to draw, and I ended up hooking up with an old military buddy out in Wyoming. Wild had become a tattoo artist after he got out, and I apprenticed with him, learning everything I could. When I was done, he pointed me this way and said his buddy, Zeke, was looking to hire for his new shop.

I never expected to get hired at Eye Candy Ink. Everyone knows about the place, and Zeke is a legend in his own right. I figured I would try and then maybe head out west. I heard Sequoia Ink was looking to hire a few more artists and maybe a place like that, in the middle of the forest, would be a better fit for me.

Even after I got the job, I was thinking of leaving for a smaller town. Before I could decide though, I saw Cat for the first time.

I can still remember it like it happened yesterday. Her

hair had been blue back then and she had it tied into two low ponytails. She was laughing, running after Maxine through the rain, and my heart had fucking kicked in my chest.

Mine.

I knew it then. All it took was one moment to have my whole world revolving around the girl.

It took me another two weeks to run into her again, and this time I got a name. I've been trying to see her more and more over the last few months but she always seems to be at work. I know that one of her bartenders quit and another moved, so she's been shorthanded but I hate seeing her so stressed.

I want to help her. I want to see her smile at me. I want to see her blushing as she sinks down on my cock.

I take another drink, shifting in my seat as my eyes drift back to the second floor.

I almost drop my beer bottle when I spot her.

She's standing at the railing, talking to one of her employees and pointing at the screen of her iPad as she shows her something.

My heart starts to race and I smile as I watch her. She's so in control, so confident, and it's sexy watching her in her element.

Her employee walks back down the stairs and Cat heaves a deep breath, crossing her arms and leaning against the railing and looking out over the crowd. She looks like a queen surveying her subjects and my cock presses firmly against the zipper of my jeans as I stare at her.

She's gorgeous.

Her hair is dyed a pale pink that looks like cotton candy around her head. I can see her usual cat eye makeup from here and she's wearing the silver charm bracelet that she always has on. I've bought her at least a dozen new charms to add to it. They're all waiting for her in my top dresser drawer along with a pink diamond ring.

She relaxes against the railing as she stares down at the crowd, but I can still see the dark circles under her eyes and the way that her mouth turns down slightly at the corners and I know that she needs a break.

I want to give that to her. I want to rub her feet as she relaxes in a bubble bath. I want to feed her grapes and steal kisses as she sits in my lap. I want to stretch her across my lap and spank her ass until it's nice and red and she's begging me to fuck her.

Our eyes lock then and I wonder if she can see the lust that I'm sure is clearly written all over my face. There's no way that I can hide it.

I want her more than anything. More than I want my next breath.

I can see her chest rise and fall suddenly and I wonder if she can feel it too. Does she want me even half as bad as I want her?

Her eyes stay locked on mine for one moment that's over far too fast and then she straightens and heads back into her office. Disappointment and a sense of loneliness hits me as soon as she's out of my sight and I sigh, forcing myself to turn back to my friends.

"You should just ask her out already, man. It's obvious that she likes you too," Harvey says to Gray and I know without any other information that they're talking about Gray asking Nora out.

The two of them are best friends but they're obviously in love with each other. Neither of them will just come out and admit it though.

"Yeah, what's the worst that could happen?" Rooney asks and Gray glares at him.

I was deployed with Gray's older brother, Jasper, a few times. Everyone called him Mack since their last name is Mackelroy and I was surprised when he showed up at Eye Candy Ink.

Out of everyone at Eye Candy Ink, I'm the closest to Gray. Maybe it's because I know his brother or because our rooms are right next to each other at the shop so we talk to each other more than the others. We're also two of the three artists who aren't related to someone from the original Eye Candy Ink tattoo shop. The third, Ames, is getting ready to marry into the family so now it's just Gray and I.

"Anyway, Ender, are you finishing that back piece tomorrow?" Gray asks, trying to change the subject and I nod.

"Yeah, I have that and then some smaller arm pieces."

The conversation turns to tattoos and the upcoming week's schedule as we all finish our drinks.

Harvey, Rooney, and Banks all were taught the trade by their parents. Gray and Ames both got certified and did apprenticeships in New York before they got hired at Eye Candy Ink.

"Ready to call it a night?" Banks asks and I can't help but take one last look up at the second floor.

Cat's there, her eyes locked on me as she leans against her office doorframe. I stare back at her, my heart beating like a drum in my ears, blocking out the other noise from the club as we watch each other.

She smiles at me as the others stand and get ready to leave and it hits me then.

Gray isn't the only one who needs to man up and claim his woman.

TWO

Cat

I CAN'T STOP my eyes from trailing after Ender as he cuts through the crowd, the people moving out of his way as he approaches them.

I don't know what it is about the man but I've been drawn to him since I first met him a few months ago. I mean, the man is at least a decade older than me and I'm sure he has way more experience than me. It might actually be impossible for him to have less experience than me. I don't think that one make-out session after prom makes me an expert at the opposite sex.

"Hey, Kitty Cat," Kayley, one of the waitresses at Se7en says as she joins me at the railing.

"Hey, Kayley," I say, trying to remind myself to be patient.

Kayley has worked at the club for a few years and it's obvious that she was expecting to get the manager position.

She tries to suck up to me a lot but I have a feeling that that's more because she knows that my dad owns the club.

I'm sure that she and some of the other employees all think that I only got this job because of my dad but the truth is that I earned it. I have a bachelor's degree in business management and I've worked at Se7en since I was eighteen years old. I've been a waitress and a bartender and every other job in between so that I know how this place runs and can operate it the best possible way.

"Mitch is looking to take a break," Kayley says and I want to remind her that covering the bartender is her job but ever since Callie quit last week, we've been short-handed and I know that I should help out.

"I'll be right down," I tell her and she gives me a fake little smile and turns to head back downstairs.

I look back to where Ender last was but I don't see him or any of the other guys down in the crowd. I sigh, turning to check my phone before I head downstairs to the bar.

There's a text from Nora, my sister Ivy, and my dad asking me how things are going and I send back a quick text to my dad letting him know that I put the ad up for a new bartender a few days ago and I'm going to set up interviews for early next week.

Ivy is overseas, attending University there. Ivy is in love with love and when she got accepted at Oxford, it was her dream come true. She's spent the last three and a half years over there and I only see her on holidays. She's about to graduate though and move back to Pittsburgh and I can't wait for her to be back in the same state as me.

I know that she's my younger sister and I was supposed to be annoyed by her growing up but that was never the case. We were always thick as thieves and we still are, even if I talk to her more over FaceTime and texts these days.

I send her back a message that I'm still in for our weekly breakfast call tomorrow morning. She's been busy with midterms so we haven't talked as much as we usually do. We always have a phone conversation over my breakfast and her dinner though at least once a week.

Nora wants to know about girl's night in a few days and I bite my lip. Things are busy here and I know that I have a lot to take care of, so I should probably skip it but I haven't seen everyone in a few weeks so I send her back a message, letting her know that I'm in and asking what I can bring.

She's probably asleep so I start to tuck my phone away when it buzzes again.

NORA: **Just yourself. I'm excited to see you! It's been too long** ☺

Cat: What's the plan?

Nora: Probably just grab some food and drinks and then Sayler and Coraline invited us over to their place after.

Cat: Sounds good! Talk to you later!

Nora: See you! 👋

I PUT my phone away and make sure that my office door is closed before I head downstairs to relieve Mitch so he can take his break.

The bar is swamped and I jump in, taking orders and grabbing beers from the cooler. Mitch comes back but I stay and help out, making my way to the other end of the bar so that Mitch can take his usual spot.

It's then that I spot Ender sitting at the bar, his eyes

locked on me. Everyone seems to be giving him a wide berth and I'm sure that some think that he's a bouncer or something with the way his black T-shirt stretches across his shoulders and the tattoos snake down his arms.

I thought that he had left with everyone else earlier but I guess he decided to stay. It seems strange since he doesn't ever look like he's having fun when he's here.

There's a different kind of energy around him tonight. Almost like he's determined to do something and I wonder what it could be.

The bar starts to die down and I make sure that Mitch and Alice are good before I head back upstairs. I can't help but look over to Ender and I see him stand as I head toward the end of the bar.

The two of us don't say anything as we walk up the stairs side by side and head into my office. The whole way up to the second floor I try to convince myself that we're just going to chat. We're just being polite since we have the same circle of friends.

I don't think that I believe it though.

The tension between us has my heart racing and my palms sweating.

I close the door behind us and then wonder if that was a mistake. Now there's nowhere for this sexual energy to go.

"Hey, how's it going?" Ender asks, his deep voice causing a shiver to go down my spine.

"Good, busy," I say, trying to figure out if I should sit or keep standing.

"The club seems busy," he says as he takes a step toward me and I nod.

"Yeah, we just lost a bartender so I have to find someone else. Plus, we could use another waitress and maybe a third janitor," I say, rambling on and on. "How's Eye Candy Ink?"

"Good, I think that we're all booked out for a few months."

I nod, searching my brain for something else to say that isn't 'can I touch your beard?'

"I was wondering if you wanted to go out with me sometime," Ender asks and I'm thrown off by the question.

He's interested in me?

He's more worldly, a war hero according to Gray and Rooney, and I've never been outside of Philadelphia.

"I'm uh, I'm really busy here at the club right now," I stall.

My heart and my brain are both screaming at me, wondering what the hell I'm doing turning down the big tattooed man.

"You have to take a break sometime," he says and I find myself nodding before I can even process his words.

"No, I mean I don't really have time for a relationship right now."

"That's a pretty lame excuse."

"I know but it's not an excuse. I just have a lot on my plate right now."

"And I'm not going to add anything. I just want to spend time with you and get to know you."

"You'll have to wait then. I need to find a new bartender, waitress, and finish payroll and that's just this week."

"Okay, I can wait. I'm not giving up that easy."

I don't know what to say to that, so I just watch him.

"I'll see you around, baby girl," he says, his voice wrapping around the nickname.

My nipples pebble in my bra and I try not to blush as I

stare at him. I want to ask him to call me that again but before I can, he's turning and heading for the door and I watch him leave, wondering why I'm so turned on by hearing him call me baby girl in that tone of voice.

I collapse back into my office chair and try to focus on the mountain of work that I need to get through but I can't. Not with Ender's voice calling me baby girl echoing in my head.

THREE

Ender

"YOU DON'T UNDERSTAND MY LOVE," Rooney tells Harvey as I walk into the shop the next morning.

"Oh my god," Banks groans as he leans back in one of the chairs and I head over, taking the one next to him.

"What are they arguing about?" I ask Banks and he rolls his eyes.

"I don't know, man. Something about an apartment?"

"What about you, Ender?" Rooney asks and I frown.

"What about me?"

"Why haven't you ever settled down? Haven't met the future Mrs. Montrose?"

My mind instantly goes to Cat but I know that I can't say I have found the future Mrs. Montrose. Not when she doesn't even know it yet.

"I don't know. Too busy with the Marines and then tattooing, I guess, to ever try to find someone that I wanted to spend the rest of my life with," I say, praying that Rooney lets it go.

"Hmm," he says eyeing me, but Banks shifts in his seat next to me and Rooney goes for him.

"What about you, Banks? You got a girl that you're not telling any of us about?" Rooney asks and I notice that Gray, Ames, and Harvey all stop what they're doing to hear his response.

"Nope," he says but I get the feeling that he's lying and Rooney must too because he doesn't let it drop.

"Really? Are you sure?" he asks and I wonder if he knows something that none of us do.

"I'm sure," Banks says tensely and I decide to help him out.

"Did you pick a best man yet, Ames?" I ask and everyone turns to look at him.

Banks nudges me, mouthing thank you and I nod.

"Not yet. The wedding is still a little ways off."

I nod, pushing to my feet and heading for my room. I need to get everything laid out for today.

"I'm just saying, I think that I would make the better best man," I hear Rooney say to Ames.

"Yeah, I'm not sure that Maxine or my two brothers would agree with that choice," Ames says as he cleans up the front counter and lobby area.

"What do you think, Ender? You would pick me to be your best man, right?" Rooney says as he starts to follow after me and I immediately shake my head.

"Not a chance."

"Right, but I don't mean out of everyone. Just out of the guys in the shop."

"Still no," I tell him as I head into my room.

"Who would you pick?" he asks, following after me and I have to think about it.

I don't have that many close friends. Out of everyone that I know, I think Gray and I are closest. I debate saying Harvey or Ames because I know that it will piss Rooney off but I have a busy day and I know that he'll be back to bug me if I do.

"Gray," I tell him and he pouts.

"We should hang out more, man," Rooney says and I can't help but laugh.

"Yeah, yeah. Don't you have a tattoo to finish?" I ask him with a grin and he bolts down the hallway to his room.

We open in a few minutes and I already have everything ready to go for the day. I just need to prepare the needles and tattoo machine and then I'll be all set.

I only have two clients today but one of them is a back tattoo that will take me at least five hours. I plug my phone in, starting some music as I get to work laying out the designs and needles that I need today. I'm just lining up all of the ink cups when Ames calls my name letting me know that my first client of the day is here.

The day is slow and by the time that I finished both clients, it's well after nine p.m. I know that I should go home take a shower and grab something to eat but I can't help it. I know that I won't be able to sleep until I get my fix of seeing Cat again.

I shower and change, grabbing a slice of pizza on my way to the club. Se7en is packed when I walk in but I pay no attention to the crowd. I don't waste my time waiting for Cat to come down this time.

My eyes drift to the bar first, making sure that Cat isn't there before I look up to her office door on the second floor.

Some blonde waitress is coming out, her mouth turned

down into a sneer as she heads back down the stairs. Cat must be in her office, so I make my way over to the stairs, nodding at the bouncers standing guard there as I head up to the second floor.

I knock but then realize that it's so loud that she probably can't hear me, so I just try the knob. It's unlocked so I step inside, my eyes going right to the desk. Sure enough, Cat is there, her pale pink hair up in a messy ponytail, a can of Coke and a half empty bag of pretzels at her elbow.

She looks exhausted and I'm sure that she's been working most of today. Judging by the stack of papers on her desk, she'll be working for a few more hours tonight. Maybe even after closing.

"Is that your dinner?" I ask, my voice coming out tight.

She needs to eat more than that. She needs to take care of herself. She needs me to take care of her.

"Yeah, I've been swamped here going through resumes and setting up interviews. I'll grab something to eat later," she says, barely looking up.

"You need to eat something. You need to take better care of yourself and if you won't, then I will," I declare and that gets her attention.

"Do you... do you want to take care of me, Ender?" she asks and I grow impossibly hard at the sound of my name on her lips.

"More than anything," I admit and she blushes, looking away from me.

I'm sure that I just came on too intense and she probably needs a minute to adjust.

"I'll be right back," I tell her.

I don't believe that she'll eat later. She'll get so busy that she'll forget so I head back out onto the street and jog the two blocks over to Wild Thyme. Harvey's girl, Coraline, is the head chef and I knock on the back door.

I'm sure that Wild Thyme has a waitlist a month long so this is my best bet at getting my baby girl something decent to eat on no notice.

A dishwasher opens the door a few minutes later and I nod at him.

"Is Coraline around?" I ask and he frowns but pokes his head back inside and I hear him call Coraline.

"Hey, Ender," she says, obviously surprised to see me.

"Hey, Cat forgot her dinner. Think I can grab something for her really quick?" I ask and she smiles.

"Of course! Give me five minutes."

The door closes behind her and I lean back against the wall to wait for my girl's food. Sure enough, five minutes later the back door opens and Coraline hands me a bag stuffed full of takeout containers that smells delicious.

"Thank you so much," I tell her gratefully.

"Anytime. Tell Cat that I'll see her Thursday for girl's night!" Coraline calls as she heads back inside.

"Will do. See you later," I say with a wave as I head back to the club.

The bouncers are starting to get used to me coming here and they wave me inside without having to wait in line. The same happens at the stairs and I head inside Cat's office, setting the bag down on the corner of her desk so that nothing spills onto her papers.

"Take a break," I tell her and she nods, her stomach growling as she smells the bag of food.

"Wild Thyme? Did you get the truffle macaroni and cheese?" she asks as she stands and looks over as I take the takeout containers out.

"I don't know. I just told Coraline that it was for you

and she made the food. She says that she's excited to see you at girl's night on Thursday."

Cat nods, popping a garlic parmesan fry into her mouth as she opens up a container. She smiles brightly as she sees the truffle macaroni and cheese and I pass her a fork, happy to see her so happy.

"So, you're still looking for a bartender then?" I ask as we take our seats.

"Yeah. We had a lot of people apply on the ad and I just need to go through the resumes and then finish the interviews."

"When are the interviews?" I ask her as she pops some more macaroni and cheese into her mouth.

"Later this week."

"Good, hopefully you can find someone then."

She nods, finishing off the macaroni and cheese and I pass her the next container. This one is steak and some roasted vegetables and she happily pops a piece of broccoli into her mouth.

"What about you? What did you do today at Eye Candy Ink?"

"I had a back piece and then just a small one on this girl's arm. Nothing too exciting. Rooney is trying to be Ames' best man," I add and Cat giggles at that.

I would happily tell her all about Rooney's antics if it got her to make that sound.

She eats in silence for a few minutes, quickly finishing off the steak and vegetables and I wonder if she skipped lunch as well. I pass her the last of the fries and then hand her the chocolate cake for dessert.

"Thanks for grabbing me all of this. You didn't have to do that."

"I know, but like I said, I want to."

"You really meant that then? About wanting to take care of me?"

"Of course."

She stands, gathering up her empty takeout containers and I watch as she tucks them all back in the bag to be thrown out.

There's a moment of silence and I can see Cat working up to say something. Her cheeks are starting to blush a bright shade of red and my cock hardens at the sight.

"What is it, baby girl?" I ask her and her breathing quickens at the term of endearment.

"I'm a virgin," she blurts out and it's obvious she expects this to be some kind of deal breaker.

"Good."

"Good?" she asks, obviously surprised.

"Yes, good. That means that my little baby girl was saving herself just for me."

I reach out, my hands snagging her waist and I drag her down into my lap. She squirms on top of my dick and I bite the inside of my cheek to stop from blowing my load right then and there. I can tell that she's getting excited but I don't want to rush this with her.

I tilt her face up, my thumb tracing over her full lips. They part under my touch and I hear her sudden intake of breath as her eyes meet mine. She leans toward me and I can't wait another second to feel her lips on mine.

Cat gasps as my lips brush against hers for the first time and my cock pulses in my jeans at the sound. I seize the opening and slip my tongue into her mouth to tangle with hers.

I have to coax her tongue to come out and play with mine but soon her arms are wrapped around my head, her tongue is in my mouth and she's grinding as best she can on the ridge in my pants.

"More, daddy," Cat begs and I almost come in my pants at the title but it seems to act as a bucket of cold water on her.

She scrambles off my lap and even though I want to grab her and hold her to me, I know that she's embarrassed right now and needs time to come around. I need to show her that I want to be her *daddy*. I want all of the responsibilities and honor that comes with that title. I want to be her world.

"I need... I need you to leave," she whispers and I nod.

"I will. I just want to say one thing first. I know that this is right and that part of being a daddy is knowing what's right for you. I know that you need time to think about everything in that pretty head of yours."

I grab her phone off her desk and open up a new contact, adding my name and number and saving it.

"You can call me when you're ready, baby girl."

Cat is blushing and not meeting my eyes and I slip my fingers under her chin, tilting her face up until her eyes meet mine.

"Just don't take too long," I warn her and she nods.

I head for the door then, wishing that I was leaving with my baby girl by my side.

Soon, I promise myself.

FOUR

Cat

DADDY. I can't believe that I called him that in the middle of us making out.

I had been so embarrassed when that word popped out. Don't get me wrong, it had felt right, but then I started to overthink things.

Why would I call him that? I don't have daddy issues so what does it mean that I wanted to call him my daddy? And most importantly, why wasn't he grossed out?

It's been two days and while I've done some research and learned that being into the daddy and little girl stuff doesn't mean that you have daddy issues. That's just a dumb stereotype. It's just a kink, an age-play and role play between two consenting adults.

One line from my research has stuck with me. It said 'she gives the control to daddy and trusts he will do what's best for her.'

That's what I want.

I've been on top of everything since I was a kid. Homework, work, getting into a good college and then excelling at my degree. I was in charge of all of that and now I'm in charge of this club. It can be a lot, especially when we're short on staff.

I just want someone to take control. Just for a little bit.

I just want Ender.

I haven't been able to bring myself to call him yet though. I need to find a new bartender and make sure everything is in order here before I try to start a relationship.

My next interview is due at any minute and I check my phone, smiling when I see a picture from Ivy. It's her in front of Big Ben grinning like a loon and I laugh. It's nice to see that one of us is having the time of our life.

I send back a kiss emoji and set my phone aside. I'll have to try to call her later tonight.

I take a drink of water as I look over her resume.

She's only nineteen and it doesn't look like she has any job experience, but there was something about her resume that made me give her a chance.

Palmer Calter walks in a minute later, her black hair tied up into a ponytail. She's fidgeting with her white button-down shirt and teetering in her high heels and I can tell that she's not used to walking in them.

"Palmer?" I ask and she nods.

"Yes, and you must be Catherine."

"Please, call me Cat. Everyone else does," I say as I shake her hand and motion for her to take a seat.

"I was looking over your resume. You don't have any previous experience?" I ask her, picking up my papers with her info on it.

"No, unfortunately not. My stepfather didn't allow me to work while I was in high school."

"Are you in college now?"

"Yes, I'm going to the University of Pittsburgh."

"What are you studying?" I ask her.

"Business," she says with a smile and I nod.

"I went there for business too," I tell her and she smiles wider.

"Did you have Professor Madison?" she asks with a giggle and I can't help but laugh as I remember the crotchety old professor. He had been one of my favorites.

"Cat!" Kayley calls from the back and I just barely manage to hold in my sigh.

"Will you excuse me?" I ask Palmer and she nods, seeming to have picked up on my annoyance with Kayley.

She's been getting pushier and pushier lately. She keeps telling me that I should hire an assistant manager and it's obvious that she thinks that person should be her.

Truth be told, she's probably right about me hiring an assistant manager to help out and give me a break but I would never choose Kayley. She'd be pushing for my job even more if I gave her an inch.

She knew that I was conducting interviews right now and that I wasn't to be disturbed unless it was an emergency, so this better be good.

"Yes, Kayley?" I ask and I can't keep the annoyance out of my voice.

"You scheduled me to work next Friday."

"Right. Shay requested it off because she has a wedding to go to. So I had to schedule you to replace her."

"But I don't like working Fridays."

I grind my teeth together to keep myself from snapping at her.

"Well, I need you to this one time. Okay?"

Kayley glares at me and I cross my arms over my chest.

"Now, since this isn't an emergency and I asked you to not disturb me while I'm interviewing, I'm going to get back to it. Please don't interrupt me again."

I don't bother waiting for a response, instead turning on my heel and heading back out to Palmer.

"Sorry about that," I apologize to Palmer and she waves me off.

"No problem."

"Well, without bartending experience, you aren't quite right for that position."

Her shoulders drop and I shuffle some papers in my hand, thinking back to Kayley and the schedule.

"But we are looking for another waitress."

"Really?" Palmer asks right away and I smile.

"Yeah, you'll have to get used to walking in heels," I warn her and she nods quickly.

"I will. I promise."

"I'll have you start tomorrow night. You can shadow Shay for a few days before we have you work your own shift."

"Okay," Palmer says with a wide grin and I smile, standing to go grab her some of the club shirts.

I give Palmer a quick tour and then let her know to be here tomorrow at seven so she can meet everyone before we open. She thanks me again before she heads out and I head back to my office. I have a break before my next interview and I head upstairs to file the new hire paperwork that Palmer just filled out.

My eyes drift over to my cell phone and I bite my lip, debating if I should call Ender now. I want to talk to him, to tell him about the interviews and my day, but I'm also curious to see what he'll do if I don't call.

I know that I'm testing him, pushing his buttons to see

what he'll do. I wonder if that is just part of the daddy/little girl role play. I wonder if I want to see how Ender will punish me.

"Cat, we need help stocking," Kayley says as she walks into my office and I want to tell her to go do her job, but I know that we're shorthanded and I'm sure that everyone could use a helping hand.

"I'll be right down. Go ahead and get started without me," I tell her and I hear her huff as she turns and stalks out.

She's beginning to be more and more of a problem. I'm going to have to fire her soon but I'll wait until Palmer is trained so that we aren't short-staffed again.

I head downstairs and back behind the bar. Kayley is barking orders and Mitch and Shay both roll their eyes at me.

"I've got it, Kayley. Why don't you go start setting up the tables."

She stomps off and the energy in the back instantly changes.

"Thanks for that. She's getting worse. So freaking bossy," Mitch says and Shay nods.

"I know. I think she might actually think that she's in charge," Shay adds.

"I'll talk to her about it," I promise them as I help to stock the bar and fill up the ice.

Shay and Mitch ask me about the new girl and I tell them that she's a waitress. The rest of the bartender interviews are happening in a few minutes, so I go grab my paperwork and get set up again at my table. Kayley is sulking up on the top floor and I look up at her. She meets my eyes and I see her roll her eyes as she heads into the back to help.

The interviews go well and I end up hiring two new

bartenders before we open for the night. They're starting tomorrow as well to get trained and used to the setup. Mitch and Shay cheer when I tell them that we'll have help tomorrow and Kayley just rolls her eyes yet again.

"I need to finish up some paperwork but I'll be down later to help out tonight," I tell them and they nod, getting back to work before the doors open.

I head up to my office and collapse in my chair. I try not to think about calling Ender but when I find myself staring at the chair that we made out in, I give in.

The phone rings twice and then I chicken out and hang up before he can answer. My heart is racing and I laugh, feeling like I just ran a marathon or something. I grin, wondering what he'll do if I tease him like that a bit.

Nothing ever seems to get to Ender but I have a feeling that a few missed calls from me and I could have the big strong military man wrapped around my finger. Part of me thinks that I already do have him.

My phone rings and I jump in my seat. When I see my mom's name on the screen, I relax but I can't help but feel a bit disappointed that it's not Ender calling me back.

"Hey, Mom," I answer and I can hear the familiar sound of a tattoo machine buzzing in the background which means that she's at work at Eye Candy Ink.

My mom is a piercer and runs the front desk at the original Eye Candy Ink shop. She's a total badass and my hero. I had even thought about going into that line of work but needles kind of gross me out. I wouldn't have lasted two seconds in a tattoo shop.

"Hey, honey! How's the club? You aren't working too hard are you?" my mom asks and I smile.

"No, I actually just hired some more people so I'll be

working less," I say and I can almost see my mom rolling her eyes.

"Now why don't I believe that?" she teases.

"What's up?" I ask and she hums.

"Nothing. I just haven't talked to you in a few days."

"Mom, I saw you at brunch on Sunday."

"That doesn't count. We need more girl time. Some one on one."

"I'd love that. Next week? I'll have everyone trained by then."

"I'm holding you to that!" she warns.

"We can dye our hair," I suggest and I can see her grinning at that in my head.

"Deal. I'll grab the dye."

"Sounds good. See you Sunday, Mom!" I say and she tells me she'll see me then.

I hang up and try to focus on work but when my phone buzzes again, my concentration is blown.

This time it's Ivy.

"Hey you! I was just thinking that I needed to call you."

"Well, I beat you to it," she says with a laugh. "What are you up to?"

"I'm at work. I fired Kayley so now I need to replace her."

"About fucking time. That girl was the worst," she says, dragging out worst.

"I know, I can't say that I'm going to miss having to deal with her bullshit all of the time. I just wish that we weren't so short handed."

"You'll find someone soon. You're Cat Fucking Schultz. You're a total fucking badass. It will work out."

I grin. Ivy has always been my own personal cheerleader and I'm the same for her. We catch up but she's headed into class so we only chat for a few minutes.

I smile as I set my phone back down, feeling lighter after our chat. I know that the whole family is looking forward to her coming back home and I wonder if we should start planning a party. Maybe Ivy will move back in with me while she looks for a space.

My phone buzzes again and I glance over to the screen. Butterflies take flight in my stomach as I see Ender's name on the phone and I waver, trying to decide what to do.

I bite my lip as I hit ignore.

FIVE

Ender

CAT IS TRYING to drive me crazy. I'm sure of it.

I'm also sure that she's succeeding.

She keeps calling and hanging up before I can answer. When I call her back, she never answers. At first, I thought that she was just busy with the club. Now though, I know that she's doing it to mess with me.

It's been three days of this and my patience has run out. I know that my baby girl is just testing me but I don't want to claim her until I know for sure that she wants me as her daddy. It has to be her choice.

"Are you going to see your girl?" Gray asks Harvey as they stop outside my room.

I'm just finishing cleaning and disinfecting everything and I know that they're waiting on me to lock up.

"No, it's ladies' night, so they're both at home. I'll sneak over later when Nora and Cat have gone home," Harvey says with a grin.

Gray's phone dings and he smiles when he sees the text. I'm sure that it's from Nora and my mind starts to work as I think about Cat and ladies' night.

"Looks like I'm going to beat you there. Nora just asked me to pick her up from Sayler and Coraline's apartment," Gray says and I hurry to finish wiping everything down.

"It's winding down already?" Rooney asks as he joins them.

"Guess so," Gray says with a shrug and finish organizing my desk, pushing my chair in as I head to join them.

We head outside and Harvey locks up while Rooney runs across the street.

"Dammit. He's going to try to drive us home," Harvey groans as he takes off after him.

I laugh with Gray as we watch them wrestle over the keys. Rooney gets the door open and Harvey dives into the driver's seat.

"Can I get a ride?" I ask Gray and he seems surprised.

Normally I walk home since my place is only like a block and a half away.

"Uh, sure," Gray says and I follow him across the street to his car.

I'm in the car before he is and Gray frowns at me, probably wondering why I'm acting so weird.

The drive is silent and I can't stop thinking about my baby girl. I'm both annoyed by her calling and hanging up on me and excited because it feels like it's finally happening. I'm finally going to claim my baby girl.

When he parks outside of Sayler and Coraline's apartment building, I'm out of the car and headed inside. I hear his phone ring behind me and I look back to see him stopped to answer it.

I take the stairs two at a time and don't bother knocking

on the girls' door. They're playing some music on the TV in the living room but they're all gathered around the kitchen island and my eyes instantly seek out Cat.

She's over by the fridge, a margarita halfway to her mouth. Her cheeks are flushed and I know that she's well on her way to being drunk.

"You," I growl and everyone's eyes widen as I stalk across the apartment, bend and put my shoulder against Cat's stomach, grabbing her purse off of the counter, and carry her out with her dangling over my shoulder.

Cat giggles as I carry her gently back down the stairs.

"Where are your keys?" I ask as we hit the lobby and she wiggles around on my shoulder, digging her keys out of her jeans pocket.

I grab them from her and head outside into the night. Gray is just wrapping up his phone call and he gapes at me as I stride across the street with Cat still hanging upside down on my shoulder.

I set her gently in the passenger seat and buckle her in. Her head rolls on the headrest and she smiles drunkenly at me.

"Hey, daddy," she whispers, trying to kiss me and I pull back.

It kills me to turn down anything she wants to give me, but I know that she's at the very least tipsy and I don't want to take advantage of her.

She pouts and I hurry over to the driver's seat, sliding in and moving the seat back as far as it will go. I merge into traffic as Cat rests her hand on my thigh and slowly starts to slide it upward. She giggles as she cups my cock through my jeans and I grit my teeth, willing myself not to come in my jeans like some horny teenager.

"Baby girl," I warn and she giggles again, leaning over

the center console to lick at my neck. "Fuck," I hiss and she does it again.

I park outside of her apartment, practically throwing myself out of the car and hurrying to help her out. She wraps her legs and arms around me and I try to think about anything but the way she feels pressed up against me as I carry her up to her apartment.

I unlock the door and carry Cat straight into her bedroom. Getting her to unwrap her limbs from around me is an exquisite torture but finally, she's spread out on the bed. When she starts to wiggle her way out of her clothes, I know that I'm in trouble and I excuse myself to go find her some aspirin and water.

When I come back, she's naked on top of the covers and she grins as she sees me.

"I need you," she says, her voice husky and I remind myself that she's been drinking.

Even if she's not drunk, it's not the right time. Being a daddy means doing what's right for my baby girl. Her needs come first.

"Drink this," I order and she reaches out to take the pills and glass of water.

She swallows down the pills and stretches her hands over her head. I clear my throat, looking away from her mouthwatering curves to grab her blankets and cover her up.

Cat pouts, trying to sit up and I put my hands on her shoulders, holding her in place.

"We're not having sex for the first time when you've been drinking. That's not how your first time is going to go," I say sternly.

"But daddy," she whines and I give her a hard look.

Her hand trails down to my hard bulge again and I grind my teeth together, forcing myself to take a step back.

"You're hard," she tells me with a devilish smile.

"I'm always hard around you, but I'm also always going to do what's best for you."

I tuck her in once again as she sighs.

"Will you stay here with me?" she asks through a yawn and I can't say no.

"Of course."

She closes her eyes and starts to snore within moments. I pick up her clothes, lining her shoes up with the others by the door. I put the empty glass in the sink and look around her apartment.

It's small but nice and in a safe neighborhood. She lives on the third floor and I know that she's been here for at least two years. Her place doesn't feel very lived in though. Probably because she's always at work.

There's a leather sectional in the living room, a flatscreen TV on the other wall. A few pillows and pictures on the walls, but that's it.

I head back to her bedroom and notice that it's much the same. Just a bed, dresser, and a lamp. She's still fast asleep, curled up on her side and I take off my shoes, moving to lie down beside her.

I don't know how long I spend watching her before my own eyes drift shut and I fall asleep. Even being beside her, it doesn't stop me from dreaming about her just like every night.

The only difference is when I wake up face to face with my baby girl.

SIX

Cat

I WAKE up groggy the next morning. I had the strangest dream about Ender coming and carrying me out of Sayler and Coraline's place.

When I roll over, I realize that it wasn't a dream.

Ender is lying next to me in bed, his eyes closed as he sleeps and I can't help but take the time to study him. He looks so peaceful, so beautiful and I inch closer to him, wanting to feel his skin against mine.

He's still fully dressed and lying on top of the covers so it makes cuddling up to him a little hard since I'm naked and he's got me tucked in so tight under the blankets. I rest my hand on his bicep, wanting to touch him and his eyes pop open at that simple touch.

"'Morning," I say, slightly embarrassed.

"'Morning," he rasps back. "How are you feeling?"

He rolls over onto his side and I take stock. He had me

drink water and take some medicine last night so my head doesn't hurt and I'm not that dehydrated.

"Pretty good. I didn't drink that much last night," I tell him and he nods.

"Good," he says as he rolls me onto my back and comes down over me.

I gasp, my eyes widening and the next thing I know, his lips are on mine. My eyes flutter shut as he kisses me, his lips molding to mine.

My hands go to his biceps, my fingernails digging into the muscles there and I hang on to him as his tongue pushes into my mouth, plundering, twisting, teasing.

It feels like he's everywhere around me all at once and I get lost in Ender, in my daddy.

My legs spread, welcoming the feeling of him between them, of his weight on top of me and I can't help but rock under him, trying to gain some more friction.

"Daddy, please," I beg as his lips leave mine and he starts to lick and nip along the smooth column of my throat.

"What do you want, baby girl. Does my little girl want daddy's big cock?"

"Yes!" I scream, willing to beg if it gets me some relief from this ache that's taken over my body.

"That's my horny little girl."

His words cause a moan to rip up my throat and I start to tug on his clothes, wanting to feel his bare skin against mine. There are entirely too many layers between the two of us.

His beard brushes against my skin, leaving a sensitive trail down my body. He nudges the blankets out of the way as he kisses lower and I feel both cold from the covers leaving but hot from what he's doing to me.

"Take your clothes off, daddy. I want to see you," I say, my voice raspy with need.

Ender obliges me, stripping off his shirt and dragging the covers all of the way off me. He slips off the bed, pushing his jeans and boxers down before he climbs back onto the bed.

He moves back between my legs and I can't help but try to rock against him.

"Be patient, little girl. Daddy's going to take care of you. He's going to take care of everything," he whispers against my hip bone and I try to stay still.

His big palms grip my knees, pulling my legs farther apart before his hands smooth up my thighs. His thumbs spread my lower lips apart and I can feel his warm breath on my damp flesh.

My hands clench, fisting the sheets as my legs start to quiver in anticipation of what he'll do next.

He leans forward, his beard hitting my skin first and tickling me slightly before his tongue licks up my center.

I can't concentrate after that. There's nothing else in my world except for what my daddy's tongue and hands are doing to me. With each lick, he drives me higher and higher until I go flying. He licks me through my orgasm and I come again.

I'm so sensitive and my sex is drenched. After two orgasms, I should be satisfied but the ache inside of me is still there. I need him to fill me.

"I need you, daddy," I moan, tugging on his hair and trying to urge him up.

He gives me one more lick, burying his face in my folds until his beard is covered in my juices. Then he moves, kneeling between my thighs and staring down at me like a conqueror.

I spread my legs wider, needing him to take me, to claim me.

"Ready for more, baby girl?" he asks and I nod eagerly.

He braces himself on his hands so that he's not crushing me and I can't stop from moaning as I feel his warm skin against mine. When his cock brushes against my folds, I swear that I almost come.

"You've got to be brave for daddy. He doesn't want to hurt you, but there's no other way," he says and I can tell that the idea of causing me any amount of discomfort is killing him.

"I trust you, daddy," I say and I can see that those words make him happy.

"Good. That's really good, baby girl," Ender says as he lowers himself, kissing me as his cock nudges my opening.

He starts to sink inside me, inch by thick inch. I gasp as he tears through my virginity and seats himself fully inside of me.

"Fucking perfect," Ender hisses and I nod.

It feels incredible to have him stretching me like this. I thought that it would hurt more but I should have known that my daddy would do everything in his power to make this perfect for me.

"Daddy is going to move now. He can't hold back any longer. Not when his baby girl's pussy is strangling his cock so good."

I nod, needing him to move too.

He starts slow, watching my face to make sure that I'm okay and I wonder if he can see how crazy I am about him. I feel like love must be a clear emotion on my face and I don't know how to hide it. I'm not sure that I want to.

"Fuck, baby," he hisses and his restraint starts to break.

I love that I seem to be the only one to drive this big

man to the brink of insanity. It's only me who can get to him.

"Oh, daddy," I moan when he passes over a spot inside of me that has me seeing stars.

"Yeah, that's it. Is my baby girl going to be a good girl and come all over daddy's cock?" he asks and that's all it takes.

I scream as I come, my whole body locking up tight as my orgasm crashes over me like a tidal wave. My nails dig into his shoulders and I hold on.

Ender shouts, his pace faltering and I feel as he finds his own release inside of me.

"Daddy," I moan, my hands rubbing up and down his back as he holds himself above me.

He kisses me and I can taste my release still on his lips. His arms wrap around me and he rolls so that I'm sprawled out on top of him. He never breaks the kiss and pulls out of me. I wince slightly but Ender notices.

"Hold on, baby girl," he says, rolling me onto my side and climbing from the bed.

He heads into my bathroom and comes back a minute later with some Advil and a glass of water.

"It's not that bad," I try to tell him but he grabs my hand and drops the pills into my palm.

"It's my job to take care of you. The pills will help with any soreness. The bath will take care of the rest."

I watch his tight ass as he heads back into the bathroom and starts the bathwater.

I'm the luckiest girl in the world.

SEVEN

Ender

IT FEELS wrong to be away from Cat but I know that we both have work to do. Besides, I'll be back with my baby girl in a few hours.

Gray and I run into each other headed into work and he eyes me as I walk up to him.

"Hey, man. What happened last night?" he asks.

I debate opening up to him but I just want to keep Cat to myself for a little bit longer.

"What happened between you and Nora last night?" I ask and his cheeks pinken slightly.

I was just teasing him but now I'm starting to wonder if something really did happen between them. It would be about time.

We eye each other silently for a minute before Gray nods and we head inside the shop. My phone rings as I get settled at my desk and I'm surprised to see that it's Gray's brother who is calling me.

"Hey, Mack. How's it going?" I ask, looking to my open door to see if Gray is in hearing distance.

"Hey, pretty good," he says.

"I'm sorry to hear about your dad," I offer.

I know that Gray went home for his funeral a few weeks ago but from what he told us, their dad was a piece of shit, and neither seem that broken up about his passing.

"Thanks, that's actually kind of why I'm calling," he starts and I wonder if something is wrong.

If he's calling me instead of Gray then I wonder if it's about him. He seemed fine the last few days but maybe he's still dealing with losing his dad.

"Everything okay?" I ask, my body starting to tense as I wait to hear about any possible threats.

"Yeah, I called Gray last night and asked if he wouldn't mind coming back to Rosewood to help me with our dad's house."

"You want me to come with him? I'm not great at construction but I can try," I offer.

"No, I'm going to hire a company to help build the house I think. It's more cleaning it out that's the problem right now. I can get it and Gray said that he might come back to help."

"Then what can I do?" I ask him.

"Keep an eye on Gray. Things have been tense for a while with us and we talked about it last night. I just want to make sure that he's okay with everything and is handling the funeral alright."

"I will," I promise him.

"Thanks, Ender," Mack says sincerely and we catch up for a few minutes.

He says that he's going to stay in Rosewood at least until he sells the old house and takes care of a few things and I offer to show him around Pittsburgh if he ever wants to come up for a visit and Gray is working. It sounds like he has a girl in town and though I want to ask him about it, I let it go. He has enough on his plate without me asking about his love life.

"The shop is opening so I've got to go, but I'll talk to you soon," I tell him and we hang up a minute later.

I have to rush to get my clients' tattoos in order and ready before they arrive but in a way, it helps. I'm not so distracted with thoughts of Cat this way.

I spend the next nine hours tattooing and by the time I'm done, it's dark out and my stomach is growling. I have a feeling that Cat hasn't eaten yet either. She mentioned that she was training people today so I stop by Wild Thyme and grab some of her favorites before I head over to Se7en.

The bouncers let me in without me having to stop and I like that I'm starting to be a regular in Cat's life. I head up the stairs and knock on Cat's door before I poke my head in. I'm not sure if she's training people up here and I don't want to interrupt but when I open the door, it's just her.

"Hey, baby girl," I say as I let myself in.

I show her the bag of food and she grins at me, pushing away from her desk.

"You're the best," she sighs as she grabs the bag from me and starts to take everything out.

I drop a kiss on her neck and she moans and leans back into me.

"How was your day?" I whisper against her skin and she relaxes against me further.

"Pretty great actually. All of the new hires seem to be fast learners and they get along well with everyone else. Well, almost," she whispers but I still catch it.

"Problem?" I ask, spinning her around to face me.

"It's Kayley," she admits, her eyes flashing and I wonder what this Kayley girl did to piss off my baby girl.

"She's not getting along with the others?"

"She wants to take my job. She never liked that I became manager and thinks that I just got it because my dad owns the club."

"That's not true," I growl, wanting to make sure that she knows just how kickass and talented she is.

"I know. I have a business degree and worked every position while I was in school but that doesn't matter. Kayley worked here full time for longer and thinks that it should have been her. She's trying to get me to make her assistant manager and creating that position isn't a bad idea but I definitely don't want it to be her. She's already gunning to take over."

"So hire someone else for the position. And fire this Kayley."

"I know I'm going to have to. She's started to boss everyone else around, even me sometimes."

"Fuck that," I growl and Cat giggles, smiling up at me.

"This is nice."

"What is? Me getting pissed off at one of your employees?"

"No, just having someone on my side. Sometimes I'm afraid to tell my parents because I know that they'll want to help but I need to do this on my own. It's nice to just be able to vent to someone."

"I'm here for it anytime you need, baby girl," I say and she smiles up at me.

"Thanks," she says as she rises to her tiptoes and kisses me gently.

"Are you hungry?" I whisper and she nods, her eyes darkening as my hands glide up her back and fist in her hair.

"Yes, daddy," she whispers and my cock pulses in my jeans.

"Are you sore?" I ask her and she hesitates before she shakes her head no.

"Food first. Can't have you getting distracted and forgetting to eat."

She pouts and I take a seat, dragging her onto my lap. She wraps an arm around my neck, smiling at me as I grab the first takeout container and open it. It's a gyro and I hold it up to her mouth, waiting for her to take a bite and swallow before I offer her another.

We make our way through all of the food just like that. She tries to suck my fingers into her mouth when I feed her french fries and between that and her squirming in my lap, I'm rock hard by the time that all of the food is gone.

"More, daddy," Cat whispers against my ear and even though I want to sink balls deep inside of her snug hole, I need to think about her needs.

I popped her cherry just this morning. She's bound to be sore. Still, I can't leave her aching like this.

I lift her, sitting her on her desk and tugging her skirt up and her panties down as I drop to my knees in front of her. I have her legs over my shoulders before she knows what I'm about to do.

She's a little pink and I know that she's not ready to take all of my inches again. It's not a shame to just have her come on my face though.

I dive in, knowing that we're at her work and need to be fast. My tongue plunges into her pussy, licking up and circling her clit. I repeat that path over and over again as my baby girl pants and squirms against my mouth.

"Daddy!" she calls as she comes and I grip her hips,

holding her in place as I suck her clit into my mouth and tease out her pleasure.

She has beard burn on the inside of her thighs but it doesn't seem to be bothering her. She smiles up at me, a dazed look on her face as I pull her to me, kissing her lips.

She moans as she tastes herself on my lips and I try to ignore my hard cock straining against the front of my jeans.

"Can I suck your cock, daddy?" Cat purrs and my legs almost give out at the thought of her on her knees in front of me.

"You don't have to," I grit out, sure that my zipper must be imprinted on my length.

"I want to," she says as she drops to her knees in front of me.

Her fingers go to my zipper and she reaches inside my boxers, easing my dick out.

Seeing her little hand wrapped around me is almost obscene and I have to grit my teeth to stop from coming before she can even wrap her lips around me.

She looks up at me from where she's kneeling and if I wasn't in love with her before, I would have fallen right then and there. She looks so beautiful but mischievous. It's a heady combination.

"I've never done this before, daddy."

"I know. Just wrap your lips around me, baby girl, and suck," I instruct and she grins at me before she does just that.

Her cheeks hollow out and dear god, I'm not going to last.

"Fuck, baby girl," I groan, my head falling back as my hands tangle in her hair.

Her head starts to bob up and down along my length and I can feel my balls tightening up already.

Her hand grips me and she starts to stroke in time with her mouth. My baby girl is a fast learner and I wonder if that's a blessing or a curse right now.

When she swallows half my length, I decide on blessing.

"I'm going to come," I warn her and she starts to suck harder, wanting me to spill down her throat.

"Fuck, baby girl!" I groan, trying to stay quiet but I'm sure that the music from the first floor is drowning us out.

Cat swallows down my release, grinning at me as she takes one last lick at the tip of my cock.

I help her to her feet, kissing her and trying to pour all of the love that I feel for her into the embrace.

There's a knock at the door a few minutes later and I reluctantly pull back. Her face is slightly red from my beard and her hair is mussed from my fingers. It's pretty obvious that we've been messing around in here.

I try to smooth out her hair. I know that she wants to keep this private and it's no one's business what we do in private.

"I'll let you get back to work. Text me when you get home so I know that you're safe. Even better, text me when you're getting ready to leave and I'll come back and drive you."

"I have my car," she reminds me and I frown.

I don't like the idea of her leaving late at night but I know that she's safe. She has a bouncer walk her to her car and I need to trust her too.

"I'll text you," she promises and I nod.

"I'll talk to you soon, baby girl," I whisper against her lips and she smiles.

I head home with the scent and taste of her still on my lips.

EIGHT

Cat

I WALK into Se7en the next day with a smile on my face. Ender came home with me last night and made love to me one more time before we both passed out. I woke up this morning with him wrapped around me and he fucked me twice more before we both had to leave to head to work.

I bite my lip as I walk up the stairs thinking about the way that he had gripped my thighs and ass as he roughly thrust into me. He had me pinned to the shower wall, my whole body wrapped around him as he pounded into me, asking me if I liked getting fucked by daddy's big cock. My answering yes had echoed off the shower walls and I came so hard that I almost blacked out. I had come back alert to find him carefully washing me and my heart had melted at the obvious love I could see on his face as he washed me off.

We still haven't said I love you yet, but it's there in every action, every caress or spank or fuck.

"Hey there Kitty Cat," Kayley purrs as I walk into my office and I jump slightly.

She's sitting in my chair, her feet up on my desk and I glare at her.

"Get out of my chair."

"I don't think that I will," Kayley says, an ugly sneer on her face.

"Excuse me?" I ask as I set my purse and the lunch that Ender made for me down on the corner of my desk and cross my arms.

"I know," Kayley whispers, her eyes darting to the door.

"You know what?"

"I heard you and that old man last night. Your 'daddy,'" she hisses, her face twisted in disgust and my stomach drops.

"That's none of your business—" I start but she cuts me off.

"It's disgusting and you did it here, at your place of work. I know that you can get everything you want because your *other* daddy owns the place, but I wonder how he and the rest of the staff will feel when they know what you've been doing in here with that man."

"It's none of their business either. How did you even hear us? Were you up here spying on me instead of doing your job again?" I throw back and when she flushes, I know that I'm right.

"That doesn't matter. All that matters is that I heard you and I know your sick little secret now."

It's not sick, I want to say but I can't force the words out.

"I want your job," Kayley demands and I roll my eyes.

"You can't have it."

"We'll see about that."

She starts to stand and I think about what my mom

would do. She's a badass woman. She doesn't take crap from anyone. Neither should her daughter.

"No one will stay if you become the boss around here. No one can stand you. You don't even have the power and it's already gone to your head. Besides, it's your word against mine. You have no proof that what you say happened did."

I smile at her as she freezes and she glares back.

"Some people will believe me," she insists and I shake my head.

"Like I said, no one likes you here. You complain and boss people around instead of helping out when we're short-staffed. They don't trust you and obviously, they shouldn't."

"Make me assistant manager and I won't tell anyone."

"No, and are you really trying to blackmail me into giving you a promotion? Do you know how illegal that is?"

She actually stomps her foot at that, her face bright red in anger.

"Fuck. You," she hisses and I give her a sweet *fuck you* smile right back.

"Why don't you get back to work?"

She stops and I can see the wheels turning in her head but I'm not going to back down. I won't let her have any power here or she'll make life miserable for everyone here, me included.

"You don't think that I help out enough? Fine, then I quit. Have fun being shorthanded," she tosses over her shoulder as she stalks past me and out the door.

I sigh, rolling my shoulders to try to ease the tension and when I go to sit down in my chair, I notice Palmer standing in the doorway.

She's blushing and it's obvious that she heard our fight.

"Hey," I say to try to ease the tension and she steps into my office, closing the door behind her.

"I'm sorry to interrupt. I just wanted to turn in the rest of my new hire paperwork and my banking info," she says and I nod, reaching out to grab the papers.

"Thanks."

"That girl is a bitch," Palmer blurts out and she looks so surprised that she said it that I can't help but laugh.

"Yeah, she is. I don't think that anyone will be upset when I let them know that she quit."

"I don't think so either."

"It just sucks that we'll be short-staffed again until I can find another waitress."

"My roommate is looking for a job. She was a waitress in high school."

"Send her my way," I say right away and Palmer smiles.

"I will... and you know that what she said isn't true, right?"

"Hmm?" I ask, pretending not to know what she means.

"About you and that man. There's nothing wrong with it. It's not sick."

"Thanks, Palmer," I whisper and she gives me a smile.

"No problem. I don't think the age gap is weird either. To be honest, I'm in love with an older man too."

"Oh yeah? Anyone I know?"

"Probably not. He's a tattoo artist over at Eye Candy Ink. Maybe you've heard of him 'cause he's really good."

My stomach drops and I wonder if I should tell her that I'm basically related to everyone who works there. My mind races with who it could be.

"His name is Banks," she says, her face only slightly dreamy and I barely hold in my laugh.

"You're his neighbor," I guess and she looks shocked that I know.

"Yeah, but..."

"I'm like his sister."

Palmer's whole face turns a flaming shade of red and I give her a gentle smile.

"I won't tell. I think he likes you too. He's been showing up late to Sunday brunch every week and the whole family noticed. He always just says that he was helping out his neighbor. I think we all assumed that you were like ninety years old and needed help around the house."

"Oh, no. It's... well, it's something else," she whispers and I know that she doesn't want to talk about it right now.

"If you need anything," I start and she nods, giving me a smile.

"Thanks. Really. I'll send my roommate your way. Her name is Rae."

"Thanks," I say and she nods as she heads for the door.

Palmer leaves and I try to focus on her and Banks or on work. Anything but what happened with Kayley. I know that as soon as I think about it, I'm going to get embarrassed again and start freaking out.

I wonder if I made a mistake.

What if my parents do find out? Or anyone else at work? How will I face them?

I know that Ender would never force me to call him daddy in public, that he knows that I only like to play in private and have no desire to make it a full time thing, but is this really right for me?

I bite my lip, weighing my options and even though it breaks my heart, I text him.

. . .

CAT: **I'm so sorry. I think that this is a mistake. I can't be with you anymore.**

I HIT send and toss my phone into my purse, trying to push the broken shards of my heart away as I focus on work, hoping that it can distract me from the pain that I just inflicted on myself.

Spoiler alert. It doesn't.

NINE

Ender

CAT: **I'm so sorry. I think that this is a mistake. I can't be with you anymore**.

I'VE BEEN STARING at the message for days and I know that I need to stop, that I'm only torturing myself, but I can't help it.

I haven't responded to the message even though I want nothing more than to beg and demand that she take me back. I'm crushed by the rejection, but I know that she has to decide that this, that I, am right for her. That's the one decision that I can't make for my baby girl.

"Hey, man," Rooney says as he stops in my doorway.

"Hey, you ready to close?" I ask, shoving my phone in my pocket as I stand.

"Yeah, Banks is just finishing up with his last client, so it will just be a minute."

I nod, straightening everything on my desk before I grab my bag.

"Did you hear?" Rooney asks with a grin.

"Hear what?"

"That Gray and Nora finally got together? Sayler told me at lunch."

"Finally," I groan and Rooney laughs.

"Right? It's about time those two realized what was right in front of them."

I grin and we head up to the front lobby. Banks is wrapping up his client's arm and I know that it won't be much longer.

"Looks like it's just the two of you left now," Rooney says as he plops down in one of the seats and stretches out his legs.

"What?"

"Just you and Banks left to fall."

I roll my eyes, leaning against the front counter.

"Why are you so obsessed with our love lives all of a sudden?" I ask him.

"I just want you to be happy, man."

"I am," I lie.

I was, I want to tell him but I don't think that Cat wants anyone to know that we were ever a thing. I try not to let that thought sting.

"Right," Rooney drawls and I'm relieved when Banks walks his client up to the lobby.

He checks her out and we wait for him to finish collecting the cash drawer and lock it up in Maxine's office in the back before Rooney starts up again.

"Are you coming tomorrow, Ender?" Rooney asks.

"Where?"

"To brunch? I just wanted to know if I should be

bringing bouquets of flowers for everyone."

"Yeah, can't have you making us look bad again," Banks teases.

The Eye Candy Ink family has a Sunday brunch together every week and I was invited last week. I had gone, bringing all of the women flowers. The women loved it, but I got a ton of shit about it from all of the guys.

"No, I can't make it tomorrow. I have other plans," I lie.

There's no way that I can be around Cat right now without ordering her to take me back. I know that this thing between us is real and right, but I need Cat to come to the same realization before we can move forward.

"Bummer," Rooney says and I'm surprised to see that he actually seems to mean it.

I'm the odd one out in the shop. Older than everyone else, not as much training or experience, not as carefree. I know that between my name, size, and demeanor, I can scare people and I think I scared the guys here when I first got hired. It's nice to see that they're starting to warm up to me.

"What about you, Banks? You got anyone special in your life? You going to bring that neighbor of yours that always seems to need help?" Rooney asks.

"No, I think Palmer has plans," Banks mumbles as he finishes up some paperwork.

"Palmer?" I ask, the name familiar. "The Palmer that Cat just hired at Se7en?"

"What?" Banks asks, his head shooting up. "What did you just say?"

"Cat just hired some girl named Palmer to waitress at Se7en," I inform him and he looks furious.

"How do you know who Cat is hiring?" Rooney asks suspiciously.

"Are you sure her name was Palmer?" Banks asks before I can think of how to answer Rooney.

"Yeah. She said that she was younger, like nineteen, and in college for business."

"Son of a bitch," Banks hisses and then he's grabbing his bag and storming out the door.

Rooney and I look at each other, wondering what the hell that was all about. *Maybe it's just me that hasn't found love.*

We lock up and I wave goodbye to Rooney as I head back home.

It feels weird to not be heading to Se7en. I'm off balance without my baby girl at the center of my world and I don't know what to do about it.

I wonder how she's doing. I can't forget about how we were together and I know that she felt this thing between us too.

I'm not that hungry and I don't seem to know what to do with myself. I keep walking around my house and I can't help but be both sad and thankful that Cat never came here. I don't know what I would do, how much more I would hurt if I could smell her all around me.

My phone dings and I can't help but hope that it's Cat. It's not.

"Hey, Mack," I say as I answer the phone.

"Hey, how's it going?"

"Pretty good. Calling to check on Gray?" I guess.

"Yeah, and to tell you that Brooks Coleman, I don't know if you remember him. He was a Ranger?"

"Yeah, I remember him," I answer.

"He's headed your way. I just found that he's finally through with physical therapy after that IED mess. He's supposed to be training at some gym there. I can't remember the name.

"Probably Kings Gym."

"Yeah, that was it. He's there training and trying to get used to civilian life. He should be in town in a week or two and I thought I would pass his number along in case you didn't have it."

"I don't, so yeah. I'll give him a call and I can show him around town, buy him a beer."

"Sounds good. I'll send it in a minute."

"How's the house coming?"

"Slow, but good. It's almost therapeutic tearing down everything," he says with a grim laugh.

"Gray and Nora are together now."

"About fucking time," he sighs and I laugh.

"That was everyone else's response as well."

"But he's doing alright? They're doing alright? He doesn't need money or anything?"

"No. he's good. He's been on cloud nine since they got together and between the two of them, they seem pretty well off."

"Good," Mack says, sounding relieved.

"He mentioned that he's coming down to help you with the house. I'm supposed to help out with the puppies."

"Oof, good luck with that," he says with a laugh. "I've heard that they're a handful."

"Thanks," I say dryly.

"I've got to go. I'm meeting someone in town, but I'll talk to you soon."

"Sounds good."

We hang up and it only takes a moment for me to remember that I'm alone. I sink down on the couch, staring up at the ceiling and praying that it doesn't take my baby girl long to realize that she needs me too.

TEN

Cat

I KNOW that it's dumb of me to be excited to see Ender at Sunday brunch. I broke up with him, I shouldn't still be happy to see him.

The past three days have passed in a blur. A painful blur. I called in one of the interviews from last week and hired her as a waitress to replace Kayley. Then had to start training her.

I thought that training would help to distract me from the constant pain in my chest but not so much. It was always there, a dull ache just behind my ribcage.

"Hey, Cat!" my Aunt Indie calls as soon as I step into Uncle Zeke's house.

"Hey," I say, hugging her back tight.

Aunt Indie always acts like she hasn't seen you in months when really, it's just a week.

"How have you been?" Aunt Darcy asks as she joins us and gives me a hug.

These two have been best friends for most of their lives. They're inseparable and also complete opposites. Aunt Darcy is calm and curvy. Aunt Indie is chaotic and thin. Together they complement each other though. The same goes for their husbands, Uncle Atlas and Uncle Mischa.

"Good. Busy," I tell her and she smiles.

I can see her studying my face and I wonder what she sees. Can she tell that I'm distracted and heartbroken? Is it written across my face?

"Everyone is out back," my mom says as she comes in from the kitchen.

"Hey, Mom," I say, forcing a smile.

"Hey," she says and I can tell by the look on her face that she knows that something is up with me.

"Need help with anything?" I ask, hoping to cut her off before she can start questioning me.

"We got it. The guys are out at the grill already and everything else is out in the kitchen. Do you want a drink?" Aunt Darcy asks and I nod, following them into the kitchen.

I can see Harvey, Rooney, Ames, Maxine, Sayler, Nora, and Gray all out in the back and I'm guessing that Coraline is busy working at Wild Thyme.

There's no sign of Ender and I'm sure the disappointment shows on my face. Maybe he's just running late.

I grab a lemonade and am about to go join my friends and family when Banks comes into the house. He spots me and his jaw clenches as he makes a beeline for me.

"Can I talk to you for a minute?" he asks, already grabbing my hand and leading me away.

"Everything alright?" I ask once we're closed into a guest bedroom.

"No, it's not. Did you hire someone named Palmer to work at Se7en?" he asks and I'm thrown off by his question.

"Uh, yeah," I say, already having an idea of where this conversation is going. "She mentioned that she's your neighbor."

"She is. She's also too young to be working as a waitress in a club."

"I mean, legally, she's—"

"Cat!" he exclaims, exasperated.

"What? What do you want me to do, fire her?"

"Yes."

"No. She's a good worker and she needs the money."

"I can..." He trails off and I wait for him to finish. When he doesn't, I start again.

"You can what? Lend her money?"

"No, she won't take it."

"Smart girl."

He glares at me and I smile.

"She wants to be independent. She wants to work. If you care about her, you won't stand in her way. You'll want her to succeed and be happy."

He looks away and I know that he knows that I'm right.

My advice to Banks reminds me of Ender and I wince. I should have taken my own advice. All Ender wants is for me to be happy and I pushed him away.

"Is Ender coming?" I can't help but ask.

"No, he said that he has other things he has to do today," Banks says distractedly.

"Oh."

Banks excuses himself, already typing on his phone and I take a deep breath.

So what? So, he isn't coming today. It's no big deal.

"What's going on?" my mom asks as soon as I step out of the guest room.

Aunt Darcy, Trixie, Edie, Indie are there along with Sayler, Maxine, and Nora.

"What are you talking about?" I try to hedge and my mom frowns at me, letting me know that I'm not fooling anyone.

"Why do you look like someone stole your ice cream?" Aunt Indie asks.

I sigh, deciding to just come clean with them. Maybe it will help to get an outside opinion.

"I was kind of seeing Ender, but we called it off the other day," I admit.

"Since when?" Aunt Trixie asks.

"I knew it!" Sayler says at the same time and I laugh.

"It wasn't very long. Just like a week."

"And you miss him this much?" my mom asks.

"Why did you end things?" Nora asks.

"Why do you think I ended it?" I ask her and she grins.

"Uh, because I have eyes and I've seen him look at you. The guy is in love with you. He would never end it," she says and I see Sayler and Maxine both nod.

"Why did you end it?" Aunt Darcy asks, her voice filled with concern.

I don't want to give them exact details and I try to think of a way to word it so that I don't give away too much.

"I'm just busy."

"Bullshit," my mom says, crossing her arms over her chest.

"I was worried."

"About what?" she asks.

"About the age gap. I think it's just too much and we were getting looks at the club."

My Aunt Trixie and my mom both huff and I know that it's because they both married older men.

"No, it's not. Age is just a number," Aunt Trixie says and I nod, knowing deep down that she's right.

"If you love him, Cat, then don't push him away," my mom says and I know that she's worried about me.

This is my first relationship and I wonder if she's excited to be talking about boys with me or worried that I'm diving into the deep end.

I nod at them and Rooney calls in from the back door, letting us know that the food is done.

"Coming!" Sayler calls back.

My mom reaches out, squeezing my hand as the others turn to leave.

"If you love him like I think that you do, then don't push him away. You're only punishing both of you," she tells me and I swallow hard, nodding.

I know that she's right. As long as we love each other, then it doesn't matter what we do in private.

I can't believe that I pushed him away, that I broke up with him when all he was trying to do was love and take care of me.

I move out to join everyone in the backyard but my head is spinning. I know that I messed up by breaking up with Ender.

Now I just need to figure out a way to apologize to him.

ELEVEN

Ender

"I ALMOST HAD YOU," Brooks says with a laugh as we leave Kings Gym.

"Not even close," I tell him, hitting his shoulder.

Brooks got to town just last night and since it was my day off, I volunteered to show him around and go to a training session with him at the gym.

It's been nice to see him again and catch up. The workout at the gym helped take my mind off missing Cat too. At least for a little bit.

"Have you found a place yet?" I ask him as we head down the block.

"Not yet. I'm staying at some pay-by-the-week place but it's getting really old. Some guy that I met here, Niall, he said that I could crash with him for a week or two, so maybe I'll take him up on that," Brooks says with a shrug.

"You can crash with me too," I offer him and he nods.

"Thanks. I'm sure I'll find something soon."

He rubs his left shoulder and I can tell that the injury he got during that attack overseas is bothering him.

"Want to grab a beer?" I ask but he shakes his head.

"I should head back and shower. Maybe ice my shoulder. Next week instead?" he asks and I nod.

"Yeah, you have my number. Let me know when you want to get together."

"Thanks, Ender. See you soon," he says as he heads across the parking lot to his old Bronco.

I slide behind the wheel of my own car and sigh, thoughts of Cat filling my head. I wonder if she missed me at brunch today. I wonder if she's been remembering to eat and take care of herself.

I start the car and shift into gear, merging with traffic as I make the short drive home. I'm parking in my driveway when I look up and spot some familiar pink hair. My heart thumps out of control in my chest and I hold my breath, willing the girl in the trench coat to turn around so I can see if it's really Cat. Maybe I'm just hallucinating.

She turns as I slam my door closed and my knees actually go weak when I see that her hair is up in two pigtails, the trench coat brushing around her naked legs.

"Hey," I say, stopping a few steps down from her so that we're at eye level.

"Hey, can we talk?" she asks and I nod, unlocking the front door and leading her inside.

"I like your place," she says and I can only stare at her.

Having her in my home feels like a dream come true and part of me is still afraid that this is all some dream or hallucination.

"What are you doing here?" I ask her, my voice coming out low and raspy.

"Well," she says, starting to undo the sash from around her waist.

My eyes snag on the movement and when she finishes untying the belt, she opens the coat, letting it drop and pool at her feet.

"I wanted to apologize, daddy," she purrs and I swear that I must be dreaming.

No way is Cat, my baby girl, standing in my living room in nothing but a pair of high heels, two pigtails, and a poofy baby doll dress that highlights her curves.

"What?" I ask, dazed.

"I said, that I wanted to apologize, daddy," she repeats, stepping closer to me.

Her hands land on my chest, molding to my pecs and my whole body tightens.

"For what?" I demand and she looks up at me from under her lashes.

"For pushing you away. I just... I got scared. Kayley confronted me, she heard us in my office and I was worried about what people would think if they knew what we did. But there's nothing wrong with what we do. I missed you. Being away from you, it just felt wrong. I just, I can't live without you, daddy. I don't want to."

"Thank fuck, baby girl, because I can't live without you either."

I grab her to me then, molding her curves against my chest and she sighs, opening to me as our lips meet and cling to each other.

"I love you," I say, my hands reaching to grab her thighs and lift her. "I love you so goddamn much that it hurts."

"I know. I love you too," she moans against my lips as I carry her into my bedroom. "I'm sorry that I got scared and pushed you away."

"I know you are, baby girl, but you should have come to me and talked about what you were feeling. Since you didn't, there will be a punishment."

She bites her lip, looking up at me with a naughty smile on her face. I can see the excitement in her eyes, and fuck, I missed this. I need my baby girl more than anything. More than I need my next breath.

I sit down on the bed, dragging her closer to me. When she's between my legs, I bend her over my knee so that part of her chest is on the bed. Her ass is right in front of me and I flip the poofy material up, smoothing my hand over the bare globes.

"If you start having doubts. If you have a question or some problem, you come to daddy. Is that clear?" I ask her, my voice firm and she nods.

I spank her, my hand leaving a red handprint behind.

"Answer daddy," I command and she moans, wiggling over my lap.

"Yes, daddy," she purrs and I wonder if she can feel how hard I am right now.

"I'm not sure that I believe you," I say, spanking her again.

She moans, her ass pushing up and I give her what she wants, what we both want.

I rain down smacks, alternating between right and left until her ass is a pretty shade of red and I can see the desire on her thighs.

"I'm sorry, daddy!" she practically sobs, need clear in her voice. "I won't run away from you again."

"Good girl, because daddy is never letting you go again," I praise her, turning and spreading her out on the bed before I reach for the button on my jeans.

I push them down my thighs, coming down over Cat as

I cage her in on the bed. She wraps her legs around my waist, urging me to thrust home and I can't deny either of us any longer.

I thrust into her, both of us groaning as I sink balls deep inside of her. It's like coming home, like heaven. My heaven.

Our lovemaking isn't slow or easy. It's rough, raw, primal, both of us trying to make up for lost time as we mate. It's fucking, but there's still so much love and trust between us.

I can feel her pussy starting to tighten around me and I know it won't be long before she comes, taking me with her.

"I love you, baby girl. Always."

"Daddy!" she screams and she comes, coating my dick in her sweet juices and triggering my own release.

I roll us so that I don't crush her and we both lie there, breathing heavily as we come back down to Earth.

"I love you too, daddy," she says sleepily and I smile, smoothing her pigtails down her back as her breathing evens out.

This, right here. This is all I need in life to be happy.

Thank god my baby girl realized that we were meant to be before I lost my mind or tried to kidnap her.

Now I just need to spend the rest of my life making sure that she's cared for and happy.

What a wonderful way to spend the rest of my life.

TWELVE

Cat

ONE YEAR LATER...

"I GRABBED PURPLE AND PINK," Ender says as he joins me in the bathroom with the hair dye.

"You and the pink," I say with a laugh as he sets the boxes on the counter.

"What can I say? I like my baby girl in pink."

"Pink it is then," I say, grabbing a pair of latex gloves.

"I'll grab some towels," Ender says and I let him squeeze past me to get to the cabinet.

I moved in with Ender shortly after we said I love you. My lease wasn't up on my apartment, so we let Ivy move in since she had just graduated and moved back to the states. I tried to split my time between the two but Ivy likes her space and besides, I wanted to spend every moment that I could with Ender, so it just made sense. I have a feeling that if I had refused or tried to split my time anymore that Ender would have just moved me in anyway.

We see Ivy and Finn all of the time anyway. It's been great having her back and I love seeing her so happy with her man.

"This is a different brand," I notice as I open the box and Ender nods.

"Yeah, it's supposed to be safer for when you're pregnant," he tells me and I look up at him sharply.

"I'm not pregnant," I remind him and he grins at me.

"Not yet."

"You want to have a baby with me?" I ask and he nods.

"I want everything with you, baby girl. You know that."

He's right, I do.

Ender is the sweetest man. He is always looking out for me and anticipating my every need. I love how attentive he is, how all he wants is to see me happy to be happy himself.

He asked me to marry him a week after I moved in. I think that my family was surprised by how fast we were moving but as long as I was happy, then they were too. We got married at city hall. We both just wanted a small gathering with family and friends there. We went to Wild Thyme after and celebrated with everyone close to us. It was perfect.

Ender had offered to plan a bigger wedding, anything I wanted he would make happen, but I didn't want the big day. It wasn't me and I knew it wasn't him either. Our small party was intimate and perfect.

"Got your gloves on?" I ask him and he nods, holding up his hands.

He's been helping me dye my hair for a year so he's pretty much an expert now. I take a seat on the stool in front of the mirror, rearranging the towel around my neck as Ender starts to apply the dye to my hair.

"How was work?" I ask him and he shrugs.

"Fine. I saw Brooks. He came in to get a piece over his ribs."

"That's cool. How are he and Rae doing?" I ask him.

"Good. They wanted to set up another double date, or I guess triple since they invited Palmer and Banks too."

"Oh, that sounds like fun."

"I'll set it up then. You still have girl's night on Thursday, right? So maybe Saturday?"

"Sounds good."

He finishes with the dye and sets the timer.

"Are you hungry, baby girl?"

"Uh huh," I say, giving him a smile and he peels off the gloves and leans over, kissing my cheek.

"Grilled cheese or something sweet?"

"Both."

He laughs but straightens and heads to the fridge to grab my snack.

I play on my phone, texting the girls back about plans for girls' night this week.

"Eat and then we'll wash the dye out of your hair," Ender orders and I happily take my grilled cheese.

"Thanks," I say as I finish off my sandwich and Ender kisses me sweetly as he sets the now empty plate out of the way and moves to help me wash my hair out.

"Ready to see it?" he asks as he towel dries my hair for me.

I look into the mirror, smiling as I see my newly dyed pink hair.

"I love it," I say, turning and wrapping my arms around Ender's neck. "Thank you for helping."

"Anytime."

He kisses me and I can't help but rub against him until I feel his cock hardening and lengthening against my stomach.

"I'm hungry for something else now, daddy," I whisper and he groans.

"Let me take care of that, baby girl," Ender says as he picks me up and carries me into our bedroom.

"Love you, daddy," I whisper against his neck and his grip on me tightens.

"Love you too, baby girl."

He spends all night showing me just how much he loves his baby girl.

THIRTEEN

Ender

TEN YEARS LATER...

I HURRY into the house in search of Cat. I need my baby girl now and our window of opportunity is rapidly closing.

"Baby girl, you better be naked and waiting for me in bed," I call out and I hear her giggling.

I head into the bedroom and sure enough, Cat is under the covers, a mischievous smile on her face.

"Good girl," I say when I pull the covers back to see her naked and ready for me.

Cat moans, squirming on the bed and I know that she's horny for me.

"Daddy's good girl in need?" I ask when I grab her ankle and spread her legs wider apart, noticing that the inside of her thighs are glistening with her desire.

"I ache, daddy," she moans with a sexy pout on her lips and I can't resist her.

My phone rings and it's Max's name on the screen. He's watching our kids and I look back to Cat.

"Answer it," she says and I do.

"Hey, Max. Everything alright?" I ask, concerned that one of the kids could be hurt or sick.

"Yeah, everything's fine. Maxine was just here with her kids and well, they want to have a sleepover over here now. Is it okay if we take them overnight?"

"Let me ask Cat to make sure but that should be alright," I tell him.

"Maxine's kids are over and they want to have a sleep-over. Is that alright?" I ask her and she thinks for a minute, making sure that we don't have any soccer games or gymnastics meets early tomorrow morning before she nods.

"That's fine. Do we need to bring anything over?" I ask Cat's dad Max and he asks for some pajamas and a change of clothes.

"I'll bring that over in a little bit."

"Sounds good. See you then," he says and I hang up.

"Do we need to bring stuff over?" she asks, starting to get up from the bed.

"Yes, but where are you going?" I ask, slipping back into the daddy role.

"To get dressed."

"Daddy needs to take care of his little girl. Then we can run over to drop everything off," I tell her and her eyes darken as I push her back down onto the mattress.

"Daddy's little girl always comes first," I whisper and she shivers as I kiss my way down her belly and between her legs.

You would think that after ten years I would be sick of

eating my little girl out, but if anything, I'm even more obsessed with her.

With two kids, both under the age of nine, we don't have that much alone time. Our daughter is in gymnastics and ice skating and our son is in hockey and football. They both play soccer and they both usually go to an arts summer camp for a week every June. It can be a lot to keep track of and to drive them to, but we make it work.

Cat hired Palmer as an assistant manager after she had graduated college with her business degree, so if we need to leave for some activity or just some alone time, she covers it. Banks and her actually ended up buying a house not too far from here, so we have playdates and sleepovers all of the time.

My baby girl comes on my tongue twice before I slide up her body and thrust home. We both moan at the feeling and I can't help but lean down, stealing a kiss and letting her taste herself on my lips.

"Love you, daddy," she says as I start to move.

"Love you too, baby girl. Forever."

Did you love Ender? Please consider leaving a review! You can do so on Amazon, Goodreads, and Bookbub.

*DID **you miss the original Eye Candy Ink series? You can read the boxset here.***

. . .

GRAB **the next book in the series, Banks, here!**

WANT **to know more about Cat's sister, Ivy? Her book is coming in the Kings Gym series! You can preorder Fighting Tooth and Nail here.**

ARE **you curious about Gray's brother, Jasper? Then check out his book, Always, <u>here</u>.**

ARE **you curious about Ender's military friend, Brooks? Check out his book here!**

BANKS

EYE CANDY INK: SECOND GENERATION

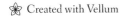 Created with Vellum

*

Banks Mitchell has a dirty little secret.

He's in love with his new next door neighbor.

Palmer Calter is everything that he wants in a woman. She's gorgeous, insanely smart, and hilarious.

There's just one problem.

She's too young for him.

I mean, she just graduated from high school, for goodness' sake.

He knows that he should just let go and move on, but how can he when she keeps showing up and looking at him like he's the best thing that she's ever seen?

When he sees some rich prick sniffing around her, he knows that he has to make a choice. Should he claim his curvy girl or let her go and try to move on?

Will pursuing Palmer ruin everything? Or will he finally get the happily ever after that he's been dreaming about ever since he first laid eyes on her?

ONE

Banks

"SEE YOU TOMORROW!" Ames and Maxine call as we lock up Eye Candy Ink.

I wave, watching them head down the street toward their car. I'm parked across the street in the lot and I can't help but check my phone as I head for my car. No messages and I try to ignore the disappointment at seeing the empty screen.

I climb into my car, heading the few blocks over to my apartment. I've lived there for three years and was actually looking to move somewhere a little nicer. Then she moved in next door.

Palmer Calter.

She was the most beautiful thing that I had ever seen. Still is.

It was her eyes that got me. I've never seen eyes so clear and gray before. They have this lilac circle around the pupil that makes them pop even more. Mix that with her midnight black hair and curvy body and she's a walking wet dream.

She just turned nineteen and is getting ready to start her first semester of college. I helped her move in and I've been looking out for her ever since.

She's so sweet, too sweet for me, but that doesn't stop me from wanting her. I've been holding myself back though. For one, I'm seven years older than her. Her parents are wealthy, pillars of the city and I'm just a tattoo artist.

I park in my spot and grab my backpack, heading inside and up to the third floor. My heart rate starts to pick up as I reach our floor. I send up a silent prayer that I'll see her, and someone must be listening because Palmer's door opens right as I reach my own.

"Hey," I greet her, slowing so we can chat for a minute.

"Hey, are you just getting home?" she asks with a bright smile as she hurries to lock her door.

"Yeah, are you going somewhere?" I ask with a frown as I run my hand through my dark hair and she turns to me with a wide smile.

"Yeah! I got a job a few days ago. Today is my first day working by myself instead of shadowing someone."

"Where?" I blurt out, worried about what kind of job starts at nine at night.

"Seven. Have you heard of it?"

"Yep," I grit out between teeth. "Cat is like my sister."

And I can't believe that she hired my girl. When she told me she did a few days ago, I asked Cat to fire her. Looks like that didn't happen.

"She's so cool! And the tips at Seven seem really good. I'm excited."

I want to argue with her, but she's already heading past me.

"See you later!"

"Wait!" I call. "You shouldn't be working at a club like Seven."

"Why not?"

"There's going to be a lot of drunk guys there. I don't want anything to happen to you."

"Well, I really need this job. Besides, Cat and the bouncers will look out for me."

"Yeah, so will I," I mumble, tucking my apartment key back into my pocket and heading down the stairs. "Come on, I'll drive you."

We're silent as we head downstairs and out to my car. The club is only two blocks away, but with traffic, it takes close to fifteen minutes. I park and Palmer is out of the car and heading for the front door. I have to jog to catch up and I nod at the door bouncer as we pass by him.

She heads behind the bar and I resign myself to sitting at the bar for the next few hours. It's a Friday night, so the place is packed and I glare around the room at all of the drunk college kids who are being rowdy at the other end of the bar.

"Hey, what are you doing here?" Ender asks as he joins me at the bar.

"Uh, just keeping an eye on someone," I say, nodding over to where Palmer just came out of the back.

"Is that your girl?" he asks, and I nod.

"Were you here to see Cat?" I ask him and he grins, nodding as he looks up to the second floor where her office is.

"Yeah, I just brought her some dinner."

I have a feeling that might be code for something, so I don't ask any follow-up questions.

"I'm headed home but I'll see you tomorrow," Ender says and I nod, searching the crowd for my girl.

"See you."

Ender nudges me, nodding over to a table in the corner, and I spot Palmer in the center of a group of guys.

"Try not to kill anyone," he says as he claps me on the shoulder and heads for the door.

"No promises," I growl as I watch my girl work.

My eye starts to twitch as I watch her get hit on by another group of guys, and I know that I'm in trouble here.

TWO

Palmer

I'M STILL GETTING USED to the pounding music and I head into the back, grabbing a Tylenol out of my purse and swallowing it. Between the bass and the chatter from a million different conversations, my head is killing me.

"Hey, are you okay?" Banks asks, pushing into the back area behind me.

"I don't think that you're allowed to be back here," I say as I screw the cap back on my water bottle.

"I know the owners. I think that I'll be fine," he says dryly.

"I'm fine. Just a little headache."

Banks frowns, looking me over like he's making sure that there's nothing else that's bothering me.

"Maybe you shouldn't be working here—" he starts and I glare at him, cutting him off.

"I need to work here. I need the money," I remind him and he sighs, growing agitated.

He runs his hands through his hair, and I can tell that he's frustrated with my answer.

"Time to get back to work again," I say as I start to head past him and he stops me, his hands going to my face.

He tilts my head up, his strong fingers rubbing at my temples, and I bite my lip, trying not to moan at how good it feels to have him touching me, caring for me.

"I'm alright," I whisper and he nods, swallowing hard.

"Are you sure?" he whispers back, his hands moving to my neck and the back of my head.

"Yeah, are you staying?"

"Of course," he says, reluctantly stepping away from me and I instantly miss his hands on me.

I nod, heading past him and out onto the floor. I pick up my tray and make my way over to a table to see if they need another round. I can't help but look over to the bar to see if Banks is watching me. My face heats as our eyes lock and I wonder if I can blame it on the heat in here.

I look away, getting back to work and the next few hours pass agonizingly slowly. I can't stop stealing glances his way or wondering what him insisting on coming here with me means. Could he possibly like me too?

By the time that the club closes, my feet are killing me and I'm ready to head home. Banks helps all of us clean up and then stops me as I head into the back to grab my purse.

"I'll pull the car up front."

I nod, watching him jog outside before I go to my locker to grab my things.

"See you tomorrow!" Cat calls as she joins me and we head outside.

Banks is parked right up front and he hops out to get my door.

"I'll give you a ride to your car, Cat," he says and she tries to wave him off.

"I'm just parked right over there," she argues, but he opens the back door for her anyway.

"Yeah, I'm not dealing with Ender or our families if something happens to you. Get in."

She rolls her eyes but slides into the back of the car and we head down the block and turn into a parking lot.

"See you tomorrow, Palmer," Cat says, playfully hitting Banks' arm as she climbs out of the car.

We stay until she's safely inside of her car before Banks pulls out and heads down the road toward our apartment building.

"Tired?" Banks asks as we drive and I nod, fighting the urge to yawn.

He turns the music on, lowering the volume, and I appreciate that he isn't going to try to get me to make small talk right now.

We pass by Kings Gym and I can't help but look for my stepbrother, Finn. He works and trains there and I swear that he practically lives there. The windows are all dark though and I'm sure that he's at home in his own apartment.

I haven't seen my parents in a few months. Not since the fight. The only people that I've been in contact with have been my stepbrothers.

My mom married Frank when I was eleven. My dad had died in a car accident when I was five and getting used to living with a new parent, let alone his two sons, was an adjustment. Finn and Hendrix are good big brothers, but they're both older than me and couldn't wait to move out. I don't blame them for leaving as soon as they could. I tried to do the same thing.

Finn is the oldest and he left our parents' house the day

after he turned eighteen. He got a job at the gym in town and started training. He never goes back home, not that I blame him, and I'm pretty sure that he hasn't spoken to Frank or my mom in years. Hendrix moved out last year, and he went as far away as he could as soon as he graduated. He's going to college in California and uses that as an excuse to not come back for visits or holidays.

I wanted to leave when I was eighteen too. My stepdad, well, he's a real asshole. Controlling and strict with a lousy temper, he's never happy with any of us. We can never meet his standards and if we tried to stand up to him, well, that never went over well. Sometimes I wonder if that's why Finn practically lives at Kings Gym. If maybe he's training for another fight.

My mom doesn't stand up to him. She never has. He's her meal ticket. He's some hotshot CEO at a company downtown and his image means everything to him. My mom spends her days at the spa and on a few charity boards. I tried to talk to her about him, but she wouldn't have it. It's like she thinks if she ignores it, that it isn't happening or like it will go away.

Neither parent wanted me to go to college. I'm pretty sure they were planning on grooming me and then marrying me off to some other wealthy family's son as soon as they could.

When I made it clear that I would never be on board with that, they changed plans.

They wanted me to stay home with them while I went to college. It doesn't look good that one of their kids fights for a living and another moved out of state to go to some college that isn't even Ivy League. I was their last chance, and I thought that I could handle it but I couldn't.

I wasn't allowed to wear what I wanted to or hang out

with my friends, and when Frank cornered me in the kitchen one morning and started screaming in my face, I snapped. I packed a bag and left that day.

Finn let me crash with him, but his place isn't big and I felt bad that I was dragging him back into the family that he tried to escape from. My mom and stepdad both came to his apartment to demand that I come home, and he was having to fight with them to leave.

Banks parks in his usual spot outside of our building and I wince as I climb out of the car. Without saying a word, Banks comes over to my side and lifts me into his arms like I'm as light as a feather. I blush, not wanting him to hurt himself. I'm not exactly a petite woman and I'm not sure that he can carry my size eighteen ass up the stairs to our places.

"You should get some more comfortable shoes," he tells me.

"Have you ever worn high heels? I'm not sure that they make comfortable versions of them," I joke and Banks laughs.

"Grab the door, smartass," he says and I reach over, opening our apartment door for him.

"I can walk," I say as we reach the stairs, but he ignores me and keeps going.

I rest my head on his shoulder, trying to resist the urge to rub my cheek against him. I try not to be obvious that I'm inhaling his inky paper scent like an addict.

I never told him, or anyone for that matter, but Banks is the reason why I picked this apartment.

I had met Rae at freshman orientation and we hit it off. When I told her that I was looking for a place off campus, she said that she was too and we came here to check out the apartment.

We walked in and there he was. He was heading out of his apartment and our eyes had met. He had smiled at me, nodding at Rae before he headed down the stairs.

That was it. One look and I couldn't get him out of my head.

I had never looked twice at a guy, let alone crushed on one. It's not like Frank would have let me date any of them, so what was the point, but Banks I couldn't forget.

Luckily for me, the apartment was nice and in our price range, so we signed the papers that day.

I think that my stepdad and mom thought that I would come home and when I told them that I had rented an apartment, they went nuclear. They cut me off. My tuition was already paid for and it would have been embarrassing or them if people learned that I was paying my own way so, for now, that's still covered. I know that that might change at the drop of a hat though, and I need to be prepared.

"Are you hungry?" Banks asks as he sets me down on my feet outside my door.

"No, just tired," I say and this time I can't hold in my yawn.

Banks looks concerned, and I give him a smile, trying to reassure him. That look, he obviously cares about me. Maybe I should make the first move, let him know that I want him too. Banks has been a bright spot in my life since I met him and I know, I just know deep down that we're meant to be together.

My heart starts to race and my palms start to sweat as I lick my lips and open my mouth.

"Banks, will you go out with me?"

THREE

Banks

"BANKS, will you go out with me?"

Those seven words have my world spinning out of orbit. I want to say yes. The word is on the tip of my tongue, but then I pause.

She's so young, she has her whole life ahead of her. She's about to start college and if we get together, she's going to miss out on a lot of experiences. Parties, meeting new people, all of it. We'll be wrapped up in each other, and I just want her to know that before we start anything.

I open my mouth again, but it's too late.

Palmer is blinking back tears and rushing to get away from me. She unlocks her apartment door and I try to follow her, but she's faster.

"Palmer, wait!" I try, but the door is slamming in my face.

"Fuck," I grit out, running my fingers down my face.

"Ouch," Brooks says from behind me and I glare over my shoulder at him.

He's Ender's friend, an ex-Army Ranger, and he's been crashing at my place for the last week since he got to town. He just got out of the military and moved to Pittsburgh while he figures out what he wants to do next with his life.

We usually have opposite schedules so I don't see him much. I only let him stay with me as a favor to Ender and Cat. The last thing they need is someone staying with them when they're just starting out. Besides, Brooks is kind of a perfect roommate. He's quiet, cleans up after himself, and always saves me some leftovers when he cooks.

He seems like a good guy, but I don't need anyone to tell me that I just messed up. I already know it. My heart broke the second that I saw those tears in Palmer's eyes.

"Yeah," I say, turning away from her door.

"It pretty obvious that you're into her. Why'd you freeze?" he asks, adjusting the backpack strap on his shoulder as I dig my keys out of my pocket and unlock the door for us.

I don't want to answer him, but maybe an outside opinion will help. I sigh as I head inside and grab a beer out of the fridge. I offer one to him and he nods, taking the bottle from me and leaning against the kitchen counter.

"She's too young. If we got together, it's forever. Shouldn't she explore more, play the field before I lock her down?"

"So, you *want* her to go out on dates or to parties with other guys? Other *college-age* guys?"

His words have me seeing red, and he laughs.

"Yeah, that's what I thought."

"The thought of some other guy touching her drives me

insane, but isn't it selfish of me to make her mine without giving her that opportunity?"

"I don't think so. I mean, she's into you too or she wouldn't have asked you out."

I take a swig of my beer, letting his words roll around in my head.

"I don't know Palmer that well, but she seems like an old soul. I think she knows her own mind. If she wants you, then you don't need to be a martyr and push her away. I mean, people marry high school sweethearts all of the time. I think when you know, you just know."

He shrugs, downing half his beer, and I mull over what he said. Maybe he's right? Or maybe I just want him to be right so that I can be with Palmer.

I'm not sure that I can trust myself when it comes to Palmer. I would never do anything to hurt her, but I also don't want to control her and keep her from experiencing all that she wants to in life.

"I'll think about it."

Brooks nods, finishing off his beer.

"I'm hitting the shower. See you in the morning," he says and I nod, staying in the kitchen for a few more minutes to think.

Should I go back over to Palmer's and apologize? Would she even want to see me right now?

I pull out my phone, debating texting her but I don't know what to say right now. Besides, it feels like this is a conversation to have face to face.

I finish off my own beer and head to my room. It's late and I should be tired, but when I lie down, I can't stop seeing Palmer's tear-filled eyes. I keep going round and round in my head, debating what to do.

I know that it would kill me to see her with someone else, but am I too old for her?

In the end, I still don't know what to do and it's a long while before I'm able to go to sleep.

FOUR

Palmer

I CAN'T STOP THINKING about what happened with Banks last night. There's a permanent ache in my chest and it took me over an hour of talking to Rae and telling her what happened to get my emotions under control and come up with a plan.

I've decided to just avoid him. I know that we're neighbors, but I have a pretty good idea of his schedule and if I just don't answer the door and ignore his texts, I'm sure that he'll get the message eventually.

That plan immediately goes off the rails as soon as I step out of my apartment.

"Hey."

"Jesus!" I say, jumping at the sound of his voice behind me.

"Sorry, I didn't mean to scare you," Banks says, shifting on his feet.

"Don't worry about it," I tell him as I finish locking my front door.

"Where are you headed?"

"To campus. I need to get my books for the semester."

"Let me drive you."

"That's okay. I don't mind walking," I object.

"Then I'll walk with you."

I can see that he isn't going to let this go, and I grind my teeth as I debate what to do next.

"Suit yourself."

I start to head down the stairs with him right behind me. We hit the sidewalk and he grabs my elbow, steering me over to his car.

"It will be faster to drive. Besides, do you really want to have to carry those books all the way back here?"

I bite my lip, debating, but he opens the door for me.

"Please, we need to talk," he murmurs and I can't resist him, so I slip inside.

I wait until he's started the car before I ask the million-dollar question.

"What do we need to talk about?"

He pulls out of the parking lot and heads toward campus.

"Last night."

"Nope. No, trust me, we don't need to talk about last night. I actually think that it would be better if we both just forgot it ever happened and move on."

"I can't."

"Sure, you can."

"No, I can't. I want you, Palmer."

That sentence seems to suck all of the air out of the car. My heart is racing out of control and I can feel my hopes growing, but it feels like there's a but coming and I try to rein myself in.

"I want you so bad that it hurts, Palmer, and I don't ever want you to doubt that."

"Then why... why didn't you say yes last night?" I ask as he turns onto campus.

"I was trying to be a good guy."

"You are a good guy," I tell him as he parks in a spot in front of the campus bookstore.

"You're young, Palmer. You're about to start college and you should be out partying or rushing a sorority or whatever kids do. I just want you to know what you're getting yourself into. What you're giving up."

"And what's that?" I ask, turning in my seat to face him.

"You need to think good and hard about what you want. If you want to go out to party or to explore your sexuality with other guys or girls, then that's fine. If you want me, then you need to be sure. You need to be all in, because I won't let you go. I can't."

I stare at him and he watches me back.

"I'm not some dumb college boy who doesn't know what he wants or is just looking to hook up."

I can't believe that this is happening and I want to tell him that he's the only one I want too, but an image of Frank pops into my head and I can't help but wonder if I'm trading one controlling man for another.

I nod, my throat dry as a desert as I lean back in my seat, trying to process everything that just happened.

Rae walks by and she waves as she spots us.

"I'll, uh, I'll get a ride home with Rae."

Banks nods, looking disappointed but like he understands.

"Text me if you need anything," he says, and I nod as I climb out with my backpack over my shoulder.

I close the door, waving as I head over to join my friend.

"What was that about? Did he apologize for last night?" she asks.

"Not exactly."

"Then what did he want?" she asks as we head into the bookstore.

"Me."

FIVE

Banks

"EVERYTHING ALRIGHT?" Harvey asks as he stops outside of my room at Eye Candy Ink.

"Yeah," I lie, frowning down at my phone.

There's been no texts or calls from Palmer for the past twenty-four hours, and I can't help but wonder if what I said to her yesterday outside the campus bookstore scared her off.

I was trying to give her space yesterday, which is why I didn't try to contact her or go to Se7en to see her, but now I wonder what I'll do if I never hear from her again.

Did I fuck everything up by telling her how much I want her?

I wish that there was someone that I could talk to but all of my friends are happily settled down and I'm not sure that they could understand it.

They've all found their other half and it's hard being the odd man out. Ender and Cat were the last ones to settle down and I think it was a surprise to everyone. When Gray and Nora got together, everyone saw it coming. The same thing goes with Coraline and Harvey and even Sayler and Rooney.

Maybe I could go see Cat. They've gotten closer since Palmer started to work for her at Se7en. Palmer seems to like her and maybe she's said something to Cat about me. It's a long shot, but I'm starting to grow desperate.

"I'm headed to Wild Thyme to see Coraline and grab some food. You want anything?" Harvey asks and I shake my head no, but then I remember that I skipped lunch to finish up a client.

"The mac and cheese and those chicken and waffle things if she's making them. If not, then just whatever the special is," I tell Harvey, reaching for my wallet and handing him two twenties.

"Be right back," he says and I know that that's a lie.

He doesn't get to see Coraline as much as he'd like so when they get the chance, they make it last. It's not a bother. I have another client coming in fifteen minutes. This one is just a small design on her shoulder and should only take me forty-five minutes.

If I'm lucky, that will be about the time that Harvey gets back with the food.

"Hey, Harvey said that you were crying or something?" Rooney says as he appears in my doorway and I groan.

"You're so full of shit," I say, trying not to laugh.

"We're all really worried about you."

"Why? I'm fine."

"Are you?"

"Yes," I insist.

"Are you?" he asks again, his voice rising several octaves and threatening to crack.

"Oh my god," I mumble, dragging my hands down my face.

Rooney is a real prankster, just like his dad. They both live to mess with people and they're masters at it.

"Seriously, man. You've seemed kind of wound up the last few weeks," he says, his index finger twirling in the air.

"You look crazy," I inform him, and he grins and comes in, plopping down in the chair next to me.

"Anything that you want to talk to me about?"

"Nope."

"Okay, I'll let Uncle Nico and Aunt Edie know. They're threatening to have an intervention."

"No, they're not," I say, glaring at him and he grins.

"They didn't say that in so many words."

"Or at all."

"But for real. The family has noticed. You've been even more broody and quiet than normal. They think that you need to get laid. I have to say, I agree."

I turn back to my desk, intending to get to work, but Rooney kicks my leg. When I turn to snap at him, I can see that he's clearly worried about me. There's only been a dozen times that Rooney has looked so serious and I bite my tongue, waiting to hear what he has to say.

"It's your neighbor, isn't it? Cat and Ender both mentioned that you seemed hung up on her."

"Ender is gossiping now?" I try to joke.

"Yeah, he's really opened up since he got with Cat. He's all sensitive and shit now. Right, Ender?" Rooney calls and Ender just grunts as he walks past my room.

I laugh, but Rooney doesn't let it go.

"So, is it her? The neighbor?"

"Yeah."

"Have you asked her out yet?"

"Yeah, yesterday. She's still thinking about it."

"Well, that's good then. It wasn't a straight-up no, so you can work with that. If she's really the one for you, then don't give up on her."

I nod, realizing that maybe my friends can understand and help me out in this scenario.

"Thanks, Rooney."

"Anytime. As this Eye Candy Ink's resident ladies' man—"

"Get out."

He laughs like the maniac that he is as he stands and heads out and it's only a minute later that Ames calls my name, letting me know that my next client is here.

I head up to the front, trying to block the jealousy when I see Ames and Maxine cuddling together behind the counter. All of my family and friends are settled down now and it only serves as a reminder that I don't have Palmer and haven't heard from her. I want her. I want what everyone else has. A happily ever after. I'm talking the white picket fence, kids, dogs, all of it, and I want it with Palmer.

I've been focused on tattooing and my career for so long, determined to be the best so that I didn't have to live in my dad's or the rest of my family's shadow. It's been a decade and I've proven myself. Now I want to be the best boyfriend, husband, father that I can be. I want to settle down, maybe even cut back on my work hours.

I force a smile at my client and lead her back to my room. She's in a spaghetti strap shirt, so I have her pull that strap down while I get the tattoo stencil ready.

"Got any plans for tonight?" she asks and I look over to my phone, wondering if Palmer has messaged me yet.

"No," I say, tugging on my gloves and fitting a needle to my machine.

"That's too bad. Maybe we can change that," she says flirtatiously and I don't reply to that, tipping my head down and getting started outlining her tattoo.

It's a rose, something that I could do in my sleep, but she makes it hard by flinching every time I touch her with the needle or even turn the machine on. The tattoo that should have taken forty-five minutes ends up lasting closer to two hours and by the time I get her bandaged up and out the door, my food is cold and I'm running late to my next appointment.

I was hoping that I could run to Se7en tonight and check on my girl, but it doesn't look like that's going to happen. I don't even know if she's working tonight to be fair. I try to check my phone every chance that I can get but when I still haven't heard from her by midnight when I finally head home, I wonder if maybe in a way, I already got my answer.

SIX

Palmer

I CAN'T STOP THINKING about what Banks said yesterday. I didn't work last night, so I had plenty of free time to play the conversation over and over again in my head. I even dreamed about it last night.

This should be a dream come true, but I need to be focused right now. My first semester at college started today and I need to succeed. I need to get my head on straight.

My phone rings, and for a second, I wonder if it's him. He seems to have been giving me some space since he dropped me off at campus, and I wonder how long that will last. Banks doesn't strike me as the type of man to give up on something that he wants.

I grab my phone, my stomach dropping when I see my mom's name on the screen. I've been avoiding her calls for the last three weeks. I know that I won't like what she has to say, but I'm not sure how much longer I can go on ignoring her calls.

What if she shows up here with Frank? I really can't have that happening.

I close my eyes, taking a deep breath as I hit accept and remind myself to stay calm.

"Hey, Mom."

"Palmer, finally! I've been calling you for weeks. Why didn't you call me back?" she demands, her voice full of annoyance and I wonder when the last time was when she talked to me like she used to when I was young.

Nowadays, she always sounds like she's chasing after an errant child or like she's disappointed in me.

I know that Frank is the reason for this change. He's mad at me and she has to agree with him. She's trapped in that marriage to him. If she leaves, she gets nothing, and she loves her new socialite life too much to walk away. I only wish that she loved me more.

"Sorry, I've been busy with work and getting ready for school."

"You wouldn't need to do either of those things if you didn't have to always have your way. You shouldn't have antagonized Frank the way you did and he would have provided for you."

I want to argue with her but unfortunately, I know that there is no point.

My mom launches into a monologue and I tune her out. Banks' words from yesterday play in my head and I wonder if I said yes to him, would I be trapped just like my mom if I wanted to walk away? He made it sound like he would never let me walk away.

That's the reason that I didn't say yes to him yesterday as soon as he told me that he wanted me. I can't stop comparing him to Frank and wondering if it would be a mistake.

The two are nothing alike though. Sure, they're both control freaks, but Banks does it because he wants to help me and make sure that I'm safe. Frank does it for his image and to feel like a big shot.

Banks helped us move in here. He sends food at least once a week because I made a joke one time about us living off of ramen since I was just a broke college kid and he told me that I need to have a better diet than that. He wanted me to stop working at Se7en but he didn't forbid me and when I made it clear why I wanted to, he supported me. He came to make sure that I was safe.

Frank never did any of that. He wants me to fail so that I have to go crawling back to him and beg forgiveness.

Banks wants me to succeed. He wants me to be happy and safe and to have everything that I want or need.

Thinking that the two of them are the same is laughable.

Banks is a thousand times better than my stepdad. Maybe that's why I've always been so drawn to him. Because he's the opposite of the man that I hate.

I think that it has to be more than that though. I was on campus for hours today, saw hundreds of guys, and not one of them interested me.

Only Banks can do that.

"Hey, Mom? I have to go. I'm sorry," I say as I hang up the phone on her mid-sentence.

I can hear her squawking at me as I hit end, but I don't care. I'm sure that I'll pay for that later but it will be worth it.

"Hey," Rae says as she comes in the door and I look over to her.

"Hey, how was your day?"

"Busy. School and work makes for a long ass day. I need

to work on my schedule for next semester so that my days aren't so long," she says as she drops her backpack on the couch and collapses next to it.

"Yeah, today was easy for me. Tomorrow is my long day. I made pasta," I tell her as I start to scoop her up a plate.

"You're an angel," she sighs as she drags herself off the couch and takes a seat at the counter.

I set the plate of spaghetti down and grab her the last of the garlic bread as she digs in.

"This is so good. Thank you. Seriously."

"No problem."

"Did you make a decision yet?" she asks me in between shoveling bites of spaghetti into her mouth.

"About what?" I ask, and she stops to stare me down.

"The hunk next door."

"Brooks?" I tease, pretending to play dumb.

Her cheeks heat and I wonder what that's about but before I can ask, she changes it back to Banks.

"Have you talked to your possessive little admirer yet?"

"No, but I'm about to," I say with a grin and she laughs, grinning back at me.

"Go get him, girl!"

I throw a paper towel at her as I straighten my shirt and head for the door.

"I won't wait up!" Rae calls as I head out and I laugh as I make the short walk over to Banks' apartment.

I take a deep breath, trying to settle myself before I raise my fist and knock.

It takes him a few minutes to come to the door and when he does, he's already in his pajamas. My mouth goes dry as I take in his still wet hair, the white shirt stretched over his chest and biceps, just the hint of the tattoos beneath that fabric.

"What's wrong?" Banks asks, pulling me into the apart-ment and looking around the hallway. "Why are you up so late?"

I take another deep breath, ignoring his questions and answering a different one.

"I'm all in."

SEVEN

Banks

I REACH OUT, grabbing her hand and tugging her into the apartment. I've got her backed up against the door a second later and my lips crush hers beneath mine.

"About time," I growl against her lips and she giggles.

The sound is cut off as I kiss her neck, sucking on the skin at the base of her throat and shoulder and then licking a path up her neck and nibbling her earlobe.

"I want you, but I don't want to rush you," I whisper and she shakes her head, her body trembling against mine.

"I want you too. So much."

I kiss her one more time before I grab her hand and lead her into my bedroom. Brooks is still out and I'm glad that we have the apartment to ourselves right now.

I reach for her, kissing her and trying to be gentle. I want to rip both of our clothes off and pin her to the bed as I fuck her hard, but I'm guessing that she's a virgin and she needs me to be soft right now.

I kiss her shoulder, her neck, her pulse point and Palmer moans, tilting her head to the side and giving me more room. Her hips start to rock against me and I bite back a moan, willing myself to take it slow.

Then Palmer's hands slide under my shirt and I can't go slow anymore. I rip my shirt off over my head, reaching for hers in the next instant, and she lifts her hands, helping me take it off.

She's so pale and curvy and I swear she looks like an angel standing half naked in my bedroom.

Her fingers toy with her pants and my mouth dries as I wait to see what she'll do next. She unbuttons them, pushing the jeans down, and my mouth drops with them.

She's got a lacy pair of panties on and I can just make out the smooth skin beneath. She takes a step back toward the bed and I follow, pushing my pajama pants down as I trail after her.

She sits down on the bed, looking nervous and I can't have that. I need to reassure her.

"I'm going to take care of you, baby," I breathe as I drop to my knees in front of her.

She blushes as I reach for her panties, pulling them off and then spreading her thighs wide. She's so wet from me and I can see her juices glistening on her pussy lips and the insides of her thighs.

"So fucking beautiful," I say, looking up at her and she blushes more. "I need a taste," I say, leaning in and licking a path up her center.

My tongue finds her clit and I roll it over the sensitive bundle of nerves until she starts to moan. Her fingers sink into my hair, holding me against her, and I grin.

My tongue sinks lower, circling her opening over and

over until she lets out a needy whine. I push one finger inside of her, knowing that I need to stretch her if I want to stand a chance at fitting my cock inside of this snug as fuck hole.

"Yes, don't stop," Palmer moans.

As if I could.

I moan, sucking her clit into my mouth as I add a second finger and curl them, rubbing against that spot that drives her wild. She gasps, her pussy dripping on my fingers and clamping down around them.

My cock is aching but I'm determined to make her come at least once before I sink inside of her and find my own release.

"Banks!" Palmer screams, her mouth open wide and a flush covering her body as she starts to find her release.

"That's it," I say as I pull back and watch her come on my fingers.

She collapses back onto the mattress and I gently pull my fingers out of her, giving her clit one last lick before I kiss my way up her body.

By the time I've reached her tits, she's regained some energy, and she sits up a bit, letting me unhook her bra and slip the straps down her arms.

Her full breasts spill free and my mouth waters at the sight. She watches me eagerly, and I grin as I lean forward and bite down on one of her nipples. She moans, arching into the touch and I lick, soothing the sting away with my tongue. My fingers slip back between her legs to play with her clit and it doesn't take long before she's back to being right on the edge.

I take turns playing with one tit and then the other until she's coming again. It feels like my cock is going to explode, so I push my boxers down, letting my cock out.

It slips between her drenched folds and we both moan at the contact.

"What is that?" She breathes and I smile.

"I'm pierced."

Her eyes widen and I grin.

"It will feel good. I promise."

She nods and I move us into the center of the bed, slipping between her curvy thighs.

"Ready?" I ask her, my cock brushing back and forth along her pussy and she nods, taking a deep breath to try to relax.

I move down, lining my cock up with her opening and slowly start to sink inside of her. I make it an inch and I'm already sweating. She's so fucking tight. I've never felt anything better in my life.

I look down at her, making sure that she's alright and the sight of her black hair spread out over my pillows has my heart racing. Her gray and purple eyes are glowing as she stares up at me.

I sink in another inch, hitting her virginity, and I hate the thought of hurting her. Palmer nods up at me, spreading her thighs wider and I push forward, popping her cherry and making her mine.

Palmer winces and I force myself to remain perfectly still, letting her have time to adjust.

"I feel so full," she whispers and I swear I almost come at her words.

She moves, her hips shifting, and I groan, closing my eyes and gritting my teeth.

"Move," she moans and I have no choice but to do as she commands.

I start slow, letting us find a rhythm together. Soon her

legs are wrapped around my hips and she's rising to meet each of my thrusts.

We speed up together naturally, both of us chasing our peaks. Her tits bounce with each thrust and the sight has me burning hotter and hotter.

"You're so fucking perfect," I moan and she blushes slightly, her eyes starting to glaze over with passion.

"I'm so close," she grits out brokenly, and I nod.

I'm right there with her.

"Come for me, baby. I want to feel you coat my cock in your juices."

She cries out, her body locking up tight as she starts to come and the sight of her pleasure has my own orgasm rolling through me.

"Fuck! Palmer!" I groan as I come with her.

It takes me a while to come back down and I lean down, kissing her as I slowly pull out. She sighs and I smile, kissing her again. My arms give out and I roll to the side at the last minute so that I don't crush her.

"That was... better than I thought it would be," she says with a sweet giggle and I pull her into my arms.

"Did you think about it a lot?" I ask with a laugh and she nods, blushing slightly.

I love how sweet she is.

"Me too," I admit.

Palmer cuddles closer to my side and I kiss her neck, breathing in her cotton candy scent as we both drift off to sleep wrapped around each other.

EIGHT

Palmer

I WINCE as I stretch the next morning, my body sore in places that I didn't even know existed before last night.

"'Morning," Banks says as he wraps his arm around my waist and tugs me closer against him.

I can feel myself blush as he nuzzles my neck, nipping at my earlobe. His body is warm and strong against my back and I can't help but wiggle against him, my ass making contact with his hard cock.

"Are you sore?" he asks, his hand slipping from my hip down between my legs.

He cups my pussy, his middle finger slipping between my lips and circling my clit. I bite my lip, moaning as my eyes fall closed. My hips start to rock, searching for more, for him and I can feel him grin against my shoulder.

His finger dips lower, pushing against my entrance, and I tense as he hits a sore spot. Banks pulls back immediately and I try to stop him, but he rolls me over onto my back.

"What time is your first class?" he asks me and I pout.

He leans in, kissing me. His tongue brushes against mine, and I try to deepen it but he pulls away again.

"What time is your class?" he asks again and I have to think to remember.

"Not until ten."

"It's nine right now, baby."

"What?" I ask, shooting up in bed and scrambling to grab my phone from the floor.

He's right and I start to race around, pulling my clothes on as I go.

"Here," Banks says as I race by the kitchen to head next door.

He hands me a breakfast burrito that he must have microwaved and I smile as I take a big bite.

"Thanks," I say as I lean over, kissing him before I bolt for the door.

"I'll text you when I get some breaks at work," he calls after me and I nod, darting into my apartment as Rae heads out.

"Want me to wait for you?" she asks and I nod, chewing my bite of burrito.

"I'll be five minutes!"

She nods, staying out in the hallway as Brooks comes up the stairs and part of me wants to eavesdrop on their conversation, but I don't have time to. I hurry into my room and tug on the first thing that my fingers touch. I only have two classes this morning, so I should be done by one this afternoon.

I shove the last bite of burrito into my mouth and grab my shoes and backpack. Brooks is just heading into his apartment as I step out and lock the door and I raise my eyebrow at Rae but she ignores me, grabbing my hand instead as we race down the stairs.

"Want to talk about Brooks?" I ask as I slide into the passenger seat of her car.

"No, I'd rather talk about what happened with you and Banks last night. Are you two officially together?"

"Yeah," I say with a blush and a grin and she laughs, reaching over to high five me.

"How was it?" she asks, wiggling her eyebrows at me and I swat her arm.

"It was really good. Not that I have anything to compare it to, but still."

"Well, it's about time. You deserve someone who loves you and puts you first."

We pull onto campus and Rae lets me out in front of my first class before she heads to find a parking spot.

"What time are you done today?" she asks as I hop out.

"I have this biology class and then an English one after, so I should be out at one."

"I still think it's dumb that we need a science credit when we're never going to enter that field," she complains and I laugh.

"I know, as a business major, when am I going to use biology?"

Rae laughs as I grab my backpack from the back seat and shut the door. She rolls the window down and I lean down to see her.

"I'm done at one fifteen if you want to meet me at the car and I'll drive us home."

"Sounds good," I tell her as I close the door and head down the sidewalk toward my biology class.

My phone buzzes and I bite my lip as I read the text from Banks.

. . .

BANKS: **Miss you.**
   Palmer: Miss you more

I SEND him a kiss face emoji before I take my seat. I have a few missed calls from my mom and I know that I'll need to figure out a way to deal with her and Frank soon, but for now, I'm putting it off.

My classes both finish before the hour since we're just going over the syllabus today, so I head out to the parking lot to search for Rae's car. My phone buzzes in my pocket and I pull it out, groaning when I see my mom's name on the screen.

I ignore it, smiling when I see Rae headed my way. We throw our bags into the back seat and she sighs long and loud as she starts the car and pulls out of the lot.

"Are you working tonight?" I ask her and she nods.

"Me too."

"Want to grab a pizza so we don't have to cook?" I ask, and she grins.

"You're perfect," she sighs. "Banks is one lucky man."

I laugh as she pulls in front of our favorite pizza place. Rae runs in to grab us a pizza and I check my phone for more messages from Banks. There's one from an hour ago when he was on his lunch break but he said it was a busy day so I'm not surprised that he hasn't messaged me more.

My phone rings. Frank this time, and I know that that's a sign that my time is running out. I just wish that I felt strong enough to face them.

Rae hands me the boxes and we head home in silence. I think she thinks that I'm just tired, but the truth is that I'm trying to work up the courage to face my family.

We drive past Kings Gym and I wonder if I should call

Finn or even Hendrix and ask for advice on how to deal with our parents.

Rae parks and we grab the pizza and our backpacks before we head inside and up the stairs. I'm laughing at Rae as she jokes about how many slices she's going to eat when we reach our floor and I look over to see my mom pacing angrily outside of our apartment door.

"There you are!" she shouts, glaring at me like I put her out when I didn't even know that she was coming.

"I'll, uh, I'll take these in for us," Rae says, side eyeing my mom before she grabs the pizza boxes from me. "Let me know if you need anything."

I nod, giving Rae a forced smile before I turn to face my mom.

"Hi, Mom."

"Don't you *hi, mom* me, young lady. Why haven't you called me back? You've been ignoring my calls, your father's calls—"

"Stepfather," I correct her which earns me another glare.

"It's time for this to end."

"For what to end?" I ask, confused and already exhausted with this whole conversation.

"You need to come back home. Where you belong. It's not respectable for a young lady like yourself to be living on your own and sleeping around."

"I don't want to move back in with you and Frank," I tell her, careful not to call it home. "I took a year off because you asked me to, but now it's time for me to live my life. I'm not giving up what I want just to please Frank and you. I'm not giving up on what I want like you did," I snap and that seems to shock her.

She rocks back on her pointy high heels, her mouth

dropping open and her face flushing with anger. My palms are sweating and I know that I just changed our relationship irrevocably.

She doesn't say anything, she just turns and storms off, stomping down the stairs and out of my view.

My appetite is long gone and I know that Rae will listen to me, but I don't think that she'll really understand it all.

"Hey, Rae? I'm running out for a bit. I'll be back by five," I call into our apartment before I turn and jog down the stairs.

I pull out my phone as I hit the sidewalk, dialing Hendrix and wondering if he'll answer. He's in college too and I wonder when his classes are. I get his voice mail and I leave a short message letting him know that I need his help with our parents.

I head down the sidewalk, stopping outside of the slightly rundown brick building. Kings Gym is pretty much a local landmark and I look through the front windows, spotting Brooks and Finn inside over by the punching bags.

"Hey, Coach," I say as I walk past the old man sitting behind the counter and he nods at me, going back to his newspaper as I make my way over to the punching bags and my stepbrother.

"Hey, Palmer," Brooks says as he holds the bag steady for Finn.

"Hey, how's it going?" I ask and he just nods as Finn grabs a towel and his water bottle.

"What's going on?" Finn asks and Brooks steps away, giving us some privacy.

"My mom came to see me today. She and Frank have been calling me a lot the last two weeks, so I guess I should have seen it coming."

"What did she want?"

"She wants me to move back in with them. She says that it's not ladylike for me to live alone at my age."

Finn snorts, looking pissed.

"You know that it's bullshit, right? You're an adult. You can do whatever you want."

"I know, it's just hard with them harassing me and getting all pissed at me."

Finn nods, taking a swig from his water bottle as he weighs my words.

"I can try to run interference for you, but they're probably not going to let it drop. You're Frank's last chance to have a kid under their thumb. He's not going to give up on you easily."

I nod, knowing that he's right. I had thought that after I got a job and proved that I was okay out of their house that they would let it go, but that hasn't happened.

"If you need anything, you know that Hendrix and I are here for you. We can help."

"Thanks," I say, leaning in to give him a hug before I remember how sweaty he is.

Finn laughs, trying to grab me, and I sidestep him, backing up toward the door. Brooks comes back over to join us and I know that I need to get back to Rae so we can get ready to go to work.

"If you and Rae want to move in with me until this dies down, you can. I don't want you getting harassed at your place."

"What?" Brooks asks, frowning, but we both wave him off.

"Thanks, I'll let you know if she stops by again."

Finn nods and I nod to Brooks as I get ready to go.

"I'll talk to you later, bro! See you, Brooks!" I call and they wave as they head back to the punching bags.

I head home feeling lighter about having options to deal with my mom and Frank. I wonder if I should tell Banks what's going on. Maybe he could have some insight too.

I bite my lip as I think about him coming to Se7en tonight to watch me. Maybe I can convince him that I'm not sore anymore and we can go for a repeat of last night.

I grin as I climb the stairs and head into my apartment.

NINE

Banks

I FINISH WRAPPING up my client's leg and walk him up front so that he can check out with Maxine. She takes over and I hurry back to my room so that I can grab my phone and check in with Palmer.

She left in such a hurry this morning that I didn't get to properly say goodbye and make sure that she was alright after last night. I should have at least given her some pain medicine and made her a better breakfast.

I grab my phone and there are no new messages from Palmer, so I decide to call her.

"Hey," she says, answering after the second ring.

"Hey, are you busy?" I ask, smiling as I sit down at my desk.

"No, just finished eating and I need to organize my planner before I head to work."

"How was school?"

"Good, we just went over our course schedule so it was a pretty easy day."

"I missed you," I admit, and I hear a dramatic gasp behind me.

I grin, knowing without looking that it's Rooney standing there and that I'm going to get shit from him as soon as I hang up.

"I missed you too," she says softly, and I can hear the smile in her voice.

"I should be off around eleven tonight. I have one more client and it's to finish up a backpiece, so it might take a while. Want me to pick you up from Seven tonight?" I offer.

"Rae is working tonight too so I can just get a ride with her."

I frown at that. She seems tense and I wonder what's going on.

"Is everything okay?" I ask after a minute and I listen as she takes a deep breath.

"My mom stopped by today."

"Is everything alright?" I ask, alarmed.

She hasn't talked about her parents very much in the months that I've known her and I wonder if her mom is sick or something.

"Yeah, they just want me to move back home."

"No."

"What?" she asks, sounding surprised by my firm tone.

"No, you're not moving back home. You love living with Rae. Besides, with our schedules, we'd never see each other if you weren't next door."

"I know, and I don't want to go back home. They just... they've been trying to control me since my mom married Frank and I don't know how to get them to see that I'm an adult and fine on my own. I know that if I moved back home that they'd be pressuring me to drop out of college next and let them set me up with someone."

I try not to growl at the thought of Palmer being set up with anyone besides me. It doesn't sound like her parents would approve of Palmer being with me.

"What do you need, baby? Do you want me to be on the lookout for them around the building?"

"I don't know if she'll come back to the apartment. I talked to Finn, and he said that he can try to run interference too. Hendrix just messaged me back to and offered to look into it if I wanted to transfer to his college in California and stay with him and his friends."

"Why are your parents doing this?" I ask, not liking the idea of her moving so far away from me.

"It's my stepdad mainly. He's just a control freak. All he cares about is his image and when both of his sons bucked him and left, he only had me left to try to mold. I don't want to be a trophy wife or a stay-at-home mom. I want to be independent and they don't want that for me."

"Then we'll make sure that they don't force you to do anything that you don't want. Make sure that Rae has my number in case of emergencies. If you need anything, Palmer, you come to me. Got it?"

"Yeah. Thanks, Banks," she whispers gratefully.

"I'll ask Brooks to keep an eye out for anyone hanging around too. Do you need anything else, baby?"

"No, just your support."

"You have it."

Palmer lets out a sigh, sounding like a weight has been lifted and I try to relax too. I just got her. I'm not about to let her go, especially not to people who don't give a damn what she wants out of life.

"Why don't you stay at my house tonight. I'll stay up for you," I tell her.

"Okay. I've got to go. I need to get ready for work or I'll be late."

"Yeah, my next client should be here any minute. I'll see you in a few hours."

"See you," she says and then the line goes dead.

"Well, well, well," comes a gleeful voice behind me and I laugh as I turn to face Rooney.

Harvey and Gray are both there with him, and I send up a silent prayer that my next client shows up early.

"What's up?" I ask, trying to play it cool and they all step forward at once, getting jammed in the doorframe.

I laugh as they squabble and try to push each other out of the way. Gray is the first to make it into my room and I roll my eyes as Harvey elbows Rooney and sneaks in next.

"So…" Harvey says, drawing out the word.

"So, Palmer and I are together now," I admit and they cheer.

"Finally," Harvey says, leaning against my desk.

"Is that why you've been singing and skipping around all day?" Rooney asks and I roll my eyes at him.

"Yeah."

"Banks! Your client is here," Maxine calls down the hallway, and I jump up from my chair.

"When do we get to meet her?" Harvey asks as they get ready to head back to their own rooms.

"Soon," I tell them, and he claps me on the back as he heads out.

"Happy for you," Gray says as he follows and I smile.

"I told Uncle Nico and Aunt Edie," Rooney says as he leaves and I groan.

I'm sure that my parents are going to be asking me to

bring Palmer around too, and I flip Rooney off as I head up front to get my next client.

I can't really be mad at him though. Not when I finally have my dream girl and I know that she's going to be in my bed tonight.

TEN

Palmer

BANKS IS WAITING OUTSIDE of Se7en when I clock out and I can't say that I'm surprised to see him there. I smile as he comes over to join Rae and I.

His hand wraps around the back of my neck and he pulls me to him, claiming my lips with his for a brief moment.

"How was work, baby?" he asks me and I grin up at him.

"Good. Busy."

"Hey, Rae. I'll walk you to your car," he says and we all take off across the street to the parking lot.

"I'm so tired," Rae groans and I wrap my free hand around her shoulders and give her a little squeeze.

"Are you hungry? We can stop and grab food on the way home?" Banks offer but we both say no.

"We'll follow you home," I say as Rae climbs into her car and she waves as we head over to Banks' car.

"I thought that you were going to be waiting for me at home," I say as we buckle up.

"I was worried about you. If they want you to quit, I thought that they might show up at work and try to get you fired."

My heart melts at his concern for me, and I relax more into my seat as he drives us down the deserted streets.

"I don't think they'd do that. It would ruin their image to be seen at a club like Seven."

Banks' hands tighten on the steering wheel as we turn onto our street.

"Have you thought about going to the police about this? If they're showing up at your house to harass you, it might be time for a restraining order," he suggests.

"I don't think I can. They didn't really break any laws and they could just say that it was parental concern."

Banks nods but he doesn't look happy about it.

"I don't want you to be stressed or worried about this. You have enough on your plate with starting school and work."

I know that he's right. I haven't wanted to burn bridges with them but how long do I really think that they're going to leave me alone? How soon before they cut me off or give me an ultimatum? It's only going to become more stressful to keep waiting for the other shoe to drop.

"I guess that I'm just hoping that they come to their senses and realize that I'm an adult and can make my own decisions. I don't want to lose them or stop talking to them."

"I know. Family is really important to me too. Rooney told my parents about us, so I'm sure they're dying to meet you."

"Who is Rooney?" I ask.

"Oh, yeah. I keep forgetting that you haven't met

anyone from the shop yet. Rooney works at Eye Candy Ink too and he's kind of like my brother. Just never tell him that I said that."

I giggle at how worried he sounds when he says that last line.

"I won't," I promise him as he parks outside of our building.

"We have brunch together every Sunday. Do you want to come this weekend? You can bring Rae if you want. That might make you more comfortable. My family is big and kind of rowdy."

"I'll ask her," I say with a smile as we climb out of the car.

Rae joins us, and we head inside together.

"Are you sleeping at my place?" Banks asks me and I nod, looking over to Rae to make sure that she doesn't mind.

"I'll see you in the morning," she says with a sly smile and I grin back at her as Banks leads me into his apartment.

"Do you want to talk about your parents or anything?" Banks asks as he locks the door and I shake my head.

"No, I just want to ignore it for a little bit longer," I say, wondering if that's childish of me.

"Okay, just so long as you know that you can always text or call me. Anytime, Palmer. I mean it."

I swallow hard, nodding up at him.

"I know. Thank you."

He leans down, kissing me and it starts off as just a peck but like every other time he kisses me, I want more.

I lean up on my tiptoes, wrapping my arms around his neck and kiss him back hard. When we pull apart, the mood in the apartment has shifted.

"I want you," I whisper and his eyes glint.

In the next second, Banks is pulling me through the

apartment and into his bedroom, where he backs me up against the door and kisses me. My body starts to heat as his hands move down my sides and grip my hips.

My hands go to his jeans and I fumble with the button and zipper, desperate to feel his cock. I've never wanted to give a blow job before but it's all that I've been able to think about today.

"Can I suck it?" I whisper, my voice husky as I look up at Banks from beneath my eyelashes.

"Fuck," Banks grits out and I take that as a good sign.

I push him back a step and sink to my knees, tugging his jeans and boxers down his thighs.

"Palmer," Banks whispers as I wrap my hand around his hard length.

"Yeah?" I ask, leaning in and taking a lip across the top of his cock, my tongue flicking over the piercing there.

"Fuck," he hisses and I grin as I lean forward again, opening my mouth and taking as much of him into my mouth as I can.

I wasn't really sure how to navigate the piercing so I was just going to ignore it, but it seems sensitive. Every time my tongue flicks or rubs against it, his thighs tense. I tongue it, rolling my tongue over it and he bites out a curse.

"Easy," Banks warns, but I ignore him.

I don't want to take it easy. I want to make him lose his mind.

I suck hard, wrapping my hand around the length that I can't fit into my mouth. I try to take more and more with each pass, my tongue dragging up the underside of his cock, nudging that piercing with each turn.

"I need you," Banks moans, his fingers tangling in my hair as he pulls me off of his dick.

I pout up at him. I was enjoying how powerful I felt making this man lose his mind.

"I'll let you suck it anytime that you want but I need that pussy right now," Banks says as he pulls me to my feet.

His hands go to my hips and I jump, wrapping my legs around his waist. His thick cock rubs against my folds and I squirm, desperate to feel him inside of me. When his dick rubs against my clit, all thoughts leave my mind.

"I love your piercing," I moan as I feel the metal barbell running just under the head of his cock rub against me.

His cock rubs against me in the most mind-blowing way as he carries me over to the bed and lays me down on the mattress.

Having Banks' hands and mouth on me has me burning even hotter and I can't wait for him to sink into me and make me scream as I come on his cock.

My fingers tangle in his dark hair as he sucks and nips at my neck. His cock is still between my legs and I shift my hips, trying to take him into my body. He's not penetrating me, just sliding along my folds and it's driving me out of my mind with want.

"My turn," he says as he starts to move lower, his lips caressing over the swell of my breast until his mouth captures one of my nipples.

He sucks the stiff peak into his mouth, his tongue rolling over the pebble until my back arches off of the bed and I'm close to begging for him to fuck me.

His mouth is so hot, his tongue teasing as he flicks it back and forth over the stiff peak. Soon my hips are rising, trying to rub against him, to take him inside of me where I ache for him, as he continues to play with my breasts.

He switches to the other one as he reaches down and I can't take it any longer.

"Please, Banks! I need more," I half cry and he takes pity on me, sliding lower down my body until his face is level with my dripping pussy.

His fingers spread me as his tongue licks a path to my core. I want to scream in frustration, but then he sucks my clit into his mouth, rolling his tongue over it and my mouth opens on a soundless cry.

He licks another path up my core, his tongue swirling around my opening, dipping inside slightly, teasing me before he circles my clit, sucking it into his mouth again.

It isn't long before I can feel a now familiar pressure filling me, cresting like a wave and I go sailing along with the surf, crashing down on the shore of my passion.

"Banks!" I cry as I start to come against his mouth, my legs wrapped around his head like a vise as I ride out my pleasure.

"You taste so fucking good," Banks says as he kisses his way back up my body.

He kisses me then and I can taste myself on his lips. It's so erotic and has me ready for another orgasm.

"I need you," I moan, breathing heavy after my orgasm.

"You have me."

He lines his cock up at my opening and thrusts inside of me. He leans down, kissing me, and I get lost in the feeling of him inside of me.

Banks starts to move and we both groan. I can feel that piercing of his rubbing against my front wall and I moan, trying to move my hips so that I can feel it rub me more.

My legs wrap around his waist, wanting to take him deeper into me. When the base of his cock grinds down on my clit, I gasp, my nails digging into his shoulders. That seems to spur him on because he really starts to move then.

"Fucking perfect," Banks whispers against my damp skin and I can feel my second orgasm growing inside of me.

Banks grunts, his fingers digging into my hips as he starts to lose control. His pace falters and he ruts into me, losing any finesse that he had.

He changes the angle and I scream in ecstasy as he hits some secret spot deep within me, that piercing rubbing me perfectly. The base of his cock presses on my clit and I fall apart, coming all over his cock as he pounds into me.

"Fuck, Palmer, shit," Banks groans, his eyes losing focus as he pounds into me.

He finds his own release with me, and I moan as he keeps slowly rocking into me.

We're both breathing heavy and covered in a sheen of sweat as he slowly pulls out of me and falls onto his side next to me on the bed. I gulp in air, my lips curling in a dreamy smile.

Banks pulls me into his arms, kissing my shoulder, his face nuzzling my neck and I move closer to him, basking in the afterglow and his warmth. It isn't long before I feel myself start to drift off to sleep.

For the first time in a long time, I feel safe and protected. I'm where I meant to be.

ELEVEN

Banks

"THAT'S IT, BABY," I croon into Palmer's ear as I fuck her against the shower wall.

"I'm so close," she whines, her head sliding up and down the shower wall.

"Good girl. Come all over my cock. I want to feel this tight ass pussy fucking strangling my dick."

"Banks!" she screams and I feel her walls tighten around my length.

I have no choice but to come with her, not when she starts to chant my name. My fingers dig into her ass and I wonder if I'm leaving bruises behind, marking her ass as mine.

"Fuck," I sigh into her neck as the hot water rains down on my back.

I lift her off my length, letting her slide down to her feet on the tile. She sags against me, a happy smile on her face, and all I can think is that I want to make her look like that every day of my life.

"Want to go out to breakfast with me? I can drop you off at your class after," I offer and she wraps her arms around my neck, smiling up at me.

"That sounds perfect. My class is at noon."

"I'll make sure that you get there on time," I promise as I turn off the water and we step out.

I towel her off and watch as she wraps it around her curvy body. It's short on her, ending at the tops of her creamy thighs and the view has my cock ready for round two in seconds. I know that we don't have time for that though, so I grab my own towel, wrapping it around my waist and heading down the hall to my room.

Brooks left early this morning to head to the gym before he went to the VA. He's been going to some support groups and volunteering there in his free time. I don't know what all he went through in the military and we aren't close enough for me to ask, but I'm glad that he's getting help.

I pull on some clothes, watching as Palmer tugs on her waitressing outfit from last night.

"You know, maybe you should start keeping some clothes over here?" I suggest, watching her as she grabs her shoes.

"Oh yeah? Are you going to clean out one of your dresser drawers?" she jokes and I smile.

"You can have the whole dresser. The closet too."

She blushes and I hope that she knows that I'm serious. She can take over my whole apartment. I just want her close and happy.

I grab her hand as we head for the door and she swings them, smiling as I raise mine and twirl her under it. I tug her close and she bumps up against my chest, a wide smile stretching her lips as I bend down and steal a kiss.

"Let's get you changed and fed," I say as I open the door and Palmer giggles.

It cuts off abruptly as we step out into the hall and she spots the man angrily pacing outside of her apartment. He's wearing some fancy suit, his graying hair gelled back and a scowl hardening his features.

"There you are," he snarls at Palmer, and I grab her, putting her behind me as I glare at the man.

"This doesn't concern you," he says to me, his tone frigid.

"What are you doing here, Frank?" Palmer asks and I can hear the slight panic in her voice.

That only makes me step in front of her more, wanting to protect her.

"We need to talk. I heard what you said to your mother yesterday. You should be ashamed of yourself talking to her that way."

Palmer shifts closer to me, her hands going to my back, and I reach back with one hand to steady her.

"It's time for you to come home. We tried this but obviously it's not time for you to be on your own. We can try again in a few years. Until then, you need to come home and apologize to me and your mother. She's arranged for you to volunteer on one of her charities with her."

"It is working," Palmer says quietly but Frank hears her.

"You think whoring yourself to this hoodlum is a good idea? Your mother and I raised you better than this. A few months out of the house and you've already turned into a slut," he snarls at her as he steps closer and I can't take it.

I snap, getting in his face and glaring at him.

"That's enough," I seethe. "Palmer isn't a whore or a

slut. She's a fucking angel. She's strong, smart, and the sweetest person that I've ever met. It's a fucking miracle that she ever looked twice at me. I know that you want to claim credit for who she is now, but it's obvious that she didn't get that from a judgmental prick like you."

Frank looks shocked but he recovers fast, trying to get into my face, but I'm an inch taller than him. He tries to reach past me to grab Palmer, and I smack his hand away.

"You don't touch her. She is an adult and can choose what to do with her life. She wants to live with Rae and go to school, then there's nothing that you can do about it. She wants to date me, then you can't stop us."

"You don't look too bright, so let me give you a heads up on something. She's just using you, just like her whore mother uses me for money and my reputation. They're both lucky that I took them in. Palmer is just rebelling and chose to do it with you, but this is never going to last."

I step closer to Palmer, wanting to comfort her.

"I'm not going to be here when this gets old," he says with a sneer at Palmer. "This is your last chance. Come home with me now or we're done. You're cut off. No more school, no more holidays or gifts, no more anything. Choose wisely," Frank says as he storms off down the stairs.

I turn, wrapping my arms around Palmer, but she pushes me away, a sheen of tears in her eyes.

"What can I do, baby?" I ask, but she shakes her head as the first tears spill onto her cheeks.

"Nothing. I just... I just need to be alone right now," she says as she pushes past me and unlocks her apartment door.

I stand there helpless as she disappears from my view and I wonder what the hell I should do now.

Did I overstep with what I said to Frank? I know that

Palmer didn't want to be cut off from her family, and I'm afraid that I just forced Frank's hand.

I watch her door for a minute before I turn and head down the stairs. I'm in over my head and there's only one place I can go to for help.

I pull my car out of the parking lot and head toward Eye Candy Ink and my family.

"Hey," I say as I walk into the original Eye Candy Ink shop and spot my Aunt Sam.

"Banks! What are you doing here?" she asks with a smile as she stands and moves to open the gate that separates the front lobby from the tattoo rooms in the back.

"I need some advice. It's about Palmer."

"Ah, and you came to Eye Candy Ink's resident ladies' man," my Uncle Mischa says with a manic grin that matches his son Rooney's.

"Oh my god. Are we still saying that?" Uncle Atlas asks as he joins us.

"Banks?" my dad says, poking his head out of his tattoo room and I smile at him.

"Banks is here?" my Aunt Trixie asks as she heads down the hall, Uncle Zeke right behind her.

"What's up?" my dad asks and leans against the wall in the hallway.

"I think I messed up with Palmer today," I admit and everyone gets comfortable.

I tell them what happened and what Palmer has told me about her mom and stepdad. They listen, letting me get it all out before they offer any advice.

"You're serious about her, right?" Atlas adds, and I nod right away.

"She's it for me."

"Then you messed up," Aunt Sam says.

"What?" Mischa asks, looking confused, and Sam rolls her eyes.

"It sounds like that Frank asshole is a real controlling prick, so I know that you were just protecting your girl, but maybe she wouldn't be cut off if you hadn't started to argue with him," she points out.

She's right. I was trying to be a good boyfriend and protect her from him but maybe I took things too far.

"So, I should apologize to her then."

Sam nods and I know that she's right.

"When do we get to meet her?" Aunt Trixie asks and I smile.

"Let me make it up to her first. Then I'll bring up introducing her to everyone again. We had talked about brunch before I fucked up. I need to make sure that she's not going to be upset with meeting my family when she just lost hers."

Aunt Trixie nods and I take a deep breath, wondering what the best way to apologize to Palmer is. I check my phone, but there are no new messages or calls from her. I just keep thinking about her crying alone in her apartment and I know that I need to check on her now and make this right with her.

"Thanks for this. I'll let you guys get back to work."

"Anytime," Aunt Sam says as she hugs me.

I hug everyone else goodbye and wave as I head back outside to my car. I climb behind the wheel and pull out my phone, sending a message to Palmer and letting her know that we need to talk and I'm picking her up in fifteen.

It's time for me to make this right with my girl.

TWELVE

Palmer

RAE HAD ALREADY LEFT for her morning class by the time I let myself into the apartment and I'm not sure if I'm glad that she isn't here to see me breakdown or if I wish that she was here so I can talk to her about what just happened.

I spent an hour curled up in bed, sobbing. I knew, deep down, that this was always going to be what happened, but I wasn't prepared. I thought I still had a few weeks left at least.

I wanted to blame Banks for this. Maybe if he hadn't challenged Frank, then I wouldn't be here, but I know that if he hadn't, that Frank would have dragged me back home this morning. It's actually probably a good thing that he was there with me and had my back.

It also just further highlights the difference between Banks and Frank. They're both alphas who crave being in control, but Frank wants to dominate everyone and bend them to his will. Banks just wants to protect those that he loves and make sure that they're happy and safe.

I pull myself out of bed and head into the kitchen. I think Rae should be home soon. I'm pretty sure that we had opposite schedules on Thursday and I know that I need to pull it together and try to come up with a plan.

I can try to take out a loan for college but will my shifts at the club be enough for me to cover rent and groceries. I'll have to get a new phone plan and health insurance and so much more. How can I ever hope to cover all of that?

I pull out my phone. There are a few messages from Banks letting me know that he's here for me and to let him know what I need. He asked if I still need a ride to my classes and I text him back no before I pull up a new message and type in Finn and Hendrix's names.

PALMER: **So Frank came to see me this morning...**

Finn: Do you need me to come over?

Hendrix: What did that fucker want?

Palmer: He told me that I needed to come home and apologize or he would cut me off. So I'm cut off now.

Hendrix: Fuck. I have some money saved. I can send it to you.

Finn: Same. Do you want to move in with me? You can bring Rae, but you'll have to share the spare bedroom. We can cover the cost if you need to break your lease.

Palmer: Thanks guys, but I don't want to drain all of your savings.

Finn: We want to help. I know we're your stepbrothers but we always considered you family, Palmer.

Hendrix: Yeah. Do you want me to come home? We can rent an apartment together.

Palmer: Let me think about it. I might be able to get more shifts at Se7en or find another part time job.

Hendrix: Okay, just let us know. We're here for you, sis.

Finn: You can come to the gym. Maybe we can teach you some self-defense moves in case Frank decides to come back.

Palmer: Thanks guys. I love you.

Finn: Love you

Hendrix: Love you

"Whew! I'm so glad that I don't have classes tomorrow," Rae says as she walks in and sees me in the kitchen.

"I know. I'm looking forward to a day off tomorrow."

"What are you doing home? I thought that you had a class at noon?"

"Yeah, um, Frank came to see me this morning."

"Oh, shit. This can't be good," Rae says, her button nose scrunched up in distaste at the sound of Frank's name.

"He told me I had to come home or he would cut me off."

"So, he cut you off then. Please tell me that you chose option b and that you're not going back there," Rae pleads and I nod.

"Yeah, I was going to go to Seven and see if maybe Cat could give me some more hours. I might have to find another part time job too."

"I've got some savings. I can help too," Rae says right away, but I know that I can't take her up on it.

She's a broke college student too and while I appreciate her offering, I don't want us both to be struggling. It wouldn't be fair to her.

"How are you feeling about all of this?" Rae asks and I sigh, stopping for the first time since this started and taking stock of my emotions.

"I was devastated at first. I'm still scared and stressed out and I probably will be until I figure out how to cover everything, but that other part of me is relieved. I'm happy that I don't have to deal with them anymore. Glad that I won't have to screen their calls or wonder if they're going to be here when I get home, looking for another fight."

Rae nods, coming around the kitchen counter and wrapping her arms around my shoulders.

"If you need anything, I'm here for you."

"I know. Thank you. You're the best, best friend that I could ever wish for."

"I know," Rae sighs dramatically and I laugh.

We pull apart and I wipe some stray tears away as she heads over to the fridge.

"Are you hungry?" she asks, and my stomach growls.

"Yeah," I say with a laugh as I join her.

"Want some leftover pizza?"

"Sure."

I grab us plates and she warms them up in the microwave.

"What did Banks have to say about all of this?" she asks and I bite my lip.

"He was the one who told off Frank actually. I was upset after Frank left, so I came in here and cried for a bit. He's sent me a few messages asking if I needed anything, so

I should probably go talk to him. I wanted to talk to Cat first and see about my hours."

Rae nods and we eat our pizza in silence for a few minutes.

My phone buzzes again, and I check it to see a message from Banks.

BANKS: **We need to talk. I'll pick you up in fifteen.**

THIRTEEN

Banks

IT'S BEEN hours since I left Palmer this morning and I can't take it any longer. I don't like thinking that she's been upset all day and I haven't been there to comfort her.

After my talk with my family, I have a pretty clear idea of what I want to say to her. My normal reaction is to step in and take over, but Palmer is an adult and I need to follow her lead here. I can't force her to do anything. I can only love and support her in what she chooses to do.

I pull into the parking lot and I'm about to turn the car off and head up to get her when I see Palmer headed my way. I hop out, getting the passenger door for her. She gives me a small smile as she slides into the passenger seat and I take that as a good sign.

She's quiet as I drive down the congested streets toward Allegheny Park. It takes us close to half an hour to get there and find a place to park.

"Are you hungry?" I ask as we pass by a couple of food trucks.

"No, I just ate."

I nod, taking her hand as we start to walk along the path.

"How are you feeling about everything? I'm sorry for taking over this morning. I just really didn't like the way that he was talking to you, but I realized that maybe I over-stepped my boundaries."

"No, don't be sorry. I'm glad that you were there. He hasn't ever hit me, but I don't know what he would have done if it had just been the two of us. He looked angry enough to physically drag me back home."

My hands tighten into fists and I take a deep breath, trying not to think about Frank dragging Palmer anywhere.

"I wanted to talk to you. I went and saw my family and told them what happened. They let me know that I might have overstepped, and I wanted to apologize but I also wanted you to know that you have options."

"You told your family about me?" she asks, with a shy smile.

"Of course. They all know that I'm crazy, head over heels, in love with you. That's why they can't wait to meet you. I told them that you might be familied out for a while so they're willing to wait until you're ready."

Palmer looks away, tears shining in her eyes and I wrap my arm around her shoulders.

"I love you, Palmer. More than anything. I'm sure that you've been freaking out all day about money and how you're going to pay for everything."

She looks away and I know that I'm right.

"You can move in with me to save on rent and bills. We can get bigger place and bring Rae and Brooks with us. I have money saved. I can pay for your tuition, rent, whatever you need, baby. I know that you want to be independent and make your own way and I only want to help you. If you won't take the money, then I can help you apply for scholarships or financial aid, whatever you need."

"You don't have to do that," she argues, but I stop her before she can go on.

"I want to. Remember what I said that day in the car?"

She nods and I tilt her chin up until her eyes meet mine.

"I'm all in. You are it for me, Palmer. All I want or will ever want. I want everything with you. I want to give you everything. I don't care about the money. I just want you to be safe and happy. Let me do this for you so that you can focus on school and getting the life that you want."

Palmer is crying now, and it breaks my heart. I wipe the tears away with my thumbs.

"Please don't cry, baby," I plead, feeling anxious.

"I love you too," she says, burying her face in my chest and I wrap my arms around her, trying to comfort her.

"You're crying a lot more than I imagined you would be when I pictured this moment," I joke and she laughs into my shirt.

"I love you, but I don't want you to think that I'm using you the way that my mom uses Frank."

"I don't. What your mom and Frank have, it's not love. It's a business transaction and I will never let our relationship be that. I'm going to love you forever and just because I pay for things doesn't mean that we aren't equal in this relationship."

She studies my face and I take her hands, squeezing them.

"We're looking for someone to help out at the front counter at Eye Candy Ink. I talked to Maxine. You can work whenever school and Seven allows and earn some extra money. Plus, we can see each other more."

She smiles and I go on.

"You'll move in with me or we'll talk to Rae and Brooks and find a bigger place. We'll see each other more and save money."

"Okay," she whispers and my heart stops for a minute.

"Okay?" I ask, making sure that I didn't mishear her.

"Yeah, okay. Thank you, Banks."

"Of course, Palmer. I'd do anything for you."

She tilts her chin up and I take the invitation, sealing her mouth with mine. My tongue slides into her mouth and she moans as I tangle it with hers.

Her hands land on my shoulders and I wrap mine around her waist, tugging her closer until we're molded together and I can't tell where I end and she begins.

Her curves are flush against the hard planes of my body and I can feel myself hardening in my jeans the longer that we make out.

Her hands tangle in my hair and she tugs it the way she does when she's horny and aching for my cock and I know that I need to get us home where we have some more privacy.

"Let's go home. Then I can take care of you properly," I whisper against her lips and she grins up at me.

"Sounds like a plan."

I take her hand as we take off running down the path and back to my car. I don't know what's going to happen with Palmer's parents or her school. All I know is that I'm never letting her go.

FOURTEEN

Palmer

ONE YEAR LATER...

"DID you want anything from Wild Thyme?" Harvey asks me as he stops next to the front desk and I look over, smiling at him.

"The mac and cheese," I say, trying not to drool as I think about it, and he smiles and nods.

I've been working the front counter at Eye Candy Ink for the past year and I love it. I get to see Banks more and hang out with my family.

Everyone here has welcomed me into the fold, and they've even extended that to Finn and Hendrix. We all had Christmas together last year at Zeke and Trixie's house and it's nice being part of a real family that just loves each other and doesn't try to manipulate or control everyone.

"Palmer will check you out," Banks says as he leads his client up to the counter.

I smile at him, blushing when he winks at me. The girl that he just tattooed tries to catch his eye, but he ignores her, leaning against the wall and watching me as I check her out.

As soon as she leaves, he wraps his arms around me from behind, and I lean back against him.

"Your next client is here," I whisper to him and he nods.

"I'll try to be quick with them and we can eat together when Harvey gets back."

"Sounds good," I say, turning in my seat to kiss him.

He heads back with his next client and the girl glares at me as she walks by but I just laugh. I'm used to the dirty looks by now, but I know that Banks never gives the girls a second look.

I get back to my homework. I just started my second year of college and things are going well for me. I was able to get some scholarships, the biggest one coming from Eye Candy Ink. Banks paid for the rest of it, though I promised to pay him back. I have a feeling that he'll never actually accept the money when I try to give it to him.

We moved in together a month after the encounter with Frank. We actually ended up switching, so that Brooks moved in with Rae and I did with Banks. The two of them circled each other for a few weeks before they got together. I knew that they liked each other and I'm so happy for them. They just got engaged last month and Rae and I have been planning our weddings together.

Banks proposed to me six months ago and I smile as I stare down at my ring. It's a cushion cut in a platinum setting. He had it transcribed and I melt as I think about the words on the inside of the band.

All in.

"Hey," Rooney says as he brings his last client of the night up to check out.

"Hey," I say, grinning at him.

Rooney is crazy, but it's impossible not to be drawn to him.

I check his client out and he collapses into the chair next to me.

"How are you doing, Palm?" he asks, kicking his feet up on the desk and nearly toppling over backward in the process.

I laugh, helping him steady himself.

"Are you leaving for Seven soon?" he asks and I nod.

"In an hour."

"I'll stick around and give you a ride then. I think Banks has another client left tonight."

"Thanks," I say gratefully and he nods, giving me a grin.

"Of course. Anything for my favorite little sister."

"What do you want?" I ask him with a laugh.

"Word is Banks is looking to pick his best man. I think we both know the obvious choice," he says, opening his arms out wide and almost tipping back again.

"I'll see what I can do," I say as Harvey comes in the front door with the food.

"Guess who's the best man?" Rooney brags and Harvey rolls his eyes, setting down the bag with my food in front of me.

"How much do I owe you?" I ask Harvey and he waves me off.

"It's on Max," he says with a grin and I laugh.

"I'll have to thank him on Sunday."

Banks comes up a few minutes later and I hurry to check out his client so that we can eat before we have to leave.

"Rooney is going to give me a ride to Seven. Isn't he just the *best*?" I ask Banks as he starts to pull our food out of the bag.

He looks up at me and then over to Rooney, letting out a sigh.

"Rooney, would you like to be my best man?" Banks ask, and Rooney screams yes at the same time that Harvey, Ender, Gray, and Ames scream no.

I laugh so hard that I'm almost crying and watch as Rooney runs off to rub it in their faces.

"Let's eat," Banks says and I take my seat next to him as he passes me my food.

"Are you really going to let Rooney be your best man?" I ask and he looks up to me.

"Yeah, I'll let him gloat for a few days before I tell him that I intend to ask all of the guys to share the title."

I laugh, offering Banks a bite of my mac and cheese.

I haven't talked to my mom or Frank in a year and there are times where I miss my mom, but I know that she made her choice. They haven't tried to reach out to me and I heard from Finn that Frank got fired a few weeks ago. I wonder how much longer my mom will stay with him if he can't provide her with the life that she's grown accustomed to.

Neither of them are invited to the wedding, and I actually asked Banks' dad, Nico, to walk me down the aisle.

"Rae said that I could stay with her the night before the wedding," I tell him and he frowns.

"Why would you do that?"

"It's customary for us to spend the night apart."

"I don't like it," he says with a frown.

"I think it's exciting. The next time we see each other, we'll be about to be husband and wife."

Banks sighs, but I know that he'll let me have this. He always gives me what I want and I love him for that. We're equal partners in this relationship, just like he promised me.

"Ready?" Rooney asks as he comes back up front and I nod, taking my last bite of mac and cheese.

"I'll see when you get off," Banks says as I lean over to kiss him and I smile.

"Love you," I whisper against his lips.

"Love you more," he whispers back and I grin as I pull away and follow Rooney outside.

I was so afraid to lose my mom and Frank and the stability that they provided, but I had nothing to fear. Life is better now than I ever could have imagined and I owe it all to Banks.

He's the love of my life, my everything, and I'm all in with him.

FIFTEEN

Banks

TEN YEARS LATER...

I SMILE at my wife as she gets ready to head out to work.

"Can we watch a movie?" our sons, Seth and Jonah, ask at the same time and I grin.

"Sure. You go pick out a movie and I'll make the popcorn."

"Okay, I think I have everything. I'll see you guys in the morning," Palmer says as she kisses both the boys and then makes her way over to me.

"I'll wait up for you," I whisper and she grins up at me.

"You better."

I watch her leave, already looking forward to later tonight when she gets home.

Palmer is the assistant manager at Se7en and has been for the last six years. Cat hired her on right after Palmer graduated from college with her business degree. Palmer loves it there and I'm just happy that she's happy.

"Come on, Dad! Hurry up!" Seth calls and I laugh as I head into the kitchen to make the popcorn.

We've been married for close to ten years and it's been the best years of my life. We had Seth five years ago and Jonah was born a year after that. We had our hands full, so two was enough for us.

Palmer is a super mom with them. She wanted to stay home with them and I supported that, so for the last five years, she's been home with them during the day and managing Se7en at night. I don't know how she does it all and I'm in awe of her.

My family has been helping out when they can and we have play dates with Rae and everyone else at least once a week.

We bought a house by my Uncle Zeke's place and it's been nice to have more room, though I know that Palmer misses being so close to Rae and Brooks.

I pour the popcorn into a bowl and head into the living room, smiling when I see Seth and Jonah wrapped up in blankets and waiting for me.

"Hey," Rooney says as he opens the front door, scaring the crap out of me.

I should be used to it by now. Everyone stops by all of the time and Friday nights usually end up being a sleepover at someone's house.

"Oh good, you made popcorn," he says as he grabs the bowl from me and heads into the living room with his kids on his heels.

"Please make yourself at home," I say dryly, and he grins at me.

"Don't worry about closing the door. Harvey is right behind me."

Gray comes in next with his kids and I give up, heading back into the kitchen to make some more popcorn for everyone.

"Hey, we brought pizza," Ender says as he pokes his head around the corner and I clear off a spot on the counter for him to set it down.

"Where are all of your better halves?" I ask him as he sets down the boxes.

"Girl's night. They were headed to Wild Thyme to see Coraline for a bit and then to Seven to hang out with Palmer."

I nod. I'm not surprised. Everyone is so busy with different work schedules and kids that we have to get creative to hang out with everyone.

"Are my grandkids in here?" Uncle Mischa calls and I laugh as I reach to grab some more plates.

I head out to the living room to greet everyone and I can't say that I'm surprised to see Finn here with his kids, along with Brooks and the rest of my family. There's barely enough room for everyone to sit and the kids have already spread out the pillows and blankets on the floor and are giggling as I get the movie set up and pass out some of the pizza.

I squeeze in between Finn and Rooney and smile as the movie starts to play on the screen.

This life is crazy, but I'm glad that it's mine. I'm lucky that I get to share all of this with Palmer and her brothers.

They heard from their parents once in the last ten years. It was after Palmer had graduated college. They wanted to try to convince Palmer to come work for Frank at his new company, but Palmer turned it down. That was a whole other fight and after that, we all made it clear that we didn't want to have anything to do with them.

They've missed so much over the years. All three weddings, the birth of all of their grandchildren, holidays, vacations, everything. I asked Palmer once if she wanted to try again with them, but she made it clear that she had the family that she wanted here with us.

I'm fine with that, just as long as she's happy.

Palmer and the kids, they mean everything to me. My family means everything to me.

With them, I'm all in.

DID YOU LOVE BANKS? **Please consider leaving a review! You can do so on Amazon, Goodreads, and Bookbub.**

DID **you miss the original Eye Candy Ink series? You can read the boxset here.**

ARE **you curious about Ender's military friend, Brooks? Check out his book, Tempted By My Roommate, here!**

ABOUT THE AUTHOR

CONNECT WITH ME!

If you enjoyed this story, please consider leaving a review on Amazon or any other reader site or blog that you like. Don't forget to recommend it to your other reader friends.

If you want to chat with me, please consider joining my VIP list or connecting with me on one of my Social Media platforms. I love talking with each of my readers. Links below!

Website
Newsletter

SERIES BY SHAW HART

Eye Candy Ink Series

Atlas

Mischa

Sam

Zeke

Nico

Telltale Heart Series

Bought and Paid For

His Miracle

Pretty Girl

Telltale Hearts Boxset

Cherry Falls Series:

803 Wishing Lane

1012 Curvy Way

Love Note Series

Signing Off With Love

Care Package Love

Wrong Number, Right Love

Folklore Series

Kidnapping His Forever

Claiming His Forever

Finding His Forever

Rescuing His Forever

Chasing His Forever

Folklore: The Complete Series

Wish Series:

His Wish

Her Wish

Obsessed Series:

Her Obsession

His Obsession

Mine To Series:

Mine to Love

Mine to Protect

Mine to Cherish

Mine to Keep

ALSO BY SHAW HART

Still in the mood for Christmas books?

Stuffing Her Stocking, Mistletoe Kisses, Snowed in For Christmas

Love holiday books? Check out these!

For Better or Worse, Riding His Broomstick, Thankful for His FAKE Girlfriend, His New Year Resolution, Hop Stuff, Taming Her Beast, Hungry For Dash, His Firework

Looking for some OTT love stories?

Fighting for His Princess, Her Scottish Savior, Not So Accidental Baby Daddy, Baby Mama

Looking for a celebrity love story?

Bedroom Eyes, Seducing Archer, Finding Their Rhythm

In the mood for some young love books?

Study Dates, His Forever, My Girl

Some other books by Shaw:

The Billionaire's Bet, Her Guardian Angel, Every Tuesday Night, Falling Again, Stealing Her, Dreamboat, Locked Down, Making Her His, Trouble

Printed in Great Britain
by Amazon